Secretary
to the
Socialite

Amanda McCabe

OLIVERHEBERBOOKS

Secretary to the Socialite Copyright 2025 © Amanda McCabe

Cover Design by Wicked Smart Designs

Published by Oliver-Heber Books

0 9 8 7 6 5 4 3 2 1

"And I knew that ... Death was so easy as the rising sun and as calm and natural—that to be infolded in Earth was not the end but part of oneself, part of every day and night that we lived ...

"If anything should happen to me ... I want to be buried in Taos with the wide sky. Life has been marvelous, all the experiences good and bad, because out of it so many things were discovered. I've had a most lovely life to myself. I've enjoyed it as thoroughly as it could be enjoyed. And when my time comes no one is to feel that I have lost anything of it—or be too sorry."

LETTER FROM MILLICENT ROGERS TO
HER SON PAUL PERALTA-RAMOS,
JANUARY 1951

Prologue: Millicent

TAOS, WINTER 1952

There is a strange freedom in dying. A lightness and clarity. It was so odd. Even as I had lived with death for so very long, had half-expected every night that I would not wake up in the morning, I had not imagined this. Life is ever surprising, isn't it? Even to the end.

It was cold that night, a bitter snap to the ice-clear air that promised snow later. I didn't care. I wrapped my sable coat tighter around my shoulders, so thin now, the bones sharp against my papery skin after all the months of doctors and surgeries and medicine bottles, and I sat up straighter against the leather back seat of my open-top car. It was my very last dance, that Christmas deer dance. I wouldn't miss it even if I froze into place.

The music hadn't started yet, but I could already feel it, so deep inside, the heartbeat that never failed me as my own weak organ always had. The drums that began low, slow, a promise of what might emerge if only we kept still and watched. Kept the faith. If it was ours, if it belonged to us, the sound would grow louder, stronger, the singers would emerge from the blackness, and it would be like the earth itself was rising up to meet us. Like something primitive and eternal and perfect.

Life goes so quickly when it is beautiful. And I have always tried to make my life beautiful, to hold every minute of it tightly between my fingers. Now it was going, going. Yet never had I possessed a moment as beautiful as this one. As if I held all my fifty years against me all at once.

I glanced at the back of Tom's head, the sweet boy from town who drove me around now that I could barely move my brittle bones myself. Over the rough, risky roads into the mountains, around my land at Turtle Walk, out here to the pueblo. He never complained, was always cheerful, full of delicious Taos gossip. He made me think of my own sons, so far away now, so distant from me in too many ways. Tom kept giving me nervous little glances, as if he expected me to collapse at any moment. He said nothing.

I had promised him I wouldn't faint. I wasn't done. Not quite yet.

Lady Dorothy Brett, my dear, muddling, maddening, wonderful friend, sat beside me, the scent of her ever-present cherry pipe smoke sharp on that cold wind, her old felt hat squashed low over her brow, white hair sticking out from underneath, making me laugh. "MR," she said, in that low, plummy English accent that always sounded so comical coming from her pug face. "Why don't you let us take you home now? It's freezing like a witch's ass out here. The doctors said ..."

I just shook my head. "Not yet. Not until I see."

She knew better than to argue with me. Everyone knew better than to do *that*. They never won.

They never had.

"I'll go get us some frybread and cider, then," she said. "You'll eat it?"

I nodded, though I knew I wouldn't. I couldn't taste food anymore. I had lost all the other appetites that burned through me for so long, for sex and love and art. But the passion for beauty was still there. It still lasted.

Brett swung open the car door, and her short, portly figure

vanished into the crowd that was gathering in the pueblo plaza. The dachshunds wanted to follow her, sensing food in the offing but I held them on my lap.

I sat back and studied everything around me, just storing it up.

I hadn't possessed a lot of years, but in them I've seen strange and lovely things. New York, Paris, the majestic Austrian Alps, the crashing ocean in California, the endless white beaches of Jamaica, people and parties and lovers and children. All of it delighted me. But nothing, *nothing*, ever reached down inside of me like this place did.

The night had gathered in fully now, but out there it didn't matter. The stars were as thick and glittering as a shower of snow in that sharp, black winter sky, more beautiful than my mother's diamond tiara had once been. In the distance, dusty purple against all those stars, was Taos Mountain.

When I first came there, first came home, Benito's ancient grandmother told me a tale about the mountain, which they call Mo-ha-loh at the pueblo. She said it was the ancient source of all life, and would protect all it had created. A woman I met in a curio shop on the town plaza put it more succinctly.

"The mountain, it either hugs you or it spits you out," she said. "It just takes to some people, belongs to them, that's all."

It belonged to me. Or—I belonged to it. I could never possess it, as I had so much else. It was free, just as I was free. But we had each other, and now I had to say good-bye.

The torches had been lit along the river that divided the pueblo into two, and now I could see the buildings around us, built a thousand years ago in the shadow of the mountain. More elegant than any Fifth Avenue mansion, any European cathedral, pure and spare, sparkling in the crackling flames.

The turquoise-painted doors were open, crowds gathered in the doorways and on the flat roofs, wrapped in their bright woven blankets to watch what would happen. To hear the drumbeats, as I did, and to wait. Time moved at its own pace here. It was a world apart.

I had searched so long, looked in so many places, only to come here now at the end. I was not born in this world. My birthplace, New York, Southampton, it was another universe. People envied it. People who didn't know the truth of it. I had to find my own world myself, the place where my heart and soul belonged. Here I was. Free.

Here my story began, and ended too. Here my story would always go on, because those of us who belong to the mountain are eternal along with her.

The drumbeats grew louder, faster, and the chime of the silver bells the dancers wore on their ankles grew with them, all in time to the night. I twisted around, straining for the first glimpse of them in the torchlight. That sight, the ancient masks, the long sweep of black hair, it always caught at me, somewhere deep inside.

The car door opened, but it wasn't Brett returning. It was Violet. The dogs went wild with joy, leaping on her, tangling in the folds of her green wool coat.

And, against my will, I felt a surge of something like happiness rise up in me, as well. After what happened, my mistakes, I thought she was gone. But there she sat, gathering the dogs up in her arms, her dark red hair like a sunset in the torchlight. She smiled at me, soft, tentative, the start of a heartbreak maybe mending—or scarring over. I knew it all so well. I had once been just like her.

"I thought you left," I said. "That you didn't approve of me, like everyone else."

"It's the deer dance, the last dance of the year," she answered simply. "I wouldn't miss it, MR."

"Of course not," I answered, and turned away to watch the crowds. The last dance. None of us could miss it, no matter how hard we tried.

CHAPTER 1

Violet

LOS ANGELES, 1947

"What kind of job did you say this was?" Jo-Jo asked, her voice full of doubt.

Violet laughed. She leaned toward the cracked dressing table mirror and carefully outlined her lips with the gold tube of American Beauty she had just bought at the drugstore. She wasn't so sure about it now. It didn't look nearly serious enough for a "confidential social secretary." She had always added a few years to her age at the employment agency. No one wanted to hire a nineteen-year-old for a *real* job, no matter what her certificate from Miss Benning's Secretarial School said.

And she needed this job. The boarding house wouldn't let her coast on credit forever.

"I told you," Violet said. She tossed down the lipstick and sorted through the mess of hairpins, half-empty boxes of Cody face powder, paperback novels, and movie mags for something a little more subdued. "It's a secretary. A confidential social secretary, who can be discreet."

"And they didn't say who you'd be working for?"

Violet shook her head. "They wouldn't, would they? Not if it's all about discretion."

"If you're working all day for some Madame Muckety calling you up all the time, you won't have time for auditions."

"I gave that up anyway," Violet said, hoping she sounded careless, light. Larky. Not that horrible sinking sensation that came over her late at night. That sense that her life was going nowhere. That Ma had been right. Once she dreamed she would be a writer, a great writer, she would scribble stories all the time. Then her brother Richard came home from the war broken, and the family all had to give everything up for him. Poor Rich. Poor all those boys. "I'm no good at it. Not like you."

And not beautiful like Jo-Jo, either, with her silken curls of platinum hair and heart-shaped face. Violet's hair was still red, despite the rinses she used, still falling in unruly waves. She still had freckles on her nose, and no bosom to speak of.

"Don't be silly," Jo-Jo said, swinging her long legs from her perch on the narrow bed. "I would kill for your hair. You look like Rita Hayworth."

Violet laughed. "On a day she got up on the wrong side of the bed, maybe. Acting's not for me, not really." She frowned as she looked at her little collection of lipsticks, remembering the long, long lines at auditions, the cold eyes studying every angle and curve. So different from the solitary work of writing she loved. "I mostly came here just to get away from Iowa."

And she was never going back there, either. No matter what happened.

"You could get married, then," Jo-Jo said decisively, as if that was all easy-peasy. The simple way to solve every problem.

But Violet knew that caused more problems than it ever solved. Poor Bill, her sweetie, dead in Normandy before he could even grow up. Chasing her through the cornfields when they were kids.

"Marry who?" she said, and studied the end of a bit of brownie-pink Elizabeth Arden left in the bottom of an old tube.

"I dunno. There's sure lots of millionaires around here. Some movie director or something," Jo-Jo said.

"I doubt any of them are looking to get married, not when they get whatever they like for free every day," Violet muttered. She wiped off the American Beauty and dabbed on some of the pink. Better. "If I get this job, I'll be making more money than in that infernal old typing pool, anyway. Maybe I could even get my own apartment."

Jo-Jo sighed, as if such a thing as a room to oneself was as distant as Mars. And maybe it was. But this job was a hope, at least. It had been a long time since Violet had one of those.

"Maybe it's with a movie star!" Jo-Jo said brightly. "Joan Crawford, or Bette Davis. Or the wife of some studio boss. That would be fun."

Fun. Violet rolled the word around in her mind, as if it was Greek or Castilian Spanish or something. Vaguely familiar, something she might once have read in one of the library books piled in haphazard piles around her tiny room. One she should be able to extrapolate meaning merely from how it was sounded, but which escaped her.

Had she ever had *fun*? She couldn't remember. She liked laughing with the other girls at the boarding house, hearing their stories of auditions and bit parts and dates. She liked going to the movies, or dancing in the parlor with them. Yet there was always a wall there. A glass wall. True, one she could see through, hear echoes, but that kept her distant. Apart. Suspended in her own lonely little world. Waiting. But waiting for what?

Once she had so loved writing. It wasn't "fun," but it *was* life. Really. Then it was gone.

Violet glanced down again at the letter from the agency. It certainly didn't telegraph the word "fun." Printed on thick stationery, efficiently typed, with a businesslike letterhead. Miss Violet Redfield was to report to a Mrs. Rogers at an address at the northeast end of the San Fernando Valley promptly at three, properly attired and with her letters of reference, to interview for the position of a confidential social secretary. The client had chosen her specifically from the agency's files to interview first.

Even in the spare, black letters, Violet could swear she heard the puzzlement from Miss Spry, the head of the agency. Violet Redfield, for a confidential position at an expensive address? Specially chosen? She'd hardly distinguished herself in the typing pools and switchboard rooms and sales counters, or during those two days as Mr. Ledbetter, Attorney At Law's, receptionist. Never mind that Mr. Ledbetter was a fat, sweaty old lecher with pinching little piggy fingers.

At least this job sounded nothing like any of those. A lady's social secretary. She just had to prove to Miss Spry, and this mysterious Mrs. Rogers, that she could do it.

Could she do it?

"I just wish I had some more impressive references," she sighed. The letter from the secretarial school, and the note from the Williamsons, who had run the malt shop where she worked after high school classes back in Nowheresville, would hardly impress a society matron or movie actress. And the terse statements from Miss Spry's agency, that Miss Redfield could type well but not quickly, was clean, neat, and respectable, weren't much better.

"That doesn't matter," Jo-Jo said, with the confidence of the beautiful. It was easy for her to be so breezy. She didn't need references for the steady stream of bit parts she got now, the bits she was sure would lead to her big break any day. "You just have to make a good first impression. Look the part."

"With my professional dress and confident, sophisticated demeanor," Violet laughed. That was even more trouble than the references.

She turned to stare at the half-open wardrobe that held all her clothes. Blouses, a couple of skirts, three cotton and rayon dresses, one "going to church" frock of lavender printed with blue flowers (not that she ever darkened a church door much anymore). Two hats. A black wool winter coat that had seen better days. One black evening gown, bought from a second-hand store but with only a few beads missing at the neckline. Three pairs of shoes, two with patched holes in the soles.

She thought of the ladies in Jo-Jo's fashion mags, the actresses and debutantes and models. All trim, tailored suits, or fairy-tale New Look skirts swirling around them like clouds of dreams. Saucer-large hats, kid gloves, alligator handbags, high heels.

Then she thought of her own purse, with its shredded satin lining and the coin purse with its broken zipper. Maybe she had $3 left from that last job, weeks of selling gloves at Walker's. It wouldn't even buy one yard for those new full skirts. For just one instant, she wished it was like the war, all of them restricted to narrow skirts, shallow hems, tiny hats. All of them on ration cards.

No. Her hand crumpled the letter with a painful spasm. Not the war. That was what brought her to where she was. Bill gone, her brother broken, herself adrift, not belonging in Iowa but not in California, either. Alone.

But would she, could she, ever have felt less alone if she had stayed in Iowa? Found a boy, kept house, had some kids, lived on a farm working like a dog just like her parents, or maybe been lucky enough to get a banker husband or something else in town. Every day the same.

Violet didn't even know. She just knew she needed this job.

"How can I ever impress your Madame Muckety with my clothes?" she said, powdering her nose with the flowery-scented Cody.

Jo-Jo jumped down off the bed, her face all alight with purpose. She got dangerous when she looked like that. "I'll find something."

"Jo-Jo, I'm not sure any of your clothes, gorgeous as they are, would work," Violet protested. She thought of Jo-Jo's closet, all the jewel-like silks and floaty chiffons and velvet jackets.

"Just leave it to me," Jo-Jo said with an airy wave of her hand. "You just see to your face. Be sure to use mascara!"

Violet knew better than to argue. Maybe, she thought, being friends with Jo-Jo would prepare her for working with a bossy society lady. If only her new boss would be as sweet about her impulsive orders as Jo-Jo.

She faced herself in the mirror again. She wasn't much to work with when it came to movie acting, the camera just didn't like her, but surely she could be a passable secretary. More powder to cover the freckles on her tilted nose, a little flick of the decreed mascara to bring out her pale blue-gray eyes, her dark red hair curled and lacquered into place.

And that lipstick. The pink seemed okay enough. She was just blotting at it when Jo-Jo returned, her arms full of clothes.

"Now," she said briskly, holding up a forest-green sheath, along with a green and cream tweed fake-Chanel jacket. "What about this? If we let the hem down a bit. And this jacket." She sighed as she looked down at Violet's shoes. "If only we could do something about *those*. But my shoes just won't fit you, and I don't think Mary's would, either. Just keep your feet flat on the floor."

Violet laughed. It sounded like the tale of her life. Keep your feet flat on the floor; don't jump too high. You're nothing special. That was why she hid her writing away.

Maybe that would never change. But at least if she got this job, trailing around after the Madame, writing her invitations and keeping her diary of charity teas or whatever, she would be able to pay her bills. Get herself some time.

Because she was never going back to Iowa again.

Violet stepped off the bus at the designated stop, at the far northeast end of the San Fernando Valley, and checked the address on the letter one more time. She glanced up, and studied the street, first one way then the other.

It was really only a few miles from the boarding house, yet surely she had shot off to some new universe. In every direction were towering palm trees, velvety-green lawns, elaborately-wrought gates and stone lions guarding driveways, a few cars, Lincolns, Austins, Bentleys, even one Rolls Royce. They glided past, smooth and silent and quick. The air smelled of honeysuckle. And everywhere was so quiet. Quiet like she had never heard before.

The quiet only money, piles of it, could bring.

Violet had once gone on a "see the houses of the stars" tour with Jo-Jo and Mary, giggling as they ate taffy and gaped at the homes of Gary Cooper and Tyrone Power. There hadn't been much to see; they were all hidden behind those gates, with only a glimpse of a red tile roof here and there. She had never gone back. Her city was very different from theirs, a place of buses and trams and drugstores and hamburger stands.

Now she was supposed to find a way to stay there, amid the palm trees and the stern stone lions.

She took a moment to smooth her tweed jacket over her borrowed dress, straighten the black felt and net hat Jo-Jo had brushed for her so carefully. She glanced down at her watch. Almost three. No running away now.

Violet remembered ladies in movies, Irene Dunne, Rosalind Russell, how they moved with purpose and confidence. She copied them as she marched up to a high stucco wall gilded with the right house numbers next to the impenetrable gates. She pressed the buzzer.

"Yes?" a fuzzy voice barked.

"I—I'm Miss Redfield. I have an appointment with a Mrs. Rogers."

"Come in. Use the small walkway to your left."

There was a soft hum, and a grilled, smaller gate she hadn't even noticed before slid open. She took a deep breath, and went inside. It clanged shut behind her.

The house, tucked away among a grove of palms and a tangle of flowering purple wisteria, was not large, but it was very pretty, like something in a fairy-tale. A cottage, half-timbered and steep-roofed, where princesses slept for a hundred years. A woman in a crisp black dress, her silvery hair drawn back in a no-nonsense knot, already stood in the shadowed doorway.

"Mrs. Rogers?" Violet said, trying not to bite her lip with nerves. The way the woman studied her with narrowed eyes made her sure she didn't pass muster.

"I am Ethel, the housekeeper," the woman snapped "If you'll follow me? Mrs. Rogers will interview you shortly."

Violet sighed with relief that she wouldn't have to work for this lady. "I—thank you." She followed the woman into the house. After the bright, warm day, the dim coolness was startling, and Violet was disoriented for a second. When she blinked, Ethel was already far ahead, vanishing into a distant room down a hallway. Violet dashed to keep up, trying not to reveal the patched soles of her shoes.

"Wait here, please," Ethel said, and left Violet entirely alone.

"Jeepers," she whispered, gaping around her like the dense farm-girl she worked so hard to leave behind.

But she'd never seen a room quite like it, not in real life. It was a museum, but a welcoming one. An alluring one. One that whispered, "Come in," instead of shouting "Don't touch! You're not worthy!"

She wandered further inside, carried in an astonished haze. She'd seen plenty of photos of stars' houses in Jo-Jo's movie mags, of course, but they were always hard, polished surfaces, glass and mirrors. Never like this.

In one corner, against the plain white-plastered walls, was a tall stove tiled in blue and white, like something in one of the old

Russian fairy-tales Violet's Russian babushka, her mother's mother, used to tell while Ma rushed around trying to make dinner for her kids and told her mother no one had time for silly old stories. This was America now, not Tobolsk. The stove was empty now, but Violet could imagine it on cool evenings. Nearby was a delicate, gilded old French writing desk, piled with papers, a cluster of framed drawings hanging above it.

She peeked closer, and saw fluffy shepherdesses and flirtatious boys in tricorn hats, picnics, gardens, swings, all like something in an old palace. Yet the large painting above the white marble fireplace was all squiggles and splashes of red and blue, puzzling and strange, full of wild energy. Who bought *both* those types of art? Who mixed them all up together?

Violet lightly ran her gloved fingers over the striped velvet upholstery of a low-backed sofa, scattered with needlepoint cushions that matched the bright, flowered rug under her old shoes. A Marconiphone nearby was stacked with albums of Bach and jazz, and art books teetered on a dark, carved table. There were also sketchbooks, full crystal ashtrays, empty martini glasses, and the smell of lilies and carnations in the air from tall silver vases.

Through the half-open French doors to the back yard she glimpsed the cool, turquoise oval of a swimming pool, heard a splash and a shout.

It was the strangest place she had ever seen, and she was hit with the feeling that she didn't belong there. She spun around to leave—and saw a woman standing in the doorway.

No, not standing, not really. Floating. As if she might drift away at any second.

Like the room, she wasn't the same as most of the ladies Violet saw in all her jobs. This woman was tall, thin like a willow branch. Her golden-blonde hair, parted in the center, softly curled around a sharp, cat-like face, a pointed chin, arched dark brows, a perfect blade of a nose and high cheekbones. The cherry-red of her lipstick perfectly matched the red varnish on the fingernails where she balanced a cigarette in an ivory holder. Long, elegant, perfectly lacquered, just like all of her.

She didn't dress like most rich, fashionable ladies who lunched, either. No cashmere twin set, or tailored suit, or full-skirted dress, no pearl button earrings. She wore what looked like a man's crisp white shirt, the sleeves rolled up to reveal stacks of bangle bracelets, a starburst brooch of red, blue, green, and purple stones sparkling at the collar. But her tailored blue linen skirt and espadrille sandals were as casual as a beach.

The woman just studied Violet for a moment in perfect, still silence, as if time had frozen. Her eyes, deep, dark velvet-brown, were unreadable.

Then a pack of dachshund dogs, a long, low, moving, barking carpet, swarmed around those beachy espadrilles, and the spell snapped. Violet took a step back, feeling all, all wrong in her borrowed clothes, all wrong in her lipstick, in her skin, in herself. Her face turned hot and clammy, and she just knew her cheeks were as red as her hair. For one wild moment, she wondered if she could flee through those French doors and jump into that pool.

It was too late for escape. The woman smiled, so gentle, and glided slowly into the room. The dogs twisted around her feet, but she just watched Violet, that quiet, deep gaze that seemed to see too much.

She held out her hand, rings sparkling on every finger, and Violet tentatively shook it. She caught a heady whiff of Schiaparelli Shocking perfume.

"I am so sorry to be late," the woman said, voice low, soft, faintly drawling with the touch of some European accent. "A terrible failing of mine, I'm afraid, always so tardy. You're the girl from the agency, yes?"

Violet could barely find her own voice for a minute. Finally, she swallowed hard and managed to say, "Yes. I'm Violet Redfield."

"Violet. Such a pretty name, isn't it? Like something from another time, something sweet and simple. I'm Millicent Rogers."

Millicent Rogers. Violet stared at her, stunned. Of *course.* How could she have not known immediately? Millicent Rogers, the Standard Oil heiress who was now taking Hollywood by storm. *Millicent Huddleston Rogers Plans To Wed Clark Gable!*, that was what the headlines had screamed just yesterday.

And now she, Violet Anastasia Redfield, was supposed to work for her?

Mrs. Rogers didn't seem to notice Violet's seizure of mortification. She just smiled that slow, feline smile and gestured to the pretty striped sofa. "Do sit down. Just move those cushions out of the way. I don't know how they got so very out of place. I had a bit of a cocktail 'do' last night, and some people do tend to be careless, don't they?" She reached for one of those cushions, all red and pink flowers beaded with tiny pearls, and plumped it. "I made them myself."

Violet was baffled. "The cocktails?"

Mrs. Rogers laughed, low, husky, her dark eyes sparkling. "The cushions. The rug, too. Needlepoint is one of my little hobbies. I am obliged to keep to my bed quite often, like some appalling Victorian maiden with a fainting couch, and must find ways to keep busy." She sat down and gestured to the spot beside her. "I am sure the agency told you what I need."

Violet carefully perched on the very edge of the sofa, keeping her feet flat on the floor to hide her old shoes, sure she was going to break something at any second. "You need a secretary?"

"Yes, I do suppose you could call it that. I fear I am terribly disorganized, you see. I need someone to take care of—well, things. My calendar, of course, some household management, communicating with my accountants, a bit of this and that. There would be quite a bit of travel, I'm afraid. Do you have a fiancé, Miss Redfield, someone steady?"

Violet fidgeted as she thought of the few awkward dates she had tried lately. "No, Mrs. Rogers. Boys are too much trouble."

She almost clapped her hand to her mouth when she remembered the gossip about Mrs. Rogers—three husbands, famous writers and spies and politicians and princes as lovers. Clark Gable, for Pete's sake. But Millicent just laughed again, that wonderful, dark, caramel laugh that made Violet feel somehow sure the world was really a glorious, fascinating place, full of interesting things, not the hard, rocky road to navigate it felt like.

Millicent put out her cigarette in the overflowing ashtray and sat back against her handmade cushions. Up close, Violet could see the tired lines around her eyes, the paleness of her skin under the careful makeup.

"Indeed they are. You're better off on your own, believe me, Miss Redfield. What about your family?"

"They're in Iowa."

Millicent frowned in puzzlement, as if this *Iowa* was a faraway kingdom she had never heard of. Violet was sure she probably hadn't. "So you won't mind the travel? An unpredictable schedule? I often need assistance at odd hours."

"I think I would like to see more of the world, Mrs. Rogers," Violet said, and to her surprise she realized it was true. She wanted to see *this* woman's world. The world she once wanted to create in her writing.

"Oh, Millicent, please. Or MR. That's what my sons call me. But never Milly. My last husband called me that. And sometimes my mother." She shuddered, the jeweled starburst sparkling like a dozen stained glass windows. She studied Violet for another silent moment. "I'm not an easy person to work with, I know that about myself. I'm often ill, you see, and it makes me irritated by everything sometimes. I have some strange whims. But I can see that you are an intelligent, curious young woman, as I once was, and I will always respect that. I'm always loyal to the people who are loyal to me. And I think I pay well enough."

She named a sum that Violet found beyond astonishing. Five times what she last made at Walker's, even more than the agency letter said. She looked around the room again, that glorious, muddled, strange room, and wondered where Millicent's travels led her. That curiosity she had tried to hide for so long, the one that this woman glimpsed in only a moment, sparked again.

"Thank you, Mrs—Millicent," she said. "I'm happy to accept."

"Good." Millicent lit another cigarette and smiled at Violet through the wreath of silvery smoke. "Now, do take off that hideous jacket, pour us both a drink from the bar over there, and tell me more about what it's like to live in Iowa ..."

CHAPTER 2

Millicent

When I was a child, my grandfather had a house called The Port of Missing Men. It was named for a shipwreck just off that shore hundreds of years ago, but I always wondered if it was some portent of my family's future life. Despite the ominous ring of it, that house was my favorite place in all the world.

It wasn't grand, like the marble mansion at Fairhaven, or my parents' unhappy gilded halls on Fifth Avenue. It was all old shingles, silvered by the years, and huge porches where a girl could read all day long to the sound of the sea and the salty smell of the wind. It wasn't a house that demanded anything of you at all. It just let you be. Let you exist, just as you were in that moment, with the ghosts of all the people who had passed through it before to keep you company.

I think I've been looking for The Port again all my life, in Austria and Jamaica and Virginia and California, and I never found it until I came to Taos. There can be no two places more different, and no two more alike. They both just take you as you are. They see through who you pretend to be.

My grandfather didn't always own The Port, of course, or all his other houses. He started as a grocery clerk, and ended as VP of

Standard Oil. He was a tough old bird; he had to build up every single thing he had from the ground. All that money made my own life both glorious and awful. But at The Port he was a different man. Funny. Silly. He would swim in the sea with me, my brother, and my cousins, play croquet with us, run about doing hide and seek in the old rooms.

Most of all, he loved art, and he loved to show it to me, talk about it to me. That was his greatest gift in my life.

After the fever, of course, it was all different. I didn't see The Port for a long time, and when I did, I couldn't swim or run or play any longer. All those months in bed, I only had books. But books contain whole worlds, don't they? I learned French, German, Greek, Latin. (When my brother, poor, god-forsaken Henry, and I didn't want our parents to know what we were saying, we spoke Latin.). I learned history, geography, philosophy. To draw and sew. Most of all, I learned even more about art.

Mummy-Da was a painter herself, and she taught me about line, color, perspective. To learn how to say what has no words.

The doctor said I would die before I was ten. I determined I would not. Like my grandfather, I can be tough when I need to be. But life after was not the same as before. After so long only talking to people in books, I wasn't sure what to say to real human beings, to people who expect so much from the Standard Oil heiress. (SOH, my sons sometimes call me now. Those three cursed letters.) I didn't know how to find a friend.

I seemed closed in my own world after that, wrapped in a haze no matter how many dances I danced, martinis I drank, men I loved. And there have been plenty of all three of that over the years. But what I learned was—sometimes things have to end before they can really begin.

After everything, my husbands, losing so much in the war, I dared to think maybe all those fairy-tales I used to read could be plausible when I saw *him*.

It was at a party. Of course. A crowd on a terrace somewhere above the canyon, I can't remember where. A warm, soft evening, smelling of wisteria and Chanel #5 and gin. Laughter, chatter, deals made. Boring. I thought about leaving, and then there he was. Clark Gable. Captain Butler.

Unlike so many other movie stars I've met, who are in real life so much *less* than you think, he was exactly right. My last husband, Ronnie, my God but he was handsome. A golden god, flying down the ski slopes. Whirling a woman around the dance floor until she was dizzy with it all. But when that was over, when you were alone and the house was quiet—that was gone. There was no *there* there.

I know you see what I mean.

I was sure Captain Butler was different. He was a beautiful man, just like they had all been—the count, Arturo, Roald, Ian. But Clark was like a man in some Hemingway story, dark and dangerous and tough, no nonsense.

He smiled at me, that white, white smile in his dark face, and suddenly the world, so gray after the war, was all brightness again. For the first time, he was *my* conquest instead of the other way around.

Maybe there could be happy endings after all. But I should have remembered, from all my reading, how fairy-tales—*real* fairy-tales, the ones of dark forests and killer witches—turn out.

CHAPTER 3

Violet

As Violet got ready for her job—*her job*—she was sure it must all be a weird dream. She would get back to that house, that magical house with its books and paintings and needlepoint, and be laughed away from the door. No one like MR would hire someone like Violet Redfield. What could Violet ever do for her?

She fidgeted in her bus seat, half-sure she would jump off at the next stop and run away. Get a job in a diner or something, where the people were just *people*, not mystical princesses. She knew she wouldn't, though. She had to see that house again; it pulled her like a giant rope. It fascinated her.

She'd even dreamed about it the night before. In her dream, that fantastical house wasn't empty, but filled with partygoers in outlandish masks. Owls, cats, harlequins, flowing up and down the staircase, dancing in looping circles around the striped sofas. Trapeze artists flew in and out of the open patio doors, and a man dressed like the Pope slid down the banister while the pack of yapping dachshunds dressed in clown costumes barked at him.

And none of it, there in that place, seemed strange at all.

The strange part was opening her eyes to the prickle of sunlight and finding herself in the same old shabby boarding house room. No trapeze, no pope, no dogs, just the dusty, sagging armchair in the corner, the mess on the battered dressing table. Had she imagined the whole thing? Like one of the stories she used to write?

"Knock, knock!" Jo-Jo sang from the hallway, banging on the door. She and some of the other girls had already left for an evening out when Violet got home from her interview, and she'd been glad she hadn't had to explain it all to them in her daze. "Are you up yet, sleepyhead?"

Violet pushed herself up in bed, shoving away the enchanted ribbons of that weird dream. "Come on in."

Jo-Jo pushed the door open with a tray of coffee balanced on one hand, like the diner waitress she used to be before her new office job. Despite her late-night date, her blonde hair was curled and bouncy, her eyes bright, lipstick red and straight. Violet thought maybe *she* should go to work for Mrs. Rogers instead. But Vi also knew nothing could make her walk away from that job now, trapezes or not.

"You're a lifesaver," Violet said hoarsely, and gulped down the coffee.

Jo-Jo plumped herself down on the armchair. "Well, what happened? Did you get the job? I'm just dying to know!"

"I did. I'm supposed to start later today."

Jo-Jo clapped her hands. "Oh, goodie! Was it all just *beyond*? Glamorous? Some society dame? Or a movie star?"

"Society lady, definitely. You should see this house." Violet frowned as she took another drink of coffee. Mrs. Rogers was assuredly high society. Everything about her, from that low, soft drawl of her voice, the way she exhaled a silvery plume from her cigarette, the glide of her walk, said *money*. Security. Certainty. But Vi didn't think she was "society" the way Jo-Jo meant. Not like the movie moguls' wives wrapped in furs, the actresses who so often looked terrified behind their diamonds and satins in real life. Mrs. Rogers was quiet, hidden.

She was different.

Violet didn't know how to explain all of that. Not to Jo-Jo, or even to herself. She'd never met anyone else like her.

"I think it will be very interesting," was all she could say.

Jo-Jo sighed. "And think of the men you'll meet in a place like that! Real, grown-up sorts who will take you out for champagne and steak, not like those chumps last night, who wouldn't even pay up for hotdogs."

Violet was sure any man who might be hanging around a place like MR's house would terrify her. MR herself was scary enough. But that was too much to think about all at one time.

She glanced at the open doors of her wardrobe, and realized she still had a much more immediate problem.

"I still don't have anything that's right to wear," she said.

Jo-Jo's red lips pursed as she studied the limp array of garments hanging there. The pitiful situation hadn't improved overnight. "What about that suit you wore at the glove counter? Surely a black suit is always okay, until you get paid."

Violet thought of that suit, cheap crepe, now faded and frayed at the edges. She remembered Millicent's espadrilles, the flashing sparkle of bangles on her wrists, the crisp white blouse. "I don't think so."

She looked again at Jo-Jo, who wore a parrot-green cotton sundress, full-skirted, held up with red ribbon straps. Maybe—just maybe, with a pair of sandals from the five-and-dime? Violet thought maybe she could scrape up some money for some shoes, and still have her bus fare.

"Could I borrow *your* dress, Jo-Jo?" she said. "I would owe you forever."

Jo-Jo looked appalled. "You can't wear *this* to work as a social secretary! It's ancient, I made it myself way back before I even came to California."

"Trust me. I think it's exactly the right thing." Violet already could tell that with Mrs. Rogers, she was going to have to think about clothes—and lots of other things—in a brand-new way.

When Violet arrived at the fairy-tale house again, no one answered her ring at the bell. No scary housekeeper, no butler, no MR herself, not even a dream-guy in an owl mask. Everything seemed shut up tight, silent, but the handle turned under her tentative touch and she let herself in.

It all looked the same, the bright sofas, the paintings, the piles of books, but a sort of stale haze hung over the rooms, like a party had just ended. Glasses stood, empty or half-full of amber whiskey, on stone sculpture bases, banisters, the floor. It smelled of sweet-sour cigar smoke, the lingering hint of Shalimar and Chanel #5 and Shocking. Empty, deserted, haunted.

But the music played on the Marconigram opera arias, as if to some vanished audience, and the glass patio doors were open. Violet followed the breeze to the marble patio by the pool.

Mrs. Rogers lay there, on a coral and white striped lounge that looked out on the empty turquoise rectangle of water, the palm trees, the stone statues with their blank, staring eyes. She wore a white, strappy swimsuit, her face and gold-blonde hair shaded by a floppy straw hat and white-framed sunglasses, her long, golden legs stretched in front of her. A bottle of champagne and carafe of orange juice chilled in a silver bucket on the table beside her, along with glasses and an alabaster ashtray, half-full of lipstick-stained butts. A book of poetry lay open next to them.

"Violet," she said, in that soft, slow voice. She turned her head just as slowly, as if moving and speaking were beyond trouble, and peered over the top of her glasses. "Don't you look lovely today. Like a bird of paradise perched in one of those gorgeous palm trees."

Violet glanced uncertainly over her shoulder, back to the

empty, disheveled house. Maybe there really was something of her ma's immaculate Iowa housekeeper in her after all, if she couldn't handle the mess just sitting around. "Are there letters I should write, or—or work I should be doing ..."

"Your work is whatever I say it is," Millicent murmured. "And right now, I say you should sit down here and have a mimosa. They're all the rage for breakfast now, you know."

Violet slowly lowered herself onto the edge of the neighboring chaise, and watched in astonishment as Millicent reached for a glass and mixed up some of the juice and champagne. Heavier on the champagne than the juice. No wonder Millicent was so slim, if this was her meal plan.

"Here, drink this, sit back, talk to me," Millicent said, handing over the glass. She mixed up another for herself, and stretched like a cat in the sun, her ruby-red toenails glistening.

Violet had no idea what to say, what a woman like this would want to talk about. She took a gulp of her drink, and had to admit it did make a tasty breakfast. "Should I—maybe come earlier in the future, Mrs—MR?"

Millicent waved this away with a flash of her jeweled rings. "My dear Violet, you must know—I never get up before noon. I just can't bear it, especially if I've been to a party. My ridiculous old body simply won't do as I command it. So I wake, I do some reading or sketching, then perhaps I feel up to going for a gown fitting or to tea. I won't need you until noon, but after that you must be prepared for anything. No day is ever quite the same." She seemed to study the pool, the wide green lawn beyond, over the edge of her glasses. "Perhaps you should just live here?"

"Here?" Violet whispered. Her—live in the fairy-tale house?

"Where do you live now?"

"Just a boarding house near the studios where most of the girls work. No place special."

"A boarding house! How utterly fascinating." Somehow, much like talking about Iowa at the interview, boarding houses seemed to catch her rapt attention. She rolled on her side to face Violet, her entire attention focused on Vi and only Vi. Violet could see why so many men were enraptured by her. "With lots of other girls? Are you dear friends with them? Go out to parties together, things like that?"

"Well—yes. Sort of." Violet thought of meal times at the house, listening to the girls' stories of dates and auditions, laughing at the trouble they got into. Knowing she could never be quite like they were. "I do have a few friends. We all work a lot, but sometimes I go with them on double dates or to the movies. I borrowed this dress from one of them."

"How delightful it all must be. I never did have real friends when I was young. It was rather lonely."

Violet was surprised. She'd have thought a lady like MR would have dashed from dance to dance with other debs, all of them in white silk and pearls, whispering together. Or maybe that was just from the movies, too, like all of life seemed to be in California. "Not even from school?"

Millicent laid back on her lounge, her hat hiding her expression. "I never really went to school. My health wouldn't let me when I was a child, so I had tutors. I did go to a place called the Madeira School for a while, when my father had a government post in Washington, DC during the war. The *first* war, in 1917. But I was a day girl when everyone else boarded, I was quite the interloper. And by then I had no patience at all for classes like Deportment." She waved her hand in a graceful arc, as if that was all they taught in Deportment class, and laughed. "I just wanted to run free."

"I know that feeling," Violet muttered. And she did. There were all those long days when she hid in the hay barn at home, with a book and her daydreams, wishing she was far away from that everyday world where nothing changed.

"So I shouldn't ask you to live in."

"I wouldn't mind at all," Violet said. There wasn't much

actual freedom in the boarding house anyway, not anymore, and here she would save on her bus fare. Could watch this new, enchanted world close up. "If you need my help."

"You could stay in that cottage over there," Millicent said, gesturing to a little stucco building beyond the pool. "I use it as a studio now, but I can move it into the house. In your off-hours, you could do whatever you like. I'm no chaperone."

Violet stared at the tiny, perfect place, overcome by the thought she might actually live there. Look out at the pool every day, have quiet nights all to herself. It was astonishing. Better than her weird costume party dream.

Suddenly, a burst of noise broke like a storm over the silent lawn, whoops and screams like in some cowboy flick. A flock of kids, sunburned, tow-headed boys in swim trunks, tumbled over the gate and launched like a tsunami into the water.

Millicent barely even seemed to notice the invasion. She just poured herself another mimosa and lit a cigarette. "Just the neighbors' sons. I let them swim after school sometimes."

"They're certainly—lively."

Millicent laughed. "They remind me of my own sons when they were tiny. But I do like it that they leave after an hour or so." She rolled over, letting the sun onto her bare back over the white straps. "Tell me, Violet darling—have you ever been in love? A *first* love, when everything is so new and sharp and bright that you're sure you'll die of it?"

Violet thought the mimosa must be going to her head, because the swift pivot of subjects didn't even surprise her. She wasn't sure anything would really surprise her in this place. She closed her eyes, let the sun warm her cheeks, and thought about Bill for the first time in ages. Bill holding her hand as they walked home from school; kissing her behind the barn; smiling at her in his crisp new uniform.

"I think I've only ever had a first love," she said. "I haven't cared about anyone else since. But I'm not even sure it was *love*."

"Why not? Who was he?" Millicent's voice was low and gentle, blurry from the champagne, but intense with interest. As if Vi's little Midwestern teenage romance was every bit as interesting as Millicent's movie stars and South American millionaires. No wonder Millicent was an object of fascination to the scandal sheets, to everyone she met. It was intoxicating to have such attention focused on her, Violet Redfield, but also a little disconcerting.

"He was a boy I'd known since we were kids. Bill. We went to school together," Violet said. "He seemed like he was just always in my life. Like I had known him forever, since before we were even born. We barely needed to say anything to each other, we just—knew." But he didn't know she wrote stories. No one knew.

Millicent sighed. "Twin souls from infanthood. It seems like a poem."

Violet laughed. "Not exactly poetic."

"Then what was it like? Why weren't you sure it was love?"

Violet thought back to when she was so young, so unaware of any world outside their little neighborhood. Of Bill's blue eyes, his freckles, his smile. The way holding his hand felt so safe and easy. "Maybe it was because we'd always known each other. Because he was sure he knew what I wanted better than I did. But when he kissed me that first time ..."

Millicent propped her head on her hand, watching Violet intently. "What happened?"

"Nothing really," Violet said. She closed her eyes and felt the touch of his lips on hers again, soft, slow. "That was the problem. I expected so much. Too much, probably. It was nothing like a kiss in a book. It was—nice. Easy. And I realized I loved him, truly, but not like a lover should."

"Then far better for you to part as friends." Millicent's voice was suddenly sharp, fierce. "Life is short and precious, Violet. Not a moment should be wasted on anything that doesn't put fire in our souls. Better to be friends, and seek what was meant to be out in the world."

Violet was startled by that ferocity. Had she ever felt so strongly about something, about grabbing what she wanted in life? Had she ever even known was that was? Writing, maybe, yes. She always felt like she was just bumbling around, fumbling in the darkness. "I'm afraid that can't be. Bill was killed in the war. I've felt so guilty since that telegram came, like such an awful person that I couldn't picture our life together there on his family farm. That I didn't want what everyone else wanted so much."

Violet didn't know why she had blurted that out. She'd never told anyone, not even her mother, how she felt so deep inside. The doubts, the longing, the fear.

Millicent leaned closer, sliding her glasses off her nose to reveal the fire in her dark eyes. She smelled of Shocking and suntan oil, of that intense, focusing energy that always seemed to burn around her. "What do you mean?"

"I—he thought we were going to get engaged when he came home. Everyone thought that. His parents, my parents, our friends at school. They all took it for granted, and thought I must be torn up when he died. That that's the reason I ran off to California, to get away from my grief. I did mourn Bill—but not in that way. And it made me a terrible person."

"My darling Violet, you must put such thoughts away. Far away. Believe me, I've learned so much in my life, and I know that guilt and regret can give us nothing. We can't live our lives according to what other people want. You were a kind friend to him, and I'm sure he died happy in that. If he had come home, you would have found it in yourself to let him go to find the *right* girl, and you would have sought out your own dreams. I am sure of it. I see it in you, just as I did in me. You did nothing wrong."

Violet choked back a violent sob that rose up inside of her. It felt like a giant knot releasing inside of her, unfurling. Letting go its hold on her at last. She'd never known anything like it. She gulped down the last of her drink, and Millicent silently refilled it.

"Who was *your* first love, MR?" she gasped, desperate to think of something, anything, to distract her. Anything but Bill, and the past, and letting it go.

She knew Millicent's first husband had been a handsome Austrian count, and expected her to say him. But Millicent lit another cigarette, laid back, and purred, "My dear, it was the most gorgeous Russian prince you could ever have imagined."

A Russian prince? From anyone else, anywhere else, Violet would have been sure that was a whopper. But here, with Millicent, the sun burning overhead, the champagne, she knew it was true. Somehow, conversations while lying in the sun were always different from any other. Rambling, strange, full of secrets and confessions. She remembered summer days with her high school girlfriends, lying out on quilts by the wheat fields with buckets of iced tea and movie mags. They had giggled about farmers' sons and the college guy who worked holidays at the soda fountain. Not royalty.

Violet wondered if she was really still dreaming.

"A prince?" she said.

"Hmm, yes, a real one. Prince Serge Obolensky. I met him when my parents took me to Europe after my debut. I was only seventeen, and they were afraid I was making a bad connection with a young man they disapproved of. They had no idea what was waiting on the other side of the ocean! I was so silly, so dangerously susceptible to a title and a pretty face. I can do without titles now, but the handsome faces ..." She laughed, a low, gravelly, wry sound that spoke of so much. Too much.

"Did you meet him in his castle?"

"Oh, no. It was after the Revolution, and the castles were lost forever. He was in Rome, visiting his mother, Princess Marie, who had escaped St. Petersburg with the most luscious emeralds. He had been a cavalry officer in the war, but when I met him, he was trying to be a stockbroker. No less dashing, though. The air of royal breeding never leaves a man, I think. I saw him later in London, and then at an absolutely freezing castle in Scotland, where we went for the shooting. Nothing to do there but snuggle together by the fire! He asked me to marry him a few times."

"But you didn't want to be a princess?"

"I thought it would be dandy back then. But you see, he was already married."

"Married!" Violet cried. That was never the way fairy-tales were supposed to go.

"Yes, to the daughter of some tsar or other. She had a life of her own, they lived completely apart. She did divorce him eventually. He married Alice Astor. And my parents whisked me off to Switzerland, where I became engaged to someone else." She studied the noisy crowd in her pool, but she didn't seem to see them at all. She seemed very far away, back there in Rome or Scotland or Switzerland, a beautiful young heiress whirling through a giddy new world. Violet could barely imagine it.

"It was such a strange time," Millicent whispered. "So disorienting. I was so young, and we had to keep leaving town every few weeks because I kept getting engaged. There were so many things to worry about—what was good for my health, what was correct behavior, what would my parents allow? What did all those men *really* want—my money? I know what the world saw, my fortune, my face, my clothes, my little scandals. But what did *I* want? I had no idea then."

Violet took another long drink of her mimosa. "Yes. It's hard to tell that sometimes." She saw what MR meant, truly she did, even if she had no fortune or beauty, had never even met a prince. Sometimes all anyone wanted was the facade, whether it was her farm family in Iowa or a millionaire father wanting to keep his daughter out of scandal. No one cared what lay deep inside.

"I did marry soon after we came back to New York, an Austrian count who didn't have a bean," Millicent said with a laugh. "My parents *hated* him, they saw to it that the marriage didn't last more than a few months. But it was fun for a while. We earned money dancing in Paris cafes, if you can imagine!

Performing tangos for tourists and such. I was very silly over him. But I tell you this, Violet darling." She put down her drink, and her voice deepened again into that rare, confiding intensity. "Love *is* delicious. Passion, sex, all of it. But freedom is everything in the end. Never give that up."

A phone rang somewhere in the house, shrill, real, an interruption in that sun-washed dream. The housekeeper came out and whispered in Millicent's ear.

MR frowned. "What is it now?"

"He says it's most urgent," the housekeeper said, twisting her hands.

"Oh, very well. I don't suppose it will go away." Millicent swung her long legs off the lounge and reached for a white silk robe. She pulled it on in a jerky, impatient movement. "Come along, Violet. We have work to do."

Violet found herself baffled, confused by the sudden change. "Oh—yes. Of course," she gasped. She put down her empty glass and hurried behind Millicent into the shadowy, cool house.

At the patio doors, MR suddenly glanced back. Her face was unreadable behind her hat and glasses. "Just promise me you will remember what I said. Freedom is everything. Never give that up for all the riches in the world. You will always regret it."

CHAPTER 4

Millicent

NOVEMBER 24, 1919

"I just don't think it's quite right." Mary Rogers circled her daughter's still figure like a hawk tracking a mouse, shaking her head, pursing her lips. The mouse just wasn't up to par. She'd seen plumper, sleeker, better prey before.

Millicent barely glanced at herself in the mirror. The couturier's assistants knelt below her stool, hemming, trimming, doing their last-minute adjustments. Millicent stared out the window at the blaze of late afternoon sun on the gold and crimson leaves of a New York autumn. It was so beautiful, so fleeting.

"White is never my best color, Mummy-Da, you know that," she murmured. "But you insisted." She well-remembered the argument in the Paris designer's atelier. The array of fabric samples on the marble tables, the models twirling around them in a luscious rainbow of gowns. Green and blue like the sea, pink like Fragonard flirts, jeweled purples and ambers and corals. Fashion was such a glorious banquet—and she was confined to one tiny end of it, eating nursery rice pudding while there was *mousse au chocolat* just beyond.

Not for much longer, though. She was almost eighteen now, and soon, very soon, she would fly through that window and taste all the sweetness of freedom. For a little while, anyway. Until she married. Then it was back into the box.

Millicent frowned. Her parents, the very people who had always kept her so carefully confined, so swaddled in cotton batting, so watched, were determined *they* would choose her husband. That after she married their selection, a man from a family just like their own, her life would go on just like it always had. Tea parties, dances, tennis, seeing the same people everywhere she went. Maybe one day she and her husband would quarrel and go their separate ways, as her parents had, but the facade would never be broken.

Little did they know. Little had they *ever* known her.

She looked back in the mirror, at her mother's reflection behind her. Mary was the very image of a New York matron, plump and pretty in her amber-colored velvet gown, diamond clips in her dark hair, a worried frown on her face. Millicent never wanted to end up like her.

"It is your debut ball, Millie," she said sharply. Millicent hated being called "Millie," but she knew not to argue with her mother. It never worked. Easier to ignore it. "White is required. I am just not sure ..."

Millicent's gaze swept down over her dress. It was the latest style, what all the English girls wore to Buckingham Palace to curtsy for the king. That was why her mother chose it. A *robe de style* of white brocaded satin over panniers, trimmed with silver-frosted white lace, white ruffled sleeves falling from her shoulders like cake icing. A green velvet belt circled her slim waist, matching the green orchid bouquet that waited in a vase on the table. The dark, wavy hair, which her parents refused to let her bob, was bound with a green and gold Grecian wreath. One of the maids fastened her father's debutante gift, a triple row of creamy pearls, around her neck. Millicent would have preferred something simpler, more modern; it would have suited her better, Millicent was sure.

"It's too late now," she said. "We have to be at the Ritz-Carlton in an hour."

"An hour!" Mary cried. "How can we possibly? Nothing is even near ready. Oh, where is your father? Is he going to ruin *this*, too?"

Millicent knew what she meant. Was Henry Rogers Senior going to drink too much before the ball even began? He had at her mother's reception for the Parisian artist Monsieur Hariot, just last month. Mary's artistic salons were terribly important to her. Her daughter's debut, a hundred times more.

Mary hurried out of the room in a swirl of amber chiffon and velvet. "Harry!" she called for her husband. "Where is the car?"

Millicent waved away the hovering maids, and drifted over to pick up her bouquet and gloves herself. The ball was meant to be about her, two thousand guests flocking to the Ritz to officially meet her, look her over for marriage. Yet it just felt like so many other things in her world. Distant for her, strange, curious. Not real, not like being alone in her room with her books and her sketches. She had been so apart at that school in Washington, different from the other girls. Apart at all the parties she had already attended that autumn, despite dancing every dance with eager partners.

Why should her own ball be any different, really? It was just another party.

She glanced over the array of newspapers on the table, the headlines and photos that heralded her upcoming debut. "Oil heiress beauty makes her curtsy!" "Rogers stunner out in the world!"

She laughed. She never had any idea what girl those articles described. She sounded like a character in some frothy musical, some bouncing giggler striding from the golf course to the dance floor. Someone Millicent might enjoy watching for three acts through various romantic scrapes, but no one she really knew.

She looked over her shoulder back to the mirror. Tall, slim, her dark hair glossy under the wreath, eyes large and shadowed. A white-clad wraith. No. That girl was someone she didn't know at all.

Her father appeared in the doorway. He wore the proper clothes, his tuxedo and white tie, his graying hair brushed and his beard trimmed, but even her mother's strictures couldn't make his eyes less bloodshot, his nose less red. It couldn't make him look interested in what might happen to his daughter. "Are you ready, then, Millie?" he asked, distracted, flicking at his onyx cufflinks. "Your mother says we'll be late. I'm not going to miss out on the champagne, not with what it's costing me. Whoever heard of two thousand people at a debutante ball?"

"Of course, Papa." She drifted closer to kiss his cheek. At least he didn't smell of brandy tonight. Yet. "It hardly matters, though, does it? If we're late. They can't really start without us."

Mary Rogers, so well-known in society for her grand artistic taste, had really outdone herself. Even Millicent, who secretly thought her mother too often took artistic matters a step too far with her old-fashioned taste, had to agree as she took up her pose at the top of the stairs leading to the Ritz's ballroom.

The hotel was transformed into an autumn fantasmic, filled by Gildman's florist with twenty tall oak trees in copper buckets, blazing with russet foliage. More pots of chrysanthemums and ferns banked along the watered silk-papered walls, and spilled like a torrent of red and gold and dark green into the foyer and down the staircase, where soon the thousands of guests would ascend. The round tables in the dining room, draped in burgundy damask, were covered with green orchid centerpieces. Hundreds of bottles of champagne were chilling, and the thirty-piece orchestra tuned up for foxtrots and waltzes.

Yes, Millicent thought coolly, it was the perfect stage set.

Mary reached for Millicent's gloved wrist, where her gilded dance card dangled by a green velvet ribbon. It was a hopelessly old-fashioned thing, Millicent thought, but her mother said the English debs had them, so there it was.

"Now, Millie," her mother said, her voice full of that low urgency she always had when she was going to make a Very Deep Pronouncement. "Be very careful who you dance with tonight. Remember—you have danced with the Prince of Wales. Twice."

Millicent sighed. She hardly needed reminding that she had danced with the Prince of Wales on his tour of the United States. Her mother did so love talking about it, even though it was the biggest non-event Millicent could imagine. He had barely talked, and was short besides. But Mary probably dreamed of being mother to Queen Millicent. As if he would ever marry an American.

"I doubt His Highness will drop by tonight," she said.

Mary frowned. "I am sure he would have, if he happened to be in New York. He did so admire you, Millie. You need to learn to take full advantage of such moments. You are always so very—drowsy. Distant. Young men will think you are aloof. Not interested in them."

Millicent fiddled with her green orchid bouquet, already bored. And the ball hadn't even started yet. "Then to whom should I show interest, if no princes show up?"

"Jimmy Thompson will be here." Mary's expression turned thoughtful, calculating. Millicent knew to beware of that look. "He has always liked you so much, and is such a fine young man. He just finished at Yale, top of his class, and his parents are sure he is destined for very great things."

Millicent plucked a waxy petal from one of the orchids. She had known Jimmy since they were kids; their mothers were good friends, on the opera board together, and the Thompsons had an estate near her family's at Tuxedo Park. He was handsome enough, fun, good-natured. Being married to him would mean her life would go on just as it always had. The thought gave her a headache.

That was the last thing she wanted.

There was only time for her to nod, when the doors opened and a flood of people poured up the stairs in a river of silks, satins, furs, and black suits. Their laughter and chatter was like incoherent, discordant music.

Millicent was sure she would be drowned in those furs, in the heady smell of Guerlain perfumes, in smiles and giggles. She pasted her own smile on her face, and tried not to scream. It seemed like even more people showed up than the thousands her mother had invited, and all too soon the tables and dance floor were packed to the gilded rafters. One of the towering oak trees crashed to the floor amid screams, though no one was actually injured.

"I said it was all too much," her father muttered, but her mother just kept chattering, and smiling, smiling, smiling.

"Millicent!" someone called, and she turned gratefully to find her friend Lela Emory running toward her in a swirl of beaded pink silk and diamonds. Lela was an heiress from Chicago, luckily an orphan, and they often found plenty of mischief together. Millicent ran over to hug her.

"Come on, let's go dance, or find some punch, or something," Lela said with a giggle. "You look in desperate need of rescue."

"Truer words have never been said, Lela darling," Millicent said. Before her mother could stop her, Millicent locked arms with Lela and plunged with her into the crowded depths of the ballroom. They pushed their way through the shrieking hoards to find a tray of glasses of champagne. No one bothered the rich about Prohibition.

"So, who signed your dance card?" Lela asked.

Millicent glanced down at the little gold-edged card. It was covered in scrawls. She tore it off and dropped it into the nearest pot of chrysanthemums. "It doesn't matter."

Lela laughed. "Well, then—who do you *want* to dance with?"

Millicent studied the packed ballroom. It was all men she already knew, had already danced with a hundred times. She sighed. "Oh, I don't know, Lela. I'm just so tired of it all, I think I'll just marry the next man who asks and be done with it."

"This must be my blessed day, then," a voice said behind her, touched with a deep, operetta-Teutonic accent.

Millicent spun around to see a man, a man she was sure she'd never met before, standing behind her. He *looked* like he came from an operetta, too, a chocolate-box prince. Very tall, slim, sharp, chiseled featured, pale blond hair cropped close. Icy blue eyes in a face tanned by the sun, as if he rode polo ponies or bounded around a tennis court all day. The deep lines around his eyes, indicating he must be several years older, just made him look more attractive. He was perfectly dressed in a well-tailored tuxedo, sharp collar, tie, cameo cufflinks at his wrists.

"Shall we dance, then?" he said. "We should probably get to know each other a bit before I propose."

He held out his hand, and, bemused and dizzy, Millicent found herself actually taking it. He spun her out onto the dance floor, graceful, confident. Over his shoulder, Millicent glimpsed Lela, and her friend pretended to swoon.

Millicent held onto him tightly as he twirled her over the floor. He was a much better dancer than the Prince of Wales, and he smelled delicious, of some lemony European cologne and starch.

"You can't marry me," she said. "You don't even know who I am."

He smiled down at her, so confident, so breezy. So perfect. "Certainly I do. You are Miss Millicent Rogers, the lady of the hour."

"I don't know who *you* are." She was sure he hadn't come through the receiving line, or she knew she would have remembered him. He would be impossible to forget. Was he even really invited to the party? Did she care?

"How very remiss of me not to introduce myself. I am Count

Ludwig Salm von Hoogstraten of Vienna, at your service. I was asked here tonight by the van Luydens, who are kindly hosting me this week, and I confess I feared it would be dull. Now I see how wrong I was."

He spun her in a graceful, dizzying arc, making her laugh. A count. Surely even her mother would like that. Unless he was a fortune hunter. Lots of those European royals were now, having lost everything in war and revolution. She suddenly noticed his cuffs were rather frayed, his jacket not the most fashionable cut.

But at that moment, she couldn't have cared less if he was nothing but some impoverished cad. Dancing with him made some of the ice around her seem to melt away, and she laughed and felt alive. Really alive. Even if it was just for a little while. Just until the next dance.

CHAPTER 5

Millicent

1947

I was up much too late again. The doctors, those solemn old men with their crisp white coats and cold stethoscopes, their frowning eyes and perfect beards just beginning to be touched with the perfect amount of silver to be called "distinguished" (Where *did* they get those beards? At medical school graduation, along with the gilded degrees they framed on their walls?) all said so. They listened to my heart, looked at my x-rays, shook their bearded heads solemnly. More sleep was needed. Fewer cocktails. No cigarettes.

"You are weakening yourself every day, Mrs. Rogers," they would murmur as they handed me rows of little pill bottles. "You must take greater care, or you won't see many more days."

Doctors. What did they know, really? I had known hundreds over the years, thousands. They had said I wouldn't live to fifteen, twenty, twenty-five, if I did not take more care. They would have me all wrapped up in cotton batting and packed me away if I let them. One cigarette did me more good than all their clucking. One minute of being alive was all I really wanted. One minute—then the next, and the next. Always moving, always seeing something new, feeling something, anything. Never still.

It was that stillness that really did a person in.

I lit another cigarette in my amber holder, and bent over to study the clutter of my work table. It was really that keeping me awake into the wee hours. I was meant to be at a party at Tyrone and Annabelle Powers' house, but Captain Butler was working late on set, and without him a party just seemed flat.

I wasn't really of much interest in Hollywood, not like New York. Not an actress, not part of the all-important work scene—every scene was a work scene in Hollywood. I'd never realized that until I had stuck around the Canyon for a while. The publicity machine was all for leading men and glamorous actresses, their next roles, their next projects. A mere heiress just confused them.

When I walked into a party on Clark's arm, for a minute that was different. I wore mostly pale colors now, gorgeous, light, floaty evening gowns from darling Adrian, gray and white and silver, with my sapphires and my Verdura starbursts, the frail queen to his dark knight. It was fun. After the war years, Hollywood was a new world for me, a bright, merry one. Gable was so very *manly*, not like my last husband, and even my sons liked him. He revitalized my flagging spirits, like something in a romantic novel.

Now, like a movie itself whose plot wore on too long, I was beginning to see the raw, frayed edges.

No man could be faithful to one woman, of course, everyone knew that, and if a woman played it right it should never matter. But with my captain—it felt different. In a way I didn't recognize, and certainly didn't like. There were women, women, women—Goddard, Kelly, Loretta Young, more of them every day. Now I heard rumors of Virginia Grey. Young, fresh, effortless, talented. Not to mention the ghost of Carole Lombard. Who could compete with the perfect dead?

And my energy was fading. With every slow, careful beat of my heart, I felt something ebbing away. Some sparkle spilling out of my fingertips, trailing away into the night sky.

I should just walk away. Move forward, as I always had before when I sensed that ending in the air. Why couldn't I do that now? What was different about this moment, this man, that made me want to scream in anguish to know he wasn't really mine?

I didn't scream, of course. Rogers never did such things, never burst out with unseemly emotions. (Except for my poor, drunk brother, and look where that got *him*.) I just poured out a finger of whiskey, tossed it back, and turned to my work. A bit of modeling wax between my fingers was just what I needed.

I'd always loved jewelry, of course. I still remembered my first solo visit to Cartier—how Papa shouted about that bill! "You presumably should have arrived at a condition in which you could perform simple mathematical problems of addition and subtraction, and to have known that you had spent more money than you had." Oh, that letter still makes me laugh! (Though I admit, I have sometimes thought of borrowing those words to send to my own sons.)

Cartier and I are old friends now. Jewelry, nice, heavy bracelets and rings, are the best camouflage for the tremors of my illness.

But it wasn't until recent years that a friend, a sculptress, suggested I try designing and making my own. It was an amazing process, from first sketch to casting the metal, and utterly absorbing. The pieces could be anything—dragons, horses, stars, hearts that, unlike mine, were full and whole. I loved the primitive weight and feel of it in my hands, knowing it was something I alone had created.

Tonight, though, the creative vision kept slip-sliding away. I was meant to be making Clark a pair of cufflinks, but the image of them wasn't clear. I put down the modeling wax, and glanced around. Since dear Violet moved into the studio cottage out by the pool, I moved my tools into an attic room. Maybe I just didn't feel quite organized there? Maybe moving Violet into the house hadn't been such a good idea?

But I knew that wasn't true. I went to the open window and lit another cigarette, studying the patch of light from the cottage windows. A shadow flickered past it, a silhouette making cocoa at the little stove. Vi was a night owl, too. I had noticed it, though of course I never summoned her at night or asked her what plagued her sleep. We were all entitled to our secrets, our demons. If I wanted to keep mine hidden, I had to let her keep hers, too.

Yet I did like her, was happy I had found her. She was a girl of quiet, neat efficiency, a girl who just got on with things without making a fuss, which I so much needed. I smiled when I remembered the rueful shake of her head as she sorted through my disheveled pile of ledgers. "Simple mathematical problems" indeed! But Violet was organizing it all.

Her clothes, though ...

I frowned as I flicked the ash out the window. Violet was pretty, striking even, with that glorious hair. Slim, graceful, quick. I had an eye for beauty—male, female, jewels, paintings, it didn't matter. Beauty was beauty. Beauty was *everything*. And Vi was wasting hers, just as she probably had all her life. But she wasn't on the farm anymore, with her childhood sweetheart and no way out. She only seemed to have three ensembles, all of them hideous, and her shoes were falling to bits.

I turned back to my table, and swept the wax into the wastepaper basket before I took out a fresh sketchbook. Maybe I wouldn't make a cufflinks gift this time. Maybe I would make a brooch. In the shape of a violet.

CHAPTER 6

Violet

"No! No, this isn't right. Why is nothing ever done right here? It must be done over again. Now! Do you hear me?"

Violet looked up from her desk, shocked by the sudden shout from MR. A flurry of papers were hurled through the air, a few flying just past Violet's head. Some were caught on a breeze from the open windows and blew away. MR had been quiet until that moment, absorbed in her own work across the room, but Violet was used to sudden changes by now. To sudden mood swings, bursts of anger. She was learning how to bend, like that breeze, and the thunder-clouds were usually worth having her own quiet room at night, having work she found interesting.

But she hated to think maybe she had messed up on something important. She held her breath and picked up a stray paper, praying it wasn't a page from one of her account books. She admitted she'd been appalled when she first learned Millicent only paid her bills, files and files full of them, twice a year. But all the couturiers, furriers, jewelers, art dealers, wine importers, didn't seem to care anymore. They knew they would get their money eventually. It was just a headache to keep track of it all.

She was happy to see it wasn't an account. Or a letter from one of MR's sons, wanting a bigger allowance or, even sadder, a visit from their mother.

It was an envelope from one of the news clipping services Millicent kept. Violet recognized the gist of the story—the "anonymous source close to Mrs. Rogers" was one of the housemaids, who thought she was stealing secret information to sell off but was really being manipulated by Millicent herself. Yet it looked like the story plans had gone awry. "Standard Oil Heiress Engagement to Gable Off? Has His Eye Roved Again?"

"I'm—not sure how this can be, er, done over," Violet said carefully. In her days of work at the fairy-tale house in the hills, she'd learned how it all went. Work didn't start until after one o'clock, then there were letters to type, dressmakers arriving for fittings, errands to run, dogs to bathe. Millicent always moved slowly, spoke softly—until she didn't. Then there would be shouts, anger, lightning, a shoe thrown.

Then all was peace again. An evening swim and cocktails, a few hours getting dressed (because MR was careful about every wave of hair, every hem-stitch, every ring on her finger), and Violet had the evening to herself. Sometimes she was called in again late at night, and sometimes not. It wasn't like any other job she had ever had. No regular hours, no set duties. It wasn't bad, even if she had met very few movie stars to tell Jo-Jo and the girls about. Only glimpsed a few from a distance.

She had her own little house, quiet and cozy and pretty, good food, a new suit and dress. Shoes with no holes on the bottoms. Art to look at, even if she didn't quite understand it. No, not bad at all.

But now, as she watched MR pacing by the windows, she realized she was actually a bit worried about her employer. Millicent hadn't been sleeping. Violet often saw the light on in the upstairs bedroom, when she couldn't sleep herself and made cocoa in her little kitchen. Millicent rarely ate much, drank a lot of champagne, and she seemed even thinner than when Vi first met her. Her hands trembled as she tried to light her cigarette, and Violet hurried to help her.

Millicent nodded her thanks, the storm already passing. There were shadows around her dark eyes, hectic red spots on her sharp cheekbones. She dropped onto one of the needlepoint sofas and watched as Violet scurried around, picking up the scattered clippings.

"You're quite right, of course, Vi darling," she said softly. "Nothing in life can be done over. So we must always do exactly as we like at every moment, and regret nothing. It's all useless in the end. We just have our memories." She exhaled a long plume of smoke. "But we must also learn not to waste our time when we know from the start it won't be worth it in the end. I think that maid has outlived her usefulness and should be sent on her way. I shouldn't mess with the newspapers anyway, they are quite vile."

Violet looked down at the papers in her hand, the jumble of headlines about Hollywood romances. Gable's famous roving eye. "MR ..." she started, not sure what to say.

Millicent gave a wry smile, and reached for the onyx ashtray. "Why don't you come with me to a party tonight, darling?"

Violet was startled. Her—go to a society party? She watched Millicent go out every night, satin gowns gleaming, diamonds flashing, her hair a perfect silvery-blonde wave after an hour with the hairdresser. Violet had never even imagined going with her, though once she had dropped off a forgotten package at Merle Oberon's house. She never wanted to go, really. What would she even say to people who had suddenly stepped off a screen into real life?

"Me?" she said.

"Of course. I do hate going on my own, and Captain Butler is working late on-set tonight. It's nothing grand, just a little dinner at Adrian and Janet's. You've met them, I think?"

Violet wouldn't say she had *met* them. Janet Gaynor and her fashion designer husband were Millicent's best friends, and Vi saw him bringing gowns for fittings while Janet waited by the pool or outside in their Rolls Royce with their poodles. Adrian even once asked Violet which shade of green chiffon she preferred for a photo shoot. They seemed all right, friendly even, but—to have dinner with them?

"I don't have anything to wear," she said, cringing at the thought of appearing on Gilbert Adrian's own doorstep in her secondhand evening gown with the missing beads. Her one new dress was a tailored day dress in dark blue, very nice but hardly ready for a dinner party.

Millicent waved this away. "Oh, I can lend you something. I have heaps of things; we'll just take up a hem or two. It will be fun. They've just come back from a visit to a town called Taos, and they want to tell me all about it."

"Taos?" The word sounded odd in her mouth.

"Yes. Out in the desert somewhere. Lots of artists apparently. You'll enjoy hearing about it, too, they're always so amusing with their travel stories. Now, come along, darling, let's have a rummage through my closet and see what might suit you."

Violet sighed, knowing it was futile to argue when Millicent got that look in her eyes. When MR's mind was made up, it was definitely *made up*.

Her doubts only grew once they were in the car, driving through the hills past mysterious gates, distant red tile roofs glimpsed between palm trees, seeming to melt in the vivid sunset light. It seemed even more strange than the first time she ventured to Millicent's house, leaving her boarding-house hamburger-stand life behind to step past a shimmering fairy-tale curtain. At least then, she had known why she was there. To get a job. Now, she had no idea what she was doing.

She awkwardly smoothed the skirt of her borrowed gown, for

about the fiftieth time. It was easily the grandest thing she had ever worn, ever even *thought* about wearing. It made her think of those times when she was a kid, and had crept up to the attic to take her great-grandmother's wedding gown from the old trunk and drape it over her cotton school dress. Great-Grandmother Louisa had come from Boston to Iowa in an old wagon decades ago, dragging the gown with her. Ivory satin and Irish lace, trimmed with velvet roses, a long train, puffed sleeves. Vi had felt like a princess in it—until she got caught, took a hiding for almost ruining the old fabric, and the dress vanished.

Wearing that old wedding gown was nothing to this. Pure, snow-white satin, falling off the shoulders in a moiré fold, the full skirt swirling with hidden panels of red brocade that flashed when she moved. A beaded red sash tied over the hips and trailed off into a flurry of ruffles. Violet was scared that if she turned the wrong way, it would tumble off into complete disarray. Like turning into a pumpkin at midnight.

She glanced at her reflection in the tinted window. They were running late, of course, and the sun slowly slipped away into the rocky canyons, leaving only a trace of palest gold and lavender light behind. Silhouetted against that glow, she didn't recognize herself. Millicent's hairdresser had piled her unruly red locks high, smoothing them into a glossy upsweep. A careful sweep of red lipstick matched the gown's sash perfectly.

"Your mother was quite ridiculous to say redheads shouldn't wear red," Millicent said, echoing what Violet protested when the maid handed her the tube of Vivid Cherries. It was very far from the crushed pink she had dug out of her dresser drawer the day she went to interview for the job.

That all seemed impossibly far away now.

"You look quite nice," Millicent finished, opening her beaded handbag to take out her silver cigarette case.

Violet turned to look at her. MR looked like—well, like MR. Like magic, a creature from *Swan Lake* in a gown of liquid black taffeta and tulle, black feathers around her shoulders, a web of diamond stars at her neck. She looked like she really belonged in a movie star's house, a palace.

"I feel strange," Violet said. She pressed her hand to her stomach, her palm sliding against the cool satin. "Sick."

"Nothing to worry about." Millicent lit her cigarette, and turned her head away to roll down the automatic window. "You've met the Adrians, they're really lovely people. And such collections of art! Wait until you see their gallery. They have a Velazquez I am very envious of, I admit."

Violet just nodded. She had no idea what she would write in her next letter to her mother. Everyone at home would think she was fibbing.

"Oh, I almost forgot," Millicent said. "I meant to give you this."

She opened her bag again, and took out something that glinted against her black satin glove. Violet saw it was a silver brooch, sharp-edged, modern, angular. Just like the ones she glimpsed in MR's workshop.

"It's a violet," Millicent said. "I hardly ever try flowers, mostly stars, so of course I thought of you when it was finished. The petals are windblown, you see, as if it was tumbling through space, not sure yet where it must go."

Violet remembered all those nights when lights shone from Millicent's window. Had she been working then, making jewelry? Making something for *her*? "For—me?"

"Of course." Millicent pinned it to the edge of the moiré neckline, where it seemed to gleam and glitter, like those stars. "Oh, we're here!"

There was no time to say anything else. The car swept between a pair of gilded gates and along a steep, winding driveway. Everything was dark, hidden behind the gathering night and the trees, until suddenly a giant, golden sparkle of a house burst into view. Every window and door of the three-story mansion gleamed with light, and Violet could hear laughter and jazz music. But the long line of cars she had expected from a movie star party just wasn't there.

"It's just a tiny dinner, Violet, I told you," Millicent said. She put out her cigarette and peeked into an enameled compact, patting her perfectly curled pale hair into place. She looked unearthly beautiful—but not happy. Violet still wondered about the purplish shadows under MR's eyes, the lines of strain around her lipsticked mouth. "It will be fun!"

Fun. Violet had her doubts there. A uniformed butler opened the car door and helped her out onto the gravel driveway, just at the foot of the marble front steps. It seemed a little silly to run off into the night now, screaming at the canyon walls like she wanted to do, so she just followed Millicent inside.

And found herself on a movie set.

It definitely didn't look like a house anyone lived in, but maybe a scene in a movie about El Cid or Queen Isabella. To her right, a gilded staircase soared up out of sight, all scrolls and swoops, lined with alabaster sculptures and antique chairs in dark, carved wood with embroidered cushions. At the landing, a stained glass window cast jeweled shards of green, blue, and ruby-red light from some hidden source onto the marble floor.

To the left was something like a museum gallery, a long corridor, carpeted in an old, threadbare rug and hung with paintings on paintings. She glimpsed the blurry glow of something like a Monet, portraits of scowling people in ruffs, a rearing horse. To the right was a set of open doors, and she could hear music flowing from that room, laughter, the clink of glasses.

"People live here?" Violet whispered. Millicent's house was beautiful and palatial, too, but somehow it was—not as formal. More like a place that grew organically to be someone's home than a stage set. She had never really appreciated the difference before.

Millicent laughed. "I told you they were collectors. They quite put my little efforts to shame, I am so disorganized about it all. Buying a little of this, a little of that ..."

"MR!" a light, sweet voice trilled from the shadows of the staircase, "I'm so glad you came after all. Adrian said you tried to put him off."

"I've not been entirely well lately, Janet darling. I probably won't stay late."

"Nonsense. It's good for you to get out and about. We all miss you horribly."

There was a patter of feet, and a sprite flitted through the glowing light of the window and floated down the stairs. Violet knew exactly who she was, because unlike most movie stars, she looked just as she did on the screen. Janet Gaynor, tiny, sylphlike, auburn curls fastened with diamond clips around her heart-shaped-face, eyes huge. She wore a halter-neck gown of pleated bronze lame that floated around her. She seemed to twirl across the foyer, and went up on tiptoe to kiss Millicent's cheek.

"It's only a few of us, and we're going to have such fun," she said with a giggle. "Adrian just returned from Taos. He bought a new property there, and he is dying to tell you all about it, as well as show off some amazing weavings he found. The artists use the same methods they had three hundred years ago!"

"He can tell me all he likes, but he won't tempt me out there," Millicent said with a flick of her hand. "It's much too far."

"Oh, pooh, MR! Just listen to him for once. If he can find other people to tell all about these new artists he loves so much, it makes my life so much easier." She turned her huge hazel eyes to Violet. "Why, hello! I'm Janet. I think we've met once or twice?"

"Yes, I—I think so. That is, I know who you are," Violet stammered, then immediately could have kicked herself. Of course she knew. Everyone knew.

"Janet, this is Violet Redfield, my assistant," Millicent said. "I don't know what I ever did without her."

"I'm so glad to meet you properly. Someone certainly does

need to keep Millicent organized." Janet took Violet's arm and steered her toward the open doors, toward the music and laughter. "Do come in, we have a new cocktail our butler is trying. I'm not too sure about them yet, but it seems they're all the rage in New York!"

Violet let Janet Gaynor—*Janet Gaynor*—lead her into the living room, and it was a whole new movie set. From a Spanish castle to an Art Deco mansion, windows looking out on a panorama of canyons and ocean. Everything was as elegant as Millicent's house, but there was none of the clutter, the welcoming effect, the sense that every object had been chosen for itself alone, and not the way it "fit" with everything else. This was all carefully arranged, a long, white room with black and silver furnishings, a pale backdrop for the paintings on the walls. *They* were a riot of color, flower still-lifes, women in bright satin gowns, crashing seascapes.

And the people were just as colorful, just as carefully arranged on the black velvet sofas and around the small jazz band that played in the corner. Gowns of emerald green and topaz-gold, tulle and chiffon and taffeta, tall, handsome men with glossy dark hair in dark evening suits.

"Have you met Sylvia and Sidney? He's a director, very avant-garde, wouldn't hire me for anything," Janet asked Violet as she led her toward an older couple sitting near the open window. "But they're very nice all the same. This is Miss ..."

"Redfield," Violet murmured, glad she could at least remember her own name.

"She's organizing Millicent," Janet said.

"Well, my dear, someone should," the avant-garde director said with a chuckle. "Though I must say I don't envy you the job, Miss Redfield."

"Are you going to trek out to the desert with her, once Janet and Adrian persuade her to go there and take her life in her hands?" his wife, a plump, kind-eyed lady in creamy chiffon, asked.

"Oh, I shan't go!" Millicent cried, draping herself languidly onto the white chair next to Sylvia's, her black-swan gown a vivid contrast to the paleness. Violet was amazed at the change that had come over her in only a moment. She had seemed tired, a little sad in the car, peevish at the house. Now her face was alight, her hands fluttering as if her energy couldn't be contained. "I'm sure I couldn't bear the heat, or the long trek."

"You travel further every year to get to your house in Jamaica!" Janet protested. "And you would certainly love Taos if you could see it. It's like nowhere else, really magical. And I'm sure Mabel would let you stay with her, she has a giant house. There are writers and artists there all the time."

"Mabel?" Violet asked, feeling dizzy, bewildered, very out of place.

"Mabel Dodge Luhan," Janet said. "Buffalo, New York heiress, you know. She used to live in Florence, wonderful gardens, but she's been in Taos with her gorgeous new Indian husband for ages."

"Well, Janet darling, that settles it—I absolutely can't go," Millicent said. "One heiress in a room at a time."

"We'll persuade you yet," Janet laughed. "Now, Miss Redfield, do have one of those drinks, take a look around before my husband finds out we have a new guest here. He'll lecture you on his collections until you just want to scream, and you won't be able to enjoy the art at all."

Millicent gave Violet a quick smile before she turned to chat with Sidney about his latest film. Feeling charmingly dismissed, Violet wandered away to take a glass of the odd-looking, sea-green cocktail from the butler, and studied a painting on the far wall, away from the music. It felt like a relief to have something to focus on, to try to gather herself before she made a gaping, Midwestern fool of herself in front of movie people.

She took a sip of the cocktail—and almost choked. It made her eyes water.

"Vile stuff, huh?" a voice said behind her.

Startled, she spun around, trying not to spill the drink all over the white perfection of the room. The man who stood behind her was young, tall, smiling, his golden hair gleaming in the light. He certainly looked like he could be a movie star himself, or a college football hero, but she didn't recognize him. His smile made her want to gasp all over again.

"It's—well, it is, erm, interesting," she said. She wasn't sure if she meant the drink, or the whole strange night.

"Adrian and Janet do love to experiment on us, their captive audiences. I don't think we've met. Are you an actress?"

"Me?" For just a minute, she wished she was, that she could impress this man. "No, I'm a—well, a secretary, I suppose. To Mrs. Rogers."

"Oh, yes. The famous MR. We all do wonder about her. They say she was a spy during the war. Passing messages for the Free French, things like that."

Violet was fascinated to learn yet another strange facet of her boss. "I hadn't heard that one. I don't think it would surprise me, though. She definitely has some secrets."

"How did you come to work for her?"

"Nothing too exciting. No espionage was involved. I was with an employment agency, and I guess she liked my qualifications. Scanty as they are."

"And do you like the job, then?"

Violet considered this as she took another sip of her drink. It didn't seem as strong now; in fact, it was pretty delightful. It was making everything pleasantly fuzzy at the edges, and she didn't even feel nervous talking to this handsome stranger. Did she *like* the job? "It's always interesting. Much better than the glove counter, or selling root beer floats. Every day is something different."

He gave her that quirky smile, and she wondered again if she had seen him before. Was he an Oscar-winning actor, and she was just too fuzzy-headed now to remember? "It's an education?"

She laughed. "It's certainly that. I think I've learned more in a few weeks than I ever could before." She studied him closer, wondering what he was doing standing there talking to her in that quiet corner. Maybe he was reporter, trying to get a story on Millicent?

"I don't think I caught your name," she said.

"Sorry. My grandma always did lecture me about how my bad manners would never take me very far." He held out his hand. "Charles Rivers."

She reached out to shake it. It was a smooth, elegant, well-kept hand, but with a light row of calluses just under his fingers. A sportsman, then? "Violet Redfield, how do you do. Are you an actor?"

He smiled. "No, a lawyer, for my sins. I've done some work for Adrian, so they invite me over from time to time. I load up on the champagne and lobster before I scurry back to the paperwork in my tiny office downtown."

A lawyer. Now that she would not have guessed. "Sounds like we have something in common, then. Though my lodgings aren't what I would call 'tiny' now. Not like the boarding house. But not like this, either. This is—well, incredible, isn't it?" Violet waved around at all the marble and velvet, the band, and the windows with their view of the world. "Is that a Renoir over there?"

"I think so. I don't know as much about art as I would like, I admit." Charles Rivers, lawyer, followed her as she drifted over to the painting that had drawn her close, a pastel scene of a woman in a flowered hat and a child in a summertime garden. It was a place she wanted to leap into, to feel that grass under her feet, the sun on her head, hear that woman's gentle murmurs to her child.

"My aunt had an old art book she used to show me, and the Impressionists were always my favorites," Violet said. "I never thought I could be so close to one of those paintings in person! Isn't it lovely? Like a dream of a summer day."

Charles gave her a quizzical glance, his blond brow arched like someone in a movie. Was he *sure* he wasn't an actor? He gestured toward the crowd gathered behind them in that black and white living room. Millicent was laughing with one of the musicians, waving her cigarette in its onyx holder. "And your employment? Has that been like a dream?"

Violet laughed. "I do keep thinking I'll wake up any minute. I've never met anyone like Mrs. Rogers."

"Neither have any of us, really. We're all very curious about her."

"Really?" Violet glanced around the room. She recognized a husband-and-wife comedy acting pair, a fashion model, a screen heartthrob who had just entered the room and gathered all the light onto himself. "But everyone here is so ridiculously glamorous."

"Because it's their job. It's what we all sell out here, even me with my cases for the studios. But Mrs. Rogers doesn't seem to have anything to sell. She just has to ..."

"Has to be?"

"Yes. She just has to be—whatever she is. Can you imagine what that might be like? To have that freedom?"

Violet watched Millicent as she laughed. No, she couldn't really imagine it. But MR didn't strike her as being completely free, either. Something inside her seemed to bind her, hold her, drive her, and Violet wasn't sure anyone else could ever really know what it was. Or if MR could even know it herself.

"No," she whispered. "I don't think I can imagine it."

"It's not real out here, you know," Charles said, his tone suddenly as wistful as she felt herself. "It's all an illusion we all work to build together. Not like where I'm from."

"And where were you from?"

"Minnesota, originally. Then I went to college out here, football scholarship."

Violet laughed. "I knew it."

"Knew what?"

"An athlete. And I know what you mean about how it's not like it was before, not where I come from."

"And that is?"

"Iowa."

He smiled down at her, making her feel all warm. All giggly. "Then we have lots in common. We are strangers in a strange land."

"Shall we go in to dinner, everyone?" Adrian called. The crowd moved slowly toward a pair of doors at the far end of the room, open to reveal a long, damask-draped dining table set with a sparkling, intimidating array of china and silver, the crystal facets of a chandelier casting prisms of light.

Violet glanced past the crowd, looking for Millicent, and saw her standing near the open windows talking with Janet. Her earlier laughter was gone, and she looked pale and drawn. She shook her head, and Janet laid a gentle hand on her arm, only to be brushed away. Janet's elfin face crumpled.

Violet was suddenly concerned, and even felt a little pang of something like—guilt. She'd been enjoying looking at Charles the Lawyer's blue eyes, drinking those terrible green cocktails, when she should have been keeping an eye on Millicent. Violet knew she wasn't feeling well lately.

"Excuse me," she murmured to Charles, handing him her almost empty glass. "It's been nice talking to you."

"Can I just ask ..." he began, but his voice was lost in the sound of the dinner-going crowd, and Violet was already making her way across the room.

"... sure that's not what it is," Janet was saying. "You know how silly these gossip columns are. If they don't find dirt, they don't get paid, so they just make it up."

"Oh, I know that," Millicent said. Her always-quiet voice was even fainter than usual. She drained the champagne glass in her hand.

"Sylvia shouldn't have said anything," Janet said. "These stupid cocktails."

"It doesn't matter, darling, really."

"Is everything all right?" Violet asked, and Janet shot her a grateful glance.

"I just have a bit of a headache," Millicent said. "Would you mind terribly if we went home early, Violet darling? I did promise you a fun evening, and I'm afraid I'm terrible at living up to my promises."

"Of course we can go home," Violet answered quickly. She touched Millicent's hand, and found it was cold. The pulse in her wrist raced. Was it more than a headache? Was it her heart?

"Are you sure you don't just need a bite to eat?" Janet asked. "The chef made these wonderful vol-au-vents ..."

"No, no. I just need my bed, a few hours of nighty-night and all will be well," Millicent said with a laugh.

"I'll go find someone to have the car brought around," Violet said.

As she made her way across the now-empty room, she saw that Charles the Lawyer had vanished. She didn't know if she was relieved, or a little disappointed. She found the butler and asked about the car, and when she returned to the living room she found one of the maids handing MR a bottle of champagne and a large silver tin. "The car should be there in only a moment."

"Thank you, Vi darling, you are a treasure," Millicent answered. She took Violet's arm and let herself be led to the marble steps, where the car was indeed already waiting. She slid inside silently, and slumped back on the seat as they moved seamlessly out into the night. Violet found a fur-lined car rug under the seat, and tucked it over Millicent's taffeta and tulle gown.

"I am sorry to drag you away from that handsome young man,

Violet," Millicent said, staring out the window at the distant lights of the city.

"He *was* rather cute," Violet admitted. "But I'm certainly not sorry to go home a little early."

Millicent nodded, and Violet noticed that when they turned out of the gates they didn't edge toward the road to Millicent's house, but in the opposite direction.

"Where are we going?"

"Oh, just a tiny little stop, it won't take long at all," Millicent said vaguely.

She fell quiet after that, and Violet couldn't think of anything else to say. She peered cautiously out the window as they emerged from the dark hills, glided past streets of bungalows, into the sleepy, prosperous hamlet of Encino.

They came to a stop at a white stucco house at the end of a lane. It wasn't nearly as grand as Janet and Adrian's mansion, not even as large as Millicent's, but solid-looking, set back from the street behind a hedge, comfortable. It seemed deserted, or at least tucked up for the night, with only one small light in a bay window downstairs.

Millicent picked up the tin and the bottle of champagne, and stepped out of the car. Her jaw was set, her eyes narrowed, as if she was intent on some very important business.

"Should—I come with you?" Violet asked uncertainly. She didn't know what was going on, but she had certainly worked for MR long enough now to mistrust that expression.

"Oh, why not, darling? I doubt there will be any secrets here after tomorrow."

Violet hurried after her across the narrow driveway and up the short flight of stone steps to the carved oak front door. Millicent dug a key out of her beaded satin handbag and let them in.

It was indeed quiet and dark, the small foyer shadowed, the living room beyond lit with only that one lamp in the window.

Just like the outside, it was nice, comfortable, but impersonal, as if the furnishings were only rented with the house. A fire had burned out in the brick hearth, which might have been cozy, but there were no paintings on the walls, few books.

Violet hovered in the doorway, yet Millicent seemed to have forgotten anyone was there. She glanced around the room with a small frown, and made her way to the foot of the staircase at the far end of the room. She was as lithe and silent as a panther, her black gown melting into the shadows. Violet didn't follow her.

She glanced out the window at the waiting car, its lights turned off but still running, and she wanted nothing more than to run outside and throw herself into the backseat. The cocktail was wearing off, her head ached, and she didn't like the feeling of that silent house. As she turned back to the empty living room, she noticed a silver-framed photo on a side table, the only hint of something personal. She gasped when she saw it was Carole Lombard, smiling and gorgeous and blonde in a mink coat, holding onto the arm of Clark Gable as he kissed her cheek. "To my darling CG—always remember. Your Fireball."

They were in Clark Gable's house.

"Millicent ..." she whispered. Had they really come to spy on MR's movie star lover? Jeepers. Just when she thought this night couldn't get any weirder.

Before she could call out, Millicent already reappeared, as swiftly and silently as she had gone. "Violet, darling, do you have your notebook with you?"

"Only this," Violet said, scrambling through her handbag for the tiny paper pad and pencil she always carried now. MR sometimes wanted to write a letter or make a list at the strangest times.

And it seemed this was one of those times.

Violet followed her into a small kitchen. It didn't look as if anyone ever cooked there, though there were some empty wine bottles in the sink. Millicent put the champagne and the tin, which

Violet saw now was stamped "Iranian Golden Caviar," into the refrigerator. She scratched out a quick note, and Violet craned her neck to over-read it. "For you and your lover's breakfast." Then Millicent left the note and the key on the table and departed the silent house, with Violet running after her.

The whole thing had surely taken about five minutes.

The next day, far earlier than work had ever begun before in the Rogers house, Millicent appeared on Violet's doorstep.

Bewildered, sleepless, maybe just a touch hungover from those green cocktails, Violet opened the door to find MR standing there in a white silk dressing gown, a cigarette dangling from her lips. She held out a sheet of paper covered with her looping, scrawling handwriting.

"Violet, darling, I need you to type this up and deliver one copy to that house in Encino, and one to Hedda Hopper's office," Millicent said tonelessly, quietly. "The chauffeur will know the way. As soon as possible."

"Of course," Violet stammered, hoping she could read the writing. *My darling Clark, I want to thank you for taking care of me last year ... You told me once that you would never hurt me, and that was true, even last night. I have failed because of my inadequacy of complete faith ... Good-bye, my Clark, I love you as I always shall.*

Violet looked up at Millicent, appalled at the thought of such intimate words flying out into the world via Hedda Hopper's gossip column. "Are you sure?"

MR gave a brusque nod and turned away, slowly making her way back toward the main house. She moved as if she was in pain, or very, very old. When she reached the pool, she glanced back, her face very white in the dawn glow of light. "I suppose it hardly needs to be said that this won't be spoken of again."

Violet shook her head.

"Good. And perhaps we should call in some extra staff to help with packing. I am giving up this house. I think I'll go see about this Taos place after all."

CHAPTER 7

Millicent

JAMAICA, 1946

The sun burned behind my closed eyes, white-hot, searing, but I didn't care. After the war years, all the long, endless hours huddled in a dark warehouse at the unfashionable end of Lexington Avenue, surrounded by piles of boxes of supplies meant to be shipped out to Allied countries for the MSRC, the color and light were delicious. At last, at last, it was warm again. The smells of the hospital—bleach, sweet-sickly medicines, old boiled vegetables—were erased by salt spray, heady jasmine, the heat of the sand beneath me. It was a bit like being born again. Starting all over.

Again.

I had so much experience of starting over. New York, Austria, Claremont, three husbands, three sons, dear Jim (dear, married, ever so busy Jim) in Washington. All of them a new path, a new way of being. A new me.

Yet this felt different. Not so much starting over as—being held suspended. Caught in one moment. There was no going back, no going forward. Not yet.

I opened my eyes and stared up at the sky. For an instant, all I could see was an endless expanse of palest blue, so pale and watery it was as if the very sun had washed it out. Faded it like an expanse of old silk. No clouds touched the dome of blue, no shadows. My eyes sparkled and glittered, and I reached into my straw bag for my dark glasses. It cut some of the limelight-brilliance, and I could see the shimmering white sand of the beach, stretching beyond my blanket. The gray-green, low lumps of the hills in the distance, so different from the towering, protective peaks of the Austrian Alps where I had long ago left Shulla House.

Jamaica had its own beauty, rugged, hard and soft all at the same time. The warmth did me some good, made me feel like I could breathe after the damp of the war.

The tremors seemed better here, the strange flutterings that plagued me now in New York. The uncomplicated sun soothed me —as did the long days on the beach, the golf course that vanished off a cliff into the sea, the casual, jolly lifestyle of the people I met there.

Yet the war, as awful as it was, had given me something I only realized now that it was gone. Not merely collecting dresses, collecting men, moving, seeing—I was needed. All those years of making houses had given me some talent for organizing. People truly *needed* me. And that clock that had always ticked away with the beats of my heart—time was always going, going, going—was there for all of us, all the time.

Now that was gone. What was left? What would I do now?

I rolled over on my blanket, letting the sun beat down on my back, bared by the new red swimsuit that would certainly have shocked Mummy-Da if she saw it. I found the crash and ebb of the waves, the iridescent blues and greens of a peacock, laced with foaming white wild and beautiful, and out there was a purpose. For the moment, anyway.

Ian. Commander Ian Fleming, of the British Naval Intelligence, sent to Washington for the war for purposes he refused to speak about. But gossip had no such reticence. He was a *spy*, the whisperers murmured.

And one could certainly well-believe it. Tall and handsome,

years younger than me, Eton educated with that delicious accent. An air of mysterious melancholy that hung over him like a dark cloud, even there in that sunshine water. Secret sorrows no one could touch. How well I understood that.

When he said he had bought a new house called Goldeneye on Montego Bay, a place where he could write some new novel about espionage and war, I had been intrigued. New places! New work! How small the world had begun to feel to me. What girl could resist flying off with him, especially when he was lying stretched out in my very own bed, that glorious long, lean body naked amid tangled white sheets?

No one needed me now in America. My war work was done. My sons settled finally in their schools (after Paul was expelled *twice!* What *was* wrong with him?), my mother gone back to France. Ian was a new adventure waiting to happen.

I rolled over on the blanket, and winced as the welts on my backside gave a twinge. I really hadn't known how *much* of an adventure Ian would be. His tastes in the bedroom were—interesting.

I had to laugh at it all now. I was surely no innocent. I had three husbands, so many lovers. I'd learned a great deal about men, their needs and desires, what drove them onward. They were simple creatures, really, especially compared to women. Women had to be always thinking, planning, strategizing, always careful, always ruthless. Men just had to *be*.

I thought of a list I made when I was a girl, my "ideal man."

Number One: He must be a gentleman, every inch of him, a "he-man."

Number Two: He must have perfect manners, be cleaver (I never could spell), have a sense of humor, an occupation in which he could rise.

Number Three: He must love me *really*, and our minds must always be in perfect accord.

I am sure there must have been more. I've never been the sort to settle for less than perfection. And yet imperfect my life had always been.

Not that my husbands were terrible men. They were certainly all "he-men," handsome and energetic, cosmopolitan. All unable to earn a living. Ludi was poor, so we were always doomed, but he was like a Nordic god. An athlete, a dancer. He even died a war hero, fleeing the Gestapo, they said. I hadn't seen him in years and years by then. Arturo—such a fiery swagger! How richly he could live, how wonderfully he would savor the moment. And Ronnie, so gorgeous. The rumors about the size of his—endowments were not exaggerated, I do assure you. ("My dear," one Palm Beach matron had whispered to me, "he can't wear Bermuda shorts without falling out.") But he couldn't hold an intellectual thought in his head for a moment.

Yet none of them lasted long. "Mummy," my son Paul told me one day, so matter-of-factly. "You and husbands just can't get along."

He wasn't wrong. I was used to getting my own way. I had seen nothing but strife and quarrels from my own parents. My health made me long for romance, for extravagance, for urgency. Marriage wasn't for me.

But men, the darling, simple, sexy creatures—men I *did* like.

I watched Ian as he swam towards the shore, the sun gleaming on his muscled back. He wasn't for much longer, I knew that now, though I might return one day to Jamaica. He was moody, reclusive, and didn't care for parties or conversation. Even the absolutely darling "cannibal" party I organized on the beach one night, bonfires and piles of papier-mâché skulls along the sand, drums echoing in the dusty, star-sprinkled darkness, had fallen flat for him. He left the party early, taking most of the rum with him. The riding crops in the bedroom were becoming tedious as well.

My time here had served its purpose. Yet as I watched Ian striding toward me across the sand, he seemed followed by the ghosts of all the other men who had come and gone in my life, who had also served their purpose. I was grateful to them all—and grateful to let them go. Grateful to always be moving forward.

Yet somehow, deep in some hidden, wistful part of me that was horribly, uselessly sentimental—I wished I had a daughter I could hand all that hard-won wisdom to. Someone who would always truly need me.

CHAPTER 8

Millicent

TAOS, LATE SUMMER 1947

"Honestly, darlings, I don't know why you insisted we leave today," Millicent murmured. She held tightly to the handle of the limousine door, which Adrian had hired to make the sixty-mile drive more comfortable. She wasn't at all sure that it was working, despite the buttery leather seats and carpeted floors. They had been climbing up steep, rocky switchbacks for what seemed like an eternity, dark stone walls rising around them like something out of a Norse myth. A land for rugged, wicked gods. Even the sunlight, so glorious in Santa Fe, seemed shut out there, except for brief moments when the car emerged to a clearing, and the sparkling, tumbling rush of the river appeared for a small glimpse.

Then it all vanished into shadows again.

Millicent slipped on her dark glasses to shut out those claustrophobic cliff walls, and glanced at Violet who sat beside her. A yellow scarf covered her red curls, and a pretty yellow and white checked coat had replaced those awful garments she first wore in California. Her silver violet brooch gleamed at the collar, and beaded turquoise and coral earrings Millicent bought her at the Thunderbird Shop in Santa Fe swayed and glimmered. She'd been quiet all day, staring out the window at the strange, almost alien scenery, yet she didn't seem nervous or apprehensive. Just—watchful. As Violet always was.

What an invaluable help she had been on the journey, Millicent thought. When a trunk full of valuables went missing from the train in Colorado, and everyone panicked, Violet calmly found it. She kept track of tickets and lodgings and the dogs and the luggage, made sure Millicent had her medicines when she felt ill, found doctors, and arranged for a new, brighter room at La Fonda in Santa Fe when the first room was tiny. Always so interested in everything around her, such a calming presence.

How very tired Millicent was of rush and noise and gossip! What had she ever done without Violet?

And what a relief it was that nothing came of that little flirtation with the handsome lawyer at Janet's party. Millicent couldn't let anyone steal her treasure away now.

"It's not much farther," Adrian said. He and Janet sat across from her, everyone's various dogs arrayed around them on the leather seat. They, too, looked perfectly calm, just like Violet, so at ease in that strange landscape. Even in their casual travel clothes, they seemed to belong, to know themselves and their own style. No wonder Millicent loved them so.

"I was perfectly happy in Santa Fe for those two weeks," she said, and so she had been. She'd made friends with all the proprietors of the shops and galleries, especially dear Mirandi at the Thunderbird Shop. She'd started learning all about the exquisite jewelry and weavings, the carved and brightly painted santos, the gleaming and intricate pottery. The buildings were charming, the parties at the hotel delightful, with cocktails on the rooftop every night as the sun set in a brilliant blaze of gold and garnet and lavender. Just the distraction she had needed after the embarrassment of California. "It was lovely there."

"Don't worry, Millicent dear, the scenery will be worth it all," Janet said.

"Santa Fe *is* lovely, and we'll be back there soon," Adrian added. "But you've never seen anything like Taos."

Millicent peered doubtfully out the window again. It was quite true she'd never seen anything like it before. Even when she lived in Austria, surrounded by the towering Alps, the mountains didn't look like this, as if they warned travelers away. And the hills in Jamaica were soft and rolling, vivid green. There was nothing soft here.

The car slowed to a crawl as it seemed to inch its way up a steep incline, teetering along the narrow path. Millicent's gloved hand curled tighter around the door handle, and Violet flashed her a quick smile.

"Where I'm from, it's so flat everywhere—you can stand in one spot and see the whole state of Iowa, stretching out all around you," she said. "I do like how a person could hide here and never be found."

"Like Jesse James on the run from the sheriff!" Janet cried. "I can just see a villain with a black hat aiming his six-shooter from behind that boulder up there ..."

Adrian laughed. "You can tell you're an actress, darling."

"You have to always set the scene," Janet said cheerfully. "And speaking of setting the scene ..."

The car seemed to give a great heave, and pushed up and over the edge of a plateau, out of the valley of shadows. And a whole new vision, a beauty of a kind she had never seen or even imagined, burst out in front of her.

"Oh, stop, please," she whispered, her voice catching. The car pulled to the side of the narrow road, and she jumped out, kicking off her high heels impatiently when they caught in the gravelly sand.

Stretching above her head, so close she was sure she could reach up and brush it with her fingertips, arced a sky of perfect, cloudless turquoise blue, the light so crystalline and pure and brilliantly golden it made everything dazzle. Far below was a canyon, bisected by the roaring, tumbling, frothing greenish waters of the Rio Grande, whispering over the rocks as if the waters tried to tell her something. Something secret and wonderful, something only this magical place could know.

The river gorge, eight hundred feet deep, cut into the earth over millions and millions of years, was a black slash in the distance, a dark ribbon through the pale tan and rosy red of the dirt, the gold of the chamisa plants. Off to one side rose the mountains, purple and blue and shadowed. Still not like the Alps or like Jamaica, these mountains were chaotic somehow, a rounded ring half-circling the valley in uneven rows. And at its center was one mountain—Taos Mountain, elegant and dignified, like a queen.

The town, low and brown, clustered at its base, and snow still lay in lacy strands on its summit. It was peaceful, eternal. Perfect.

Welcoming.

Millicent took off her glasses and let the scene wash over her, into her. It seized her very soul as nothing else ever had. She felt something in her being she didn't recognize at first, couldn't even begin to sort out. Then she realized. It was goodness.

It was home.

She pressed her hand to her lips, holding back a ragged sob. Rogerses *never* cried. They never even wanted to cry, like ordinary humans might. When Captain Butler broke her heart, she'd longed to scream, to shout—but tears? Never. Not until this very moment. With this perfect light shining down on her, drawing her in and in as if it would never let her go.

Violet came up beside her. She held a wriggling dachshund under her arm, another nipping at her ankles, but she didn't seem to notice. She looked just as captured by the scene as Millicent herself, her lips parted in awe, her gray eyes large and shimmering.

Millicent threw her arms out wide, and spun in a circle. She forgot her stuttering heart, her heavy limbs, her careful movements, forgot all but that sky, that endless, endless sky, twirling above her.

"Why has no one ever told me about this?" she shouted.

CHAPTER 9

Violet

"Are you sure you'll be okay here alone??" Violet asked Millicent. The hotel room at Taos's version of La Fonda, dark and full of drifting shadows with the heavy red curtains drawn at the windows, was filled with heavily-carved old Spanish furniture. It smelled of lilies, MR's Shocking perfume, and sour-sweet medicine. Millicent was only a pale, thin face on the pillow, the blankets drawn up close around her despite the warm day outside.

It had been that way for days now, since soon after their arrival in Taos. Millicent, enthralled by a new town, new people, everything, had gone and gone, moved and moved, looking at pottery and jewelry, eating by the fountain at El Patio Restaurant, running from cocktail party to party, until she collapsed. When she fainted onto the hotel lobby floor, Violet was terrified.

"Of course I'm sure," Millicent said hoarsely, impatiently. "I just need a little rest, that's all. I have done this before, you know. Many times. I always get better."

She might have been through it before, but Violet hadn't. Oh, there had been doctors aplenty in California, pillboxes, long naps, flares of sharp temper, yet it was easy to hide in the big house there.

Here, in their suite of rooms in the old hotel right on the plaza, everything was right in the open. Just as it had been after her brother came back from the war, and his horrible nightmares filled every corner.

"Dr. Pond says ..." Violet began.

"Oh, Dr. Pond!" Millicent snapped. The dachshunds, who were tucked up beside her, growled at being disturbed in their quilted nests. "The man comes all the way from Santa Fe to say what I already know! I just need a little *rest*. To not have everyone bothering me all the time."

That was not exactly what Dr. Pond said. He warned that Millicent's heart was growing weaker, more enlarged. Slower every day. The high altitude didn't help. "It's the valves of her heart, you see," he had whispered to Violet in the quiet hallway. "They have to work harder and harder now. The poor circulation is what's causing the pain in her arms and legs. Rest for a few days, and the medication I've left, should help for a while. But she mustn't exert herself once she feels better, or the pain will return."

Violet knew what was behind those words. MR would never be completely well; she never had been. The worst could only be kept cornered for a while.

She also knew that all the doctors' warnings of over-exertion would be in vain once Millicent felt stronger. She would run out and seize onto life all over again.

"MR ..."

"Oh, just go, Violet!" Millicent shouted. She threw the teacup from her bedside table across the room, where it smashed onto one of the Alhambra-throne chairs. "Just because I'm stuck in here, you don't have to be. It's a festival day, they said. Go and see it, and tell me all about it when you return. Ethel is here if I need anything." As if Ethel, the surly housekeeper, would be much help at all in a crisis.

But Violet knew by now when staying would cause more trouble than leaving. "Okay, I'll go," she said, surreptitiously checking the level of morphine in the brown bottle. "I admit I am a little curious." They'd been hearing the echo of music from the plaza all day, laughter and merriment. So different from the dark, quiet world of the room.

"Take that new camera with you, in case you see anything interesting. I need some inspiration for new jewelry designs to keep me busy."

Violet frowned at the brand-new Polaroid Millicent had insisted on buying. Violet couldn't quite master how it all worked yet, but she obediently packed it into its case. Millicent nodded, and rolled over in the blankets, suddenly quiet.

Once she was sure MR was sleeping, Violet stopped in her own room, two doors down the hallway, to change out of her shorts and into a pink linen dress. She studied the camera for a minute, turning it this way and that. "Just point at something and press the button," MR had told her impatiently, but Violet still had her suspicions. She tucked it into a large handbag, and smoothed her hair back into a neat twist she covered with a silk Hermes scarf that was one of Millicent's cast-offs. She decided she looked respectable enough for a quick outing.

And she had to admit to a tiny, fluttering excited feeling at being freed from the hotel room. Ever since they had arrived, after that first magical glimpse as they drove over the top of the cliff and spied the mountains and the river, she had been running after MR to parties, making sure she had what she had needed, and then tending to her sickbed. It was not a hardship—Millicent mostly drew and read, until a storm overtook her and there were shouts and objects thrown. But Violet longed to see more of the town, the countryside, the new people.

She grabbed up her heavy bag, packed with the camera and a thermos of tea along with her lipstick, and shut the door behind her. The hotel was quiet at that time of day, the halls narrow and dark, smelling of dust and lemon polish. She hurried down one staircase and then another, marveling at the paintings and display cases at every turn. Scenes of Spain mostly, ancient castles and matadors in sparkling suits, ladies in stiff black gowns and glaring frowns. The chambermaid had said that the old owner of the hotel, James Karavas, had come from Greece with a taste for European art and historical display, and now his son Saki carried on the tradition.

It seemed like a good enough spot for Millicent to land in, even temporarily, Violet thought as she paused to study a real matador's suit of lights in a glass case, all creamy satin and sparkling beadwork. Behind it was a Renaissance settee of carved mahogany and gilt, cushioned in gold velvet. All so eclectic and strange, unexpected and mysterious. Almost like MR's villa in California, which had so enthralled Violet when she first saw it, but without the lightness of touch.

She went down one last flight of stairs into the lobby, her footsteps muffled on thick red carpet. More dark furniture lurked there, x-backed chairs and benches in groupings within alcoves, a fire blazing in a large grate, more stern ladies in black staring down from gilt frames. A line of new guests waited at the reception desk, all flowered hats and white suits, porters piling luggage onto racks.

Violet paused at the quieter end of the long, high-ceilinged space to study a sepia-toned photo on the wall. Two men, with bushy mustaches and large straw cowboy hats, sitting on the ground next to a broken-down wagon.

"Ah, the founders of our fair town!" a voice boomed behind her. Violet glanced back to see Saki Karavas, La Fonda's owner, watching her. Portly, red-cheeked, with hair and an elaborate mustache so black she wasn't sure it didn't come from a bottle, he had his usual genial smile on his face, around the ever-present cigar he seemed to love. His barrel chest wrapped in a red velvet smoking jacket. The maids said they knew to become very industrious with their dusting when they smelled that cherry-smoky scent.

He had been most hospitable indeed when he found out Millicent was the "Standard Oil Heiress."

"I didn't know they had such informal photographs in 1919," she answered lightly.

"1919, my dear?"

"Isn't that when Mr. Blumenschein and Mr. Philips came to Taos? Or maybe it was back in the 1100s, when the pueblo was built."

Saki laughed loudly, puffing around his cigar. "You have been reading up, I see. Ah, no, Miss Redfield, those are indeed Blumenschein and Philips, and their famous broken wagon wheel. They were going to Colorado, you see, to paint the mountains, until their wagon broke down here and it took many days to fix the wheel. By then, they were enchanted by this place, as so many have been before and since. If not for them, there would be no art, no poetry, nothing to even tell people like your Mrs. Rogers that we are here."

Violet looked at the men again, their fading faces, their fateful wagon. It reminded her of that day she landed on Millicent's doorstep, under those palm trees, and found herself in an alien world. A wonderful world. A place where you could be a new person. "I can definitely see why they would never want to leave. I've never seen anything like it myself. That view of the gorge, that black slash in the earth. The light and the sky ..."

"Are you an artist yourself, Miss Redfield?"

Violet laughed, thinking of those old notebooks hidden under her bed at home. All that scribbling in the middle of the night. The stories that wouldn't leave her alone. "No, just an ardent admirer, Mr. Karavas."

He laughed again, and squashed out his cigar in the nearest brass spittoon. "As am I, Miss Redfield, as am I."

He gestured toward a portrait hanging on the wall beyond the photograph, of a woman with lustrous dark hair in a bright blue dress, sitting on a portal with a straw hat in her hand, the mountain in the distance behind her. "That is my mother, painted by the great Russian Leon Gaspard."

"She is beautiful," Violet answered, remembering her own Russian grandmother. No one had ever painted her looking so elegant, though there was that one photograph of her in her fine wedding gown that Violet kept locked in her suitcase.

"She was, she was. And Gaspard has become quite famous, you know. Many people want to buy that painting from me." He took out another cigar from his silver case. "Are you going out to the festival, then? There is much to admire here at such celebratory times. Our own St. Geronimo." He waved at a carved and painted statue of a bearded man in a brown robe.

"Just for a little while. Mrs. Rogers is resting." Violet curiously studied the little saint, who looked so sad to inspire such a festival. "Who *is* St. Geronimo?"

"St. Jerome? He was a priest and theologian in the 300s, and is the patron of Taos. We celebrate his protection every year with music, feasting, dancing ..."

"It sounds very colorful."

"Colorful, yes, yes! One day you must go out and see the dances at the pueblo. They remind me of when I was a child in Greece, and everyone would parade the statues from the church through the village, dancing and singing." Someone called his name, and he glanced back to see a porter looking terrified. A frown flickered over his mustached mouth. "Do excuse me, Miss Redfield. I will send some wine up to Mrs. Rogers with her dinner, I just got a case of a lovely Pol Roger she might enjoy. It strengthens the blood, you know."

"Of course. Thank you, Mr. Karavas." Violet put on her hat and made her way outside, into the noise. A jazz band played in the bandstand, under the shady trees of the plaza, while couples danced on the flagstones. She tried to take photos of it for MR, but she wasn't sure they would come out very well.

Violet came around the corner of an alleyway, and froze for a second at the sight in front of her, in stark contrast to the colorful joyousness just behind her on the plaza. Two men knelt there, one of them being violently sick into the gutter.

"Can I help?" she said impulsively. She knew that if she was sensible she would run away, back to the crowd; she was in a strange town, after all. But her heart wouldn't let her just leave someone in such trouble. It made her think of her brother, poor Richard, making his way home from the one tavern in town at dawn, staggering drunk, trying to forget nightmares he couldn't talk about.

The man who tried to hold his sick friend upright glanced up at her, and Violet fell back a step. Not because he was fearsome; but because he was too beautiful. His face, all sharp angles and planes, high, cut-glass cheekbones and a blade-like nose, was framed in glossy black hair, falling in a wave over his brow. His skin glowed bronze. He was more handsome than anyone she had met at Millicent's Hollywood parties.

But he also looked furious. His chocolate eyes narrowed as he stared at her.

"You a nurse?" he said roughly.

"No, but I ..." She looked again at the man who was vomiting into the street, and she remembered her poor brother again, poor Rich, with a pang. "I've seen stuff like this before. We need to keep him upright." She pulled her thermos of tea from her bag along with a handkerchief and dampened the linen. It wasn't clean water, but it would have to do. She stepped closer and gently mopped the sick man's clammy brow.

"I don't think I've seen you around town," the handsome, sober one said.

"I just got here a few days ago," she answered. She tried to get the sick man to take a sip of the tea.

"Well—welcome to Taos," Mr. Handsome said, a wry, laughing tone to his laconic voice.

Violet laughed, too. "It's not so bad. Usually." She nodded to the sick man. "Is he ill? My employer has a heart complaint, I can get medicines from her if we need them."

"Just whiskey-sick." Between them, they hauled the man upright and leaned him against the adobe wall. He sagged and staggered, but at least he wasn't throwing up. "We try to keep him out of town, away from the bottle, but ..."

"I know," Violet said gently. No one could have kept her brother away from a bottle, either, not even if they locked him in jail. "When it's on them, there's not much anyone can do. Was he in the war?"

"Of course."

"So was my brother. He helped liberate the camps. He can't get over it."

Mr. Handsome took the thermos and gently trickled some of the tea into the other man's mouth and onto his chapped lips. "He's my cousin," he said simply, and Violet could see now that was true. If the man wasn't so ill, he would be even *more* handsome than his relative, with a Renaissance-angel face. Such a shame. "Doesn't a lady like you have better things to do than help a drunk Indian?"

"No," Violet whispered, feeling her face turn hot at the thought that she could be lumped in with all the people who would turn their noses up in disgust if they saw this scene. Women whose own husbands and brothers and sons fought this same battle. "Not a single thing."

He gave a simple, curt nod, but she thought his frown relaxed a bit. "This is Benito, by the way, Benito Suarez. I'm Lorenzo Serna. I need to get him back to my aunt at the pueblo. She's been up since dawn worrying about him vanishing again, as well as cooking for dozens of people for the fiesta."

"Does he vanish often?"

"More lately. Sometimes he does fine, finds some work, some kind of distraction. But ever since he got back from Italy there's been a darkness in him. He can keep it at bay sometimes, but then it rolls over him all over again. We always find him, though. Not many places he can go here, not if he needs to buy his whiskey."

"Yes," Violet murmured, remembering her little hometown, the few shops where everyone knew what you bought and where you went after. No place to hide. At least here there were the mountains. The possibility of disappearance. "Maybe that's part of his problem. In a small place like this, like where I came from, everyone knows and cares about you. But there's no escaping them, either. No finding yourself." Benito's head lolled onto her shoulder, and she gently cradled his clammy cheek. "There's no escaping anything."

"That can be true." He stared at her hard, closely for a long minute, his face unreadable. She just looked back, and finally he nodded. "Who are you?"

"I'm Violet." Unable to look at Lorenzo's fascinating face for another second without fidgeting, she glanced down at Benito. His eyelashes fluttered and he murmured softly. "I think he's coming around."

"Benny," Lorenzo said, and Violet was amazed at the way his tone changed. Became light, teasing, as a person cajoled a child out of a tantrum. "There's a lady here, so mind your manners, ah? We're taking you back to Aunt Inez."

"Don't wanna let her see me like this," Benito slurred. He tried to roll his head back, to look up at Violet, but he almost tumbled back to the ground.

"Well, you have to. Or would you rather I call Uncle Tony again? We can't let you stay here in this alley."

"Why not? Good a place as any." His head fell back, and his eyes closed.

Lorenzo glanced up at Violet, and she nodded. They understood each other in that tiny movement. "One, two, three," he said, and they heaved Benito to his feet. Lorenzo took most of his cousin's weight on his own shoulder, but Violet managed to slip her arm around him and steady him. He felt so thin and bony, like a bird who might snap at any moment, and he smelled sour and sweet all at once. It reminded her much too much of those dark days with her brother.

Lorenzo led them around the edges of the bright, noisy plaza to a side street. A battered old Ford coupe was parked by the back wall of a shop, its chipped paint dark green against the tan stucco. Lorenzo heaved his cousin into the back seat, and Violet clambered in beside him to keep holding him upright.

"Sure you're okay there, Violet?" Lorenzo said as he took the wheel, and turned the key with a wheeze-gasp. "It'll be a bumpy drive."

"I'm fine." Violet shifted around on the cracked upholstery of the seat, and took out her thermos to try to coax Benito to take a sip.

The car coughed into life at last, and they drove out onto the main (only?) street of town, lined with shops and cafes, and then filling stations and rusty mechanics' yards, leaving the bright fiesta behind. They turned at a fork in the road from pitted pavement onto dusty trail. To one side was one last gas station, to the other the rusted iron gates of a cemetery, and then they seemed to leap into countryside. Fields and horse paddocks undulated away on each side, with that solid, snow-capped mountain always watching, watching.

It *was* beautiful, peaceful, a glory of green and dark purple and turquoise sky, but Violet couldn't gape at it the way she wanted to. She had to hold Benito upright, keep him from hitting his head on the doorframe, from getting sick all over the seat. After a few minutes jolting along the mud-puddled road, he stared right at her with wide, dark eyes and said hoarsely, "Say—who are you?"

Violet gave him a sad smile. She could see then how very good-looking he was, beneath the pallor, the bone-thinness. Almost unreal, like some of the actors Violet saw in California. It made everything even more sad.

"My name is Violet," she said simply.

"Are you Lorenzo's girlfriend? My mom is sure he has one. He's always disappearing, see."

"He said the same about you. You're always disappearing." She hated the jealous pang of thinking the handsome Lorenzo had a girlfriend.

He tried to smile, a tight rictus of his sculpted, though chapped and pale, lips. "I always did have the most girlfriends of all of us. Never a redhead, though. Lucky Lorenzo."

He fell back into pained silence as they jolted onto another track, this one narrow, barely more than a horse path, lined with straggling hedges, gray fields beyond. A cluster of sheep watched them curiously as they squealed past. They finally stopped in front of a house, a two-story farmhouse of the same pale brown mud walls, peeling blue paint on the window frames. Laundry flapped on a line, while dusty dogs rolled on the ground and chased each other in and out of the open door.

A woman rushed out, shooing them out of her way. She was older, frazzled, graying black hair straying out of her braid, her oval face heavily lined. Yet it was easy to see she was related to these men, with her fine, high cheekbones and shining brown eyes, her elegant height and slimness.

"Lorenzo! There you are finally. Did you find that crazy *tseh*? I told him last time ..." She seemed to see Violet for the first time, and she took a flustered step back. She smoothed her hair, and the faded calico apron that covered her dark dress. "Oh. Hello."

Lorenzo turned the car off, and the sudden rush of silence after the sputtering, roaring engine was deafening. She could hear everything, the patter of distant drums, the chirp of birds and the dogs barking.

"Auntie Inez, this is Violet. She helped me haul Benito out of the alley and into the car," Lorenzo said. He leaped out of the car in one quick, graceful motion and reached for his cousin, pulling him onto the pathway and holding him steady as he swayed precariously.

"Well—that's nice of you, dear," Inez said. She patted her hair again, seeming embarrassed. Violet remembered her own family's pride, the deep shame when some tavern barman hauled her brother home again and again.

"I'm glad I could help a bit," Violet said. She climbed slowly out of the car, unsure of what to do now. "My own brother sometimes has these, er, fits, too. The war, you know."

"We should get Benny to bed," Lorenzo said.

"Of course, of course, it's all ready. Do come in, Miss—Violet." Inez waved her hand toward the doorway, and shooed some of the dogs away.

Violet followed them into the house, ducking her head under the low door-jamb. Just beyond the doorway was a kitchen and dining area, two long tables spread with linoleum and lined with bowls and platters of food, steaming chile stews, mutton chops, vegetables, bread, jars of homemade jam. The dirt floor under her feet was hard-packed and swept, covered with a faded rug and lined with mismatched chairs and stools. "Are you having a party?"

"It's a feast-day in town, dear, everyone will be in and out all day, especially once the dancing in the main plaza is over." A frown flickered over Inez's face. "At least, I hope they will still come."

"They won't have heard about Benny's latest yet, Auntie," Lorenzo said.

"No, I don't suppose so." Inez waved towards the feast. "Violet, dear, do help yourself. I won't be gone a minute."

She and Lorenzo led Benito, nodding and swaying again, away toward a narrow staircase, and Violet glanced around, even more unsure about what to do. In Iowa, manners were everything, and she wanted to be polite now. Then she noticed a rusty-red stain on the skirt of her sundress.

She found a water pump outside, around the edge of the house, and let a spray of cold, clear water rush over her hands. She scrubbed at the spot until it grew fainter, and she wished she had a hairbrush. She splashed the water over her face, and the chill made her feel a little steadier. She found her tube of lipstick in her purse and slicked a bit of pink over her lips.

"... a stranger see!" a faint voice came from an open window, set high in the brown plastered wall.

"Better than one of your neighbors seeing," Lorenzo said. "Benito didn't want me to call Tony again."

"Of course not. We can't go bothering him every time, can we? What would that *kwee* wife of his say? Does this lady know Miss Mabel, too?"

"I don't think so. She said she was new in town. And she kept a cool head about her to help."

There was silence for a long moment. "That was kind of her, I'm sure. We just don't need more talk. It's hard enough." Her voice broke a little, as if she tried not to cry. Violet had heard that often enough with her mother.

"She doesn't seem the talky sort."

Violet frowned. She'd often been told she was too quiet as a child, too deep and strange, absorbed in her books. She'd been trying to chatter more, with the example of MR's sociable friends around her, be lighter and brighter. Maybe not being "talky" wasn't always so very bad. Maybe there were some people she could just be herself with.

"You should go see to her," Inez said. "Make sure she has something to eat. These girls are so thin nowadays."

Violet hurried to the edge of the yard, closed in with wooden pole fencing, in case someone came out and thought she was eavesdropping near the windows. She found herself looking out at the mountain, just beyond a field of horses and cottonwoods, and its solid presence steadied her.

Lorenzo appeared in the doorway, looking around until he spotted her. He gave her a nod and came towards her, slapping a battered hat over his cropped black hair. In the sun, she saw again how good-looking he really was, with a sun-browned health unlike his cousin, tall and lean, moving with a colt's grace.

She felt herself blushing, and she turned away, swearing it was just the sun. She took a pair of dark glasses from her purse and slid them over her eyes before he could see what she was thinking.

"All right, then?" he said, leaning against the fence beside her. His tanned forearms were corded with muscle, and he wore a gleaming silver bracelet on one wrist.

"Oh, yes. I just tried to wash up a bit." She brushed at her damp, crumpled skirt. "I'm afraid I didn't do a very good job of it."

"You look great," he said, then he looked away, as if embarrassed by his mild compliment. "I'll drive you back to town as soon as you have something to eat."

Violet glanced back at the house. It looked so quiet now. "I don't want to intrude on your aunt's party ..."

"She'll be insulted if you don't." He turned toward her with a grin, his arms crossed over his chest. "Besides, she's a really good cook. Much better than my mother, but don't ever tell either of them I said so."

Violet laughed. "I admit I wouldn't mind some home-cooked food at all. My employer hasn't been feeling well for a few days, so it's just been room service trays."

They walked together to the end of the fence and onto a pathway through the field. A warm breeze waved up around them, smelling of cedar and lavender and the faint tang of sheep manure. Much like home, Violet thought. The mountain shifted and shimmered, watching them, knowing.

Lorenzo took out a tarnished silver case. "Want a smoke, Violet?"

"No, thanks. But I don't mind if you do."

As she watched, his long fingers deftly rolled a narrow cigarette. He propped it at the corner of his lips and lit it with an equally tarnished lighter, some sort of engraving faded on its side. "So, what's your work? If you're not a nurse."

"A secretary. We just got here from California, via Santa Fe. I haven't been able to see much yet." She looked around, at the clusters of adobe farm buildings, the rounded lumps of horno ovens, a few children chasing the mangy dogs. The glorious deep purple and blue and green of the hills. "It really is so beautiful here. Not like where I came from at all."

"And where would that be?" He smiled down at her, a dimple flashing in his carved cheek that made him even more ridiculously good-looking. "Sorry. My aunt always did say I'm a nosy one."

She smiled back. She couldn't help it, really. "I'm from Iowa. Flat cornfields as far as the eye can see."

"Iowa, ah?" He exhaled a plume of silvery smoke. "How did you get from there to being a rich lady's secretary in California, Miss Iowa?"

"Who says she's rich?"

"If she wasn't, she probably wouldn't have a secretary she takes traveling with her. We see artists and such here all the time, people who haven't got a dime, but we see rich people here, too. They grab up our jewelry, poke around in secret places here at the pueblo, ask nosy questions."

"Like your Uncle Tony's wife?" Violet said, then wanted to slap herself. She'd forgotten she was eavesdropping there. Asking nosy questions, indeed!

Lorenzo narrowed his eyes through the smoke. "You know Mabel?"

"I don't know anyone yet. But I've heard of Mrs. Luhan. She sent an invitation to dinner to Mrs. Rogers, we just haven't been able to go yet." Violet *had* heard of Mabel Dodge, now Luhan. They said she ruled Taos from her large house just beyond pueblo land, that she knew everyone, and everyone did as she told them.

Violet would wager that wouldn't include MR. Or this man, either.

"She'll try to collect you," Lorenzo said.

"Collect us?" Violet laughed.

"That's just what she does." There was no judgment in his

quiet tone, just fact. "Like being a nurse or an accountant, she's a collector of souls. It's her job. She likes people, you see, she's curious about them. But just like a piece of sculpture she likes, she can't leave it on the shelf."

"She might want to collect Mrs. Rogers," Violet said, though she doubted Millicent could ever be "collected" by anyone at all. She was too closed in with herself. "But I doubt she would want me."

"Oh, she wants everyone." He ground the cigarette out under his scuffed boot. "Have you always been a secretary?"

Violet wondered at the quick change of subject, the easy elusiveness of him. "I used to work at a glove counter, and a soda fountain, among other things, before I got this job."

"That's why you left Iowa?"

"Not really. I mean—I wanted to work. I had some vague idea of acting, but I found out pretty fast that wouldn't be great for me. I just wanted to get away, see somewhere else, meet some new people." She didn't mention that old writing dream. It seemed silly now.

A smile quirked at the corner of his lips. "I had that feeling once."

Violet looked around her, at that place that seemed so eternal, so solid. The houses filled with his family. "You've always lived here?"

"Until I went to war." He nodded at a tin-roofed farmhouse across the field. "That was my parents' place, until my dad died and Mother went to live with my sister over by the river. She likes the noise and the company of being on the plaza, her friends coming in and out all day, my sister's kids to pester her. I took over her fields. I like the quiet out here."

"So you're a farmer?" *That* Violet could understand.

"And I do some silversmithing, some mechanics. It's what I learned in the war."

Violet thought of her brother, the camps. "In the Pacific?"

"The SeaBees. Building airstrips on tropical islands, fixing trucks and planes, whatever needed doing." He went quiet, and the silence was so heavy, as if he was far away. Back on those islands. "It was nice to get back here after that. I haven't had wanderlust since."

"I can see that," Violet answered softly. "If this was someone's home, why would they ever want to leave?"

"You ever want to go back to Iowa?"

Violet shook her head. "Never." Not after all the things she had seen and learned with MR; all the things she sensed might lay ahead. "At least, never yet. I do miss my family, but I love the other places I've seen. Especially this." She nodded at the mountain, so graceful yet solid, so permanent. So welcoming. "And I'd never have met Mrs. Rogers in Iowa! Or you, or Mr. Karavas, or Mirandi at the Thunderbird Shop in Santa Fe."

"And what do you think of us, of Taos, so far?"

Violet looked around at the mountains, the glorious blur of dark green, yellow, purple, the endless stretch of that sky. "I think it's the most beautiful place I could ever have imagined."

He glanced at the mountain, his eyes narrowed almost as if he had never really looked at it before. "It's not so bad."

"Not bad?" Violet laughed. "You must take it all for granted, having grown up here."

"Oh, I don't take anything for granted now."

Violet thought of the war, the stories everyone heard even in the middle of Iowa, the blood and starvation and cruelty. The men who didn't come back, like Bill, and the ones who were never the same, like her brother. "No. I suppose not." She turned her back to the mountain, but it felt like it still watched her, saw everything and said nothing. "You asked if I always wanted to be a secretary. I guess that's the most a girl could really hope for, at least one like me, who could never get to college. But when I was a kid, I had a secret dream."

His lips quirked, and he nodded. Did that mean he was interested? He was hard to read. And she had seldom wanted so much to impress someone. Just MR. "And what was that?"

"I wanted to be a writer. Like Mrs. Wharton, or Willa Cather. Or Virginia Woolf. Even like a Tolstoy, creating whole people with just words. I had a Russian grandmother, you see, and she would tell me such stories about the old country, even though she left when she was very young. The beauty and strangeness of it all. A lot like here, maybe."

"And you wanted to turn those places into stories? Make them real?"

"Yes," Violet said, amazed he understood. "When I wrote some of those ideas down, it felt like I wasn't even in *this* world any more. Like I had escaped, and I could control what happened to me. Make it all better, safer. Beautiful. Like that mountain." She paused, and bent down to pluck one of those strange little yellow, sticky flowers at her feet. "I never told anyone that. My parents would have thought such daydreams a waste of time."

"So why don't you write those places down now?"

"I don't think I still have those words in me."

Lorenzo was quiet for a moment, studying the end of his cigarette. "I'm not very artistic myself, I admit, but I've met lots of people who are. Painters, poets, they flock here to our little town. Have ever since I was a kid. I even posed for some paintings back then, watched how they created those better worlds you talk about."

Violet smiled. "Yes, I can see that, you being a model."

His cheekbones flushed with a dull red, and she laughed to see him actually blush. "They paid well. And one of those artists told me why they all came here to Taos. Because the sky is magic. Maybe you could find your words here, under a magic sky."

Violet could only nod, only stare at him. Only wonder at finding a spot of magic at last.

"Lorenzo," his aunt called from the doorway. "Are you talking the lady's ear off? Let her eat something, for heaven's sake. And put on this shawl, dear, you must be freezing." She handed Violet a shawl woven of bright red and blue stripes, and wrapped it tightly around Violet's shoulders. It smelled of juniper and smoke.

Violet smiled at Lorenzo. She thought Lorenzo Serna was one of the least "talky" people she had ever met. He said almost nothing, in fact, but she felt like he saw things no one else did. Or even could. She gave him a nod, afraid she had said too much to someone she had just met, and hurried inside. This place *did* change people. She felt herself shifting and shading inside already. Maybe this was a magic place, after all.

CHAPTER 10

Millicent

When she opened her eyes, for a long moment she didn't know where she was. The creaky old colonial rambler in Virginia, Claremont? The house in Jamaica, salty and sweet, sandy-floored? The stuffy heat, the darkness torn by flashes of light, was suffocating, burying her under cotton wool and quilted satin just as that little cot had once done when she was a child.

Was she a child again, pushed back through time, everything after her fever just a dream? She thrashed against the blankets, opening her mouth to call out for her nanny. To beg someone, *anyone*, to hear her and come save her from the tearing talons of those chasing shadows.

A pillow knocked over a lamp with a thunderous clatter, and she remembered where she was. The hotel room, in New Mexico. She'd run as far as she could.

Millicent sat up in the middle of the tangled bed, her heart pounding in her ears, so loud, so unsteady. Her hair clung to her forehead in the heat, her satin nightgown twisted around her legs. At least there was no lover there for once, to see her like that. So bare and vulnerable and trembling like a child. There was no one to see.

She was completely alone.

She drew in a deep, slow breath, as she had long ago learned to do when her heart was in a bad state. The first instinct was always to panic when her heart was in a bad state. The panic when it turned tickety-tock-boom on her, when rooms turned fuzzy around her and she fell in on herself. But giving in to the old fear meant defeat. And she wasn't ready to run up the white flag just yet.

In—breath. Out—breath. One, two, three. Slowly, like climbing up those steep Austrian crags she once scrambled along with her sons like a herd of goats, she regained a measure of steadiness.

Once her hands quit shaking, she felt around in the darkness for the fallen lamp, and hoisted it back up onto the table. She switched it on to reveal the usual clutter of her solitary bedrooms, amber pill bottles, water pitchers, whiskey bottles. Her army of makeup pots lined up on the dressing table, the blue linen suit she wore before that old enemy struck hanging on the wardrobe door. Herself, waiting to be put on again.

She heard sounds from beyond the window, the echo of guitar music, its beat pounding against her, laughter. A sharp crack. Guns? Fireworks? It was like something heard from a different planet.

Even though the curtains were drawn tight—striped red and blue like the woven cushions on the carved, dark wood furniture, like the rug underfoot with its intriguing design of arrows and birds—she knew it was night. She could always feel the darkness when it drew close, soft and comforting like an old friend. Like something she could hide inside. Tonight it just felt like a prison, as if it made her want to claw her skin off to be free of everything.

She heard that creaking sound again, and she couldn't be still a second longer. She pushed back the blankets and caught up the lace-edged dressing gown snagged over the back of a chair. She wrapped it around herself, not bothering with the sash, and padded across the room, dodging around trunks and suitcases to the window.

"Damn it all," she gritted out when the curtain caught, and she yanked at it until it fell back on the iron rod. And then suddenly, just below her window yet seeming a hundred miles away, she saw —life.

Sparse green patches of grass amid flagstones that formed the plaza below her window were surrounded by a low, crumbling adobe wall, with a large stone cross at one end and a bandstand at the other. Every foot was filled with people, laughing, dancing, drinking.

She stared and stared, taking in every face out there in the night. Every flower and embroidered shawl and smile. She felt sure she'd never seen so much color in one place, so much sheer, raw *life*. Her hand, long, white, thin, trembling, weighed down with diamonds and rubies, curled around the curtain in a fist, as if she could catch that color in her palm and hold it tight. As if she could grab onto life itself and force it to her will.

Force it to stay with her. To be *hers* again, just as it was theirs.

She watched a circle of dancers, their ruffled, lacy trains twisting around them as their hands clapped over their heads, as they spun and twirled. Then, just beyond the dazzle of their fringes and roses, she glimpsed a familiar face. Violet, pale and simple and slightly rumpled in her pink sundress, her hair brilliant red under the lights strung from the trees. She also wore a shawl over her shoulders, but it was different from the embroidery and fringes of the dancers, woven in bright stripes.

Violet half-turned and tilted her head back to say something to the person beside her. A man, tall and lean, his shoulders shifting muscles and sinew under a white shirt, his face hidden by a battered hat.

Violet laughed at whatever he said to her, and Millicent realized she'd never seen her secretary—her friend—like that before. Light, easy, giggling. Usually she was so serious about her work, about all she did and said. So careful.

As Millicent watched, feeling a pang of something strangely like jealousy, Violet spun around and hurried out of sight, under the front portal of the hotel. The man stood for a long moment, half in shadow, his face turned up for just an instant, just long enough for her to see dark eyes and sharp cheekbones. No wonder Violet smiled.

There was the light patter of footsteps up the stairs, the low click of the door handle as it turned. Violet's lavender-water perfume, some fresh, clean, green bit of breeze that still clung to her from outside, interrupted the staleness of the room's warm air.

"Oh, MR, you're awake," she said, surprised. She bent to pick up scattered shoes.

Millicent frowned, put out and irritated in some way she couldn't understand. She hated not understanding. Not controlling. She turned away. "Yes. I was alone when I woke, I didn't know where I was."

"I'm so sorry." She heard the door close, the sound of Violet straightening up some of the clutter. "I didn't know I would be gone quite so long. Mr. Karavas said he'd send up some dinner, make sure a chambermaid looked in on you. Where is Ethel?"

Millicent whirled around on her, hot anger flowing through her veins, making her heart pound dangerously all over again. "Ethel is just the cook and the maid! It is *your* job to look after me. I know I told you I would be a demanding employer, but surely I pay enough to be? A girl like you could *never* find a position such as this one on your own!"

Violet looked stunned, her hands freezing on the blouse she was folding. That bright shawl slipped on her shoulders. "Mrs. Rogers ..."

"And dinner *was* sent up, but it was the usual gray slop Mr.

Karavas likes to call 'room service.'" It was as if she watched it all from high above, out of herself, as it always was when the red mist swung low and she lashed out through it. At husbands, sons, whoever was near. She caught up the untouched tray with its silver dome-covered plates, and hurled it against the red-painted wall.

Violet stared at the rivulets of gravy dripping down, her mouth open in silent astonishment. And just like that, as quickly as it came, that mist was gone. Millicent's legs gave out beneath her, weak and shaking, and she fell to the carpet.

"MR," Violet gasped. She ran to catch Millicent's arm, and Millicent leaned on her shoulder, tears like a sharp pain at the back of her throat. How fresh and lovely and young and alive Violet smelled, of clean air and lavender and mountains. How escape seemed so impossible. Violet had a future. Millicent only had the past.

"I'm sorry," she whispered. "I don't know what comes over me like that."

But she did know. It was the same thing it always was. Jealousy and longing, longing for life as it was when she was young and healthy, free and thoughtless and as wide as the sky. Violet had all that, and so much more than the girl even realized. But she didn't deserve abuse for it.

"It's all right," Violet said. "Come on, let me help you back to bed." She led her back to the rumpled nest of sheets, tangled from Millicent's restlessness, from those awful dreams. So efficient she was, so calm, so cool.

"Oh, Vi. You must promise never to leave me. Never to go away." Everyone always did go away in the end, of course—but she intended to hold on by her Cherries in the Snow red nails as long as she could. "I can't do without you, no matter what I might say in one of my beastly tempers."

Violet smiled quizzically. "I'm not planning on going anywhere."

Millicent shook her head. "Not now, maybe. But you are young, healthy, curious. You'll tire of all this. I tire it of myself."

"Oh, MR." Violet's smile widened as she smoothed and tucked the blankets around Millicent's aching limbs, searched for the satin pillow that always had to be near. "You are so right—who else would hire me to be their social secretary? There's travel, art, interesting people. I'd never have even seen this place without you. So you're stuck with me now." She picked up the pieces of the broken china from the floor, tossing them carefully into the wastepaper basket. "You're also right that I should have stayed with you. Someone else needed my help, and I was gone longer than I planned. Let me call a doctor. Dr. Pond, maybe?"

Millicent waved her hand impatiently. Now that the storm was past, she was just so very tired. Bone-chilled weary. "No doctors tonight, I can't bear their poking and prodding. There's nothing they can do."

"Then some food. You haven't eaten all day. I'll have the porter bring another tray."

"Don't bother, darling. It will just be more of the same. I don't know where Mr. Karavas gets such staff. I wish we could go back to that lovely little restaurant we ate at the first day. The one with the fountain."

"El Patio?" Where Millicent had scandalized the locals by wearing white shorts and espadrilles, her long, coltish, tan legs bare.

"Yes, that's the one. El Patio. I've never tasted such food!" Millicent let her heavy head drop back on the pillows, and closed her eyes. She saw it again, the bright, intense sunlight dancing on the waters of the fountain, the blue pots of red flowers against the tan walls, the taste of the sangria on her tongue that was just like drinking light itself.

"I could probably go fetch a meal from their kitchen. Maybe some tacos? Chicken tortilla soup?"

"Maybe later, darling." She reached for Violet's hand, the skin so warm after her day outside, smelling of the desert air. "Sit with me for now. Tell me where you went, what it's like out there. All of it."

Violet sat down on the edge of the bed, her gaze very far away for a moment, as if she saw something beyond the hotel window. Far beyond Millicent herself. "You won't believe it, MR! I went to the pueblo."

Millicent opened her eyes. "The pueblo?" How she had dreamed of it after all the tales she heard, all the paintings she looked at. The ancient buildings against the purple of the mountains, the glowing turquoise of the painted doors, the sparkling river.

"Yes. I went out to see the festival on the plaza, and found a man whose cousin had become quite ill. I offered to help take him home, and their family lives there at the pueblo. Not in the main buildings, but on a farm."

Millicent remembered the shadowy man she saw Violet standing with outside, standing far too close together. She knew attraction when she saw it, knew that pull of soul to soul that came all too rarely. And yet all too often it was only an illusion. "Vi, darling, you are much too good-hearted. Running off to the middle of nowhere like that!"

"I know. Not like *me* at all," Violet said teasingly. "Where on earth could I have learned such shocking behavior? What a terrible influence you are on us farm girls."

Millicent laughed, and swatted at Violet's arm. "Enough of that, insolent child! What did you see there? What was it like?"

Violet sighed. "I didn't see those buildings in the paintings, just that farm. But it certainly wasn't like any farm at home! Like something from hundreds of years ago, all natural beauty and peace. You would so love to see it for yourself, I know you would."

"And I intend to. Tomorrow."

Violet laughed. "Not tomorrow. You have to get better, as you know if you don't rest now you'll just get worse in the long run."

Millicent felt a burning flash of that anger, that fury that she couldn't always do everything she wanted when she wanted. That helpless rage at her betraying body. She shoved the satin pillow to the floor.

"You know I'm right, MR. And don't throw things at me!"

"You *are* becoming insolent. It's a bad habit, Violet Redfield." Yet Millicent felt a grudging respect for it, too. Violet was starting to find herself, her spirit. Maybe it was this place. Magic things could happen here, she could already feel it. It showed you who you really were, deep inside. "Very well, though. Not tomorrow. This weekend."

"If the doctor says so. Now, please let me get you something to eat. I won't be gone long, I promise."

Millicent nodded, too tired to argue. "I'll let you have your way—this time. But only because it's late and I need my beauty sleep."

"I thought so." Violet picked up the satin pillow, and stood up to cross the room, snatching up more discarded gowns and shoes as she went.

"Oh, Violet, can you hand me those letters on the dressing table? I didn't have time to read the post before you and the doctor gave me that infernal sleeping potion."

"Of course. Anything I need to answer tonight?"

"Certainly not, Vi darling, it must be nearly midnight! I'm not *such* an ogre employer as all that." She glanced through the envelopes Violet passed her, tossing aside bills from milliners and furriers and couturiers. "Ah, a letter from Paulie. I do hope he doesn't need money again. And it looks like some invitations, what fun! Word must be getting out we're here, thanks to Janet and Adrian." She opened one creamy, heavy-milled envelope. "Do you know a Mrs. Luhan?"

Violet was tucking away a pile of silk nightgowns into the drawer. "I think I might have heard of her. She has a big house just outside of town, and knows all the writers and artists who come through. Her husband is from the pueblo. He might be the uncle to the men I helped today?"

"Married to an Indian? How delightful! Well, it seems we're summoned to her demesne next week for dinner. Maybe your new friends might be there, Vi, darling?"

CHAPTER 11

Mabel

G *lamour Girl Goes To Wilderness! Escaping Gable Broken Heart!*

Mabel squinted down at the newspaper spread on the bed. Even with her thick glasses and the bold, black print, the words seemed to squiggle and squirm before her. How dreadful it was to get old, she thought for the thousandth time in her advancing years. When she was young, energy had burst out of her like thunderstorms over the mountains, powerful and inescapable. She'd had to keep moving, Italy to New York to France, to radical protests and salons and bookstores. All the way to the Taos deserts.

Energy storms still rolled over her at odd moments, catching her unaware, propelling her forward. Pouring that life force into artists and writers, dancing in the moonlight as Tony drummed. But what she had never done, never been, was a "glamour girl."

Mabel studied the photo of the said glamour girl. She was indeed something, tall, slim as a reed, bright blonde hair waving around a heart-shaped face, cat-like, almond eyes, a Charles James gown structured of satin and tulle swathed around her, diamonds at her ears and throat.

Mabel thought of Italy, her garden there, her magical world of parterres and fountains and olive trees, smelling of lemons, a dream of so long ago. The New York apartment, draped with bohemian shawls and filled with the talk of people who declared they would make a revolutionary world that never came to pass. Her son, her friends, all that tall talk, all those grand ideas. Her husbands, her various lovers, so much passion and fire. This Mrs. Rogers, too, had surely seen such things. Possessed such things. Maybe they could understand each other.

No one had really ever understood her. Not her parents, so cold, so distant. Her first husband, that dotard. Maurice, who thought he could possess her. Only Tony understood. Only sometimes.

Mabel looked up, out the window of her room at Los Gallos. Her home, her perfect little kingdom, the place where everything was exactly as she expected it to be. The meadows and mountain and gardens.

The rising moonlight reflected on the cypresses Tony had planted so many years before. In Italy, a cypress meant mourning. Not here. "Our hope," he called it. As it grew, towered high, so would their love. The tree was hers. It *was* her. Strong. In the great blue-black bowl of the sky, the stars were scattered in their hundreds, thousands, sharp as glass. Only the solid mountain, never sleeping, pierced their glow with a spot of darkness.

"This is mine," Mabel said, but her voice cracked appallingly. "*I* am queen here."

No blonde glamour girl was going to take it from her. Others had tried before. Her town, her home, especially her husband—oh, they had tried. But she held onto what was hers. She always would.

She pushed herself up from her chair, the bulk of her body familiar to her now, and shuffled into her gallery, floor to ceiling windows that looked out to the mountain. All her life, all her wanderings, her strivings and efforts and seekings, she had searched for she knew not what. Until she found it in a place she never even heard of before, an ancient place of peace and beauty and eternity.

The wilderness.

She pushed open one of the tall windows, and let the wind rush in, bringing the smells of pine and woodsmoke and sage.

At the edge of the garden was Tony's wigwam, a small, circular structure of bent branches that gleamed in the night from the glow of a lamp inside. She heard the low thrum of a drumbeat, the murmur of a song, as Tony sat out there in the night. Her husband, her strong, quiet, man. The only one who always understood her.

Being a glamour girl wasn't everything in life, after all. And here, things like that wouldn't matter in the least. This Mrs. Rogers would soon find that out for herself.

CHAPTER 12

Violet

"Would it be possible for us to engage a car for this evening?" Violet asked the girl behind the La Fonda reception desk. And she *was* just a girl—small, slim, black-haired, her face still plump with teenage puppy fat. Her navy-blue suit and white blouse were much too large for her. One of Mr. Karavas's many nieces. Or cousins, or great-nieces. That was the way everything seemed in Taos. A family business, connected everywhere.

It made Violet think of her own hometown, with a wistfulness that surprised her. She didn't want to go back there, but it had been a sort of comfort to know everyone, to know they knew you in return. Where you belonged. The problem was, once you were put into that box you couldn't get out again, no matter how hard you tried.

The girl's eyes widened with nervousness, and her hands twisted in the sleeves of her too-long jacket. "I—I'm not sure. There aren't many cars here, you see, Miss Redfield, and nothing someone like Mrs. Rogers would want."

Violet thought of all the kids on horses she had seen all over town, the bicycles and creaking motorbikes. But Lorenzo had a car. And he was a mechanic.

"Surely there must be something in town," Violet said. "Mrs. Rogers has sent for her own car to be brought, but it has to come from Virginia, and Miss Gaynor has already gone back to California. Mrs. Rogers has been invited to the Luhans for dinner, and I think it's too far for Mrs. Rogers to walk, yes?"

Violet wasn't sure MR should go anywhere at all, really. She still looked so pale from her bout of illness, and tired quickly. But being shut up in her hotel room was certainly doing her no good, either. She didn't sleep, and her temper grew worse.

It was no good for Violet or Ethel, either. Violet ached to see that glorious mountain again, to hear its voice calling to her, to watch the blue-purple-yellow expanse of the sky change above her head every second, and she would steal a car if she had to in order to get out.

She remembered Lorenzo again, his long, elegant hands as he casually steered the car, the rare, quirking smile he gave her. She wouldn't mind seeing *him* again, either.

"Mrs. Luhan!" the girl cried. "Oh, you can't be late there, you just *can't*." She sounded almost terrified, the poor thing.

Violet could already see a problem ahead, car or not. Millicent was *always* late.

"Why is that?" she said. "The note says there's a cocktail hour to start. Is it like Windsor Castle or something? One sherry on the stroke of six, and then you're booted right out?"

The girl turned even more pale. "I—I don't know. I've never been there. But no one can get on Mrs. Luhan's bad list, you'll never meet anyone here again. That's what they say, anyway."

Violet found herself intrigued. What did one have to do to get on a socialite's "bad list?" She'd love to see that group of names. She leaned over the desk and whispered, "What really goes on out there at Los Gallos? I heard it's an artistic salon, painters and writers and such. I'm sure that sort of people do often get into some trouble. Especially way out here where no newspaper can see them."

The girl bit her lip, obviously in some agony of indecision. Violet knew that feeling well. She was a "confidential secretary," after all. Yet sometimes she thought she would burst if she couldn't tell someone like Jo-Jo a really juicy bit of gossip.

But nothing about Millicent, her illness, her insomnia, her tempers that passed so fast, her bad dreams. Never anything about Millicent.

Maybe this Mrs. Luhan was like Millicent in one of her bad moods? Mabel Luhan was an Eastern heiress, too, after all. The daughter of big money from Buffalo, New York, with a string of husbands and lovers behind her. Regrets, memories, fascinating tales to tell. Violet had learned that women like that didn't think like everyone else.

Millicent's moods passed like thunderstorms, though, raging one second and vanished the next, and everything was friendly again. As long as everyone remembered their place. Yes, indeed— maybe Mrs. Luhan was like MR in that way. Or why would everyone seek her out? Just as they themselves sought her out now, if a car could be found.

"Mina," a voice boomed from the back office. "What is taking so long with those files? People are in a hurry here; they don't want to hear you chatter on and on."

Mina jumped back as if burned. "No, Uncle Saki," she called back in a shaking voice. "Miss Redfield was just asking about hiring a car."

"A car? For Mrs. Rogers, is it?" Mr. Karavas emerged into the reception area, his smoking jacket a dark blue velvet that day, an expensive cigar lodged in the corner of his mustached lips.

"Yes," Violet answered. "We're meant to go to Los Gallos for dinner with Mrs. Luhan, surely too far to walk."

"Walk! Guests here at *my* hotel never walk, Miss Redfield. Mina, what did you tell her?"

Mina turned even more pale, if that was possible, and nearly vanished into her suit collar. "I—didn't know where to find a car

Mrs. Rogers might find acceptable, Uncle Saki. Your own Cadillac is in the shop, isn't it?"

"I think I do know a mechanic, perhaps he could help," Violet said, though she wasn't sure what Millicent would think of Lorenzo's old car. She would probably find it great fun, an adventure, as she did everything else.

"Nonsense! Mina, find young Tom McCarthy. He can take Mrs. Rogers out to Los Gallos. Now!"

Mina ran off into the office as fast as her scuffed court-heeled shoes could carry her.

"I didn't mean to cause such inconvenience," Violet said quickly.

"There can be no inconvenience from my guests, Miss Redfield, whatever you need, you just come to me. My life is only to be of service." He gave her a low bow.

Violet somehow doubted it was *all* service. To himself, maybe. "Mina says Mrs. Luhan was even friends with Mr. Lawrence, before he died. I loved his *Women in Love*."

Mr. Karavas's face darkened, and he chomped down hard on his cigar. "Mrs. Lawrence no longer speaks to Mrs. Luhan. At least not today; she might tomorrow. You would be wise to never let their names pass your lips, Miss Redfield."

Violet nodded somberly, even though she longed to know the whole story of *that*. She certainly knew how to "mind her lips," ever since she was a kid who had to hide her books under her bed for fear they would be taken away and she would be sent outside to "make herself useful." Besides—being quiet meant she heard everything that was most interesting.

She wasn't sure about MR, though. One never *did* know with her. Sometimes she kept her thoughts as tight as a drum, and sometimes she told everything. But she was in her own Millicent World so much of the time lately, half in and half out of the prosaic old world. It should be an interesting evening, Violet knew that much.

"I do have something you might enjoy seeing later, Miss Redfield, just between us. If you're of an artistic nature, as I suspect you are."

"Indeed?" Violet said, most intrigued.

"Yes. Some paintings I acquired once from Mr. Lawrence, after they had been banned from being shown in England. I said I would keep them for him, you see, for safety. For only a nominal fee. But he never came back for them. I do show them to very few people."

Violet knew what sort of pictures he must mean; the sort of naughty problems DH Lawrence used to have with the censors. And Mr. Karavas thought *she* might like to see them. Her—Violet Redfield from the cornfields. She had come a long way. All thanks to Millicent.

She was not one tiny bit shocked, as her mother would assume she should be. She felt—sophisticated. Almost Millicent-like herself.

Almost.

"I would find that most interesting, thank you," she said.

He touched her hand, his fingers moist, plump. "Excellent! Next week? They are in my vault, you see."

"If Mrs. Rogers does not need me then."

Mina came dashing back, her blouse untucked from her over-large skirt and her hair straggling, as if she had hurried a bit too much, and Mr. Karavas luckily removed his damp hand.

"Tom is on his way now," Mina gasped. "He can use his father's car."

"Excellent, excellent," Mr. Karavas muttered. "You must know, *agapitos*, if you want to run a fine hotel, you must anticipate every guest's need before they even realize they have it. Most vital."

It sounded much like Violet's own job, she thought. Anticipate what Millicent would need or want—which changed from instant to instant—and be there to make it happen.

"You will like young Tom, Miss Redfield, his family is one of the finest in town, they own much property and know everyone," Mr. Karavas said. "Just let us know if you require anything else at all."

"I will. And thank you, Mina, you have been a wonderful assistance. I'll just go fetch Mrs. Rogers." If Millicent had finished her bath and toilette, which was a considerable doubt.

As Violet turned to leave, Mina called out, "Oh, Miss Redfield! I nearly forgot. This came for you today."

She handed Violet a letter, and with a sinking feeling Violet recognized her mother's firm, slanting handwriting. It had been a few weeks since she'd heard anything from Iowa, thanks to the move from California, but every letter before then said the same thing. *When are you coming home, where you belong? When are you going to marry and settle down properly?* "Thank you, Mina."

"And this for Mrs. Rogers."

Violet glanced over the stack of envelopes. More bills, of course, a letter on thin blue international letterhead from Millicent's mother in France, another from Paul which no doubt asked for another allowance increase. She wondered if MR's mother wrote letters like Violet's own family—slightly critical, all "for your own good, dear." "When are you coming home?" But Violet's mother's letters had far less about the Cote d'Azur and Cartier's, and were more about harvests and Corn Princess parades. Violet and Millicent both had brothers who struggled, though.

"Thank you," she said again. "We'll be down soon. It was so kind of Mr. McCarthy to come for us so last minute. Does he have a professional chauffeur license?"

Mina laughed, which made her look like the young, carefree girl she should be, until her uncle shot her a reproving glare. "Not exactly. But I'll ring your room when he arrives."

Violet wasn't entirely reassured by the laughter. She remembered the winding ride through the mountains to get to Taos, the bumpy gravel, the hills that seemed to climb and drop like a roller coaster. But beggars couldn't be choosers or they wouldn't ride.

She nodded, stuffed the letters into her handbag, and rushed back up the stairs past a few other guests coming down for dinner.

In their rooms, it was the usual mad scene. Millicent sat in front of her mirror, Ethel trying to fix her hair since no professional hairdresser could be found in town, while Millicent sorted through her lipsticks. She was wrapped in a pearl-colored satin dressing gown, while dresses were scattered over the bed and chairs, a riot of black, red, bronze, green.

"There you are finally, Violet," Millicent said impatiently. She still looked pale and drawn, her jaw gritted against pain, but Violet knew better than to try and make her stay home and rest. "Did you have to walk back to Santa Fe to find a car or something?"

Violet picked up a violet-purple Ceil Chapman cocktail dress where it had landed on the carpet. "Almost. But Mr. Karavas found someone here to drive us, a man named Tom McCarthy. He'll be here any minute."

"And here I am, just trying to look presentable." Millicent frowned, and her fingers trembled on the gold tube of Elizabeth Arden lipstick. For the first time since those strange moments in Gable's house, Violet thought MR seemed—could it be nervous? "I do want to fit in here. I have a sense I may want to stay around for a while. Yet I can't even get my hair right! Do stop pulling it like that, Ethel."

"Well, Mrs. Rogers, I am a cook, not a hairdresser," Ethel snapped. She'd been with MR for years, and knew even better than Violet when to speak out and when to retreat.

"I could hardly get Etienne to leave Los Angeles, could I? We'll just have to find someone. Pay them well to come out here to the desert, and they won't say no. Maybe you could learn, Violet?" She glanced at Violet in the mirror, taking in the plain French twist of her red hair with a flicker of disdain. "No, Violet must do what she does best, keeping me organized. Someone else can curl my hair."

"Speaking of organizing," Violet said, digging through her handbag for the letters. She filed the bills with the others, and handed the rest to Millicent, who glanced over them as Ethel finished setting the waves of her blonde hair. Violet couldn't help but realize with a worried pang that the golden waves were thinning, losing some of their sunlight luster.

Millicent glanced at the letters. "Oh, Mummy Da. She's found some other handsome young artists to 'patronize' in Nice." She tucked the letter under a bottle of Shocking. "And Paulie, again. I'm sure he wants a larger allowance, but I don't see why he can't live within the one he has. It's more than I ever had at his age, and I did just send him some new shirts. My father would say money does not grow on trees."

Violet glanced at the litter of gowns on the bed, Charles James, Dior, Balenciaga. She'd met Paul Peralta-Ramos a couple of times, when he visited his mother in California from his Eastern school. She'd very much liked him, he was polite and funny, and knew such a lot about art, just like his mother. And he was darkly handsome, like his father. He would go far, surely, even though he was not the intellectual his brother Peter was.

Yet Millicent had once flown into a rage when Paul asked for money for new suits. As if she was about to starve on the street.

Violet remembered something she'd read once. Maybe something in Fitzgerald? The rich *were* different. They saw money differently.

Millicent put Paul's letter by her mother's, and only then did she notice Violet still held one envelope. "Something from Iowa, darling?" Ethel pinned up a curl of hair and fastened it with a diamond clip, while Millicent studied a compact of pearly powder. "Not bad news, I hope."

"I haven't read it yet," Violet admitted.

"Oh, but you simply must! I'm dying to know what happened to the Millers' litter of piglets after your mother's last letter."

Violet did hate to read her mother's letters aloud, but MR was always so interested, like they were bits of news dropped from another planet. A Dickens serial for the 1940s. Her mother's worries for Violet's unmarried future, her brother's struggles, her father's work on the farm, her cousin's new job at the school. It all sounded so far away and strange, especially here with the mountains and the desert and people like Lorenzo Serna.

But as Millicent finished her makeup, Violet slit open the letter and scanned the close-written lines. "All the piglets survived, but one."

"Oh, that is nice! And how is Edna faring at the school? Has her beau proposed yet?"

"Hmm, not yet, it seems." Violet scanned the next paragraph, and suddenly gasped, unable to hold it in.

Millicent's hand froze as she pressed foundation along her jaw. "What is it, darling? Did your father's cows escape again?"

"No. My brother Richard is—engaged." She could hardly fathom it. For so many years, he had barely been able to rise from his bed, had startled at every loud noise. No one had known if he would ever recover from the war. Now he was going to be married. How had he even gone on dates? "To Jane Rasmussen, the daughter of the bank vice-president in town." And who had been the homecoming queen their senior year of high school, the Corn Princess. "A Christmas wedding."

"Oh, you must go!" Millicent cried. "Weddings are such fun. I had three myself, though I fear they were such hole-in-the-wall events. I liked the privacy, of course, no vulgar flashbulbs going off in one's face, but I did miss all the veils and orange blossoms and such."

Violet cold hardly picture it. Her brother and Miss Rasmussen? What earth-shaking changes was she really missing by being so far from home? Was her mother right, she should go back where she belonged? "Maybe. There's plenty of time to think about it all." She read on a bit further, and saw her mother said that Rich and Jane's house, provided by Mr. Rasmussen, would surely have room for Violet if she wanted to live in town rather than on the farm. She couldn't even imagine such a thing, not anymore. Not now that she was just beginning to see herself, Violet, as a whole person in the world. "But there's no time to think of all that now. Mr. McCarthy will be here with his car soon."

Millicent sighed. "I wish I had said no to this dinner after all. Mrs. Luhan sounds exhausting."

"But she does collect so many writers and artists around her! You said you want to stay here a while, fit in, yes?" Violet said. "And there might be dancers from the pueblo. Remember how you loved to watch them in Santa Fe? Now you can talk to them about it, learn the history."

Or maybe it was she, Violet, who wanted to do that. Wanted to know more about that magical place she had only glimpsed. She longed to know every single thing about it all.

Millicent glanced at some of her treasures lined up on the windowsill, pottery gleaming in shimmery reds and blacks and earth-colored mica, baskets closely woven in figures and patterns. The tray of silver and turquoise jewelry on her dressing table. It *was* all very beautiful, unlike anything Violet had ever seen before. She did want to talk to some of the artists herself, and not be shunted off to a secretary's little corner. She knew Gertrude Stein had once been great friends with Mabel Luhan when they lived in Europe, and that Miss Stein would banish mere wives to the kitchen while she talked to Great Men like Hemingway and Fitzgerald.

She certainly hoped that wasn't a habit of Mrs. Luhan.

"You're right, Violet darling, of course. Once an invitation is accepted, it must be followed through." Millicent did cancel often in California, but only when she was very ill. She seemed determined to press ahead now.

At last her hair and makeup were done to her satisfaction, her lips painted a crimson glow, her hair swept up into diamond clips that disguised that new thinness. She rose and shed her dressing gown, revealing the exquisite pink silk Parisian underpinnings.

After a few long moments' indecision, she let Violet help her into a black and white print Chanel with a matching bolero jacket embroidered in red roses. She smoothed the close-fitting skirt while Violet found a pair of red Ferragamo shoes, a black alligator handbag.

Millicent pinned one of her jeweled Verdura starfish to her shoulder, donned a pair of pearl earrings that her father once gave her and were a great favorite, and tossed a red shawl around her carelessly. She looked exactly like the Hollywood star she had nearly been.

"Are you going to wear that, then, darling?" she murmured, glancing at Violet.

Ethel swept up the discarded lipsticks on the dressing table, ignoring them both now.

Violet glanced down at her dress, a black, sleeveless sheath with black beads at the neckline, her silver violet brooch pinned at the shoulder. She thought of her mother's words—she belonged in Iowa, not in the middle of the mountains with famous people. "I did hear that Mrs. Luhan is a bit—bohemian. Am I too *boring*? Too ordinary?"

Millicent laughed merrily. "My darling, no one here knows what ordinary even is. You must learn to be yourself! That's why we came all this way, isn't it? To find what *we* want."

Violet remembered the way she felt when she looked at that mountain. As if it welcomed her back at long last. As if she could breathe, for the very first time. As if she could run and run and jump into the sky, free, if she was only brave enough. Was she brave enough?

Millicent picked up a coat from a chair, a piece she had brought with her when she lived in Austria, black velvet embroidered with white edelweiss and trimmed with narrow white satin ribbons. "You are part Russian, yes, V.? I think this coat was embroidered in Moscow, long ago. You should wear it now."

As she slipped the sumptuous fabric over Violet's shoulders, a knock sounded at the door. "Mrs. Rogers, your car is here," Mina called.

"Thank you, my dear, we shall be there soon." Millicent leaned down leisurely to check the seams of her stockings. "Violet, do you think these shoes *really* work? Maybe I need the Chanel shoes s with the kitten heels?"

Violet didn't even know where those shoes could be packed. "No," she said firmly. "Those are perfect."

"I just don't know ..."

At last, they made their way downstairs, where Mina waited to lead them outside. Luckily Mr. Karavas himself was nowhere to be seen.

But Benito Suarez was.

He paced close to the reception desk, twisting his straw hat between his hands. For a moment, Violet almost didn't recognize him. The man who had been sick all over the alleyway, pale and clammy and reeking, was now tall and slim and handsome, as good-looking as any of the movie stars Violet met in California. His features were finely-carved, a slim nose and strong jaw, towering, cut-glass cheekbones, dark eyes, and gleaming black hair brushed back from his brow. He wore a white, pressed shirt and brown tie with black trousers, respectable even without a coat.

He also looked deeply, deeply embarrassed, his eyes not quite meeting hers, his booted feet shuffling on the worn burgundy carpet.

"Miss Redfield," he said. "I—well, I hoped, that is—I wanted to come here and apologize."

Violet was achingly aware of Millicent standing right beside her, watching the little scene as avidly as she would any opera. She stood very still and straight, her hair shimmering, her eyes wide. That very stillness was the thing that told Violet she was paying the most intent of attention. When she was bored or in a hurry, her fingers would flutter, she would look all around, her toes would tap in her expensive shoes. Not now.

"Mr. Suarez," Violet said. "I'm surprised you remember my name."

He blushed like a schoolboy, and kicked at the carpet again. When he glanced to the side, he looked a bit like Lorenzo, a younger, more callow, more dissipated version of his cousin. Violet almost wished Lorenzo was here now, to know how to manage it all.

"I admit I just remember a pretty redhead. I thought it was all a dream. Then Lorenzo told me what happened. *Everything* that happened." He twisted his hat harder. "That's how I knew it was—bad. Though I imagine he didn't tell me quite everything."

Violet could understand that. Lorenzo Serna seemed like a man of few words, of unreadable eyes. A man who just quietly took care of things. "I've seen worse, Mr. Suarez. Don't worry about it any longer, please."

He smiled, shy and sweet. "Lorenzo did say your brother was in the war."

"Yes," Violet murmured, reminded of that marriage announcement. "He had a hard time when he came home."

"I was in Italy. It was—well." He smoothed out his hat, but the straw brim looked mangled beyond repair. "Lorenzo was in the war, too, and he never had such—well, such troubles. My aunt said I was wrong to let an outsider see me like that."

"It *was* in the middle of town," Violet couldn't help but remind him. She knew she was an 'outsider' in Taos, but it stung a bit to hear it. "Lots of people were there."

He shook his head. "No excuse, that. I never really do have an excuse. Just nothing else to do, I guess. But again, I'm sorry."

Millicent finally moved then. She took a gliding step toward him, long, white, bejeweled hand, diamonds and rubies mixed with new turquoise, held out, a smile on her crimson lips. Her silken skirt rustled, the silver bracelets lining her arms singing. The unique music of Millicent. Benito looked thunderstruck, just as

Violet was on that first interview in California. Like he'd fallen into a different world.

"How do you do," Millicent said in her low, slow, musical voice. "I'm Millicent. You must be one of the people dear Violet said she met at the pueblo. I was terribly jealous, she remarked how very kind you all were."

"She—she was the kind one," Benito stammered. He took her hand, holding it carefully like it might break. "I'm Benito Suarez."

"So pleased to meet you. But I am sure it's nonsense that only Violet was kind—though she is *always* kind, I could not do without her. She said your aunt's cooking was second to none, and the mountains gloriously beautiful." She turned his hand in hers, examining the wide, engraved silver cuff on his wrist. "Just like this bracelet. What craftsmanship! I've never seen anything quite like it. What's this symbol?"

From anyone else, it would be easy to wave away such words as distracting flattery, polite chatter, but Violet knew well that MR took her jewelry seriously indeed. She gently touched her own silver violet brooch at her collarbone, and thought of Millicent's intense concentration for hours and hours as she bent over her workbench.

"It's a thunderbird. It means power, protection, strength," Benito said. "My cousin made it. He's a silversmith."

"Lorenzo?" Violet blurted. "I thought he was a mechanic."

Benito's mouth hardened. "We Indians have to be jacks of all trades to make a penny, Miss Redfield. Or jack of none, like me."

"Oh, I am sure that cannot be true," Millicent said. "You must be good at something."

"It is. No job, you see, Mrs. Rogers. No one would hire me."

Millicent's dark-penciled eyebrows arched. "Well, *I* will hire you! It's become clear I shall need a permanently on-call driver, once my car arrives from my house in Virginia. My chauffeur refuses to stay here, insists on returning East right away. When I am settled somewhere, you must be my driver." She glanced around the dimly lit lobby, the matador jackets sparkling in glass cases, the paintings of Indians and mountain landscapes, the dark red wallpaper. "I have a feeling I will be staying here for some time."

Violet felt a tiny spark of alarm, remembering what she had heard of Benito, his binges and rages, his unpredictability. "MR ..." she began, but Millicent just waved her away.

"Thank you so much, Mrs. Rogers," Benito said, staring at Millicent as if she was a goddess. Which, of course, she was. Temperamental, true, but as kind as she was beautiful, always taking in strays like Benito. Like Violet herself. "You won't be sorry."

"I never am," Millicent said. "Regret is such a waste of time. Now we must go. Good-bye, Mr. Suarez. I'm so glad to have met you."

"And me you. Thanks again, Mrs. Rogers."

He watched them go as Violet hurried behind Millicent out of the lobby, but he didn't follow.

The sun was just beginning to set when they stepped out of the hotel. It was much quieter than when Violet watched the festival; the main square held only a few people, couples sitting close together on wrought iron benches, children chasing around the towering cottonwoods. The shop windows were being closed, shutters drawn, the light mellow-marigold yellow on the adobe walls. But the sky made up for any lack of color below, all rose-pink, lavender, azure, bronze, streaking away over the mountains.

But Violet couldn't quite revel in the glories of pink and purple and gold, the shifting shapes of clouds. She was certainly used to MR's changes by now, the temper that flared and vanished, the sadness, the pain, that melted into laughter. Decisions made, then changed. Hiring Benito Suarez, a man she had just met, a drinker with black moods, as her driver of all things, was a new one. He was a stray, too, like Violet, but she worried about Millicent's safety.

"MR," she said carefully. "Mr. Suarez was—well ..."

"A man of deep troubles. Yes. I can see it in his eyes. Such beautiful eyes, so sad." She glanced at Violet, a bemused smile on her lips, her gaze misty. "Do you think I can't read men, Violet darling? That I don't know what they're like, through and through?"

Violet shook her head. MR knew art, clothes, books, history— but most of all she knew people. Especially men. She could indeed read them, read what they wanted most of all, and she gave it to them. She made them feel they were the only one that mattered in all the world. Until the next one came along. The romance was all.

Yet she had misjudged Clark Gable.

"No, MR," Violet said. "You do know that."

"And, of course, I can hire who I like. I answer to no one. I tend to know which people I want in my life after knowing them only a moment. I found *you*, did I not?"

Violet couldn't deny that. She also couldn't deny who signed her wages checks. Without Millicent, she might have to go back to Iowa.

She studied the buildings around them, so golden-brown in the sunset, that glorious sky, that purple mountain watching her in the distance. She smelled the sharpness of green chile roasting, the sweetness of tortillas, heard the faint strains of guitar music somewhere nearby. Yes, she definitely did not want to go back to Iowa. Now when she had just found this strange, wonderful place.

She thought of the bracelet Lorenzo made. The thunderbird— power, protection, strength. Millicent gave her all that. And maybe now she could find it for herself, too.

The trill of a car horn broke through the hum of conversation and guitar music on the plaza, and Violet turned to see an enormous red Hudson jolting to a halt at the curb. It stuttered, growled, and jolted once more before stopping again. Violet could barely see a tow-head above the steering wheel.

The kid waved at them with a shy smile. "Mrs. Rogers! I'm

Tom. My dad says Mr. Karavas wants me to drive you out to Mrs. Luhan's."

"My goodness, but he must be younger than my son Arturo," Millicent said with a laugh. Arturo, her youngest son, was a teen, but this kid looked about eleven. Yet Millicent just sailed ahead, climbing into the back of the car when young Tom hopped out to open the door for her. She was as calm as Cinderella in her pumpkin coach.

"Vi, darling, are you coming?" she called merrily.

Violet glanced back at the dark hotel lobby through the open double doors. It was either get in the car with the toddler chauffeur, or stay alone in the haunted, silent corridors with more greasy room service food.

"Don't be a ninny," she whispered. Hadn't she once ridden on the back of a tractor driven by her brother when they were much younger than Tom McCarthy? Barreling through the rows of corn with nothing but a rubber cord to hold onto. Since then, she had done more, braved more, than she had ever dreamed, with Millicent. This was just the next step in the adventure.

She laughed, and ran to jump into the back of the car, her black and white coat floating around her in the sunset light.

CHAPTER 13

Millicent

Millicent had to admit, Mabel Dodge Luhan knew how to create a home. And after all her own house-building, she should know.

Los Gallos, as it was called, had impressed even as the car swept through the open gates, past the gatehouse and the gardens, to a three-story main home topped with a glass atrium, all pale adobe and light and welcome, the doors and windows to the portal all open. Inside there were colorful Indian rugs on the floors, soft chairs, fires in kiva grates, paintings hung three deep on the white-washed walls, Spanish santos and Indian pottery on every shelf, books and dogs and conversation.

The aperitifs were served (promptly, of course) in what the maid called the Big Room, a vast space that somehow still managed to be cozy and comfortable, before they were ushered down a set of tiled steps into the sunken dining room, where an oval table was surrounded by old Renaissance leather chairs. And the company was just as interesting and varied. Hal Bynner, the poet who lived in Santa Fe, and his longtime boyfriend, the handsome Robert; Frieda Lawrence, large and blonde and German and blowsy and drunk, with her young Italian husband Angelo, friends with Mabel once more; Martha Reed, a beauty from the East; Claire Morrill, who owned the town's bookstore and seemed to have read everything. Painters, writers, wits, and Mabel's lovely blonde teenaged granddaughter Bonnie Evans, taking it all in, as Millicent once had at her own parents' house. It seemed true, what they said. Everyone did come to Mabel's.

Millicent took a sip of what she had to admit was a very fine Bordeaux and nibbled at some elk in cherry sauce with tomato and spinach salad. ("From my own garden!" Mabel had said, "The key to the sweet taste is bull fertilizer from the pueblo, you know." As if she was out digging her plump, beringed fingers into the soil herself.)

It was a lovely house, Millicent thought with something that seemed almost like—could it be *envy*? The dining room they sat in was down five blue and white tiled steps from the Big Room, and seemed set below the real world itself. Tall French windows, uncurtained, looked out at the dusty, purple-blue night, and the low ceiling, laced with seasoned sapling logs, was painted to look like the stripes of the Indian blankets hanging on the Big Room walls and spread on the terracotta floors under their feet. Huge silver bowls filled with roses and sweet peas scented the air, with the piñon smoke from the fireplace and the rich meal. It was lovely, welcoming, unusual. And if there was one thing Millicent knew, and could admire in others, it was home-making.

She took another sip of her wine and studied the large, octagonal oak table, as solid as an island, surrounded by those fine leather chairs. Conversation and laughter hovered in the smoke like a cloud of perfume, just as a dinner party should. Heavy silver, engraved with Mabel's New York family's crest, clinked on the translucent china, glowing under the light of a Venetian glass chandelier. Yes—a fine party indeed. One she only had to enjoy, not orchestrate every detail. She could certainly appreciate it all.

Yet she couldn't quite believe the woman at the head of the table had put it all together. Millicent glanced at Mabel over the beveled edge of her glass. Mabel Luhan had traveled, true, surely as much as Millicent had herself. Perhaps more. A wealthy Buffalo family, a villa in Florence, an apartment in Greenwich Village, years as queen of this wondrously intriguing little town. It was all there, written on her round, wrinkled, sun-browned face beneath a chopped-off, outdated bob, her thick glasses glinting.

She hardly looked like a queen in a white linen caftan, silk scarves wound around and around her lined neck and dangling into her soup. She laughed, chatted vaguely, waved her plump hands.

Yet Millicent knew the boss of a scene when she saw one. She caught Mabel staring at her with narrowed, dark eyes through those ridiculous glasses, and Millicent smiled at her serenely. She had no intention of bossing anyone, running anything. Not now, not any longer. She only wanted art, beauty, interesting people, the things she had possessed all her life. The things she saw in abundance wherever she turned in Taos. She didn't intend to be hostage to anyone now; she didn't need Mrs. Luhan's acceptance.

But she could see that it would be helpful. Everyone around that table was someone she wanted to know. Artists, writers, poets, thinkers, wits.

She held out her glass for one of the servers, a lovely young lad with long, black, red cloth-wrapped braids, dressed in a white dinner jacket. He said something quiet in Tiwa to Tony Luhan, who sat at Millicent's right, and glided silently away.

"My nephew," he said to Millicent. "I have many."

She smiled. Tony was a very quiet man; he'd barely said four words since they sat down. Yet there was something wildly attractive about him despite his silence and his advanced age, a strong, confident presence, unshakable. His velvet-brown eyes seemed to say what his words did not, filled with the wisdom of ages. Another place Mabel Dodge had done well for herself. Millicent wondered if, now that she felt her own age in every bone, felt her feet sink into the soil of this magical place, she should find a Tony for herself.

She thought of a handsome man with a silver bracelet on his lean wrist, and smiled secretly.

"I have three sons of my own," she said. "I wish they would find some regular employment, but alas, they are wanderers."

"Manuel wants to be a writer," Tony said. "So he likes to meet my wife's guests."

"I can see why. She does gather a fascinating crowd around her." She gestured toward the cluster of poets with her glass. She thought of Ian back in Jamaica, the tap of his typewriter, the strange world of spies and secrets he created. "I wish I had the talent of my pen. I'm not sure I've ever read anything that really captures New Mexico. The sage smell of the air, that sky—so clean and clear a blue, those always-moving clouds. The drama of it all, and yet the serenity! I've never seen such a place. Such a stillness."

Tony just nodded, slowly, carefully, but Millicent felt a world of approval there. She wondered what it must be like to actually be from such a place, to be part of it in blood and bone. To *belong*.

"Oh, I consider myself a creator of creators!" Mabel called from the other end of the table. Her voice was hoarse, rough. "I knew as soon as I saw this land, the meadows and the stream, that people of rare creativity had to come here to be inspired. To put their artistic truth out there in the world, sent out from the top of the sacred mountain!"

"An artists' colony of the first order," someone said. "Like Yaddo, maybe ..."

Mabel flipped her damask napkin. "No, not like that! Not a *colony*, not a retreat from the world. Taos is outward-looking. A place where change, real change, can be affected. Setting the stage is *essential* to creativity of all sorts."

Millicent remembered stories about how many artists had fled Mabel's house, especially DH Lawrence, once her closest friend, who turned into her bitter foe, even though his blowsy widow now sat across the table. Yet Millicent had to raise her glass to Mabel's undoubted successes, which glowed from the very paintings on the walls, scenes of adobe houses glimmering in the sunshine, the mountains, the tumble of flowers, the moonlight. All created there at Los Gallos.

Millicent's glance fell on Violet further down the table. She was laughing, too, her face glowing with the sunny days behind them. She looked so content, just as Millicent felt deep to her toes. Surely it had been right to come here, to stay here. Right for them both.

"I'm sure your nephew is very fortunate to be surrounded by such beauty, such fascinating people," Millicent told Tony.

"Hmm," he hummed low and deep in his barrel chest. He took a slow bite of the elk. "We have what's really important here, true."

"The sun, the moon, the earth ..." Mabel said with another flap of her napkin.

"It has to be protected," her husband said. "But so many youngsters want to try their hand at business these days. Bring plumbing to the pueblos, cars, highways, factories. No time for earth-love now."

"They don't know what they do!" Mabel cried. "I've seen the world out there, it's nothing to this life. We already have what's important, it must be protected." Without prompting, the quiet lad in the white coat refilled her glass, and she fell into silence over the wine. "Only the people of the Pueblo understand how to live reciprocally with the world. Always taking care of the world we white men ruin."

"I wouldn't be so hard on them," the pretty woman across from Millicent murmured. Millicent remembered she was called Martha Reed, and owned a dress shop in town. She wore a beautiful dress of white, carefully pleated silk trimmed with red velvet, perfect with her sleek, dark hair, as intriguing as the creations Millicent found at Charles James. Miss Reed flashed a rueful smile at Millicent. "The young men were the ones who went away to war, who saw everything out there smashed to bits. It's no wonder they have a hard time finding their place again, even here in this beautiful place. Maybe *especially* here."

"So true," Millicent murmured. She remembered the bleak war years, the young Frenchmen who came to Claremont for help, so youthful, so bitter. "This does seem a place of extremes. Every corner is filled with beauty and terror."

"Sun and shadow," Miss Reed said.

"Have you lived here long, Miss Reed?" Millicent asked.

"A few years. I run a little shop next to the Taos Inn. It's not Schiaparelli, but I enjoy it very much. One does meet the most fascinating people!"

"And you must sell such charming things." Millicent nodded at her white dress, her coral necklace and earrings. "I would love to visit."

"Do come by anytime, please. I would be inundated with orders once it was known Mrs. Rogers browsed my shelves! But you needn't feel obliged to buy anything at all."

"I doubt I could help myself."

"What are you talking about down there?" Lady Dorothy Brett shouted, that cut-glass Belgravia accent so strange coming from that craggy, sun-battered face. Paint splashed on her loose smocked blouse, as if she came straight from her studio to dinner. She banged her ear trumpet on the table, making Miss Reed wince, but Mabel just carried on eating. "Poetry? Toby here is all blocked up!"

"Toby?" Millicent whispered, appalled that she couldn't recall being introduced to anyone named Toby. Was her keen social memory, hammered into her so long ago by Mummy-Da, slipping?

Martha gigged behind her napkin. "Toby is what she calls her ear trumpet. He rarely serves the purpose, but she can't be persuaded to get a modern hearing aid."

Millicent laughed, always delighted by eccentrics. "Yes, Lady Brett, poetry," she answered loudly.

"It's the only topic worthy of discussion," Hal Bynner declared. "The reason for the nature all around us. Surely the key to real progress is to maintain the harmony between man and nature, the expansion of beauty in every aspect of life." He smiled at Millicent. "I know Mrs. Rogers must agree with me on the necessity of beauty."

She smiled at him in return. He was quite a charmer, and a fine poet besides. "That is true, Mr. Bynner." She'd always tried so hard in her life to find that core of calm and serenity—it was all that carried her through sometimes, that quiet watchfulness, that waiting for storms to clear. Here, all around her, she saw a place that seemed *all* calm and serenity.

"I confess I'm fascinated by the ideas of creation I see here, of the natural flow of life and death," she said. "I feel I've been looking for it so long."

Mabel set her glass down with a thud, the wine splashing onto the fine linen cloth. "Just so! People have to be *ready* for Taos. Not everyone is meant for its gifts. Well, that is enough of *that*." She pushed her chair back, the heavy wood squealing over the tiles, and marched out of the dining room, past an astonished maid carrying in the dessert tray.

Millicent glanced down at her still half-filled plate. In her mother's house, she'd grown up being filled with the importance of impeccable manners. Even after, everywhere she had been, everyone she knew, she was amazed anyone could act like that. A few people followed Mabel, but Tony just went on eating as if nothing had happened.

Bonnie Evans, Mabel's pretty blonde teenaged granddaughter, seemed to sense Millicent's astonishment, and laughed nervously. Her cheeks were as pink as her ruffled silk dress. "Oh, Mrs. Rogers, you shouldn't mind my grandmother! She does get, um, indigestion sometimes."

Martha Reed laughed. "She decides when a conversation is over, at least in her own mind. We just don't pay attention."

"Try the apple crumble," Frieda Lawrence declared in her thick German accent. She scooped out a large portion onto her own plate and poured cream over it. "I never miss it. A good Bavarian recipe, I gave it to Mabel's cook myself. My husband did say Taos was one of the magnetic centers of the earth. It takes us all in strange ways."

Those still at the table just kept on eating, so Millicent smiled and nodded, laughing to imagine what her mother would say. They were a long way from New York now.

CHAPTER 14

Millicent

LATER THAT EVENING

I fitted one of my Viceroy cigarettes into an ebony holder and lit it up, that tiny, floating, flickering flame a glow in the dusty night that soon vanished. It left me in the darkness, all light and sound behind me from the open windows of the house. I inhaled the sharp, delicious cherry-ness of that smoke, and let the glorious night wash over and around me.

The wooden pillar of the portal was rough against my shoulder as I leaned against it. Someone played a phonograph from the Big Room, a Bing Crosby song, much the pity, and there was a sweet giggle from Bonnie Evans, a shout from Lady Brett, the murmur of Violet as someone handed her a sherry. The golden glow of lamps, no harsh glare of electricity, cast puddles on the flagstone floor around me, catching the embroidered hem of my dress. The moon rising beyond the mountain answered with its own incandescent light, peeking behind shifting clouds, outlining that rounded, motherly peak.

I was reluctant to admit it, but Mabel Luhan, despite appalling table manners and her airs of the Queen of Poetry, had made herself a glorious life here at Los Gallos. I was no stranger to making homes myself—The Port, Austria, Jamaica, California, Argentina, Claremont. But I'd never quite managed to find a place like this. What was her secret?

I stepped off the portal and walked slowly across the courtyard, past hammocks and old remains of bonfires and rosebushes and the outlines of sculptures. The sounds of the party turned fainter the further I wandered, leaving me quite deliciously alone in the night.

One of the magnetic centers of the earth. I was certainly no great fan of DH Lawrence's books, so overwrought, and his taste in wives raised some questions. But I was sure he was onto something with that. I had never seen a place like this before, in all my wanderings. Every breath I took of the cool, crystal air seemed to spread peace down to my very toes, heavy and delicious. I never wanted to move. Never wanted to take another step again. It was as if I had been traveling this way all those years. Seeking this very thing.

But what if I was too old for it now, had come too late? The tiredness was heavy in me now, almost always, and I felt the time sliding through my hands like a silk scarf, slippery. I could hear the music from the phonograph, a tango now, its rhythm thudding and steady and passionate. Once I had danced to just such a song, through a cafe in Argentina in Arturo's arms. That seemed a very long time ago now. And I was wonderfully alone.

I tossed my cigarette into a terracotta planter at the edge of a low, rough mud wall. Beyond was a meadow, an expanse of black in the night, and I turned my back on it for the house.

Through the topaz windows, I glimpsed Mr. Bynner and our hostess talking to—talking *at*—Violet. I could almost feel sorry for her, the darling thing, but I had learned one thing about Violet she probably didn't even know about herself. Violet could become anything at all, anything she wanted. She was a rare, truly kind soul. She needed me to look after her.

I remembered the handsome lawyer she had flirted with at

Janet's house in California. He was surely rich enough. Maybe I should have urged her to talk with him again? Write to him? A man like that could help her a great deal. I was afraid my own assistance couldn't help her be what she wanted in life, not really. No matter how much I wished I could.

As I watched through the window, Mabel pressed her hand to her forehead as if it ached, and Tony whispered to her, his touch gentle on her arm. She laughed, and her lined, round face glowed. I could see why she had stayed here so long, and maybe even why everyone else was willing to pay the price of being in her orbit to stay, too. She did remind me of my mother in a way, though Mummy-Da would never have been so ill-dressed, of course. Yes, I had met a few Mabels before, but none so very *Mabelish*.

And that husband of hers—he was something different, too. Old and craggy now, but such soul in those vast dark eyes, those silences as deep as an ocean. He said few words, where usually men were such chatterers, going on and on about themselves and their woes and them, them, them. Tony Luhan wasn't like that at all. His words were doled out carefully. Yet when he looked at me, so steady and deep, he seemed to see everything. To know it in an instant. Just as I felt I saw it all in a flash, in the purple and black shadows of the mountain. The mountain that seemed to be summoning me home.

I laughed at myself as I lit another cigarette and sent the lacy smoke out into the night. It wasn't like me to be sentimental. When one has so little time, one has to get on with it. To move, move, take it all in, make it all mine. This place told me to be still at last. To just *be*.

And to think I almost hadn't come here at all. What a tragedy that would have been. For I knew, I just knew, as I stood alone there in that purple enchanted night, that everything which had happened to me—my husbands, my lovers, my work, my homes—just served to carry me here. To my end.

I glanced over the house, Los Gallos, and the moonlight

gleamed on the porcelain chickens who looked down at every corner of the roof. Mabel had built something truly remarkable here. I envied it. No matter how hard I tried, how many houses I created, I never quite captured that rare light in a bottle. A place of beauty and truth, that made others discover that truth in themselves. She was a lucky woman, that bossy cow.

I suddenly caught a glimpse of myself in a darkened pane of glass, pale, elongated, my Chanel perfectly cut, elegant. All wrong for this place. I had never let myself be *wrong* before. I smoothed my palm, shaking slightly, cold, over the slippery, silken skirt, and my head spun. That old, chilly, light breathlessness threatened to overtake me, as it did all too often, and I inhaled deeply of my cigarette.

A drumbeat cut into the night, sudden, deep, thudding. Like a heartbeat, but steadier than my own.

At first, I was sure I imagined it. Sometimes things happened when the fever seized me, I heard snatches of music and saw ghosts. But now I shook my head, and the song was real enough. Its deep pattern broke the silence of the night, reminding me that even in this enchanted valley there was something beyond us.

I tossed aside the cigarette and followed the music around to a cluster of buildings behind the house, a kitchen and a garage, and an open sort of shed. They were rough, prosaic, and didn't seem to quite belong there. Or rather, they shouldn't have. But like all other things at Los Gallos, they just seemed part of it all.

But the man who stood over the drum there definitely belonged. It was the beautiful man I had met in the hotel lobby. Benjamin? No, Benito. The one with the bracelet.

My stomach caught and lurched, deep inside, as it all too often did at the sight of a beautiful man. Beauty was *always* my weakness. Gowns, paintings, flowers, houses, jewels—men. Especially men. My husbands had been lovely, as had Ian and Roald and Captain Butler.

Yet I'd never really seen one like this. I drifted closer, quite unable to do the clever thing and run away. My life had never been one of doing clever things.

As I glided into the light, he glanced up. Startled at first, his song interrupted, as if he'd been so absorbed in what he did he didn't know anything else, but he quickly smiled. A white, beautiful slash. "Mrs. Rogers."

"I am. And you are—Benito, yes?"

"Yes." He retrieved his drumsticks and put them away, smoothing his ruffled hair. "Your secretary rescued me."

"Of course. Violet is so very good at rescuing wounded creatures."

"Did she rescue you, too, then?"

I trailed my hand over the smooth surface of the drum. It felt warm under my touch, living. "Yes, in a manner of speaking. Violet is one of those people whose heart is too kind for their own good."

That glamorous grin turned rueful. He really was beautiful, even more than Clark had been. But so very wounded. Extraordinary. "She sounds like my cousin Lorenzo. Or my Uncle Tony. They're always on a rescue mission."

I wanted so very much to know what haunted this beautiful boy, why he needed rescuing. For he did, I knew it when I looked into his extraordinary eyes, dark green and hazel. Tony's eyes said he was secure in his place, his world. Benito's said he wandered lost. I knew how that felt.

"Tony Luhan is your uncle?" I said.

He shrugged, his muscles fluid under his white shirt. "In a way, I guess. We're all related at that part of the pueblo. He treats us all as nephews and nieces, helps us when we're in a jam."

I smiled. "A true *pater-familias*."

"Something like that. Whenever someone gets into trouble, they send for Tony."

Tony sounded like my grandfather. But in the end even that

formidable old bastard couldn't save us from ourselves. "What does Mabel think of that?"

Benito snorted on a laugh. "Not much. She wants to save us all herself, us poor, lost Indians. But she doesn't like Tony going home to us when they argue. He sleeps with Candelaria then, even after all these years."

I was very intrigued. "Candelaria?"

"His first wife. He divorced her back then, to marry Mabel, but Mabel still pays her. Alimony of sorts. He sleeps with her when he comes home."

"My heavens," I murmured, trying to take in the sweeping romance and scandalous adultery of two such stolid old characters. It rather gave me hope. I took out my cigarette case and offered one to Benito. "I suppose they must really love each other then, in their strange ways. Tony and Mabel."

Benito lit my cigarette then his own, the golden glow on his sculpted face, his haunted eyes. "Got used to each other, maybe. Who'd put up with both of them except each other?"

I exhaled a long plume of smoke and smiled at him. "You don't believe in true love, then?" That seemed a sad thought, for such rare beauty was meant for grand passion, in books anyway. And books had been my reality in my illness for so long.

"Nah. Just reality. Life's not like in the poems Mabel likes so much, is it? It cracks up even when you think you've put it back together again. Never whole. Never trustworthy."

I remembered what Violet said, that she had helped this man when he was very inebriated. That he had been in the war, and this still troubled him. Just like Ian and his whips. My heart ached for him, this beautiful boy, and I wondered if after all I did have some of Violet's softness myself, buried deep inside. Maybe that was why I hired him on such a whim. But then, I did like my whims.

Yet Benito didn't seem to want to talk about the past, to let even a hint of softness in. I understood. Pretending was always so much easier. Yet how could that be, in this place that seemed to demand the very deepest of truths from every soul. With that mountain seeing it all.

"Is this what you do, then?" I said. "Come out here and drum."

He shrugged. "Sometimes. I do a bit of everything here, when I'm able. Build chicken coops, work on cars ..."

Able—when sober? I thought of my brother so long ago, stumbling on the stairs, the despair of my parents. Poor old Harry Junior, my brother. Just like Violet's Richard. "Well, perhaps if you work on cars you will be good at helping *me*, then. I need a driver, a regular driver, once my car arrives here. It's at my house in Virginia, but I've sent for it. You still want the job, yes?"

He stood up, straight, so tall and lean, and he looked over my head. I glanced back to see that Mabel had come out onto the porch, squinting through her glasses into the night, but I knew she couldn't see us there. "It's all right," I said.

He stared at me, closely, with that expression I well-recognized from so many men. The expression of interest. "I'm sure you could find a better driver than me."

I laughed, thinking of that dreadful, jolting ride with that boy stripping the clutch at every turn. I wasn't sure my neck would ever recover. And if I could see that look from Benito, from any handsome man again, again, just once in my life ... "I don't think so. And I never did get my own license, my sons would say no government worth their salt would let me pass."

"Yeah, but why me?"

I gave it some thought. Was it really just his beauty, the way he looked at me? Or had I really been infected with some of Violet's kindness? "I just have a feeling for people, I suppose. I follow my instincts when it comes to them." And that was true. I knew as soon as I met people whether I liked them or not. My husbands, Violet. This man. "I think we might get along. And I want to know so much more about this place. I need people to show me."

He laughed, but there was no humor, no delight in it. It

sounded rough and raw, far too old for that beautiful face. "This place? I'd be careful about that. Once it gets its barbed hooks into you, it won't let you go. The more you struggle, the sharper it gets."

"Did you struggle? Want to escape?"

He shrugged again. "Not anymore. There's no use in it, is there? We're always stuck with ourselves. Can't run from that."

I wasn't so sure about that. We could at least try. I'd been trying all my life. "No," I murmured. "Can't run from that."

"So," he said. "This job."

I nodded, forcing myself back into the present moment, the cool night breeze, the smell of sage. Maybe we couldn't really escape ourselves, not in the end. The past always lurked, and the future waited so patiently. But we could pretend for a while. And this place, barbed hooks and all, felt more real than anything else I had ever known.

"It's yours if you want it," I said. "But I warn you, the hours might be long. I can tell there is a great deal I want to explore here."

"Because you have an instinct for people?"

"Yes. I admit it doesn't always work out as I hope," I said with a laugh. Captain Butler hadn't worked out at all as I expected. "But when it does, I find it all quite spectacular. Life is too short not to follow one's instincts, don't you think?"

He looked down at the drum. "It's too short, that's for sure. Yeah, I'll take the job, Mrs. Rogers. At least I can try to help my ma with some extra money, I've sure caused her enough trouble. But people will say you're a fool to hire me."

"I never bother with what people say about me. What do I care about that? I do what I see is right."

"Right for you, missus?"

"Of course. I can't possibly say what's right for other people. That's up to them to decide. I don't bother them, they don't bother me."

A smile quirked at the corner of his lips. "And how does that work out for you?"

I laughed again. "Not always so well, but more often than not —just as I would hope. I live as I see fit."

"That works well enough for a rich white lady, I bet. Mabel does it, too. The rest of us ..." He turned away, his shoulders held stiff. "For an Injun like me, it could get me lynched in that arroyo over there. Sometimes only being stinkin' drunk works."

I was appalled, and fascinated. So much anger in those few words, so much pain.

A slow, dragging footstep on that stone pathway pulled me out of that tiny, separate world with this man and the drums and the night, and I glanced back to see Mabel slowly pulling her bulky, caftan-clad figure toward us with an elaborately carved walking stick. She peered at us through her thick glasses, and I had the itchy feeling those hazy eyes saw too much.

"Mrs. Rogers?" she said. "There you are. Your Miss Redfield was worried."

I tried to laugh it off, waving my cigarette holder toward her. Ash flaked off and floated to the ground like snow. "I just needed a breath of fresh air. Your gardens are so glorious here. What a wonderland you've created."

"My little utopia, yes. I've worked so hard on it all. It doesn't come in a day, you know." She turned her head sharply to pin poor Benito with those owlish eyes, her lips pursed. "Nearly done there, Benny darling? Tony needs you to make sure the tractor is running for tomorrow, he wants to look over the farm."

"Just about, Aunt Mabel," he said with a grin, all that pain seemingly vanished.

"Good, I'm very happy to hear it." Mabel's bobbed head swung back toward me, making me feel horribly as I once did when my nanny would scold me. Was talking to the Indians off-limits here, for a woman like me? Surely Mabel Luhan would be the last one in a place to scold anyone on *that* score. "Your secretary was looking for you, Mrs. Rogers. She did seem worried."

"Oh, dear Violet, she does get concerned for me. I've been ill, you see, just a bit of my old trouble. I feel very well now. Your magical mountain has revived me, just as I hoped. I'm so eager to explore a bit more, and your Mr. Suarez has agreed to work as my driver. So kind of him."

"Benny? A driver?" Mabel's round-faced expression was impossible to read as she looked at her husband's nephew. He fidgeted under her steady eyes, and turned away to put the drumsticks in an inlaid box. "I'm sure his family will be happy to hear about that, there are few enough jobs around right now. But I think ..."

"Then it's quite settled!" I said with determined cheer. Surely I could get around even her to find my own way, as I could everyone else. I was greatly tired of all this tiptoeing about. I'd so wanted to leave that behind me in this wide-open, starkly honest town. "Once I move out of the hotel and find my own house, I'll need more staff, as well. I just have Violet, and Ethel, my cook, right now."

I spun around and marched out of the shed, headed back to the courtyard. Mabel had no choice but to follow me, her cane tapping frantically. My head whirled at that sudden movement, and my legs trembled under me, just as they had earlier. Maybe I hadn't yet recovered as I had hoped.

"Mrs. Rogers!" Benito called after me, and ran to catch up. His dark hair gleamed in the moonlight. He held something out to me, a glint of silver. His thunderbird bracelet. The supernatural being of power and strength.

"Mr. Suarez ..." I whispered.

"You take it. It seems to belong to you. A thank you gift, for the job."

"I couldn't."

"It's meant to be yours. And I could see you admired it earlier."

"I did. It's lovely." I took it from him and slid it onto my wrist with my other bracelets. It was too large, of course; I had lost weight on the hotel food, and my wrist was like a pitiful twig now. But the weight of it, heavy and solid, stopped some of that constant trembling, and it was warm from his skin. "It's so beautiful."

"Not like your diamonds," he said, sounding almost bashful. "But if you like the style, I can introduce you to silversmiths who can make you others. Weavers, potters, artists, too."

"She can find painters enough here at Los Gallos, Benny," Mabel snapped. "And it's getting cold out here."

"Of course," I whispered. I couldn't find any real words to express how I felt just then, how very beautiful the bracelet on my arm seemed to me. The delicate inlay, the glinting silver. Yet it was strong, like the thunderbird itself. Cartier and Verdura, with their great artists, filled my jewelry case, but I had never been quite so moved by a piece of art before. "Call on me next week at the hotel, Mr. Suarez. My car should arrive by then."

I followed Mabel and her tapping stick back across the courtyard toward the house, still lit up in glowing amber and blue from chimney to portal. I was happy to slow my steps to hers, to take it all in, the house and the night and the hammocks and easels scattered across the garden. It really was extraordinary.

"It's kind of you, Mrs. Rogers, to help Benito like that." Mabel paused outside the half-open French window, watching the others play cards and drink sherry inside, their laughter and chatter like clouds. Some of the dogs ran out and clustered at her feet, whining and barking. "Such good jobs are hard to come by here, and the money will help his family."

"It will help me, too. I don't drive, and of course I don't know my way around here. All these winding roads ..."

Mabel suddenly looked up, directly at me, piercing through.

"But, as I'm sure we're going to be great friends, I need to warn you."

"Warn me?"

"Poor Ben is—well, troubled. Changed, they do say, when he came home from the war. He drinks, you see. I think your own Miss Redfield witnessed what happened a few days ago?"

I stiffened. I couldn't bear being lectured at all, like I was a child in the schoolroom again, frowned at by my mother. "She helped him home after he had too much to drink at a fiesta, I heard. I've seen such things before, believe me." And so I had. My brother, my husbands ...

"It's not just a bit of over-imbibing at times. It's like ..." Mabel's plump hands, beringed with turquoise stones, fluttered like partridges as she seemed to look for words in the air. "It's as if the devil gets into him sometimes. He worries Tony terribly. It's a tragedy, how so many of our young people can't reconcile life here with what they've seen and done in the outside world."

"I do understand," I murmured, and I *did*. I saw so well. "Maybe steady work can help."

"Perhaps," Mabel said, yet she sounded doubtful. Perhaps she thought a woman like me, like her, an outsider, wouldn't know how to begin to help. But just as I had felt drawn to help with so many other troubled men, with Violet, I had to try with Benito. I wasn't sure why. I just felt it strongly. It was like he was my last chance.

I stepped toward the portal, but Mabel's hand on my arm stopped me. For all its plump softness, it was like an iron band, those rings digging in.

"Did I hear you say you may be looking for a larger home, Mrs. Rogers?"

"Yes, if there's something suitable," I answered. "The hotel is a bit confining, and though I have an offer to stay at the Dicus' guest ranch for the winter, it can't really be permanent."

Mabel's gaze was again unreadable behind those glasses. "And you do want your stay to be more permanent?"

I glanced back at the mountain, black and solid against the sky. It felt as if I stood on the edge of my very last great adventure. My best adventure. "I think so, yes."

Mabel hesitated for a moment. "I do have a friend, Judge Kiker, who is selling some land. The building isn't much, just an old morada ..."

"Morada?"

"A chapel. There are walls and a roof of sorts, no foundation. It hasn't been used in ages. But there are many acres, a stream nearby, lovely views. I think something could be done with it. The judge was going to use it as a summer camp for his children, but he's decided to sell it instead. And I don't need it."

I sighed, trying not to let those ridiculous excited butterflies that always arose in my tummy at the thought of redecorating get out of hand. "It does sound intriguing," I said softly, and so it did. "When could I see it?"

"Oh—next week, perhaps? I could write to the judge. It *is* rough, Mrs. Rogers, but so was this old place when I first saw it. I'm sure you could devise something more elegant. Perhaps I could help."

I wouldn't be a hostage to anyone else, not at this point in my life. Not ever again. I wanted my very own place. "I would like that," I said simply.

Mabel nodded. "An occultist once told me my life would be a bridge. A way to bring together people. I've tried to live my life by that ever since. I understand where you came from, Mrs. Rogers—I was caught by East Coast money myself. By husbands. Four of them! I needed this place, I searched the world for it. And I sense that you might need it, too. Shall we go in? Tony does fuss if I catch a chill."

I was sure Violet would "fuss" if I became ill, too, but I couldn't resist one more glance back at the mountain. And I took that conscious first step forward into the rest of my days. I knew I wouldn't be sorry in the end. No matter how long, or how little, it lasted.

1927—AT SEA

The ocean air smelled of that peculiar blend of salt, inky seaweed, and the starchiness of clean linen, that singular scent I wished I could bottle and sell. It would be better than Mitsouko. I never tired of it, no matter how often I inhaled it into my poor battered lungs. How I abused them, with cigarettes and champagne! But being in the middle of the ocean always revived every bit of me.

I stretched out my legs on the deck chair and wrapped my sable coat closer around me. It was a chilly day, despite the yolk-yellow of the sun overhead, and not many people ventured onto the deck of the *Santa Elisa*. Just me and my little Pekingese curled at my feet, and the wonderful foaming, frothing gray-green ocean roiling below.

It suited me perfectly. The whoosh-whoosh of the waves, the shriek of the seabirds high above. After the hordes of reporters haranguing us all the way across the dock, the well-wishers besieging our nightclub table last night, the quiet seemed unreal. Heavenly.

I picked up the newspaper folded on my lap and laughed at the headlines, the grainy photos of me in the pearl-gray chiffon dress turned white by the camera, the tulle-wrapped picture hat I foolishly thought might hide my face. *An American girl's chance for happiness greater if she marries another American, Standard Oil Heiress Says! Doesn't Follow Her Own Advice!*

I laughed. Indeed I had *not*. Twice now.

My dog whined, and I handed him a caramel from the dish beside me, took a sip of champagne, and laughed a little more. The last time I had been in the middle of the ocean like this, I was pregnant with Peter, puffy with tears and huge, fleeing from poor Ludi. Now I was going the other way, with darling Arturo.

Tall, dark, dashing, fascinating in bed (he did this *thing*, you see, with his tongue. Maybe it was South American). From an Austrian aristocrat to an Argentinian one. Six months after my divorce; the papers loved that detail. But I wasn't entirely sure that Arturo, for all his family's reported ranches and pampas and all, had much more money than the Salms, my first husband's family.

I held out my hand and admired the way the sunlight flashed on my new emerald ring. Arturo was generous, of course. Just as worthy to be collected as that ring, or the new Van Cleef bracelets on my wrist. Those eyes! So endlessly dark. His touch as he pulled me close on the dance floor, making everyone sigh as if we were in a film. A man's man, good at polo and shooting and gambling. I'd known that ever since we first met in Paris, way back in 1921, and it was even more attractive when we met again last year. I knew he was the one for me.

But he was quite unable to meet my father's American standards for suitors. My father had found Arturo a job at a brokerage house in New York for when we returned from the honeymoon. I had my doubts that would work out at all, though my father did seem to live in hope no matter what.

It hardly made any difference to me. After all the strife and shouting about the divorce, all the trouble with the wedding (Arturo's family *would* insist it be Catholic, so there was all that silly bother with the pope and annulments), I had what I craved all along. Delicious freedom.

I had tried other ways, of course. The farm in Vermont, bought with the money from my grandmother, meant for a bolt-hole. But Mummy-Da was there so often. Who could blame her, of course, with Daddy's drinking and my brother Henry's ridiculous ways. I couldn't deny her, not with the way she took over little Peter's care when I was so hopeless. It rather took away the hope of privacy, and Daddy's constant shouting about disinheriting—exhausting.

The doctors always said I couldn't bear it. That I needed quiet and rest, always rest.

Quiet, yes, maybe. But rest—surely I would get enough of that when I was dead, which could be sooner than I would like.

I stared at the waves breaking against the ship far below, choppy, dark, receding and returning, always, always. That was how death was for me; I could push it away, but it would return and return. Faster, stronger, until I couldn't keep it at bay any longer. That was another thing Arturo's strength gave me. Life.

I had never known anyone quite so able to grab and seize a moment as he did. From that first moment we met again, when he took me in his arms and held me close, so close, there on the dance floor in a tango. "We wish to be left alone," he snapped at the reporters in his rich, slipping-sideways accent. And such a miracle—they left us alone.

Even when he carried me out the side door of the nightclub and into his car, and we drove and drove and drove, the lights of the city fading around us as we found a country lane where we could drink champagne and laugh and kiss until the sun came out all rosy-gold. And in that glow I found the spark of life again. The rush and light and thrill.

Maybe it wouldn't last. It had vanished so fast with Ludi, back when I foolishly thought love lasted forever. Probably it never did. But I would see a new place with Arturo, make a new start. Buenos Aires! The words themselves were redolent of sun-heat, tango music, cocktails, spice.

And right now, I had that life in my hand again. That freedom. Even if it faded, even if I had to search for it again and yet again, it was mine *now*, and now was all I had.

I leaned back and stared up at the darkening sea-sky. A wave of feminine laughter, a wave of awareness that tingled down to my very toes, made me glance along the polished deck. Arturo sauntered toward me, all 6'4" of him, dark, glowing, elegant as a race-horse. He tilted his gray fedora to two ladies in fox furs, making them giggle even more, making me blush, too, I felt so silly for admitting. He certainly was very good with the ladies. And he was mine. For the moment.

At least I knew one thing for sure with him. Life would not be boring.

Not yet.

CHAPTER 15

Violet

IN TAOS

Violet took up the large, striped woven basket and a straw hat from the leather-backed chair in the small foyer of the Dicus' guesthouse, and fished in her purse for a pair of dark glasses.

"I'm off to the market, MR," she called. "Is there anything else for the list? I have Ethel's menus for the week."

Millicent had been locked away in her little sitting room, making sketches for new pieces of jewelry, all morning. It had been that way for days now, ever since they moved out of the hotel. Violet typed up letters, went for walks with the dogs, read to MR when her head ached. Tried not to think about going back to the pueblo. Had that place been a dream, one she wouldn't ever see again?

"Mrs. Luhan's cook is coming to teach Ethel how to make *calabcitas*. Maybe we need extra squash? I can't imagine she'll learn quickly," Millicent called back. "And take Fanny with you. The poor darling is so bored, I think."

Violet eyed Fanny, who sat perched on a pile of Millicent-made needlepoint cushions. Fanny was MR's favorite dachshund, a chubby, malevolent, barky creature who liked no one but Millicent and enjoyed chomping any available ankle. Fanny looked like the last thing she wanted was a walk.

Violet sighed. "Okay, Fanny. Let's make a bargain. I'll carry you halfway to the plaza, and you don't bite me."

Fanny squeezed her liquid brown eyes shut as if in agreement, and Violet clipped on her leash then led her out into the sparkly-bright day. Once outside, they both seemed to cheer up, and set off at a brisk trot down the dusty pathway toward the market.

Summer was slowly sliding into fall, Violet could feel it in the softening air, see it in the gold-tinged light, all turning orange at the edges, cutting some of the dazzle. She could still wear her white shorts and a crisp, dark blue cotton blouse, knotted at the waist, but she knew soon she would need some new clothes. She studied the women she passed as she and Fanny turned at the main road toward the plaza, calling out greetings to the neighbors she'd met since they moved into the little guesthouse. Most of the women wore printed cotton shirtwaist dresses and wide-brimmed hats, like her mother at home, and some had the most beautiful pleated skirts and ribbon-trimmed shirts to match. Flowered sundresses. Wide-legged trousers and silk blouses. Violet envied their easy style.

Yes, she definitely needed new clothes.

She paused to peek at herself in an office window. Her hair was growing a little too long, her blouse a little faded, but there hadn't been much time lately to think about that.

Yet things had been less busy the last few days, as Millicent mostly started keeping to herself. Working in her little sitting room/studio, listening to the phonograph at night, Mozart and Ella Fitzgerald and tangos. And walking alone on the narrow paths past the cottonwoods, the dogs at her heels, smoking. What did she think about, worry over? Violet was very concerned, but she also knew well no one could coax confidences out of Millicent when she was keeping her own counsel. Maybe one night, after too many gin fizzes under those magical stars, it would all spill out.

In the meantime, Violet did her own work, and crept outside

whenever she could, alone like MR. Looking, absorbing, letting the essence of the place inside of her. It was wondrous, the light and clear air, the way it smelled and sounded and felt. It made words come into her mind again, words she wanted to get down on paper.

But Ethel fretted that MR didn't eat enough, and grew thinner and thinner, as Violet worried, too. The fancy sauces at Frenchy's restaurant, the green chile at El Patio and the Sagebrush, were often pushed away for another cigarette, a martini. Ethel wanted to find tempting dishes to cook, hence the long list in Violet's market basket. All the best produce would be gone if she didn't hurry, so she couldn't idle her way along the street all day.

She tugged at Fanny's leash, and the dog growled at being pulled away from her newfound patch of shade, but she waddled behind Violet well enough. She knew the basket meant there would be fallen treats waiting on the ground just up ahead, and Violet could put off her promise to carry the heavy dog for a while.

They passed the open courtyard of the old Kit Carson house, and she peeked inside to see Mr. Berninghaus had set up his easel there. The half-finished scene of the courtyard garden glowed in the sunlight, pinks and yellows and sand-tan. Not for the first time, Violet wished she had a talent for the brush and canvas, could capture the otherworldly colors of this place. The marine-blue of the sky, the turquoise of the jewelry, the splash of pink and red hollyhocks and the wild climb of yellow and red roses against tan adobe, the piercing light.

But maybe, just maybe—it could be caught with a pen and paper and words, too? There were poets as well as painters to be met at Los Gallos. She shook her head. She'd have to be brave, as brave as MR, to try writing again.

"Good morning, Mr. Berninghaus," she called. "Your painting is coming along beautifully."

Oscar cocked his head to one side and studied the canvas with a fierce frown. His hair stood on end, his clothes splashed with blue paint, a streak of sienna on his cheekbone, disappearing into his beard. He looked like a real artist, just as she had imagined them back in Iowa. "That blue still isn't quite right ..."

He always said that, whenever Violet saw him painting there in the courtyard, even when they met him at Mrs. Luhan's house. Even though he had been in Taos for decades, he never thought the scene was right. Maybe that painting would never really be done. Maybe that was how he liked it. Surely the hardest part of any work of art was letting it go free into the world, like a child.

"Well, I think it looks perfect," she said. "It has the feeling of the day, doesn't it? That slip from summer into fall."

He smiled just a tiny bit. "Does it really? Hmm. The feeling of the day. You don't think your Mrs. Rogers might like to buy it? When it's finished, that is, and who knows when that will be."

Violet thought MR might well want to buy it. Millicent had been buying up all sorts of things, both there and in Santa Fe. Beautiful, strange, entrancing things, pottery, weavings that glowed ruby and sapphire and storm-gray, jewelry, carvings. They mixed with the pieces she brought from California, the Fragonard drawings and abstract splashes of paint, the cushions and Persian rugs and Russian carved tables, in a glorious jumble.

"You do have to finish it first," she reminded him. But she thought she'd rather like to have it herself.

"Wiser words were never spoken, my young friend," he said, and set to fiercely mixing more blue on his palette. Violet laughed, and tugged Fanny on their way, taking a short cut in the alleyway behind the Taos Inn.

On the corner that led to the plaza, she started to turn, but a shop window caught her eye. It was right next to the inn, a tiny space facing onto a side street, but the bright colors behind the glass popped and glowed, sage green, sky blue, rose pink, sun yellow, just like the colors of the day itself, like that painting.

Martha's of Taos read the painted sign overhead. Violet remembered meeting her at the Luhans'—Martha Reed, of the elegant, sleek dark hair, the laughing eyes, the beautiful white dress with its lashings of ruby-red that matched her lipstick. This must be the "little shoppy" she talked about.

A dress on one of the mannequins caught Violet's attention, pale green trimmed with darker green ribbons, its skirts spreading out like something in *Gone With the Wind*, miles of pleats. At first she didn't even notice the woman hanging painted silk scarves in the window, until she rapped on the glass. Violet swung her head around, and saw Mrs. Reed herself, smiling and waving, her ruby lipstick glowing. "Do come in!" she called.

Violet patted at her messy hair, suddenly shy. She shook her head, but Mrs. Reed came out in a cloud of L'Heure Bleu perfume, her red pleated skirts swaying. "You're Miss Redfield, right?" she said, stooping to pat Fanny, who didn't even try to bite her ankles with their red gauze espadrille ribbons. "From Mabel's dinner."

Violet was surprised she remembered. She'd felt so tongue-tied at that dinner, everyone talking, so smart and cultured. But Martha smiled again, open and friendly, and Violet liked her. "Yes, I'm Mrs. Rogers' secretary."

Martha laughed, a silvery sound, hoarse from cigarettes. "Oh, yes, who could ever forget *her*? So glamorous, just like a film star. She doesn't look like anyone else in Taos. She quite lights up a room without even trying."

"So do you," Violet blurted. And she did, with her elegance, her evident interest in everything around her.

"Oh, Miss Redfield, how kind you are. I'm an old mountain lady myself now, grizzled and worn. But you—I think you do underestimate *yourself*." She glanced at the window, the green dress. "Do you like my skirts?"

"They're beautiful."

"I hire my own seamstresses, mostly Navajos and ladies from the pueblo. Some of them take fourteen whole yards of fabric, calico or silk, hand-dyed and all pleated by hand, too. The dyes are brighter than they're used to, maybe, but my customers like them." She carefully studied Violet, making her want to fidget. "You should come in and try on that green. It seems made for hair just like yours."

Violet was so tempted. She remembered the sorry state of her closet, the women she saw around town in their lovely cottons and turquoise jewelry. "I have to go the market. Our cook will chase me out with a kitchen knife if I'm not back soon."

Martha laughed. Violet wondered what *her* story was. Everyone in Taos seemed to have a fascinating one, a compelling reason that brought them to this place. "Another day, then. I won't sell the green until you try it on."

"Of course. Another day, very soon." Violet turned away with one more wistful glance back at that dress, and tugged Fanny ahead again. The dachshund growled at being prodded along, just when she had found a cozy patch of shade once more. "Sorry, Fan."

They stopped to drop letters into the post, one from MR to her mother in France and three for her sons in their various schools and travels, Violet's to Jo-Jo in California and one to her parents about Rich's engagement. She glanced down at the address before she put it in the box, and it seemed so strange to think about the cream-painted farmhouse, still there just like always, her parents sitting on the porch, also just like always. It seemed so far away, and centuries ago.

She looked back over her shoulder at the mountain always watching over the town. That was life now. That was her present. Her future—it was white and cloudy, hidden. But that was all right. Millicent had shown her that was all right. More, that the present was all they really had. Violet was determined to enjoy it as much as she could, for as long as she could.

The market stalls lined the edges of the plaza and spilled up the steps of the bandstand, where a guitar trio played and children danced and leaped and shrieked. She examined the carrots and sweet potatoes and corn, the late tomatoes, the sweet baked bread and little apple pies, practicing the Spanish words she was trying to learn, filling her basket as Fanny munched on some fallen spinach. Violet added one of the pies, hoping it would coax Millicent to eat more at dinner. And she was determined to lure her to Martha's of Taos. Shopping seemed to perk MR up like nothing else.

"Well, if it isn't Miss Iowa."

Violet's stomach did a strange flip-floppy-queasy thing at the sound of that voice, and she clenched her fist on Fanny's leash. Her face turned hot, the pale redhead's curse, and she turned to see Lorenzo Serna sitting on a low wall behind her, a crooked little, unreadable smile on his face. Was he hoping to see her, then, just as she was ridiculously happy to see him? She couldn't tell. Couldn't decipher anything about him. But she'd been wondering for days if she would see him again, and here he was.

He looked much the same as he had that strange, dream-like day at the pueblo—a white shirt, sleeves rolled up to reveal smooth, bronzed forearms, dungarees, a hat shading his face, hiding his eyes in the shadows. But without those fierce lines of worry for his cousin. With that smile. He seemed so relaxed, so happy, so part of this place. So secure in himself.

"I think this town has knocked the Iowa right out of me, Mr. Serna," she said, remembering the address on her letter, the house that seemed like it was on a different planet. "How are you? And how is your cousin?"

He hopped down from the wall, making Fanny growl. He patted her in apology, faint hints of grease under his nails. "Call me Lorenzo, yeah? After what you saw that day, Mr. Serna sounds wrong. And I'm just the same as always, thanks. Working on getting the last of the summer crops in. Bennie says your employer offered him a job."

"You heard that, then?"

"Chauffeur, they say, once her car gets here. The idea of a steady income seems to be doing him some good. My aunt says he hasn't passed out drunk once since."

Violet could see that Millicent needed someone to ferry her around; she was a terrible driver, always landing in hedges when she tried it. And Violet wasn't all that great behind a wheel, either. But could Benito Suarez be trusted with such a task? She remembered her brother's benders, that time he nearly ran a girl on a bike down as he tried to get home from a tavern. "Is he—well, capable of driving, do you think?"

Lorenzo laughed. "He drives well enough when he's sober, I guess. He knows some mechanics, too. Surely she doesn't have to go far to get anywhere from the hotel?" He tilted his chin toward La Fonda on the other side of the plaza.

"We're not at the hotel now. We moved out to a guesthouse for now, maybe until she finds something she likes better. She wants to go out, find more artists, do some exploring. Mabel told her about some land that might be for sale, I think." She remembered the pottery and jewelry that already filled their small rooms, and smiled. They would need a bigger place very soon. Without even thinking about it, she and Lorenzo walked together, past the open doors of the shops, onto the narrow, dusty paths that snaked away from the plaza. Chickens clucked across the trail, and Fanny barked back at the sounds of dog-calls in the distance. Lorenzo took her heavy basket, and Fanny settled down to waddle beside them, strangely content, just as Violet was.

"I didn't even know Mrs. Rogers had seen your cousin again, after we met him in the lobby of the hotel for a few minutes," Violet said after they strolled in silence for several minutes.

"He said he saw her at a dinner at Los Gallos." He adjusted his hat, casting the angles of his face into shadow again. "Everyone in town meets there eventually."

"A dinner?" Violet tried to remember if Benito had been there that night, but he hadn't. There was that hour MR vanished into the garden ... "I can see that. I was overwhelmed by all the names and people, all of them artists and poets and scientists."

"What did you think of the place?"

They were close to the edge of town, the buildings further apart, the sun splashing on the ground around them. "I've never really been anywhere like it before. Well—maybe to Janet Gaynor's house in California, which was so glamorous, so full of art. But not like Mrs. Luhan's at all. All that philosophy and poetry—I guess it was a little overwhelming." She laughed at herself, the country goose around all the Big People. "But then again, everything has been a little overwhelming since I came to work for Mrs. Rogers."

"In a good way?"

"Sometimes. A very good way, yes. I've learned so much, not just about art and poetry, but about life, too. About myself. It shows me I just have a lot left to learn." She glanced at the mountain, which was so silent, so watchful. Like a mother. Like a place to belong. She wondered if it was possible this was what it felt like to be one of those contented people who thought life was, on the whole, pretty good. It was strange, and nice.

"You looked a little sad just then," Lorenzo said, no pity in his voice, just a fact.

She looked up at him in surprise. No one talked so easily to her, so honestly—not at home, where there were so many expectations that a girl would just conform, fit in, not fuss. But this man seemed to see everything around him. Like the mountain. "Not sad, really. Just—well, wistful, I guess. I just mailed a letter to my mother. My brother is getting married, you see, to the daughter of one of the richest men in town. He had such a hard time after the war, just like your cousin. No one could have expected such a thing. And my parents seem to think—well ..."

"That they want you to come home and settle down, too."

Again, that statement of fact. That little smile. "Yes, I think so. They thought when I left for California, I would just end up running right back. Like a scared rabbit or something. I would see the big, bad world, and scurry into my hidey-hole with everyone I had always known again."

His smile widened. "Not scared yet?"

Violet grinned back. She couldn't help it, his smile was infectious. And rare, she imagined. Too rare. But he was so easy to be with. "Not a bit. I admit California wasn't really for me, and I couldn't really live in France or Austria or New York, like MR. Everywhere is home for her. Or maybe nowhere. But here ..." She swept her arm around to the sky, the meadow, the shadows on the adobe walls, the splashes of late hollyhocks pink and white and yellow. "Here feels peaceful."

Lorenzo shook his head. "Peaceful now, maybe. But we've had wars and plagues and plain, everyday cruelty like everywhere else. We all have families that drive us crazy, too."

Violet nodded. "Did you maybe want to stay away, too, after the war? Mr. Luhan says the young people here just want highways and offices and industry, like they saw out in the world."

He took a battered silver case from his pocket and rolled a cigarette, quietly thoughtful. "Wanted to, maybe. I even tried it for a while, worked on a pipeline in Alaska. But if you belong here, it pulls you back. Every time."

"I can see that. Yes, I can definitely see that."

"You feel it, too? It takes some people like that."

Violet scuffed the toe of her sandal in the dirt, feeling a little silly to admit her feelings. "Is it really possible to feel such a thing, in such a place? Even for Miss Iowa?"

He shrugged. "Sure. My grandmother always said, if the mountain thinks you belong to it, then you do. Why do you think so many artists come here, just passing through, and stay and stay? If this place wants you, it ties you down, dazzles you, and you can't get away. Beware, Miss Iowa."

"'*There be none of beauty's daughters with a magic like thee, and like music on the water is thy sweet voice to me,*'" Violet whispered.

"Byron."

"Yes," Violet said, surprised the old, beloved words still lurked in her mind. She thought of long days hiding in the hayloft, or sunbathing with her friends, reading poetry. "One of my favorites. He seems old-fashioned now, I guess."

Lorenzo took a long drag on his cigarette, sending a plume of hazy-gray smoke into the air. "I think he takes us out of ourselves better than most poets. Nothing much to do for most of the time in the war except read."

"You couldn't make your jewelry then, I guess." She gestured to the bracelet he wore on his tanned forearm, heavy silver incised with perfect lines and triangles. She suddenly thought of one of the new bracelets on Millicent's wrist, always there now, Benito's thunderbird.

"I didn't have my tools, fell out of practice. I'm just getting caught up again."

"I'd say you've certainly made up for time. That's beautiful."

He held it up, the sun shooting along the silver grooves. "I'm getting there. It's still never the way I see it in my head. But I guess it means we always have to go home in the end."

Violet shook her head. "I won't." She suddenly knew this, deep in her bones. Going back would mean losing herself again. "Iowa isn't my home. It never really was, though I love my family. Maybe I really am waiting for the mountain to show me the way."

"She always will, if she likes you. You just have to be patient. We all have to be patient." He took another drag on his cigarette. "My grandma used to tell us a story when we were kids. That the Blue Lake is where the spirits of the gods are still living today. We go over there to pray, and we go over there to worship. The stars and the moon and the sun and the sky and the clouds and the air and whatever nature has provided for us. I would laugh at her back then for how serious she was, but now I wonder if she was right. Some places are just special."

"My grandmother just told me tales of old Russia, the motherland. Running away from Cossacks through the snow, that sort of thing. I would write stories about it at night, brave girls named

Olga or Larissa who would save their families and marry the tsar." Or named Anastasia, her own strange middle name. "I haven't thought about all that in ages."

They walked past a gas station, seemingly the last building on the road. "Have you written anything since you came here?"

Violet remembered confiding in him about her writing, the first person she had ever told such a thing. She was surprised he remembered. "Not really. It's been so long since I even tried, and I have a lot of work to do for Mrs. Rogers."

"But what will you write about, when you pick up a pen again? Tsars and Cossacks?"

She laughed to remember the old, melodramatic stories hidden under her bed. They seemed like nothing compared to sneaking into Clark Gable's house in the middle of the night with MR. She looked up at the mountain, which had come closer, become more watchful, on their walk. "No. I think I'd like to write about this place, but I don't think I have the words in me."

"You'll find them. Just like I found my silversmithing again. It's all there waiting for us."

He sounded so sure of that, so filled with that quiet confidence, that she felt like she could actually do something. No one had thought she could before, except MR. "The mountain will help me?"

He laughed. "You scoff, Miss Iowa. But you'll be surprised."

"You think she likes me, then?"

He narrowed his eyes, pretending to study the always-waiting blue-purple mountain. "I would say so. She certainly seems to like your employer."

"Does she?" For a moment, Violet was surprised, but she knew she shouldn't be. She thought of Millicent pacing the gardens at night, staring at the mountain, the darkened meadows, watching, watching, waiting. "How do you know? You haven't met her yet."

"This is a small place. Everyone's heard about Mrs. Rogers."

Violet remembered what Martha Reed said. And it was true;

MR was quiet, but dominant. Every room she entered belonged to her, she didn't even have to reach for it. She didn't even have to try. "She is hard to miss."

"My nieces have started 'playing Millicent.'"

"Playing Millicent?"

"They color their lips with chokecherry juice since their mothers won't let them buy Coty lipstick at the five and dime, and use twigs for cigarette holders. Then they saunter up and down the riverbanks."

Violet giggled to picture it, an army of tiny Millicents stalking the pueblo. "She'll love that. And she talks about visiting the pueblo all the time."

"There's a dance coming up soon, she'd be welcome. All the weavers and potters love her already."

Violet thought again of the new items in MR's rooms, the way she studied them so closely for hours. "I'll tell her that. But, Lorenzo ..."

"Yeah?" He crushed the end of his cigarette under his boot.

"Do you really think she'll be quite safe, hiring your cousin?"

He was silent for a moment, his face tilted down. "If he can stay off the bottle, keep those demons at bay—sure. Better than relying on young Tom McCarthy, I think. Just tell her to keep a close eye on her jewelry."

She nodded, hearing the doubts, the hope in those words. She knew MR wouldn't be dissuaded from a course once she decided on it, and for some reason she had decided to help Benito Suarez no matter what.

They had reached a pair of ornate, rusting iron gates set back from a graveled lane. They guarded a cemetery, stones and wooden crosses leaning together between bright bouquets and tall lilac hedges that would surely be filled with vivid purple in the spring. "Sierra Vista," the iron letters read.

"My sister is there," Lorenzo said quietly.

"Your sister?" she gasped. He nodded, and she thought of the old ruins of the church at the pueblo, the crosses circling the crumbled tower, the ones she had seen photos of. "Not at the pueblo?"

He shook his head. "Want to go in? It's quiet there, nice. Lots of those artists are buried here, too, Higgins and Couse, people like that."

Violet nodded, and tied Fanny up to the fence so she could take a nap in the shade. They put the market basket out of the dachshund's reach. He held out his hand to help Violet climb over the rails, low and rough there, and he kept holding it as they walked down the meandering, overgrown path. It *was* quiet there, so quiet she wondered if he could hear her heart thumping at just holding his hand.

"I see what you mean. It's lovely here. So peaceful." And it was. Not sad at all, just pretty and quiet, with a view of the mountain and flowers everywhere.

At the back, along another fence and a towering hedge of that lilac that would smell delicious in the spring, was a dark gray granite cross with a faded bouquet of yellow roses at its base. *Mary Juanita Serna Bixby, 1923–1946.*

"She was young," Violet whispered.

He took off his hat, holding it in a tense hand, and nodded shortly. "I was still gone, after the war. She was pregnant, the baby came too soon and a doctor couldn't get there. She lived on an orchard farm, out past Embudo, isolated." He spoke in a quiet monotone, his gaze steady on that cross, but Violet could see past that. Could hear pain.

"She was alone?"

"Her husband was there, but he couldn't do anything. He's buried just there. They say he had an accident not long after she died, but ..." He shrugged. "This is the Catholic part of the cemetery."

Violet swallowed hard, remembering when her brother tried to take his own life once, in one of his fits of depression. "So they aren't at the pueblo."

"He was a white man. A white clay person, my grandmother would say. Mary had to leave the pueblo when they married." He gently touched the top of the cross. "She loved him a lot. I was young when it all happened, just before I left for war, and pretty dumb in lots of ways, but I could see it. They just belonged to each other. Might as well have tried to stop the lightening."

"She left her home?"

He nodded.

"But—your uncle. Mr. Luhan. He married Mabel, and everyone seems to listen to his advice." She thought of the dinner party, of the smiles the two of them would exchange, the way they touched hands, even after being married for so long. The quarrels and secret languages and speaking glances.

"He had to leave the kiva, the religious center, when he divorced Candelaria and married Mabel, but he's on the political councils still. And Mabel helps out a lot here, especially with her connections back East. She was tireless about returning Blue Lake to the pueblo. She's won some respect. But he can't live full-time with us again. He can't practice the old religion."

Violet heard a deep sadness in those words, and slid her hand out of his. "I'm sorry about your sister."

Lorenzo just nodded, and turned away from the stone cross. "Come on, then, Miss Iowa. I'll walk you home."

"Thanks, but only if you agree to carry Fanny. I did promise her she wouldn't have to walk all the way again."

He laughed. "Sure thing. We can't have Miss Fanny upset."

"I can't lose my job!" Outside the gates, Bonnie Evans, Mabel's pretty blonde granddaughter, was riding past on a paint mare. She waved at Violet, and called out to Lorenzo, her blue eyes wide and fascinated. Violet sighed, wondering if the "small place" gossip would land on her and Lorenzo next.

"Violet, is that you?"

Violet heard Millicent calling from her little sitting room at the back of the guesthouse as soon as she stepped inside. She put down the basket and wearily tugged off the scarf that held her hair back, shaking it free as Fanny ran off barking. Violet glanced out the window, but Lorenzo had already vanished.

That strange feeling of contentment mixed with disquiet still lingered.

"Yes, it's me, MR," she called back.

"Finally! You were gone so long."

"The market was busy, and I stopped for a moment at Mrs. Reed's shop to look around." For some reason, she decided not to mention Lorenzo and their walk. "She says she can't wait to show you her newest skirts."

"Oh, yes, they're quite unusual, aren't they? We'll go later today. And dinner at Frenchy's? That little man who owns it is horrid, of course, but the food isn't awful."

Millicent glanced down at her full basket and remembered Ethel's planned *calabictas*, but with MR plans changed fast.

"I've been busy, too, Vi darling, do come and see." Violet couldn't stay mad at MR long when she sounded so excited.

Violet followed Fanny to the little, glassed-in sitting room at the back of the guesthouse which Millicent had turned into a quasi-studio. It was lined with shelves, piled high with art books and sketch-pads, random objects scattered on low tables. Millicent declared she found the bits of pottery and jewelry inspiring, and had to keep them around her. Her workbench was set up near the wall of windows, but only scraps of metal were scattered on it now as MR molded and re-molded wax. The dachshunds slept on a folded red Navajo carpet, dappled with topaz light filtered through the trees outside.

Millicent leaned over the workbench, her hair a pale halo. She did look thinner, her jeans held up with a broad, glinting silver concho belt. But Violet was happy to see she *did* look better than ever, or at least better than she had since those last desperate days in California. Her bones were still sharp through her shoulders, her skin pale against her coral lipstick, but her eyes shone with a happy light.

"Isn't this flower darling?" she said, holding up a sketch, turning the paper this way and that in a dusty beam of light. "I've never seen so many things of beauty in one place. They all race through my mind, all the time. How can I ever capture it?"

Violet nodded. Hadn't she felt the same, walking through town, the colors and light and mountains all around? "I don't think we can. We can only hold it for a split-second, and it's gone. Like fireflies." She laughed to remember those most ephemeral of creatures, running along the creek banks with her brother when they were kids, trying to catch light in jars.

"How right you are. But we have to try. Isn't that all life is? Catching bits of beauty?"

Violet took the sketchpad and examined it as Millicent lit a cigarette. The alabaster ashtray was filled with them, but Violet knew very well that MR would never heed the doctors' warnings to cut back and get some rest. She could only tuck the cartons out of sight, behind a large, glossy-black vase, and hope Millicent forgot they were there.

The sketch opposite the cluster of hollyhocks was quite extraordinary, a brooch or pendant in the shape of a pointed star, all sharp and tumbling.

"Wonderful," she whispered. "Like when we sit out in the garden at night and watch the stars." Like last night, lying on blankets under the cottonwoods with MR and the dogs as they stared up at the black bowl of the sky, the swirling sparkle of stars unlike anything she could ever have imagined. So bright and close, like a diamond necklace tossed onto a table, so near she could almost touch it. Once in a while, one of those stars would shoot past, sharp-edged like the sketch, shimmering, gone before you could even really know it was there at all. So beautiful and unreal it made her want to sob.

Those stars were like MR herself.

"Yes," Millicent said, taking back the sketch and turning it one way and another, frowning. "A star. Unpossessable, beautiful, so sharp and burning if you dare touch it." She sat down in her needlepoint armchair, her shoulders slumping as if on a wave of sudden tiredness. "Oh, Violet darling. Before I came here, I looked so hard, so very hard, for a place where I could be the person I was meant to be. I've seen such strange and lovely things that excited me, but never anything that just reached down and belonged to me. Not that world of perfect clothes, perfect parties, too much money. Just me, just being. Freedom, I suppose. But here—I think I can begin to see it. Can't you?"

Violet nodded, her throat thick as if she would cry. But why cry? Here was something wonderful, in front of both of them. They had found it at last! If they could hold onto it. "Yes," she said simply. "I see it."

MR studied her for a long, silent moment, that light through the windows making her glow in such a translucent way she already seemed beyond them all.

"Yes," she murmured at last. "Yes, it is happening to you, too, Vi. I see it. You're changing. How like me you are. Who would have thought it?"

"Oh, MR." Violet laughed, abashed. "I'm not like you at all. No one ever could be."

Millicent shook her head. "But you are. You see the real beauty in things, too; you want to be free to find yourself, wherever and however that might be. Just trust me on this, darling—don't make my mistakes. Do what you want, do what you want knowingly." She lit another cigarette, despite Violet's little subterfuge with the vase, and Violet noticed the sun shooting along the thunderbird bracelet on her wrist.

MR seemed to notice it, too, and turned it over in the light. "I never knew there were so many people like you in the world, Violet, not really. Beautiful souls who don't even realize what they are."

"Millicent ..." Violet said, but faltered, not sure what she needed to say, what her worries really were. Yet she, too, had been one of Millicent's strays.

"The art here is beyond anything I ever imagined," Millicent said. "The truth of it all. I'm eager to meet more artists, weavers and potters and jewelers. How much there is to learn from them! I do envy Mabel that."

Violet tidied up a stack of magazines "Envy Mabel Luhan?"

"Yes. She knows the Indians, and they know her. Trust her, I think. It takes time to earn such trust, more valuable than rubies. And time is one thing I can't buy, isn't it?"

Violet tried not to frown as she realized something alarming— how much Millicent seemed to dwell on death lately. How it seemed to occupy her mind even as she lived as intensely, *more* intensely, than ever here in Taos. "MR ..."

Millicent abruptly stood up, swaying a bit on her sandals, and stubbed out her cigarette in the overflowing ashtray. "And time runs out right now! Come along, Violet, find your hat. We're going to visit Lady Dorothy Brett at her studio."

CHAPTER 16

Millicent

"A re you sure this is an artist's studio?" Violet's tone was full of doubt, and it made Millicent laugh. She remembered the studios she visited so often in Europe and New York, bright places filled with props and models and color. Her mother's longtime lover, Monsieur Boutet de Monvel, was the epitome of that old-fashioned sensibility. But this wasn't at all like that.

In her experience, studios were as varied as the artists and their work. As varied as life itself, messy and tidy and colorful and gray and uplifting and depressing. That was what made them so fascinating. Seeing life itself created and renewed on easels.

"What do you think an artist's studio should look like, darling?" she said, picking her way carefully up an overgrown pathway.

Violet frowned thoughtfully under the floppy brim of her straw hat. "I'm not sure. There weren't very many artists where I came from. Some of my mother's friends did watercolors of wildflowers." She glanced around the mess of the garden, and laughed. "I think I'll be making up for the lack of artists in my life while we're here."

"Of course you will. We've already started."

"But are you sure Lady Dorothy is a—well, a *real* artist?"

"What do you mean? She certainly seems eccentric enough to be an artist."

"Well, at the Luhans' dinner, she did seem a bit like a character in a Dickens novel."

Millicent laughed again. She did love Violet so, with her funny way of looking at things. "Of course she is. That's why she's so delightful. And an artist is an artist if they say they are. Things like academies and beaux-arts societies are just names really." She stepped over a broken fountain. "Just don't tell that to my mother and her lover Monsieur Monvel. They would be shocked."

The door to the ramshackle adobe hut flew open, and an arm in a billowing, dingy white sleeve waved at them. "Come in, come in!" a cut-glass English voice called, reminding Millicent of manor houses and rainy gardens, Elizabethan mazes and cakes on the lawn. "There's tea!"

Of course there was. Millicent smiled at Violet, who smiled back, her eyes brightening with the adventure. Another reason she did love the girl. She might hesitate for a moment, but her curiosity about the world always took over. A feeling Millicent was very familiar with.

The inside of the studio was as wonderfully cluttered as the outside, as eccentric as the owner. A small room but full of color and movement, canvases stacked along the walls and lined up on easels, a large couch by the fireplace tossed with pillows and a bright, woven Navajo blanket. Empty cups and plates everywhere, half-squeezed tubes of paint, brushes in glasses. Wildflowers in painted pottery vases.

Dorothy Brett looked just as she had at the Luhans' dinner, short and stout, her large bosom loose under a paint-splashed smock, her white hair bundled on top of her head and straggling free. In one hand she held Toby, her ear trumpet, and in the other a half-smoked cigar that accounted for the many scorch marks on the ancient carpet.

The smell of smoke and turpentine hung heavy in the still, stuffy air, the very smell of that creation Millicent craved. Canvases were everywhere, in all different stages of being born, and one sat on an easel beside a table laden with palette and more squeezed-out tubes stained with color, a large jar of water jammed with brushes.

Brett wound up an old gramophone, a Gershwin song, as Millicent studied one painting after the other. Just as it always did, the outside world, illness and bills and money and sons, vanished in color and shape and movement. *That* was the real life. The real truth. And she saw Brett had the gift.

Millicent had fibbed just a bit when she told Violet anyone could be an artist who called themselves one. She would dearly love to be an *artist* herself, and she tried. How she tried! The closest she came was in her jewelry, but even then, the visions in her head rarely came out through her fingers. She was best at finding beauty in the work of others. Making sure it was seen. So no—art wasn't just art just by calling it so.

Yet neither was art only what her mother collected in France. Mummy-Da and Monvel loved only smooth, perfect scenes of life, landscapes and portraits and historical scenes. Her mother did see the beauty in art, it was her great gift to her daughter. But she also saw money in it, status, position. That kind of painting, Monvel's painting, had its place, of course. But so did what Brett was doing here. Her work breathed of this magical place itself, it was real, it was life.

Millicent tilted her head and studied a scene of a dance, a line of tall, willowy men wrapped in colorful blankets, feathered head-dresses, a sense of movement and energy.

"I like this one," Violet said.

Millicent glanced back to see her standing near a small canvas hanging on the whitewashed wall, a scene of people climbing a mountain path, wrapped in more bright blankets. Lonely and perfect and eternal-lasting.

"One of my favorites!" Brett cried, in that Mayfair voice that seemed so wonderfully strange coming from her weather-beaten face. "What do you like about it, Miss Redfield?"

Violet frowned as she considered this. "The feeling of it, I think. They are together, but alone. Not lonely. Just themselves, in the moment, the place."

"I do think you're exactly right, Violet," Millicent said. She took a mug of tea from Brett's hot plate and glanced at an array of simply-framed photographs on the wall by the door as Brett's motley array of dogs poured in and out from the garden, barking and pawing and whining. There was one image of Brett with Frieda Lawrence and Mabel, sitting smoking on a porch, grinning and squinting into the camera, friends in that moment, wrapped up in life together, an old love and an old rivalry. An image of a large Elizabethan house with a lawn sloping away from it, incongruous in the untidy studio.

"Is this your family's home?" Millicent asked, waving the mug at a scene of the half-timbered manor house.

"Mmm, yes," Brett answered, all the noise and passion and rush that was in her when she talked about her paintings muted. She stirred a lump of sugar into her tea. "Horrid place. Lovely gardens to sketch, though. I never went back after I went to study at the Slade. One can't be a debutante *and* be Bloomsbury."

"I never found it so difficult," Millicent murmured. She remembered dancing in Paris cafés with Ludi, pretending to be poor.

Brett laughed, a harsh, exuberant donkey-bray that was quite infectious. "Well, *you* wouldn't, would you? But not with my family. And I never was beautiful. Beauty gets a person out of a lot."

"I suppose it does." Millicent was surprised; everyone knew that, of course. A man needed to be rich to get a free pass, a woman had to be beautiful. But to be both—that could so often be a burden as well as a gift. But few would just say it aloud as this fascinating woman did.

"You know people in the Bloomsbury set?" Violet said, her eyes wide.

"Oh, yes. Writers mostly, always talking about their souls and the meaning of life and art. It was the first time I was ever happy, when I made friends with them. That's where I met the Lawrences." She gestured to a photo of a bearded man squinting into the camera, the mountains behind him. "I came here with them, you know. In the '20s. Now I could never bear to live anywhere else. My old life was just wrong. This is my place."

"Yes. Of course." Millicent studied the photo, and the one of the three women leaning against each other. "You must miss him."

Brett's face creased even more, like an apple in the sun. "Of course. He was a strange one, but he could really *see* things. Wonderful, invisible things, and he could make others see them, too. He was an s.o.b., but he was brilliant. Frieda and I don't have as much to argue about anymore without him there."

"I think you are the same as him," Violet said. "Not the s.o.b. part, but a—a seer of beautiful things."

"Indeed you are," Millicent agreed. She'd thought perhaps she could find a friend in Mabel Luhan, because they had so much in common—strange Eastern families, the gift and curse of money, a love of marrying lots of husbands. But the evening at Los Gallos had shown her that would not really work. Mabel wanted to rule things, rule people; Millicent just wanted to *be*. But this woman— this strange woman—could be her friend. They both knew how to find their own path and follow it, only for themselves.

"I'll buy this one, if it's for sale," Millicent said, nodding at Violet's favorite. "And that one." A group of dancers at the pueblo, all color and life. "Is four hundred enough? It's all I have with me." She opened her alligator handbag and took out the envelope of cash. She knew from Mabel that Brett hadn't a bean, that she painted all day and ate at friends' tables at night. But such art deserved to be supported, needed to be created.

Brett's mouth fell open. "Just for the two?"

"I'm sure I'll want more later, once I've found my own house, my own walls for them." She glanced at another painting, a large scene of a buffalo dance against the backdrop of the mountain. "What an enchanted place that must be."

Brett took the money and tucked it into her smock. "Do you want to visit? I could take you one day, introduce you to some of the potters and weavers. And you, Miss Redfield. They're not always completely sure of outsiders, but they trust me a little now. They know I wouldn't bring someone who can't appreciate their art."

Millicent felt such a longing sweep over her, a sensation she hadn't known in so very long. A yearning toward something, toward a new reality. Something she couldn't buy, but could only earn. "Could we? Truly?"

"There's a dance soon, we'll go then," Brett said decisively. "But I assure you, they'll know all about you long before then. I'm certain they already do."

"This is a small place," Violet murmured.

Brett glanced at her. "Indeed."

"Oh, I know all about small places. I'm from New York. Everyone knows everyone's business there." Millicent sipped the last of her tea, and glanced at the platinum watch on her wrist. "We have to go to Martha Reed's shop now, do you want to come?"

Brett snorted. "Me? A dress shop?"

"Her clothes are very beautiful, works of art I would say." Millicent nodded at the dance scene, the swirl of brilliant colors. "And I think you appreciate beauty in all its forms, even in appearances, just as I do."

Brett reached for her enormous, battered sombrero and clapped it over her wild shock of white hair. "Well, then, let us go!"

When Millicent swept into the small shop with Brett and Violet behind her, she glanced quickly around, taking in the glass display cases, the armoires hung with calico and velvet creations, the little clutches of ladies sitting on the tufted chairs in the corner sipping coffee, no doubt having an afternoon gossip like ladies did at the Plaza tearoom in New York. They stared from beneath their flowered hats, mouths open mid-gossip, but she had already glided past them.

Her attention was on the delectable array of colors, spread everywhere like a sun-shower of gold, pink, blue, green. Her fingertips were irresistibly drawn to the soft nap of a velvet jacket, beautifully cut, trim lines, shining with silver buttons, the darkest scarlet-red.

She imagined one of her starfish Verdura brooches against that fabric, or a drape of those turquoise necklaces she saw so many women wearing around town.

Just like the one Martha wore now. She came out from behind her glass counter, light, graceful, elegant in one of her own pleated creations of sprigged sky-blue calico and a darker blue velvet jacket, her dark hair glossy and parted in the middle, swept back with engraved silver combs Millicent had to admit she envied. Her lapis necklace lay as blue as the Taos clouds against the velvet. Perfect for the place, just as Millicent always believed style should be.

"So, you did come back, Miss Redfield!" Martha said with an easy smile. Millicent quite liked her already. "You've come to buy the green dress, yes? It suits you too well to belong to anyone else." She gestured to a mannequin in the window, wide pleats of aspen-leaf green printed with a tiny pattern of flowers and vines, trimmed in emerald satin ribbon.

She was quite right. It was perfect for Violet. Her eye could be trusted.

Millicent touched the velvet again. What if darling Charles James could see these creations? Couldn't he refine them just a teensy bit, make them perfect for *her*?

"Oh, no," Violet said. "That is, yes, I do love it. But I've brought my employer, Mrs. Rogers, who was so eager to see your shop."

"I'm certainly happy to see you again, Mrs. Rogers, and somewhere quieter than Mabel's dining room!" Martha said with a laugh, arranging a few painted silk scarves on a table. "It can be hard to get even a tiny word in there. And you, Lady Dorothy! I don't think I've seen you in here before."

Millicent bit back a smile to think of Brett in one of Martha's ultra-feminine skirts. But surely a new smock couldn't hurt ...

"No, sorry," Brett muttered around the stem of her unlit pipe. She plumped herself down on one of the tufted sofas and waved Toby around, much to the horror of the gossiping ladies.

"This is quite lovely," Millicent said, leaning down to examine the braid trim of the jacket, the intricately etched design of the silver buttons. It made her think of her new bracelet, of all the beauty and art out there yet to be discovered. She'd made just a weensy beginning today, with Brett and Martha. "I think I would need a necklace like yours to complete the outfit."

Martha trailed a red-painted fingernail over the oblong, incandescently blue stones. "It's called a squash-blossom. These silver beads are interspersed with the 'blooms,' see, like crescent moons. The center piece is the *naja*, a protection talisman, maybe. The turquoise and lapis are blue, like the sky that brings the all-important water in the desert. A man I know at the pueblo created it, I'm sure he could make you one just like it, or to your own design. They say every necklace must be different, to suit the spirit of the wearer, with its own blessings on the stones."

The ladies in the corner gasped and giggled, as if such beauty was beyond them. Such meaning.

Millicent turned her back on them. She'd known too many clucking chicken-women like them in her life, she wasn't going to tolerate it here. "That would be truly lovely. I can certainly use all the blessings I can find." She glanced at Violet, who was looking at a display of embroidered blouses. "Vi, darling, why don't you try on the green? Mrs. Reed is so right, it's perfect for you."

Violet shyly smiled as Martha took the green off the mannequin and led Violet to the small, curtained-off dressing room in the corner.

"Your father is an artist, I think?" Millicent said, examining a tray of beaded bracelets.

"Yes," Martha answered, with an arch of her perfectly plucked dark brow. "Doel Reed. He started the art department at Oklahoma State University. I also studied art history at college, though I found my eye was better than my hand. How did you know?"

Millicent laughed. "I keep track of artists, and so does my mother. And you do have such an eye for color."

"I just like to find beautiful things."

"As do I. I think we'll be good friends, Mrs. Reed."

Martha flashed a beautiful, red-lipstick smile. "I think so, too. And you really must meet Manuel, the jeweler who made my necklace. His work is extraordinary. Enchanted, I would say."

The ladies in the corner gave a final huff, gathered up their parcels and purses and left, making Brett laugh. She gulped down their abandoned coffee.

Martha watched them go dispassionately, without even one of those arched brows. "Thank heavens. They do drink up all my coffee and eat my French macarons, and don't even buy a scarf."

Millicent smiled. She'd met plenty of *their* sort before. She wouldn't have expected them in Taos. "They do seem rather—humorless."

"Oh, I wouldn't worry about them." She leaned closer and whispered, "Wives of rich oil men, things like that."

"Believe me. I learned long ago to *never* worry about people like that." Millicent picked up the velvet jacket and measured it against her shoulders, the fabric delicious against her skin. "Now, I will take this jacket, and that rose-pink skirt and blouse, and those scarves. Blue, yellow, pink. And the green for Miss Redfield, of course, if she likes it." She felt that old familiar rush through her veins, the love of fashion, the thrill of finding something pretty, unique. She'd always used clothes to tell her story, and it had been too long since she'd felt that pleasure in it. She felt herself tingling alive again.

Martha's face flashed astonishment, quickly hidden in a smile. "Are you quite sure you don't want to try them first?"

"Oh, no, I'm quite sure they will work." She had long given up trying things on in public, since her body was much too liable to betray her with its tremblings and shakings no one could be allowed to see.

Violet stepped out of the small dressing room, and Millicent was sure it was just like summer itself washing through the little store. Green and fresh, like a meadow smelling of clover, clean as daisies nodding in a breeze. How very well it suited her, Violet turned into a Demeter of green calico and red hair, sun-touched, freckling skin. How well it suited this place, made her seem to *belong* here. How Millicent longed to belong, too, just as she had with everyone, everything, everywhere in her life, yet it had never been quite right. Never like she wasn't just playacting, just floating over like a mist of perfume. This place was very different. It was *real*, she knew that down to her very bones. It demanded more. It demanded that she try her very hardest.

And Violet, that darling, unaware, sweet girl, didn't even have to try. She was just here, herself, finding her true path as Millicent had always tried to do for herself. It made a lump of something cold and melting grow in her heart, something of sad yearning and dawning happiness all at once. It was all changing, all shifting, all becoming what it *should* be. And for once, she couldn't control it at all. Every bit of her waning strength would not move it an inch. A different power worked over them all now.

She did not even care. This was home. This was her beginning, and her end, too.

"How do I look?" Violet said, twirling in her miles of green.

She did look different now than she had when Millicent first met her, stepping into the California house in that dreadful suit, scared and brave. She smiled and laughed, glowing like the sun, and Millicent remembered how once, so long ago, she had longed for a daughter.

"You look like the springtime fairy," Brett said, waving a coffee cup and Toby around. "I should paint you!"

"Yes," Millicent murmured. "It's all so wonderfully perfect ..."

CHAPTER 17

Violet

AT MABEL'S AGAIN

S he'd never seen anything like it. Maybe it was a dream?

Violet had thought that a million times since the day she stepped off the bus into Millicent Rogers's palm-studded garden. Every day brought new strangeness. But now she was absolutely sure she would blink, and when her eyes opened she would be back in her narrow bed at home, wheat-colored summer sunshine through the old white curtains.

She squeezed her eyes shut, longer this time, and to her delight everything was still there when she opened them. No open fields and weathered red barns, but Mabel Luhan's beautiful house, the purple night pulled in close around it.

Los Gallos blinked amber-light from every window, glowing down on the crowd gathered around the courtyard and clustered on the portal. On the dusty earth, dancers swirled and dipped in the moonlight, to the sound of drums and flutes that seemed part of the night itself.

The beat echoed down to her very toes, bare and dirty in her sandals, and she knew she wouldn't be surprised if she suddenly flew up into the sky like a top spun off its string. Everything seemed a real part of her in that spot of time, and she a part of it. All together in that tiny slice of time.

She leaned against the railing of the portal and stared up into the sky, the tangled skein of stars bright and blinking.

"Miss Redfield," she heard Mabel call, in her low, rough voice, strangely touched with the sound of every place she'd made her own—Florence, New York, Long Island, New Mexico. Violet smiled at her, feeling a bit nervous, as if those blurry dark eyes could see all her fancies. It was like being at school again, under a stern teacher's stare.

And maybe they could see everything. Mabel seemed to have made a whole life, a whole purpose, in *seeing* other people. She wasn't a painter or a writer, but her life was an art in itself. Just like MR's.

"Mrs. Luhan," she said. "What a glorious evening."

Mabel cast a narrowed glance over the dancers, the plume of sweet woodsmoke, the night itself, and nodded in satisfaction. She'd surely ordered it all to be just so.

"The drums do get into your soul, don't they?" she said. "When I first came here, I could hear them at night, from a distance. I knew they were calling me. That I was finally at home."

It was just as Violet felt, when she lay awake at night and let the cool air wash over her from the open window, piñon-scented and cool, so perfect. "Yes," she said simply.

"You do feel it, too, I think. That means you're meant to be here. It called you." She tapped her carved walking stick on the flagstone floor. "And what about your employer?"

"Mrs. Rogers?"

"Of course. Do you think *she* is meant to be here?"

She thought of MR, wandering beneath the trees late at night when she couldn't sleep, her arms thrown out as if she would gather it all close to her, possess it all. But they all knew it could never be possessed at all. "I think only she can tell you that."

"But she seems to have vanished tonight. Like a beam of

moonlight. Yes—that's what she reminds me of. A silver slice of the moon, beautiful, quick. You grab onto it, but—poof, it's changed already. It takes on the shadows around it."

Violet studied the winding dancers, moving in and out of the smoke. She saw Benito, who had driven them there, but no Millicent. When had she left?

Was she suddenly taken ill somewhere out there in the darkness?

Violet stood up straight and glanced back into the house, through the open doors and windows. People drifted through the rooms, eating, drinking, laughing, but no Millicent. A tiny ice sliver of worry touched her deep in her stomach. The dream of the night and the drumming faded. MR *had* looked pale that evening when they left the guesthouse. She'd argued with Mrs. Dicus about all the stray dogs Millicent was collecting, and like all strife it left her drooping and tired. Yet she'd insisted on coming to the party. What if she'd fainted, and was lying out there in the darkness?

"... the mountain wants her own, true, but only if they are their authentic selves," Mabel was pontificating, waving her stick around. "Only our real hearts allow us into this place. If we ..."

"Excuse me, Mrs. Luhan," Violet said, and jumped off the portal to hurry across the courtyard. Mabel stared after her in open-mouthed astonishment, but Violet hardly noticed. Millicent still wasn't among the dancers, or the crowds who lounged on the hammocks and folding chairs at the edge of the firelight. She gathered up the pleated folds of her new green dress and plunged into the night just beyond.

Past the main house and scattered guest cottages were garages and studios, a dairy and chicken coop, and then gardens and a meadow. It wasn't totally dark, even out there. Torches flickered on the gravel pathways and out of windows, touches of some other lives. The mountain was still there, too, a hulking black shadow over the stars. But she didn't glimpse any people or hear anything, just those drums and the distant barking of dogs. No Millicent anywhere.

Then she heard another song, no bird or dog, but—Bing Crosby? Tinny and distant, but growing louder as she followed it.

She came around a corner and found herself facing the open doors of a garage. The familiar scent of grease and turpentine floated out to her, on Bing's crooning voice.

"Hello?" she called timidly, stepping closer to the open door. She saw a car, a lovely blue Bel Air, the hood opened.

A head appeared around the edge of that open car hood, and she smiled in relief. *Lorenzo.*

"Well, Miss Iowa," he said with a laugh. He had a smear of grease on his cheekbone, and he wiped at it with his bare forearm. "Imagine running into you here."

"I thought I imagined your music at first. I wouldn't have taken you for a Bing fan." She came into the light, studying the shelves and tables around her. The car parts, the buckets, the stacks of mysterious, alchemical-looking liquids. "It seems deserted out here."

"Had enough of the party, huh?"

"Oh, no. The music is wonderful. I'm surprised you aren't out there?"

"Putting on my Injun for Mabel's friends? Nah, too much to do out here. And I'm a terrible drummer. Tin ear. Maybe it's why I like Bing." He laughed, low and rough, musical despite his words. He closed the hood with a snap and reached for a towel to wipe his hands. "I should probably turn in my card for my Luhan half. They're all great at music, they have a natural ear."

"And you like Bing Crosby." She laughed, too, trying to cover her sudden discomfort. She had enjoyed the dancing so much; but she didn't want anyone "performing Indian" for her. She didn't want them performing anything at all.

"Someone else's music—that's different. I can appreciate it. I just sound like a scalded cat when I try to make it." He studied her carefully for a minute, making her fidget. Why did he always do that to her? "If you're not running away, where are you going?"

"Millicent—Mrs. Rogers—I can't find her. She was out there with the dancers, and then I started daydreaming ..."

"Imagining what you're going to write next?"

Violet shook her head ruefully. "Maybe. Not really. I don't even know what I was thinking, honestly. And then ..."

He snapped off the radio. "I think I can help you. Come on."

She followed him out of the garage, back into the night. Just at the edge of the gatehouse was parked Millicent's station wagon, pale in the shadows. Lorenzo nodded toward the back seat, and Violet peeked closer. Millicent lay there, wrapped in her white fox fur stole, asleep.

"She walked past the garage earlier. I thought she might be a ghost at first!" Lorenzo said with a laugh. "You never do know at Mabel's."

"A moonbeam," Violet whispered, remembering what Mabel said.

"So I came to the door to check. I saw her get into the car, and thought she might need a quiet minute. Those can be hard to find around here."

Violet gently eased the door open to make sure Millicent was really just sleeping, not ill. Her pulse beat steadily, and her cheeks were pink and healthy. She was fast asleep, for the first time in days.

"She seems okay," she murmured, tucking the fur closer around Millicent's thin shoulders. "I'll just leave her to sleep a little longer."

She left the car to its silence, and followed Lorenzo back toward the house, the drumming and laughter growing louder. "I think—I might need some quiet myself."

Lorenzo nodded. He never did need explanations, Violet realized. It made him so easy to be with. She didn't have to think about things, worry about things, she just *was*. He led her to a cushioned bench under one of the aspen trees, the wind whispering through the leaves. She could see the glow of the fire there, hear those drums, but she wasn't in the middle of it. It was distant from her, yet part of her. Part of the whole world.

Lorenzo propped his booted foot on the bench next to her and took out his cigarette makings to roll one, part of the night, part of everything around them. Comforting and exciting all at once. How did he do that?

She noticed Mabel and Tony at the edge of the circle, Mabel's tunic dress glowing white. She waved her stick, as if agitated about something, and Tony just nodded slowly.

Lorenzo blew a smoke ring in their direction. "It might not always seem so," he said softly, "but they really do love each other. Always have, I guess. It's taken decades for the family to see that."

She watched them, Tony taking her hand in his, Mabel talking and talking still, nodding, smiling. They wandered off into the house, hand in hand. "But you've seen it?"

"Sure. They fit together, that's all. Their good and bad reflect each other."

They fit together. Violet nodded. Hadn't she seen that with her own parents, wanted it for herself? But it always seemed far away. It never could have been with dear Bill, who didn't know her at all. "Have you ever been in love?" The night gathered around them seemed a cloak, an invitation to confidences.

He laughed. "Once, I think. It didn't last."

"No?" She felt something weirdly like jealousy. Toward the unknown woman? Toward anyone who had known love like that? "A girl from the pueblo?"

He shook his head. "A woman I met in California, during the war. I was on leave. Maybe that's why it felt so urgent. So full of emotion."

"What happened?"

He shrugged. "I went back to war, and she went home, I guess. She was from Sweden, doing war work in America."

Violet frowned to picture a golden, statuesque Nordic goddess so different from herself. So perfect. "But you still think about her?"

"Sometimes." He studied the glowing end of his cigarette. "Where I came from, marriage didn't have a lot to do with love. Your parents found someone from the right house, someone with a good dowry or family connections with your own. Maybe that's why they don't understand Tony and Mabel. She just brought him trouble, they think."

Violet nodded, remembering how Lorenzo told her Tony had to leave the kiva when he married Mabel. But wasn't marriage a bit like that where she came from, too? Someone your family knew, someone with a good job. Someone suitable.

"But Mabel completes his life, too," he said. "That's all. Life's too short for anything else."

"Completes his life," she whispered. That was all anyone could ask for. Millicent hadn't found that in three tries. Maybe only the really lucky got it. "Yes. Some people come into your life to make it better, some worse."

"So what about you, Miss Iowa?"

"What about me?"

"Have you been in love?" He sounded light, faintly teasing, and it made Violet laugh even though she didn't like the answer.

She thought of poor, lost Bill, of that handsome man she had met at Janet Gaynor's. Charles Rivers, the lawyer who looked like a football star. They both felt so long ago now. Not to mention that *one* time. She never really thought of that anymore. "Not really."

His brow arched. "Never?"

"There was a boy I went around with in high school. People expected us to marry one day, I guess. Like your pueblo family. He was suitable." And MR had told her never to regret what happened, never to take less than real love. She was right, surely. But Violet still felt a pang over all that had happened in her old life. "He was sweet. All I knew at home, really."

"But you didn't marry him."

Violet swallowed hard, trying not to cry, not to look back at all. This place was her world now, her reality. But the past wouldn't be shaken off quite so easily. "He didn't come back from the war. But I wouldn't have married him. It would have ruined our lives, I see that now. I just always had a—I don't know ..."

"A restless feeling?"

"Yes. Exactly. I wasn't sure where it was leading me. I still don't know. I just knew I couldn't stay there. I would wither away." She glanced up at the moon, shimmering silver in the endless Taos sky, and she knew the moon at home would never look like that to her. Like the world was endless. Full of possibilities.

"I felt the same, once."

"But then you came home. I don't think I can ever do that." No—she knew she couldn't. Not after knowing Millicent. Not after seeing what life could really be, if a person was honest with themselves and brave.

Lorenzo blew one last smoke ring and crushed the end of the cigarette under his boot. He sat down beside her, his shoulder brushing hers. She wanted to lean on it, inhale him, be there right then at that one moment with him. "Some of us are born where we belong, whether we know it at first or not. Some of us have to search it out for ourselves."

"Yes," she whispered. "I guess we do."

The drumming ended, but the beat of it still echoed down through her toes, tying her to the earth. She stood up and kicked her sandals under the pleated hem of her new dress, and made a little twirl.

"Wanna dance?" Lorenzo said.

She laughed. "Now that there's no music?"

"I'm sure we can make our own." He took her in his arms, his hand resting at her waist, his other taking hers, their fingers entwining, palm against palm as he swung her in a slow circle, bringing her close. Her heart pounded, so loud she was sure he could hear it. That the whole world could hear it. "'*Sunset glow fades in the west, night o'er the valley is creeping,*'" he sang in a low, rough tenor. "'*Birds cuddle down in their nest, soon all the world is sleeping ...*'"

"You don't have a tin ear at all!" she scolded hoarsely, trying to keep everything light, silly. Trying not to think about how it all suddenly seemed so different. So very, very real.

He twirled her in a wide circle, ending in a low dip that made her giggle. "Not always. It comes and goes."

"Comes and goes," she whispered, her head spinning. "Yes. I can see that ..."

CHAPTER 18

Millicent

STILL AT MABEL'S

S he woke up with a great, trembling start, so strong she knocked her fur stole off her shoulders, afraid for a moment, so afraid. Where was she? Was the darkness all around death at last, claiming her when she was least aware?

She pushed herself up, a scream clawing its way up her throat. Before it could fly free, she remembered. The party, the sudden weakness that seized her limbs, finding the car. She was just going to rest a moment. Surely it had been more than a moment, but how long? She shook back her tangle of hair and peered outside.

And she froze, as if something deep, deep inside of her, some hidden fragment of soul, stood still and at attention for the first time ever, in all the frantic and crazy moments of her life, all the running. The sky above seemed completely endless, so black, black as forever, but sparkling with whirls and swirls of stars that actually twinkled and blinked like living things, more glorious than she'd ever longed to possess in any jewel. The moon, silvery-amber, with a misty halo of pure gold, cast a dream over the whole world, all the buildings and aspens and flowers and smoke. And the silence beyond the cracked-down windows; it was the most perfect she'd ever heard, even more than the piney mountains of Austria.

It surrounded her with peace, a warm blanket of it, enfolding her into the earth itself. Making her a part of it all, of everything that had ever existed here. Only the faintest echo of drums reminded her she was still there. Still really alive.

There was no future then, no fear, no past to haunt her either. No Millicent Huddleston Rogers. Just *her*.

It was glorious. Wondrous. It was terrifying.

She knelt on the leather seat of the car, where she remembered seeking refuge from that old exhaustion, the old flashing pain, after dancing around that bonfire. The pain she had felt every day seemed vanished, too, taken away by that enchanted mountain that watched her now in the darkness, she could feel it there. Always there, like the loving mother she never really had.

She smoothed back her hair and her rumpled new skirt, those yards and yards of rose-pink pleats. She studied the scene outside the car. It was parked at the end of the drive, near Mabel's long, low guesthouse by the gates, and she could see the glow of the fading bonfire, red and pink and orange, the plumes of smoke breaking into the night. The sweet scent of piñon hung in the air, illuminating the windows of the house.

She heard a low moan, and twisted around to see that she was not quite alone after all. A man lay on the ground at the edge of the drive, just past the car, face-down, his white shirt glowing, the only sign he was there in the shadows.

"Oh, shit," she muttered. She seldom cursed, but this seemed to warrant it. Was he dead? Mabel wouldn't like that, not in her perfect little paradise.

She slid out of the car and hurried toward him, stumbling on the stones in her thin new sandals. He moaned again as she knelt down beside him.

"Are you ..." she said. "Hello? Can I help you? Call for—well, for Tony, maybe?" Tony did seem to be the problem solver around here, with his quiet, stoic ways. Mabel would just shriek and faint.

"Not Tony!" he groaned. So, not dead after all. But terribly drunk, to judge from the sour smell of whiskey. Had he bathed in it? It made her think of her poor, lost brother.

He rolled over, and Millicent was shocked to see it was Benito. He had seemed fine when he drove her there earlier, but not now. The beautiful man was pale as chalk, his eyes red-rimmed, his hair rumpled and dusty, a raw fury seeming to emanate from his very core. And yet he was still so horribly beautiful, like a tormented Prometheus. Millicent felt a pang of sorrow.

She'd quested for beauty all her life. Paintings, clothes, jewels, men. Oh, yes, especially men. Ludi with his European aristocratic mien; Arturo with his hot temper, his dark eyes; Ronnie, handsome and stupid as a Greek statue. No one quite like this, though. With those tragic, liquid eyes, filled with the sorrows of all the world, that perfect face, so young but so, so old with sadness. Just like her.

She couldn't help but run one carmine-tipped nail over his sharp blade of a cheekbone, the satin of his skin, so pale under the sun-brown.

"Are you an angel?" he whispered hoarsely.

She gave him one of her soft, slow smiles. "I'm Mrs. Rogers, remember? You drove me here." She held up her wrist, the thunderbird bracelet catching the moonlight.

He looked away. "So I'm fired."

Millicent shrugged. "Not necessarily."

He covered his face with his hands, hands she saw were shaking. "Why would anyone hire me like this?"

She looked up into the sky, that endless sky that never died, that saw everything. "I've seen worse in my life. You wouldn't believe some of the things ..."

"They can't be as bad as what *I've* seen." His voice, like his eyes, was so old. Ancient. She knew how that felt.

"No one ever accused me of settling for the ordinary, the easy," she said. And she never had, not really. Even when she was young and smuggled flasks in her garter just as all the Bright Young

Things did, or when she married a European title as all heiresses did. Those things were apart from her, not part of her, not real rebellion as she once imagined. Not *her*. She's spent her life smoothing tempers so she could do what she thought she wanted —her parents, her husbands, always smoothing, smoothing.

Now she was no one's pawn. Not to men, not to money, not to her parents. Not to her name. This was *her* place, her life—what was left of it. At long last.

And something in this wounded boy called to her. Not just that familiar old sex drive—desire that tugged at her deep in her belly, though there was that. Something sad and old and death-haunted that she knew too well from her every day.

She glanced toward the house. The fire had died down, and pale pink-gray light peeked over the horizon. Day arriving, ending wild dreams. She thought of Mabel and her silent old husband, the wonderful Tony. Mabel was a silly, bossy woman in so many ways, just like Millicent's own mother. But Mabel followed the call of her own soul. She was no hostage to men, not for security or money or social position. She did not care.

And now neither did Millicent. Here, she was unknown. She was really free. And what was she going to do with that?

"We should get you inside," she said gently. "It's almost dawn." The silence was near total now, except for birds' song heralding the day. She would have to find Violet soon.

Benito turned his face again, abrading his cheek on the gravel. He didn't seem to notice. "They'll see me like this. Again. That redheaded lady—the nurse who isn't a nurse ..."

"Violet? You know she won't care." And Millicent knew very well little fazed Violet, her dear, cool-headed, efficient Violet, with her eyes that saw everything and never told anything. She'd even seen that humiliation with Captain Butler, seen Millicent pale and sick and angry. Whatever would she do without Violet? "No one will care. They were all three sheets themselves when I crept away."

"Not my uncle," he said, fear in his rough voice.

Millicent would imagine that, yes, Tony would not be happy. But he wouldn't show it. "No, perhaps not. But we have to go. We can't sit here on the ground forever."

And suddenly his lips were on hers, tasting of bourbon and mountain air, quick, rough, hard. Strange and awful and perfect.

"Sorry," he muttered, looking away. Maybe he was ashamed to kiss *her*, a white woman, a stranger years older than him. Yet she was not ashamed. She never was. Shame was such a waste of time. Especially with the mother mountain looking down, surrounding her with a goodness and understanding she'd never known before. Maybe now *she* could help someone else, instead of being the ill one, the frail one, the one who needed rescuing.

"Come on," she said, and took his hand in hers. The palm was rough, ridges of calluses along the base of his fingers. So unlike Ludi's and Arturo's smooth manicures.

He stumbled on the uneven ground, and she put her own arm around his waist though she felt none too steady herself. He leaned on her shoulder, warm, strong, but so vulnerable.

She found Violet sitting on the portal with that man, Benito's cousin or something—what was his name? Violet had said. Larry? Lorenzo. They sat close together on a cushioned bench, their heads leaned towards one another, laughing easily. Millicent felt a sharp twist deep inside, something strangely like—jealousy? Fear? The thought she could ever lose Violet at all had never even occurred to her. More fool her.

Lorenzo's smile faded as he looked at Benito, leaning unsteadily on Millicent's shoulder, Ben's face gray now. Benito broke away from her and stumbled away, past his cousin, silently into the house. He tripped over the steep doorstep, and vanished into the shadows, his footsteps limping, unsteady, fading.

"Are you all right, MR? You don't look well. I never should have left you, but you were sleeping so quietly," Violet said, fear overcoming her laughter. "I have your brown drops in my handbag …"

"No. No, I'm quite fine," Millicent said. She tried to laugh, and tucked her hair behind her ears, the curls catching on her heavy pearl earrings, that perfect gift from her father so long ago, her favorites. She had lived her life always making sure she was absolutely impeccable, her clothes perfect, her lipstick fresh, her hair coiffed, but she feared that was all gone now. "So very silly, I fell asleep in the car, of all things. I found Mr. Suarez on my way back. I do hope you weren't too worried, Vi darling."

Violet just shook her head. She looked different, too, as if that strange night had somehow changed them all. There was a new knowledge, a new contentment, in her gray eyes. All Millicent's dawning, vibrant hope seemed to fade in the rose and gold light creeping along the courtyard, through the lingering smoke. She sat down wearily on the turquoise-painted bench next to Violet, and rested her heavy head on Violet's shoulder, the soft, lavender-scented green cotton of her dress like the best pillow, the best sanctuary. She closed her eyes, feeling that safety come over her again.

"You remember Mr. Serna, I'm sure," Violet said, wrapping her arm around Millicent as if to hold her up.

"Oh, yes." Millicent glanced toward him with one of her most charming smiles, the one that always melted anyone she so chose. But Lorenzo Serna just looked wary. It made her feel terribly uncomfortable, in a way she wasn't accustomed to and didn't much like. Men always liked her. He just briefly nodded. "You made this bracelet. Your cousin was so very kind to lend it to me. I do wish I could buy more of your work? Or learn some of your techniques? I make some of my own pieces, though I am certainly an amateur."

"She made this," Violet said, gesturing to the silver violet pin on her ribbon-edged neckline.

"I don't have much time for silversmithing these days," he said quietly. Then he turned to look at the sunrise, all vivid pink and red and gold and tangerine-amber now, his profile stark and solemn. Closed. No—Millicent wasn't used to that at all. Yet he had not been closed to Violet.

A frown flickered over Violet's face, as if she was also worried, puzzled. But she drew Millicent back down to her shoulder, and together they watched the new light, purple and caramel, creeping slowly across the tan adobe of the buildings, the shining yellow-green of the aspens. And with it came the promise of new life itself.

CHAPTER 19

Millicent

NEW YORK, 1935

"Millicent! Millicent, look over here!"

I clung close to Ronnie's arm as the attorneys forged a path ahead of us through the great phalanx of reporters. Their shouts and screams, the phosphorescent yellow explosion of their cameras through the black net veil of my hat, it was all so barbaric. How my father, dead nearly a year now, would have detested it all! Yet it was his fault we were here now. His stubbornness, his unending quarrels, his selfishness. Always *him*. Even when he was rotting in the ground.

Father and his money. It always tied us to him, to each other, whether we wanted it or not. Money showing its ugly face, ruining relationships, ruining love. My brother, Arturo, Ludi, my step-mother. Stepmothers, I should say. None of them could be seen separate from the money. No one would ever be a true friend again.

One reporter grabbed at the sleeve of my sable coat, and Ronnie knocked him flat on his slimy ass. Dear Ronnie. Everyone wondered why I married him so soon after Arturo finally divorced me. Ronnie might not be the brightest of bulbs, but he was sweet. And strong.

207

"Ronald Balcomb!" Mummy-Da cried from her home in France when she heard of the quick wedding in Vienna. "But he is quite as dumb as a fence post, darling. Though I do hear he has a penis the size of a horse ..."

Dear Mummy-Da. Always so classy. Not that she was wrong. He *was* dumb. And spectacular in bed. All the Palm Beach ladies said so. So did Claudette Colbert and Norma Shearer. And Lady Ashley, who really should know. It was true he mainly talked of golf during dinner parties—hours and hours and hours of golf. But his bright golden looks, his outdoorsy shining health, his no-nonsense strength was just what I needed now, as the photographers pressed closer and closer, making my heart pound until I was sure I would faint. And what a scandal that would cause.

He shoved our way through until the courthouse doors slammed behind us.

Inside, all was blessed silence, marble coldness, that crisp scent of officialdom. The reporters still shouted from outside, but it was muffled, far away. Ronnie and I followed the lawyers up a flight of stone stairs to a bench-lined waiting room, and my stepmother Pauline waited there, pacing in her black Mainbocher suit and mink stole. Her face was half-concealed by a dotted lace veil, except for her red lipstick.

I couldn't say Pauline and I had ever truly been friends. She was too social-butterfly, too concerned with what "everyone" thought. Too preoccupied with dull parties. Though she was certainly not as dreadful as wife number two, Marguerite. Pauline was friendly enough, and seemed to make my father happy. I was happy to host their engagement dinner. The night Henry got so drunk and shouted at my father "For God's sake, can you stop hanging a marriage license on every slut you fuck?" That terrible dinner that changed everything. The party that forced the two of us to be allies now. Even my mother, who could never abide a scandal, would not side with my brother Harry now.

The week after my father died, it all broke upon us. Everyone knew he hated poor Harry, especially after that scene at the party. And then there was that dreadful business of the dead showgirl at Harry's house. Even I never embarrassed my father as my poor brother did. None of us knew then how deep the hatred went, though.

Father divided his estate in thirds—one to me, one to Pauline, one to my son Peter. Harry was all out. Peter even inherited the Southampton estate, with The Port and the grand, gilded beach house my parents built when they first married. It was time for battle to commence.

I sighed deeply, stirring the net veil of my hat. I had just rid myself of Arturo and his tiresome jealous rages when Father slugged us with all this. Ronnie and I had hoped to start a new life, far away in Austria, where the fresh mountain air could revive my health and he could ski to his little heart's content. Now we were back in cold, smelly, loud New York.

"Millicent, darling," Pauline said, kissing the air above my veiled cheek. She smelled of Shalimar, heavy and spicy. "How perfectly dreadful it all is!"

"Yes," I murmured. And things were about to become even more dreadful. The waiting room doors opened and Harry strode in. As usual, his hair was rumpled, his face red, his suit wrinkled, his tie askew. My poor brother, once so handsome, so sweet.

Pauline stiffened. How she had hated Harry since his insults at that dinner! Not that I could blame her. Manners were everything. Civilized people kept their dirty laundry to themselves. Now we were wallowing in it. Ronnie's hand tightened on my arm as Harry lurched forward and tried to hug me. He reeked of rum.

"Milly!" he slurred. "And—Arturo?"

"This is Ronald, of course, as you well know," I murmured, stepping back, my court heels slipping on the stone floor. Harry swayed as if he would collapse entirely, his nose purple, his eyes watering. Yet I remembered how it was when we were children, running on the beach at The Port looking for shells, reading fairy-tales. My heart ached for it all. I wanted, longed, to run away, to pretend this wasn't happening. That we could be happy as other families were.

But I had to protect Peter now. My brother was lost. Peter was just a child. I might not be much of a mother, but I would protect my boys with every ounce of my failing strength, always.

A clerk called us into the courtroom, and I broke away from Harry to follow Pauline and Ronnie. It was a plain room, lined with more benches in front of the judge's seat high above, windows swathed in blue cloth. A typist sat at her table, spectacles and plain brown suit at the ready.

Our attorney, Mr. Langton sat at one long table, while some shyster in a plaid suit (plaid!) Harry had found somewhere was at the other. Adam Larkin, one of my father's executors, also waited, a mountain of papers before him. I held my breath as the judge, a fearsome, portly crow in his black robes, appeared.

This is just a stage scene, I told myself. *Not real at all*. Even I, who had made a life of illusions, couldn't quite convince myself.

The judge scowled at his own tumbling stack of papers. I knew what they said all too well. I spent sleepless nights going over and over them, cursing my father.

"So we are here today to confirm the breaking of the Colonel Rogers trust set up in 1899, yes?" the judge said, right to the (hideous) point.

To break my grandfather's trust, my father had gone to great and destructive lengths. He also insisted all death taxes due and lawyers' fees be paid out of the capital of the estate, at least sixteen million, and paid immediately. It all brought the estate from one hundred ninety million to about twenty million altogether. All because my father thought my brother a rude drunkard. I had begged Harry to stop drinking, to find a purpose in life, to no avail. It was all too ridiculous. It punished us all.

"I also see here that Mrs. Pauline Rogers is requesting an

outright bequest for her third of the estate in lieu of property," the judge said.

"Indeed I am!" Pauline cried. "My husband was quite incompetent when he wrote that will. *Quite* so. I implored him to stop drinking so much, to think straight before it was too late."

Mr. Larkin sighed. He had heard it all before a million times now.

"And I see here that Mrs. Millicent Rogers, now Mrs. Balcomb, has demanded the return of estate jewelry valued at over a million dollars," the judge said, shifting to another stack of papers. I did hope never to see another notarized paper in my life. "An emerald and diamond bracelet valued at $85,000, a diamond ring at $95,000 ..."

"Those were gifts!" Pauline cried. She took out a lace hankie from her snakeskin handbag and sobbed into it.

"... also a loan of $45,000 in cash," the judge continued, unperturbed.

"Another gift! I was his *wife*," Pauline wailed.

None of it mattered, of course. In the end my brother lost, and my father's will stood. I got my jewelry back and I could leave that damned courthouse behind. Leave it all, except, for the gossipy newspapers blowing around, landing even in my own car.

I threw the newspaper to the floor and reached for the retractable bar set in the car door, pouring out a measure of straight gin. I tossed it down and poured another, letting the bitter, piney liquid flood through my cold body.

"Mary Milly, don't you think you should ..." Ronnie said hesitantly. "Shouldn't you slow down?"

"Don't call me that," I snapped, unbearably irritated by him. By the whole world, even, that had once seemed so full of glorious beauty before, such promise. I hated it in that moment. "No one calls me that but my mother."

I couldn't pretend now. Myself, my heart and soul, would

never be separate from money. Who were my true friends? My true loves? I would never really know. Not really. Not for sure.

I closed my eyes and let my head fall back on the buttery leather of the car seat. All the old pain, the old exhaustion, was still there. Always waiting. So patient.

"Just get me far away from here," I whispered. But where in the whole wide world could I ever go to find real peace?

CHAPTER 20

Violet

Violet wrote another word, a sentence, a paragraph, the Cross fountain pen Millicent gave her floating over the page, black and clear and wonderful and full of life. When had this last happened? When had she last felt like this? Far outside of herself, yet more herself, more Violet, than ever. It was like the stories she once wrote in her parents' attic, secretly. Scribbled tales of princesses and fairies and wicked witches and tsars and escape, a way out of the everyday world. Flying free.

She had never really thought much about writing again, writing as a *real* thing to do, even in LA when everyone who didn't want to act had a screenplay. At home, books and paintings and music weren't real, they were just little hobbies, like her mother's watercolors. Cornfields that needed harvesting were real; washing dishes was real; getting married was real. Here, everything seemed possible. Even she could feel it, rising up inside of her like a blue bubble. A cloud. Ephemeral and undeniable all at the same time.

She glanced down at her notebook, filled with black blots of words, images, ideas. Fanny the dachshund snored on her cushion in the corner, and Millicent napped upstairs while Ethel baked sweet-smelling bread in the kitchen. Violet's small bedroom, with its little desk, its battered bureau, its narrow bed spread with a quilt, the red Navajo rug on the floorboards, was still there. All was quiet, still, seemingly the same as every afternoon. Yet the whole world looked different to her now. She was writing again.

She tapped the pen on the edge of the desk and stared out the open window, the fresh breeze stirring the white gauze curtains. Kay Dicus was working in her garden, harvesting the last of the summer vegetables while the chickens clucked around her, the mountains endless purple and blue and gold in the distance.

She looked down again at the pages. It had all come to her when she couldn't sleep last night, when she heard MR pacing restlessly next door, when the moon glowed through the white curtains, hazy as lace. A story not of princes and lost maidens, but of this land itself, ancient and ever-new, filled with magic that seemed just as real as European witches and curses, just as irresistible. Of men with unfathomable eyes, of mountains that loved or hated you, of dusty roads and the smell of oil paint and chamisa. Of a land that was forever.

Maybe it came from that night at Mabel's, the drums and the dancing and the darkness. Maybe it was this light, so bright it blinded with its dazzle, the turquoise sky, the eternal-ness of it all. Maybe it was being so far away from all she thought she once had to be, a daughter, a wife, a smalltown girl. A girl who did what she was told. Millicent didn't ever do what she ought. She just lived. She had shown Violet that life wasn't something that happened to a person, it was what they created. Even for little Violet Redfield. Miss Iowa.

That was how the words came at last. Like Brett's paintings, colors and shapes and emotions and whole worlds. She didn't have that gift yet. But maybe she had a beginning.

She remembered something Mrs. Luhan said at that first dinner. She had come to Taos to create a new place for artists, not a "colony," but something outward-looking, a new community, an adventure that could change the world. Mabel saw Taos as pure, timeless. How she wanted them to absorb the smell of the morning air, the color of the sky, deep, crisp, alive. Yes—the smell of blue itself. The way one fell into vast spaces and was lost in the eternal real. The green and gold meadows, the vast pinkish expanse of the desert, the ever-changing clouds. The romance of it all, the strange, striking harmony. The light and the shadow. Man and nature, one. Beauty in every aspect of life, even the hideous parts, the strange and frightening.

The people who belonged there, and nowhere else.

Violet didn't know if she was one of those people. She only knew she felt so different now. Light and free. The past was gone. Let go like a puff of cloud over the gorge.

She remembered how it felt to sit on Mabel's portal with Lorenzo, listening to the heartbeat of the drums, the crackle of the bonfire, while that endless night sky stretched over their heads. As if she was being born, opening unsuspecting eyes to the world. Lorenzo said little then, he never did. Not in the few times she'd seen him, even when they danced. But she liked what he did talk about, about what really mattered. And she sensed he, too, felt that primeval longing in the night. Millicent did, too. They all needed no words for what was eternal.

The mystical quality of the light, the grandeur, the brilliance and drama and subtlety. The perfection of real life.

Now she wanted, so much, to capture it all in words. Was she good enough? *Could* she even begin? She remembered Freida Lawrence, devoted to the perfection of her husband's work. Violet knew well she was no DH Lawrence. But could she find her own way? Her own stories? Could she even have anything someone else would want to read?

She looked down at her desk. It was tidy, notebooks in a pile, a few books, a pottery vase of pencils, a bouquet of late roses from the garden, the photo of her family outside their farmhouse, one of Millicent in Santa Fe, resplendent in a Charles James suit and turquoise necklace. Violet's letter from her mother about Rich's engagement sat under an onyx paperweight MR bought her on the plaza. There was another letter, newly arrived, not yet opened. She knew what her mother wanted; for Violet to come home, marry, settle down, stop this silly wandering. If even poor Richard could do it, so could she.

Maybe she should. She would know what to do in that life. Can vegetables, make jam, wipe kids' dirty mouths, hang out laundry. Here, she had no idea what the next turn would reveal. What MR would show her. And she liked that. She liked the not knowing, the discovery, the fun, the uncertainty. The life.

No, she didn't just like it. She loved it. She loved Taos, loved this notebook, the sky, the snoring dog, loved Millicent.

And maybe, just maybe—she could also come to love the quiet, mysterious, gorgeous Lorenzo, in a way she never loved sweet, simple Bill. Lorenzo, who could never be hers.

"There's time," she whispered. Time to figure things out. To see more of this world. Learn more. Try more. Taste all that life.

The roar and snap of a car engine from beyond her open window interrupted her whirling brain, and she glanced past the billowing curtains. For one giddy, silly instant, the sound of a car made her think Lorenzo was actually there. But why would he be? He had his own work to do, and surely never thought of her. His silly Miss Iowa.

Of course it wasn't Lorenzo, or his darkness-haunted cousin MR had taken a strange shine to. It was a hired station wagon, battered, paint peeling, Kay Dicus stepped over her baskets of vegetables and shielded her eyes with her palm to watch the arrival; the dachshunds lounging in the shade barked in crazed joy at this unexpected midday excitement. Even Fanny roused herself.

Tom McCarthy was driving again, and the car skidded to a halt, half in a hedge. The back door opened, and a lanky, tall figure stepped out, his curling dark hair blowing in the wind, a grin on his face. He glanced around at the guesthouse, the garden, the dogs, swept off his battered fedora, and threw back his head to laugh.

"Paul!" Violet gasped. It was Paul Peralta-Ramos, Millicent's second son, who should be at school getting ready for college. She'd met him once or twice in California, and found him great company, joking, artistic, full of hijinks. *Too* full, according to his mother. And much too handsome for any young girl's good.

What was he doing in Taos?

It was true he had been writing his mother asking for an increase in allowance, but he didn't look in a begging mood now. He looked puzzled, excited, happy.

And surely money was not the only reason for traveling so far. Taos was never easy to reach. Violet knew he adored his mother, she saw the way he watched her, smiled at her, sought the approval that too seldom came. Maybe he wanted that approval now? Was that why he came all this way?

Violet shoved the notebook into her desk drawer and locked it before a quick glance in the new tin-framed Spanish mirror. She wore a pair of white shorts and gingham blouse, her red curls tied back in a blue scarf. But her casual garb couldn't be helped now. She shoved her feet into a pair of sandals and ran down the stairs with Fanny at her heels. Millicent's door was still closed, quiet beyond.

"Paul?" she said, coming out just in time to see him pile his cases by the fountain as Tom roared away in a spray of dust. Paul's cat-like face, the masculine version of his mother's, was sun-tanned, his eyes bright.

"Hi, there, Vi," he said cheerfully, giving her a wave. "Aren't you looking grand? The desert must agree with you. I admit that drive has me a little woozy. How high up are we, anyway?"

"About seven thousand feet, I think. You should be careful, it does make some people feel sick. Drink plenty of water."

"Not you, though. You're blooming!" He picked her up and twirled her around in a dizzy circle, making her laugh.

She's always liked Paul, or Paulie as Millicent called him, as if he was still five. He was open and friendly, curious, affectionate, and he suited this place already. "And you, sir, are a terrible flirt! I could be your—well, your older sister."

He shrugged with a grin. "I get it from Mother, I'm sure. She can never help herself either." His smile suddenly turned serious, and he looked much older. "How is she, really? I hope she's blooming, too."

Violet thought of Millicent, her tired eyes but her contented air. "She does seem to love it here. The art, the fine weather, the interesting people. Hasn't she written to you?"

He glanced away, swiping a hand through his tousled hair, and Violet thought of MR's sadly distant relations with her sons. "Sure, but I've been traveling a bit. I might not have received them all."

"Or written many yourself?"

"I do send postcards. You know the SOH, Standard Oil Heiress. She doesn't like to be crowded." He hoisted up a case under his arm. "Besides, I never have as much news as Arturo. He wants to get married, you know."

"No!" Violet cried. Marriage did seem to be in the air lately. "He's only nineteen."

"My mother was only about twenty when she married the count. But Art's nervous to tell her."

"Why? Is the girl someone unsuitable? A chorus girl or something?" Millicent was friendly with everyone, conversing with maids and movie stars equally easily. But when it came to her own family, that was a different matter. She wasn't a snob, but she could be very picky.

Paul laughed. "No, Dusty is great. I'm sure he'll want to bring her here to visit soon, she loves horses and the outdoors and all that. I told him I'll break the news for him while I'm here."

"Paulie?" Violet heard Millicent call. She glanced back to see MR framed in the doorway. She wore a blue satin and lace house robe, her silvery hair in curlers and tied up in a net scarf, the dogs swarming toward her, barking. Though she looked pale, purple-shadowed under her eyes, her magenta lipstick was in place, silver bracelets stacked on her wrists. She frowned a bit.

"Hello, SOH," Paul said, a tentative smile on his face. He went to kiss her powdered cheek, but he didn't twirl her around as he had Violet, impulsively exuberant. "Good to see you again. Vi says you're enjoying yourself here."

"So we are." She patted Fanny on her doggie head. "But what are *you* doing here? Did you write to tell me you were coming? The mails here are so uncertain."

"They probably come by mule up the mountains," Paul answered. "No, I didn't write. I've been out traveling, you know, and was at the Grand Canyon. Your letters were so interesting I just had to stop here. I want to see the gorge and the pueblo, maybe some of those dances. You didn't mention the dust, though."

Millicent's lips pursed. "And you need money, too, I'm sure, Paulie."

He scuffed his booted toe sheepishly in that dust. "Well—maybe just a little. To get me to California. But mostly I wanted to see *you*. It's been too long."

Millicent's suspicious expression softened a bit, and she stepped forward to gently touch his cheek. "So we shall do all the lovely Taos things while you're here. You can tell me about your travels, and there might be *some* money to spare—a very little bit. If you spend it sensibly for once. Shall we have dinner at El Patio tonight? The food is simple, but authentically local, so fun."

"I look forward to it, then. It sounds groovy."

Millicent shook her head. "You boys and your language! And after all that expensive schooling."

"You had to bully the masters at Groton to keep me on."

"So I did." She sighed and smoothed the bow of her scarf. "How tiresome it all was. But you're *here* now, and we will have a lovely time. Vi darling, can you make sure Kay has a room for Paulie? I need just a tiny bit more rest. We'll go out to the shops later, if I feel up to it."

"Yes, of course," Violet said. Paul watched his mother go back into the shadowed house with a frown.

"She's not really getting better, is she?" he said quietly.

Violet touched his arm. "She'll never really be better, you know. Yet she is happy here. Peaceful. You'll see."

"And now she has you to help her." He smiled down at her, and for an instant she remembered her brother, the way he used to be. "She does rely on you so much, Violet, she writes that to me all the time. My brothers and I are so glad you're with her."

"So am I." And she was. She'd learned so much, seen so much, things she never imagined before she met Millicent. Before she saw what life could be. "Come on, let's find you a room. You can tell us what you've *really* been doing on your travels."

In the end, Millicent was too tired to leave the house by afternoon, so Violet was dispatched to show Paul around the shops of the plaza, hardly a tough duty as she loved hearing his funny stories, seeing his enthusiasm for the town, laughing as he flirted with the pretty local girls. She loved going to the plaza, too, whenever she could, watching the kids ride their donkeys home from school on the dirt roads, looking in on Mr. Karavas at La Fonda to hear all the gossip or peek at the naughty DH Lawrence paintings, browsing Reyna's Indian Shop. Watching the plein-air artists at work. And perhaps, just maybe, there was a teeny-tiny hope of glimpsing Lorenzo again, since she hadn't seen him since that party at the Luhans'. But that never happened. Maybe Mabel kept him away, not being the best of friends with MR; maybe he was just busy. As Violet was herself.

She laughed at Paul's stories of his hijinks on his travels, tales he begged her not to tell MR, but Violet could see, as clear as the azure Taos sky, how much he adored his mother. He asked constant questions about Millicent's life in New Mexico, about her suitors, her art collections. About what she said about *him*, what she thought of him and his brothers. It made Violet rather sad to see such eagerness, when MR rarely talked of her family at all.

Violet shook away the memory of letters that piled up on MR's desk, her muttered irritations about her sons and money. Paul's open, eager young face, his dark eyes so like his mother's, were too anxious for some approval. Violet knew too well what it felt like not to be what your family expected. Not able to be that at all.

"She wishes you would work harder at your studies, yes," she said carefully, taking a bite of the chocolate ice cream he bought her from the corner store. "But she says you share her love of art more than your brothers do."

Paul laughed, and took a bite of his own butter pecan. "I think Artie only worries about luuuvvv right now. But it's true Peter only thinks about the old ways of art and books, thinks those are the best—he is so European. He's a bit of a fuddy-duddy for being so young."

Violet smiled and shook her head. "Your mother says it's because his father was an Austrian aristocrat."

Paul took the last bite of his ice cream. "How can that be when he barely knew his father at all? I'm hardly South American despite *my* father."

"Not like a South American in a movie, no. Not suave and tango-y. You even sort of remind me of the boys where I grew up."

He gave her a curious glance. "Iowa?"

"Yes. You're sweet and funny, and honest. But as handsome as a South American in a movie."

"Well, thanks for that," he laughed. "But how did *you* feel there in Iowa? That you were a real—Iowan? Is that a word?"

Violet smiled. "I didn't feel like that, not one little bit. I couldn't wait to get away, to figure things out for myself, I guess." She remembered Bill, how everyone thought they would marry, how she should be over the moon about that, and she hated the pang of guilt that still brought. The guilt of being content now. The joy of finding writing again.

"I guess I feel the same about school. That there's more out there for me."

Violet stopped to glance in a shop window, a display of tourist pottery. "My grandmother was Russian, running away from the steppes long before I was born. She married and had babies and grew old a long way from her home. Maybe that's why I feel like I'm looking for home, too. Like you."

Paul nodded eagerly. "Yes! Looking for home. Do you think you might have found it here, then, Violet?"

She glanced around the plaza, the bandstand where a guitarist played, the giggling girls, the sky and clouds and air. The way no one cared about her personal business or what her parents might think. The art and books all around. "I think I just might have."

"I think I could, too, if I had the chance. I've never smelled air quite like this before, never felt so much like myself." A shadow seemed to pass over his handsome, young, open face. "No one has ever been more of a wanderer than my mother. But she seems different here, too. Still. Peaceful."

"Yes." Violet knew what he meant about Millicent in Taos. The nervous, restless woman in California was gone. Here she stood still. She just *was*.

"Hey, what's that shop over there?" Paul spun around and loped across the plaza to Tony Reyna's Indian Shop, toward the large windows filled with bright weavings. All the schoolgirls stared after him in awe.

Violet loved Reyna's shop herself. There was always a new, vast array on the shelves, a treasure cave of pottery and jewelry and katsinas from local artists. Drums lurked in corners, silver and turquoise gleamed in the cases, and rugs woven in all shades of garnet, sapphire, coral, gray, and umber made footsteps soft. It was dim and cool after the bright noon sun, and the air smelled of dust and pine.

"What a place," Paul muttered, already drifting to the towering shelf of pottery. Gleaming black and red slip polish, painted Hopi pots, double-necked wedding vases.

"Violet! How nice to see you again so soon," Eva Mr. Reyna's niece who often manned the store, called from on top of a ladder where she dusted the higher shelves. She waved her feather duster. "Who is your friend?"

Paul seemed to remember himself then, and tore himself away from his wide-eyed perusal of the art to smile at her. Eve was very pretty, after all, with her shining dark hair set off by a blue Martha Reed dress, so maybe Artie wasn't the only son interested in luuuvvv. He held out his hand to help her down from the ladder and bowed like a courtly old gentleman. "I'm Paul Peralta-Ramos. Here visiting my mother, Mrs. Rogers."

Eve's pretty face brightened. "Really? My uncle says she's his all-time best customer."

Paul laughed. "She often is. But I'll try to give her a run for the title, then."

"Let's hope so. I have to earn my wages! What do you like? I saw you looking at the pottery. Zuni, maybe?"

Paul looked puzzled, and chagrined. No man wanted to look dumb in front of a pretty girl. "I—hardly know."

Eve gave him an understanding smile. "Why don't you just look around, see what speaks to you? There's the right piece waiting for everyone. Violet, how about some tea? I just put the kettle on the hot plate."

"That sounds wonderful, Eve, thanks." It had been a dusty day, and Violet's throat was parched from laughing with Paul. She took off her straw hat and fanned herself with it. "And I could use a new pair of moccasins, if you have any in my size."

"I'm sure there's something. I just got some in from one of the bead workers." As Eve brewed the tea on the hot plate in the back room, and Paul happily sorted through the shelves of pottery, Violet rummaged in a crate of moccasins, red, turquoise, tan, all beautifully beaded.

"We just got this in, too. From my cousin, he's a wonderful silversmith." Eve brought out a tray of rings and pendants, engraved silver studded with turquoise and coral. Scalloped silver buttons, engraved with star patterns; bracelets in exuberant sunburst designs; ketos; tiny Zuni turquoise cluster bracelets.

Violet laughed. "You do have a lot of cousins. More than I have back in Iowa, and that's saying something."

"I heard Mrs. Rogers just hired one of them as her chauffeur," Eve whispered, glancing warily at Paul, who was still obliviously studying the pottery. "Benito."

"Oh, yes," Violet said carefully. She had to wonder why everyone seemed to react like that at the mention of Mr. Suarez and MR. Like there was something lurking behind his name, just out of view. "She's a terrible driver, I'm afraid, she landed us in a ditch last time she tried to drive off the guest ranch!"

"And I'm sure we're all grateful he found a good, paying job, they're hard to come by these days," Eve said, but her lips were still pursed as she rearranged the rings. "Just be careful, Violet, yeah? You might end up in the gorge itself with Benny behind the wheel."

Violet stared down at the shoes arrayed around her. "Because of the—the drinking?" She thought of the times her brother ended up in ditches and on sidewalks, the worry it all caused.

Eve nodded, not quite meeting Violet's gaze. "He can't help it, really. It's like a demon on him. It's just ..."

"The war. I know. So many came back that way. Haunted."

"Too many. And they say your Mrs. Rogers does, er, well ..."

"Have an eye for a handsome face?" Violet said lightly, trying to fight off that overwhelming tug of discomfort. It was surely one thing an Iowa farm girl and a Pueblo Indian woman had in common, a powerful aversion to confrontation. To minding other people's business. MR was the same—always evading, always smoothing. Her storms of pain and anger were so brief, and always followed by cooling balm. Was it their parents' legacy, in all their own ways?

"He does have that. A handsome face. The handsomest I've ever seen, despite it all. Just—take care. We do like you around here, Vi."

"I'm glad to hear it," Violet answered with a laugh, and she determined to keep a closer eye on MR, too. She was too fragile lately. "And of course I'll be careful. I can't seem to be anything else."

Eve turned away to pour the tea. "My mother does say you're a sensible one, for a *biligana* anyway," she teased. "And Mr. Paul over there is no slouch in the handsome department, either. Is he staying long?"

"I don't think so. He's taking a cross-country trip, a bit of an adventure before he goes to college." Plus MR never liked guests to linger, even, or especially, her own sons and mother. They sapped her strength.

Eve sighed. "Too bad. I get tired of seeing the same boys over and over, y'know?"

"I do indeed know. There were only about fifty boys altogether at my high school." And Bill the only one she would have considered dating.

"Find something that calls to you?" Eve said as Paul joined them, pouring him some tea.

"I think so." Paul held up his pot, a small but elegant piece with a creamy slip background, painted with a serpent chasing its own tail in shades of umber and green. "I love the color and movement, the way the creatures just seem about to swim out at us."

Eve nodded. "The *avanyu*. A Tiwa guardian of water, a plumed serpent. The changer of seasons. A fine choice, Mr. Peralta-Ramos."

Paul flushed happily. "Call me Paul, please."

"I'll wrap it up. Did you pick out some shoes, then, Violet?"

"Oh, yes, I think these brown ones will be great with my new green dress." She glanced up at the clock, and realized they would be late for their dinner at El Patio. Luckily, she knew they were always on "Taos time" now. And "Millicent time" always ran even later.

Of course, they *were* the first to arrive at the restaurant. El Patio was still quiet, bartenders chatting as they mixed sangria, a few old men who had surely been lounging in the corner gossiping all afternoon smoking their cigars, a girl playing lazily at the piano. Only a few of the tables around the open-air, flagstone-floored courtyard, were taken up by customers, and MR's favorite spot by the fountain was luckily open. The evening air was still warm, smelling of roses and frying tortillas, and the rich, spiced red wine of the sangria.

The waiter immediately led them to the table, leaving napkins, handwritten menus, and a pitcher of that fresh, fruity drink.

"This place is amazing!" Paul enthused as he stared all around. He nodded to the piano player, who blushed and fumbled the keys. "I could imagine I was in Italy again, back when I was a kid."

Violet nodded, thinking of the wandering childhood he and his brothers must have had. Living in New York, London, France, Italy, Austria, Switzerland, everywhere and nowhere. "I do love it here, too. The food is wonderful, and it's all so comfortable and easy. Like dining at a home! A four hundred year old haunted home."

"Haunted?" Paul said, avidly interested. "Is that a ghost back there mixing the drinks, then?"

"I doubt it. They say it's Teresina Bent, Governor Bent's daughter, looking for her murdered father. This was once his office, you see."

"I think there was a ghost nanny when we lived at Shulla House in Austria," Paul mused. "She used to rip our blankets off as we slept on the coldest nights, then vanished in a scent of camphor. Or maybe it was our grandmother! Though she wore Mille Fleurs."

Violet laughed. "She sounds like my grandmother, too. Always preaching the virtues of fresh air and cold baths."

"Ours isn't so bad. She was always there, you know, when we were kids. A bit strict, but she always organized our schooling and took us for holidays at her house in France. She always listened to our concerns." He frowned as he looked down at the menu. "She was the one who had time for us."

Violet ached for him in that moment. "Did you like living in Austria, then? Except for the ghosts."

He smiled again, like the sun peeking out from the clouds, easy and friendly. She could see why the girls liked him so much. "Sure. There was always skiing, hiking, skating. It was right in the mountains. And Ronnie was a peach. My mother's best husband, I think. He was funny and athletic, always listening. Peter and Artie liked him, too."

"So what happened to him?"

Paul laughed. "What happened to the count, and to my father. My mother couldn't get along with them. She likes *getting* married; not so much *being* married."

Violet laughed, too. She could see where Millicent was coming from with that. Violet wasn't sure she would like being married, either. "She seems all right now."

"I hope so. But I was sad to leave Shulla. It was the most like a home we ever had, the most time we all ever spent together."

"You left because of the war?"

"Of course. A Nazi officer told my mother he was taking it over after the Anschluss. She probably stayed longer than she should have, but she arranged to get Jewish friends out on Italian passports and into Switzerland, and there was Peter to think about, too, with his Austrian father. But she had a heart attack in '38 and that was that."

Before Violet could answer this extraordinary story, told so matter-of-factly, there was a stir near the door, and she knew Millicent had arrived. She looked beautiful as ever, her daytime sleep thrown off, her silvery hair perfectly curled, her legs long and tanned in white shorts paired with a calico Martha's blouse and espadrilles, piles of turquoise bracelets on her wrists, her diamonds in her ears. She held a large valise in one hand. She glided and smiled as if on a different planet from mere mortals altogether.

"Oh, darlings, I *do* hope you had a lovely day," Millicent said in her soft, slow voice, airily kissing Paul's cheek before she sat down. The waiter leaped to pour her a drink, blushing at her grateful smile. "Tell me all you did."

Paul was grinning at the giggling piano player, whose fingers fumbled over the keys again.

Millicent tapped his hand with her red-tipped finger, bringing his attention back to her. He smiled at her, rapt as if he looked at a goddess.

"What did you buy, then, darling?" she said, nodding at his box as she waved her hand to order a basket of tortillas.

Paul eagerly unpacked it, holding the small pot up to the light. The eye of the serpent seemed to gleam knowingly in the dim light. "It reminded me of that story, SOH."

Millicent turned it, studying the details of the *avanyu*. "Story, darling?"

"*The Mermaid and the Prince*. The one you sketched for us when I was a kid. When you were ill in bed. We would come and sit next to you, and you would tell us the tale. The mermaid who had to leave her sea home to marry her prince on land, and she is homesick and lonely."

Millicent laughed, a delighted, silvery sound that made Paul smile even more. Violet remembered something MR herself had once said about parenthood—she was better at whimsy than organization. Storytelling, while her mother arranged the schools. "Of course! I'm sure I still have it somewhere. Oh, Paulie, this *is* a pretty piece. You have a good eye. The finish is impeccable, the line quite alive. I'm sure your artistic ways come from me." She waved at the waiter, who poured her another drink, and opened her valise. "Now, my darlings, you must look at this. Just rough sketches, of course, but ..."

"Sketches of what?" Violet asked.

"That property Mabel told us about, of course. The one Judge Kiker is selling. Janet and Adrian say they don't want to buy it, they're too busy with Palm Springs, and Mabel isn't interested, so I thought I might take a look after all. They sent me these drawings."

Paul frowned. "You want to *live* here?"

"Well, why not, Paulie? California is no use to me, and it's so cold at Claremont, my old bones can't bear it. And Jamaica is lovely, but so far away. I like it here. One can just be *quiet* for a while." Millicent unrolled the papers. "It's not much now, just four walls and a falling-in roof, really. No floor at all. They say it was once a *morada*."

"A *morada*?" Paul still looked doubtful.

"An old chapel," Violet said. "One used by the *penitentes*."

"So mysterious!" MR said with a delighted laugh. "And there's so much land. Views in every direction, toward the mountain, a wildflower meadow behind. I'm sure I could make something of it."

"But what about your health?" Paul argued. "The mountains in Austria were bad for your heart, and I'm sure it's even higher here. And it's a long way from your doctors."

Millicent gently touched his cheek. "Oh, darling boy. You are sweet to worry about your old mother so. But surely you know by now, life is so full of beauty. Marvels and terrors and delights. We have to hold onto it while we can. I know I've taught you that?" She took a long sip of her wine and gave a satisfied sigh. "Now, do look at this blueprint, it would make such a splendid space for parties ..."

CHAPTER 21

Millicent

SHULLA HOUSE, AUSTRIA, 1937

"Are the boxes ready? Let me see them! It has to be just right."

"Of course they're all here, *ma belle*, don't worry so. It will make wrinkles," her friend, Van Day Truex, said with a wave of his fingers. Van Day was an interior designer, a professor of design in Paris, a painter, and the man who knew more about art and fashion than anyone else she knew. Even her mother loved him, had adopted him as a sort of son after the disappointment of poor Harry. Who else could Millicent find to help her clear out a whole schloss in three days?

Before that dreaded Gestapo man took possession. The thought of him touching *any* of her well-collected beauties with his pale, clammy fingers made her want to vomit into the Sevres bowl she held.

He could have the house, the place where she had been so happy, where she had gathered her family around her in the cold, pure air. There was nothing she could do to stop that. The Germans were the masters of Austria now, and there was nothing more she could do there. No one else she could help after smuggling out so many people, hiding her money, flying her American flag high above her door. But she would be double-damned if he touched her Fragonards!

She studied the piles of wooden-slatted cases stacked high around the drawing room that barely looked like the same elegant, *gemutlich* space of Yule logs and spiced wine just a few months ago, a place for card games and charades and flirtations. It was a warehouse now, all Beidermeier furniture, Aubusson rugs, paintings and sculptures packed away. Only the gorgeous green and white tiled stoves in the corners, the large deerskin sofas too heavy to move, remained. Everything else of the life she created here was packed in those cases.

And they had until the morning to get them safely away. Out of those foul Nazi hands.

Thankfully the boys were already gone, sent to school in Switzerland in her mother's care for the time being. She had to deal with Salm's ridiculous demands concerning Peter, but that was the least of her worries now.

Fraulein Shweig, Millicent's efficient secretary from Salzburg, had the all-important ledgers, checking numbers and lists and keys. Only Millicent herself and her mother had the other keys, and there were three lists with crates numbered. Everything was referenced again and again. Everything was ready. She had to start a new life—again.

Suddenly, she felt so weary, the energy that had carried her on the wave of urgency for so many days ebbing away. She couldn't bear it another moment, those mountains of crates, they seemed sure to topple and crush her into the bare marble floor. Her head ached like an iron band closed around it, and she ducked out onto the wide veranda for a gulp of that clear, cold air. She could not be sick now! Not now.

Shulla House—how she had loved it when she first saw it! It was like a fairy-tale. She was divorced from Arturo—no more of his hot flares of jealous temper, no more tiresome quarrels! Ronnie was so different, as sunny and simple as his blond good looks. A stockbroker, nine years younger than her, funny and sweet, easy to be around. Athletic, energetic, handsome as a stone Greek god.

About as smart as one, too, sadly. He mostly gabbed about golf and tennis at parties, but no one seemed to mind. Least of all glamorous women. Millicent hadn't minded, either, when she managed to beat those beauties to the post and carry him to the altar. But things seemed so different now.

Austria had been a truly fine place to settle, back then. It was distant from her family's scandal in New York, her mother wasn't far away in Paris, and the boys seemed to like it there. The four of them were together far more often than usual, and Ronnie, a professional-level skier, adored the slopes right outside their gates. He liked teaching the boys the sport, too. Anything to keep him distracted. There was a tennis court, stables, several golf courses nearby. And Millicent thought the style of the Tyrol would be an amusing change. She matched dirndls and felt hats with Charles James coats and Schiaparelli shoes. It, and the house, made all the fashion magazines.

She loved Shulla House, her gingerbread schloss with its vast rooms and large terraces. It had enchanted her from the moment she first came up the drive between the towering, shady pines.

She hadn't liked the inside quite so much. So bare, so full of deer horns and such things. The Germans made some excellent cheese and beer and bread, but with interior design they hadn't a clue, the poor things. It was all dark wood and stone austerity, lamps made of those horns, shepherdess figurines smirking about.

But Millicent summoned Van Day to help her, and sat down to make it all her own. Bright carpets, those massive tiled stoves to keep the mountain chill away, fine European style with just a fun dash of that folksy, peasant, lederhosen charm. She had made it elegant and cozy, furnishing the large bedrooms she loved with curtained, carved beds and fireplaces. She'd adored those vast terraces where she could sit with the dogs and the boys in the evenings, sipping mulled wine and watching the sun set over the jagged mountains while Ronnie skied, waving as he whizzed down the slopes.

At Christmas, her mother came to visit, and all the boys were there at once, one more fling in their lost little world. Millicent made sure the house was lit from chimney to basement, and added every Yule tradition she'd ever read in a book. She couldn't remember much about Christmas from her own quiet childhood, except perhaps a little tree beside her sickbed, new books and hats, chocolate boxes. At Shulla, there were several trees, towering and bedecked in sparkles, piles of brightly-wrapped, beribboned gifts, games and music, snapdragon, cakes and fruit tarts and minced pies and spiced wine in pewter goblets. A huge party for the local children, with a gift for them all.

New York and the courtrooms seemed far away then. Austria was a fairy-world of forests and fresh bread and puppet shows in town squares, of Millicent's new loden coats, peaked Tyrolean caps, scarves and dirndls and edelweiss.

"I don't want to hear one word of politics while I'm here," her mother had declared, tossing her sable coat toward the Christmas trees. "It is a holiday, Mary Millicent, and all this dreadful Nazi talk is such a bore."

But the Nazis wouldn't wait for them. There came the day when they woke to the bells tolling the news of the Anschluss, and Millicent knew her little idyll was over. Nazis were immediately preening around the town in their tacky uniforms, strutting like banty roosters. How she hated them, and their beady, icy blue eyes. She knew then she had to pack up, pack up *everything*, and go.

But not before she helped as many people as she could. They showed up at the kitchen door, their suitcases in hand, their eyes wide with fear. She fed them, found them papers, got them out. She could do no more. Not there, anyway. There was surely work for her in America, important war work.

One life ending. What would the next one hold? When would she find a real home at last?

CHAPTER 22

Millicent

"It looks gorgeous, MR," Violet said, holding tight to both her hat and the magazine as the car almost leaped up in the rutted dirt road, jarring back down hard enough to rattle one's whole skeleton. Getting it paved in some way after the house was finished would certainly be my next priority. Benny simply wasn't a good enough driver, even when he was sober, to do this every day. "I do like this photo especially."

I slipped on my dark glasses and peered over her shoulder at the glossy fashion spread in *Harper's*. Me sitting sideways on a chair, black sateen Navajo skirt and crisp white blouse with a pink neckkerchief, my silver and turquoise bracelets stacked up my arms. The makeup artist and hairdresser had done their work well, I looked healthy and elegant. "Excellent. That should sell a few skirts for Martha." I braced myself against another deep pothole. "What does the Cholly column say today?"

I knew I shouldn't even read the wretched thing. Gossip columns had been the bane of my life since I was in toddler hair ribbons. They picked apart my marriages, my romances, my gowns and shoes and eyebrows and lipstick, until I wanted to scream. But I couldn't seem to help looking at them. They were like dispatches from an outside planet to our little valley, a note dropped in from another life, an old self. Days here in Taos slipped by so perfectly, pearls on a chain, each as glowing with perfection as the next. Planning my house, finding artists, trying to teach Benny to make jewelry, to pour gold and silver and forge metals, casual dinners at Brett's or Frieda's, walking along the rivers and meadows and hillsides in the magical air.

Sometimes, when I looked out at all that wondrous beauty, a strange sadness would come over me. Life here was governed by nature, beyond our control, quiet and deliberate, without the artifice I had hidden behind for too long. Here there was just me. Exposed.

Yet I always knew that other world, the world of rush and noise and clackity-clack, lurked just beyond, the world where I was not me but Millicent Huddleston Rogers. It waited past the gorge. It was never good to forget it entirely.

Violet flipped over to the Cholly Knickerbocker column and frowned as she scanned it. She tried to shut the magazine, to put it away. "We're almost to the house," she said. Violet always tried to protect me.

"Go on, then, read it fast," I said impatiently, catching one of the dachshunds before it could throw itself out of the car after a fleeing rabbit. "No gossip rag could ever hurt my feelings, you know."

Violet still frowned, but she read. "'*All is not well, one hears, between the two leading ladies of Taos, N. Mex society. That sleepy little town is quite awake now that Millicent Rogers has pitched her tent there and Taos's first lady, Mabel Dodge Luhan, resents her intrusion. Both ladies just love the Indians. And just in case you don't know, Mabel is married to one, Tony, who wears long pigtails!*'"

I gave a bark of laughter as I imagined Mabel chasing after me, waving her walking stick with menace, hardly able to see me through her thick glasses, her bulky figure in those Isadora Duncan caftans flying along. I might be a sick woman, my heart faltering more with every day, but I could still be fast when I wanted. And to call the majestic Tony just a man "with long pigtails" ...

"How delicious," I said, "that anyone could think two pitiable old ladies such as ourselves capable of such a feud."

"You are hardly old *or* pitiable," Violet said. She snapped the magazine shut. "And pity is certainly the last thing I would feel for Mabel. But ..." She paused, looked away over the desert beyond the road.

"But what?" I said impatiently.

"I did hear that Mabel actually talked to Judge Kiker about possibly divorcing Tony."

"Divorce Tony? After all these years?" I choked. The thought was so absurd. They could only ever be thought of as a unit— MabelAndTony. They were so entwined in this place, so much a part of everything. "She's just having a temper, like my mother used to. I surely have nothing to do with any of it."

Violet bit her lip. "He *does* have dinner at Turtle Walk, Millicent's name for her house, often. Frieda Lawrence says Mabel rails about it."

"To keep an eye on his building crew! Most of them are his nephews, after all. I can't help it if he eats dinner with them, you know I always have meals in my room. Why would I want such an old man anyway?" But there *was* something about Tony, something I kept hidden in my own heart and spoke of to no one at all, not even Violet, something stoic and proud and quiet I had come to appreciate, crave. But no matter what he did, or said, he belonged to Mabel. There had always been plenty of men in the world who belonged to no other woman that I could claim. I did not poach. "Where did you hear that about the judge?"

Violet shrugged, still staring at the landscape beyond the car. "Just town talk, I guess. Villages do like to gossip as much as city magazines."

"So they do, more fool everyone." I wondered if she heard it from Benny's taciturn, vaguely disapproving, all too handsome cousin, Lorenzo. I hadn't seen him much since that strange night at Mabel's, but Violet had started vanishing on her days off. She smiled and hummed more when she was writing my letters or going over accounts, too, a soft look coming into her eyes. I recognized that look all too well from my own mirror.

But right now she did look so worried about that silly column. I laughed, grabbed the magazine from her, tore out the offending page, and tossed it out of the car window. It flew away on the wind, just as I let that old life go. *This* was my home now, my place, and I could see it was Violet's, too. She would have more years here than I would, years she had to fill for both of us, and I refused to let anything spoil it for her.

The car swung around the old, rusted gate onto my land, and I took a deep breath. *My* land. My home. A place for running free. Well, not *running* maybe, not anymore, but I could imagine. I could feel like it.

Eighty acres, the only structure on it crumbling away when I first saw it, but the lack of any house was far made up for by the vistas. Perched on the side of a mesa, it looked one way down rolling meadows towards a river, and in the other way toward the great prize—Taos Mountain, with the pueblo nestled at its base. The fields spread all around like a velvet blanket of green and gold and amber, purple and gray shadows sliding past. It was beyond beautiful, raw and earthy and ever-changing, the perfect place for my final grand adventure. As soon as I saw it, I knew I would buy it, make it mine.

We turned another corner, and the house rose before it, a hive of activity as workmen scurried around. They must have heard we were coming, to be so very busy, or maybe Tony was keeping his eye on them somewhere. I smiled to wonder what Mabel would think of that.

The place was very different from the tumbling-down ruin I first saw, five rooms with barely a roof and no floor at all, water hauled from the river. It would never be large, but it was nearly eight rooms now, of fresh adobe bricks and with a new roof whose vigas Brett was painting for me, terracotta-tiled floors, a portal that looked to the mountain, a courtyard where there could be dinners and dances. I had sent for some of my furniture from Claremont and New York, my great gold-draped bed Roald Dahl gave me, Renoirs and Fragonards, and French settees and escritoires, which I would mix with my new rugs and pottery and paintings. It would be habitable in no time, I was sure.

"We'll be able to move in no time at all," I said brightly.

Violet tilted her hat to shield the glare of the sun, and frowned doubtfully when she looked at the gaping holes where windows would go, the stacks of bricks off to one side half-covered with a tarp. I knew she was thinking of that "blessing" incident. A shaman from the pueblo had come to bless the nearly-finished house, and declared the placement of my bedroom incorrect. I needed to move it six inches to sight the sacred mountain from the bed in the center of the room. So down came the wall. I wanted this place to be absolutely perfect. Once the wall was moved, the windows had to be replaced as well, as the plate glass made the light too intense. Once it was done, I would paint the walls deep red and yellow, the ceilings night-blue. It would be my refuge.

"Do you think so, MR?" Violet murmured.

"Of course I am sure! Onward and upward. We won't be in the whole house yet, maybe, but the back rooms should be quite all right. I want to be in my own space for the holidays."

The car screeched and ground to a halt near what would be the small front courtyard of the house, once it ceased to be a building site and was tidied up. (Despite my hopes of Benny as a driver, he had not quite become the chauffeur *ne plus ultra*, but there was time yet.)

I feared I could see why Violet was doubtful, the place was an utter mess. A Spanish crew mixed up more adobe bricks, piling them up to dry in the sun. Soon they would form new walls to my turtle, new rooms. The current plan for eight rooms I was sure would lead to more, once I had the real feeling of the place, a sense of what it wanted to be. Making a house was not something to happen in a day or month. And this was to be my finest house.

The usual peace of the land, the mountains and stream and blue sky and birdsong, were broken by the discordant hammering on the roof, the whir of drills, shouts in Spanish and Tiwa. I had to remind myself, as I watched all that screaming chaos, that very soon it would all be done and I would be left alone there. The fields and hilltops would be all mine. But I needed that house first. I could hardly pitch a tent in the meadow and call it a day. Simplicity only went so far.

I wanted perfection, and I would wait for it, though it did rather seem to take forever. The peace of Taos, which I loved and craved so madly, also meant nothing and no one was ever in a hurry. Not like I had been for my whole life. My new life, their new ways, intoxicated me, yet I could feel my energy fading a bit every minute. Some days were like swimming through nursery tapioca, pale and blurry and slow-slow-slow.

Brett appeared in the doorway, and waved her paintbrush. She was doing the designs of the ceiling vigas in my drawing and dining rooms, making them distinctive, and usually I loved nothing more than sitting down on the drop-cloth and mixing colors until we found the perfect shade, going over sketches. Today, though, I found myself rather out of breath, and had been ever since I got out of bed, my hands shaking. I wanted to sit alone for a moment, make sure I had my smile-mask on.

"You go ahead, Violet darling," I said. "Take Brett the picnic basket and see what she's been working on this morning, she must be starving, the poor dear."

Violet studied me closely, too closely, that concerned pucker to her lips. "Are you sure, MR? We can sit here in the car a little longer. Or get Benito to drive you back to the guesthouse, so you can have a nap. I can bring you notes about the work."

I was suddenly very fed-up with being whispered over, worried about, wrapped in cotton wool. There was no *time* for such things, didn't they all see!

"I'm fine," I snapped, and shoved the basket into Violet's hands. "Go, go!"

She looked doubtful, but luckily she climbed out of the car and made her way toward the house before I started actually shouting. I never *wanted* to be cutting toward Violet—what if she left me entirely? I found, to my wonder and frustration, that I needed her. She kept our little household running like a fine Swiss clock, food bought, bills paid, artists discovered, orders sent East, even Mummy-Da kept placated and happy and far away. I hadn't been wrong to follow my instincts and hire that poor, nerve-wracked girl in her hideous jacket that first day. She had become a dazzlement of organization.

More than that, though. I liked her. She was nearly as prodigious a reader as I was, and on quiet evenings when there was no party or dinner at El Patio or drinks at the Sagebrush, we sat in the cool stillness by the fountain and chattered about books. Poetry, art, jewelry, dogs, anything. Violet was easy to talk to, easy to listen to, easy to be quiet with, which was so rare. I had never known a friend like that before. She loved this place, felt it soul-deep, as I did. We were so different. Our lives before could not have been more opposite. Yet I knew her now.

So no, I could not let her go. I wouldn't lose her through my terrible temper and impatience, as I had too many people (though, truly, most of them deserved to be lost). I had to hold onto her with all my waning strength. But what would happen to her *after*?

"MR ..." Benny said, and I slowly turned my head to study him from behind my dark glasses. His beauty was almost too dazzling in the intense sunlight, the troubled depths of his eyes.

Poor Benny. He was not like Violet, blossoming under that wondrous azure sky, finding his core of strength. I tried so much to help, gave him this job, taught him what I knew of making jewelry.

Hid the bottles when I could. And he did try when he was with me. I saw that. I tried to remember all he must have seen in the war, all the darkness that smothered his soul.

I didn't listen to clucked warnings, gossip. We all deserved a chance. A change. I had so many.

"Yes, darling?" I said.

"Could I ..." He waved toward a group of men half-hidden behind one of the new walls, passing a flask.

I sighed. "Yes, of course. I'll be here all afternoon." Most of the crew were surely his cousins. I had turned to Tony for help when I first bought the property and knew no one who could work on it, and he had brought in his nephews from the pueblo. I learned later it caused a bit of a stir in town; the Spanish work crews didn't like being left out of any work. Caused a stir with Mabel, too, it seemed, which was so silly. Tony and I only ever really talked about the house, when he talked at all. He was old, set in his ways, devoted to his funny old wife, no matter how I liked his quiet ways. He wasn't really my type, was he?

I watched Benny as he strolled, snake-hipped and loose-limbed, his black hair gleaming in the sun, to boisterously greet his cousins. He, it was true, was assuredly my type. Handsome as the night, and just as troubled and complicated. Sadly.

I took a deep breath, and carefully climbed from the car, the dogs swarming around me. I waited for the sandy earth beneath my moccasins to feel steady again. Ralph Vigil, the foreman, waved and hurried toward me with my newest blueprints in his hands. He was a kind man, steady, strong, funny with his many children, and I was glad he was in charge every day at Turtle Walk. He said nothing, but held onto my arm until I felt still again, silent and casual, and I flashed him a grateful smile.

"How are things progressing, then, Ralph?" I asked, straightening the red wool shawl over my shoulders.

He laughed. "Since we had to move that bedroom wall?"

I had to laugh, too. "Oh, I know, I know. I am impossible. I don't know anything about the technicalities of building, but I do know what I want. I'm the one who has to live here, after all."

Ralph shrugged; he was a good foreman, steady, understanding, patient, knowledgeable. Like everyone else I met in Taos, he seldom got angry, seldom moved fast, seldom seemed to worry. It both delighted and maddened me, this world of *manana*.

"We're about done with that bedroom now," he said. We walked around to the back of the house, where my bedroom would look out, perfectly square now, onto the mountain. "A bit behind on that dining room floor, though. The boys from the pueblo were out yesterday."

I pursed my lips. "Another festival?"

Ralph shrugged again. "Can't be helped. They work hard when they're here."

Yet there were so very many festivals. I couldn't really be angry, though, when I looked at my house, rising before me, a little larger every day. It *was* my Turtle Walk, rooms spreading out like the shell, one way and another according to the views. My heaven.

Ralph showed me the new tiles that had arrived to be set in the kitchen, the half-finished carving of the fireplace. As we came around to the side garden (well, one day it would be a garden, once the building tools were cleared away, a place to grow kitchen vegetables and herbs), I saw Brett sitting in her folding chair in the shade, the basket open in front of her. She happily waved a chicken leg in one hand and took a drag on her pipe with the other. Dear Brett. How she always made me smile! How I admired her art, her dedication to it, her gusto for life.

I glanced around, looking for Violet. I finally saw her standing under a pine brush lean-to where they kept some of the heavier construction equipment. She leaned against a horno oven, laughing, a ray of sun filtered through the wooden slats to shine on her vivid hair, like a Dutch painting. A man leaned over the open hood of a tractor, talking to her, making her laugh like that, so carefree and easy.

He stood up, wiping his hands on a rag, and I saw it was Lorenzo Serna. Benny's always-stern cousin.. He never seemed stern with Violet.

And she never seemed quiet and wary with him. In fact, they looked so at-ease, so natural, standing close, laughing-laughing. I felt a touch of some chilly disquiet, some worry about the future. Violet was no heiress like Mabel, able to thumb her nose at the world. She needed to be taken care of.

"Mrs. Rogers?" Ralph said.

I spun away from the sight of Violet and Lorenzo Serna. It was *her* business, surely, who she laughed with. I had no room to lecture anyone on their romantic escapades. I'd certainly had plenty of them in my life; nothing *but* them, nothing that lasted. And I had enjoyed them all, no matter how much I might wistfully wish for something different now. No regrets.

But Violet was not like me. She was an innocent in so many ways, and that was a precious thing.

"What do you think about how the kitchen's coming along?" Ralph asked.

"Lovely, Mr. Vigil. Perhaps, though, the dining room along this side could be just a teensy-weensy bit longer? I do want to have grand parties here, you know …"

VIOLET

"How's the writing coming along, then, Miss Iowa?" Lorenzo asked, tinkering with something too complicated-looking on a tractor. He brushed the back of his hand over his cheek, leaving a greasy streak Violet wanted to touch away. She folded her arms under the cardigan draped over her shoulders instead.

"Not bad at all. I've surprised myself."

"Surprised yourself? You didn't think you could do it?"

Violet thought of the way she felt when she first looked at the blank page, the way she wasn't sure words that once flowed through her mind like water might come again. "Not really, no. It's been a long time since I put pen to paper. I wasn't sure I could do it anymore at all. And it did feel rusty at first, like trying to walk after you've been down with the flu " She patted the yellow-painted side of the tractor. "Like this, I guess, if it was left out in the wind and sun too long."

"Just needs some oil, and a little patience."

"Exactly. I told myself I would just put down a few words, just some practice. An experiment. But the more I wrote, the easier it was. Not that it's *easy*, really. It's the hardest thing I've ever done, harder than getting on that bus to California. Some days I don't want to sit down at my desk at all. But when I do—it's exactly where I should be."

"Nothing worth really doing is easy."

"Like your silversmith work?"

He held up his wrist, where a new bracelet gleamed. A sinuous, snake-like twist of silver, modern and spare and elegant.

"You're working again, too!" she cried. She grabbed his hand to examine the bracelet closer, his skin warm against hers, smooth as satin under the roughness of fine black hairs, the chill of the silver. She wanted to curl her fingers around him tighter, hold on.

"Just a little. I can't let my tools go to waste. What do you think of it? It's just something new I tried."

"It's absolutely beautiful. You should sell this design at Reyna's. People would snap it up."

He laughed ruefully, but she dared to think he also sounded a little pleased. "Nah. Not thin enough, it's too rough at the edges, see. I'll work on refining it, though, see where it goes."

"Just like I'm working at the rough edges of my story. There's still a lot of them."

He reached for a wrench, letting her go. "What's it about, then? Your story."

She shook her head teasingly. "Uh-uh. I can't talk about it until I'm a lot further along. I'll put a jinx on it, and won't finish."

"A jinx?" He smiled up at her from under the shadows of the hood, and she tried to deny it made butterflies flutter up in her tummy, her heart beat just a little faster. But it wouldn't quite be denied, it was still there, pitter-pattering. "Is that like a curse? We know all about that where I come from."

"Then you must know my grandmother, or someone just like her. She used to warn us about a *sglazit*, a Russian sort of evil eye thing, that will sour anything you may touch."

"She sounds like my grandmother. She said everything we touched would wither if we broke taboos."

Violet thought sadly of his sister, her death so far from home because she reached for what she wanted, what was forbidden. She made herself smile again, giving him a little nudge. "Then you know why I can't talk about my book. We can't have it wither or sour."

He laughed. "Understood. What about your other work, then? How's it with your boss?"

"It's fine." She remembered how pale Millicent looked after the ride from town, the way she stayed in the car. The way she rose later and later in the mornings. "Paying bills, arranging parties, same as always. MR pays well, so I'm trying to save up a bit. It's getting hard not to spend too much at Martha's!"

Lorenzo glanced at her up and down, her new dark-rose calico dress from Martha's shop, her cashmere cardigan and new hair-style, and his smile widened, making her blush. "I'd say it's worth it."

She gave a little spin, making the pleated skirt flare out. "I do like it. I've never seen such beautiful clothes as what she sells! But I do need to save, too."

"Very prudent. What will you save for?"

Violet glanced back at the house, slowly rising up like its turtle namesake, peaceful and glistening in the sun. "I don't know.

Maybe my own little house someday. I've never really been able to look ahead like this before."

"I know what you mean. In the war, no one could ever think ahead even an hour. And now ..."

"Now?"

"Sky's the limit now, eh?" he said with a strange smile.

"Maybe not quite that high. But to finish writing a book, save for my own place. Grow a little garden. Maybe that's possible."

Lorenzo slammed the hood closed and leaned back on it, his arms crossed, bracelet shining in the light. "Have you shown her your writing? Mrs. Rogers."

"No, of course not!"

"Why not? Think she might not like you moonlighting?"

"No, of course not," Violet said again, hating that small touch of doubt. MR did tend to be possessive of things, people, places. In the best way. "Artists are her favorite people. Look at Brett. She gave up everything in England to devote herself to painting, and MR loves her for that."

"Brett doesn't do her bookkeeping or arrange her dinner parties."

"Are you saying she might resent my hobbies?"

Lorenzo shrugged. "I don't know her to say one way or another. But some people, like Mabel for instance, like to control their orbits. It's what they've always done, what they're used to. And your writing isn't a hobby, is it? Don't let them do that to you, Violet. You're too good for that."

Violet swallowed hard, not wanting to think about this, not wanting to admit that sometimes MR *was* controlling, was demanding, did like to think the world was ordered to her. It was the way of rich people, true, but MR was also kind and generous. She wouldn't resent Violet's secrets. Would she? *Could* she? "How do you know I'm good?" she said instead. "My book might be the worst thing since—since Bulwer-Lytton."

"A dark and stormy night?" He laughed, and she loved the

sunlight-sound, the dissipation of her doubts. "I doubt that. But I mean *you* are too good, you yourself. You're kind and thoughtful and generous. Don't let anyone take advantage of that, or steal it from you."

"You think so?" She slid closer to him in the shadows, the two of them wrapped in their own moment, their own little place. He smelled delicious, of sunlight and lemons and Lorenzo. "Maybe my goodness might deserve a little kiss, then?" she dared to whisper.

He grinned, and caught her around the waist to pull her close. "Maybe it does at that."

CHAPTER 23

Violet

Violet was deep into writing a new chapter when her other-world haze was pierced by the sound of a car circling its way up the Dicus's drive. She frowned, and reached out to part the lace curtain fluttering at her open window. MR hadn't said they were expecting anyone that day. She was still closed up in her bedroom after a late night at Frieda's, the guesthouse silent in the crackling, cool autumn weather.

A large, fancy Daimler slid to a stop by the fountain, not lurching and squeaking like when Benito or Tom McCarthy drove by. It couldn't be Paul again. In fact, a uniformed chauffeur stepped out, opened the back door, and helped a lady in a sable jacket and tilted, veiled hat step into the sun.

She peeked up from under that dotted net, and Violet gasped. Janet Gaynor! Looking just like she had when she left Taos months and months ago, her coppery hair shining, her face elfin, her lips perfect with Elizabeth Arden red. She remembered that night in Los Angeles, the gorgeous house, the glamorous couple, and it was like the past leaped into the present. The outside world piercing into their peaceful valley.

A man climbed out of the car behind her, and stood studying

the courtyard, the fountain, from under the brim of his gray felt hat while little Susan, the Dicus' daughter, gaped at them. He was too broad-shouldered to be Adrian, the hair curling from under the edge of that hat too blond. He threw back his head to laugh at something Janet said, and Violet was shocked to see it was Charles Rivers. That attorney-football hero she met at Janet's house over those green cocktails. And he was even more handsome than she remembered.

They looked like they were parachuted in from another world, a world of glamour and sparkle.

She tried to duck away, to change out of her jeans and head-scarf, but they saw her before she could manage it, and waved at her. She waved back, and went down to greet them.

Janet kissed her cheek on a wave of Shalimar, and Charles took off his hat to run a hand through his golden hair, leaving it rumpled and even more beautiful, and gave her a rueful, white grin. "You probably don't remember me, Miss Redfield."

"Of course I do, Mr. Rivers. The dinner party. Those green cocktails." Breaking into Clark Gable's house. But no one needed to know about *that*.

"Charles, please. Yeah, those cocktails. Your butler is crazy, Janet."

"Oh, don't I know it," Janet said. She tugged off her kid gloves, studying the little guesthouse, the dogs in the doorway, the fading flowers in their blue pots. She waggled a little wave at the dazzled Susan, who promptly ran away. "Isn't this just adorable? How are you and Millicent settling in, then, Violet?"

"Very well. The new house should be ready to move in soon, or at least part of it. Luckily, since Millicent's new collections are crowding us out here!"

Janet laughed, a little, silver-bell tinkle just like in her movies. It made the peace and dust and reality of Taos seem so—unreal. "We saw those photos in *Harpers*. That jewelry! She always did have the enviable eye. And where is m'lady?"

"Still asleep in her room, I think. She's been staying up a bit late."

"Well, I'll just have to wake her! I'm dying to see all her new discoveries." Janet marched inside, an unstoppable tiny general in furs and pearls, and Violet was glad she wouldn't have be the one to dare wake MR today. Better to let someone else beard the bear in its lair.

She smiled at Charles, feeling suddenly shy. "Should I show you to one of the powder rooms? They're more like tiny closets, I'm afraid, but they're quiet. I know the drive up from Santa Fe can be a bit—well, a bit harrowing."

He laughed, and she was struck by his sunny openness, the friendly glow in his sky-blue eyes. "I think I'd rather look around a bit, get some fresh air. This place is incredible! I've never seen anything like it. If you have the time to show me?"

"Of course. I could use a little fresh air myself, I've been working all morning."

She led him down the dusty pathway past the main house, to the stream beyond. Kay Dicus, hanging out laundry, waved and gave Charles a curious look before patting her hair self-consciously. Violet knew the feeling.

She waved back. "That's our landlady, Mrs. Dicus. You'll be an object of great interest all over town before you know it. A new face is always of enormous interest here, especially a handsome one."

He grinned at her. "You think they'll say I'm handsome?"

She laughed at him, and reached out to unlatch a gate into the sheep meadow. "Of course you are, and you surely know it. Really good-looking people always do."

"You don't, though."

"I don't—what?"

"Seem to really know how beautiful you are."

Violet was startled. She thought of MR and Janet, of Benito, people who were dazzlingly beautiful, and she glanced down at her faded jeans held up by one of MR's concho belts, her old blue cotton shirt. "Now you're just being a flatterer, Charles Rivers."

He held up his hand. "Scout's honor, I tell the truth. You can trust me, I'm a lawyer."

That made her laugh again. "Not reassuring, I'm afraid."

"Well, I *was* a Scout, once upon a boyish time, and I'm afraid it's stuck with me. All this cussed wholesomeness."

"You can take the boy out of Nebraska ..."

"Minnesota. Or the girl out of Iowa. It stuck to us, though, like an irritating little cockleburr."

Violet sighed, and thought of her mother's letters, the images that crowded around her late at night. The farmhouse, her brother, her mother bustling around the kitchen. "Too true. But I feel like this is my home now." She waved around at the meadow dotted with bright yellow autumn chamisa, the purple-dark mountains, the endless turquoise sky dotted with fluffy, sheep-like clouds that caught on the hilltops and cast long shadows.

"I can see why. It's gorgeous. And so quiet. I can actually hear the birds! Bet you can see stars at night, too. I'm not sure when I could last do that."

"Not many birds in LA, true." She perched on the top beam of a fence and leaned back on her palms. He jumped up beside her, his eyes wide and thoughtful as he studied the scene, like an archaeologist in some exotic ancient place he had never imagined before. He smelled like expensive cologne, unlike Lorenzo and his sunlight.

"Not many at all. I do miss it all sometimes, the space and silence. It seems to suit you, too, Miss Redf—Violet. You look even prettier than you did that night at Janet's house, truly."

Violet felt her cheeks turn hot despite the autumn breeze. She remembered the fabulous white and red gown she'd borrowed from Millicent that night, and scuffed her old sneaker along the fence. "Is that the Scout or the lawyer talking?"

"Both. Honest. This place suits you."

"It does. More than anything I've found before."

"And your work?"

"I enjoy it. Never the same thing every day. I never know what will happen with MR!"

"She can't be an easy boss."

"Not really, I guess. She likes things to be a certain way. But she's generous, and always interesting," Violet said carefully, thinking of Cholly Knickerbocker's silly column. How could she trust him, or anyone really? Maybe Millicent's suspicion was wearing off on her.

"I can imagine. She makes you work all morning while she sleeps in."

"I don't mind. It's nice to pay the bills and organize the books while it's quiet, and it's gorgeous here in the mornings. All that fresh light." She kicked the fence again, thinking about her abandoned notebook waiting on her desk. "And sometimes I have my own projects."

"Do you think you'll do this for a long time, then?"

Violet hesitated, Millicent's pale cheeks and slow movements flashing through her mind. "Probably not."

"Then will you stay here later? Find someone else who needs a secretary?"

"I haven't really thought far ahead." She tried to imagine working for someone else the way she did with MR, Mabel perhaps. She couldn't picture it. But neither could she imagine what else she might do, beyond that little house she had told Lorenzo about. "If I've learned one thing from MR, one really important thing, it's to live every day fully in itself. Enjoy the moment. It's all we really have."

He gave her a quizzical glance. "And that's been an easy lesson to learn?"

She laughed. "Not at all. My parents were always great planners, and that's hard to shake off." She thought of people like Tony Luhan, like Lorenzo, their quiet smiles, their patience, their peace.

"This place is helping, though. I'm hoping maybe you *can* take the Iowa out of the girl."

"Then maybe I can take the Minnesota and the California, out of the boy. It's impossible to stop and smell the roses in LA."

"Then have you thought of trying someplace else one day?"

"Sure. Don't we all? I liked Paris after the war. Battered, but still so gorgeous, full of a vivid magic. I would sit on a bench by the Seine and imagine what it would be like to live there, maybe on one of those river boats. Or a garret high up in Montmartre."

"Paris," Violet sighed. "I've always wanted to go there."

"You should, you'd love it. Totally different from this place, of course, but it has a similar energy. And the bread is amazing."

Violet laughed again. It was strange how light she felt around him, how at ease, considering his looks, his sophistication. "I do love good bread. You'll have to taste the bread at the pueblo, warm from the horno ovens." She turned away as she remembered the best bread she'd ever had, at Lorenzo's aunt's table. "Why aren't you in Paris, then?"

"Well, that's the tragic thing. I've gotten too used to the spoils of my California work. The house, the cars, the parties."

"An occupational hazard, I guess. For a lawyer or an heiress, either one." She tried to imagine Charles in a Parisian garret, or Millicent as an artist. Would either of them be happier then? "But you're here now. None of that stuff matters in Taos. How long are you staying? *Where* are you staying?"

"At the Taos Inn. I'm really looking forward to trying out their bar tonight. And for how long—it depends on Janet, I guess. I told Adrian I would keep an eye on her, he's stuck working on a new movie."

"You're a good employee. I wouldn't imagine most lawyers would travel quite so far for their clients."

He ran his hand through his hair again, a rueful smile on his face. "Well—I admit I volunteered. When I heard you were here."

Violet was startled. "Did you really?"

"I wasn't just flattering about how pretty you are, you know. Or how interesting. So different from anyone I've met in a long time. I've often thought about that dinner party, how disappointed I was that you ducked out early."

Violet laughed a bit to remember *why* they "ducked out early," so Millicent could break up with her Captain Butler. Her Cinderella ballgown felt even more Cinderella-ish now that she knew she missed the prince. "I've thought about that night, too." It had been one of the strangest nights of her life, how could she forget it? Yet she had remembered Charles Rivers, too. That little spark that warmed her deep inside when he smiled. She hadn't felt so comfortable with a man since Bill.

Charles even reminded her a bit of Bill, handsome, uncomplicated, easy to read. Easy to be around.

Unlike Lorenzo, who wasn't so easy to read at all, and could never be called "uncomplicated." And yet she understood him, and he understood her, in ways she couldn't even fathom yet.

"Have you really? Thought about it?" he asked.

"Sure. Who wouldn't? You're pretty memorable yourself."

"You think so? I feel like an old bowl of oatmeal next to all those movie stars."

She laughed. "You could hardly be that. But I often feel like old, cold oatmeal myself."

"*You* could hardly be that. Not with that hair." They were quiet for a long moment, watching the cloud-shadows move over the mountains. "Tell me more about what you do here, life in this place. Is it ever boring?"

"No, never. Not to me, anyway." She told him about Millicent's house, going up slowly on her mesa, impromptu dinner parties, Mabel's Los Gallos and all the people who congregated there with their paintings and poetry and dances and feuds. But she couldn't find the words, not yet, for the essence of her happiness there.

She saw little Susan Dicus running across the meadow, MR's

dachshunds trying to bound behind her on their minuscule legs. "Mrs. Rogers wants to know where you are, Violet!" she called. "She's having lunch brought in. And there's a movie star in the living room!"

"Tell her I'll be right there!" Violet called back. She smiled at Charles. "Hungry? When MR 'gets lunch in' she orders dozens of tamales and enchiladas from El Patio."

"Famished! Must be this altitude. Everything looks and feels clearer, more honest, here, doesn't it?"

She studied him carefully, wondering if a big-city lawyer might understand after all. "Well. That's Taos for you."

MILLICENT

She peered through the window at the scene in her courtyard, framed by the old fountain and the sky and the lace-edged curtains, like a painting. A French still-life maybe. *Dejuner sur montange.* Ethel had carried out a table and chairs, laid out the platters of tamales and bottles of wine, Millicent's new, handmade blue pottery plates and goblets from a store on the plaza.

Janet sat at its head, her fashionable hat and fur jacket gone, copper hair shining like something on Millicent's jewelry-making bench. She was telling a story, her little hands fluttering, making Violet laugh.

Next to her sat a man, Janet's lawyer. Millicent barely remembered him from the awful dunner at Janet and Adrian's, the night she saw off Captain Butler. She certainly didn't remember him being quite so handsome. The lawyer, not Captain Butler. He rather resembled Ronnie, husband number three, all golden good health, hearty laughter, expensive grooming. He didn't wear a tuxedo now, of course, but a white shirt with the sleeves rolled up, muscled forearms gleaming in the autumn sunlight, and no hat as the wind ruffled his hair. He laid his hand lightly over Violet's as he said something quietly in her ear, and she smiled at him.

Hmm.

Millicent could only hope he was somewhat smarter than sweet, silly-headed Ronnie, with more to talk about than golf and skiing, for Violet's sake. Because he did seem to like her. Quite a lot.

Millicent narrowed her eyes as she studied the way their heads bent close together, watching him very carefully. Violet deserved only the best, and she needed someone to see to her best interests. If there was one thing Millicent could unerringly spot in life, it was masculine intent. And she saw it stamped on his face, unmistakable.

It felt a bit odd to be spotting such interest for someone else, like a fusty old maiden aunt/chaperone/careful mother, but it felt good, too. Even with everything, her breathless weakness, that horribly waning light, she could be of use to someone. Someone she cared about.

Violet did deserve so much in life. A man like Mr. Rivers, so obviously prosperous, so obviously smitten with Violet (which showed excellent judgment on his part), could be just the golden ticket Violet needed when Millicent—well, when later. He could look after her, as Millicent couldn't always. Could give her love. Or at least sex, which was no small thing.

She let the curtain drop and turned away. The guesthouse was silent with everyone outside, even the dogs. She crossed the shadowy hallway and gently opened the door to Violet's room.

Unlike Millicent's own chamber, Violet's space was tidy. No dresses and shoes scattered on the rug, overflowing ashtrays, stacks of books and magazines, open lipsticks and spilling powder-boxes. The bed was spread with a neat blue quilt, one of Brett's paintings on the wall casting color and light. The dressing table held a photo of her family in front of their farmhouse, along with carefully-capped lipstick and a silver hairbrush.

Next to the window was the small table Violet used as her desk. Millicent's own household account books were stacked to one side, next to a brass tray and pen-holder, some volumes about art and local history.

In the center was a pile of papers, covered in Violet's neat handwriting, held down by a chunk of pink quartz. Curious, Millicent feathered through it, and saw to her shock it seemed to be a story. A novel. Dozens of pages of it.

Violet had said she used to write a bit, when she was a girl, but Millicent had no idea she still did it. She'd never said a word about it.

Not that it should be a surprise, she realized. Art ran through Taos like a rushing river, flooding inspiration everywhere. It was in the dry, warm, piñon-tinted breeze. She herself had been in a sort of fever with her jewelry-making, designs bombarding her brain so she couldn't sleep. Of course it touched Violet, too, with her sensitive heart.

Curious, Millicent sat down and read the first page, and the next and the next. She found herself feeling drawn in, caught by this story, which seemed to be the tale of a woman's artistic searching through wartime and family strife. Captured by the cadence of Violet's words, her vivid imagery, her insights.

Stunned, Millicent reluctantly put down the chapters and stared out the window. Violet's work was no idle, amateur scribbling. It should, it *must*, be finished, published, seen. Above even men, Millicent knew beauty, knew real, true art, when she saw it. Beauty was everything, and it poured from Violet's fingertips.

She nodded decisively. That was it, then. Violet had to marry that rich, handsome young lawyer. He could support her, protect her, as nothing else could until Violet's work stood on its own. She would have no worries, a large house of her own, nannies for her children, an adoring husband, for as long as she needed them. Millicent had worried about how to really take care of the girl. This was it. She could be a matchmaker.

She thought briefly of Violet and Mr. Serna, there under the lean-to at Turtle Walk, and dismissed it. Someone rich and careless like Mabel could do that, but Violet needed help. Millicent would see that she got it.

She carefully put the manuscript back as she found it, and stood up with a crisp, efficient movement that came only with purpose. She loved a good plan so much, and she was determined to be the stalwart field marshal of matchmaking until all was exactly as it should be. Time was ticking away—for all of them.

CHAPTER 24

Millicent

AT THE PUEBLO

It was cloudy when I woke up, gray and low, the mountains hidden behind their silvery veil, and the damp made me ache as it always did. Made my body freeze and refuse to move out of bed, which infuriated me. I'd been looking forward to this day, longing for it, for weeks. A festival at the pueblo. I refused to let a little misery stop me from doing whatever I wanted. When had I ever done that? And I had never wanted anything more than this.

I dragged myself out of bed, dislodging the dogs from their heaps of blankets, and used that hated cane to hobble to the window and throw back the curtains. There were few gray days in Taos; even when it was cold, the sun burned brightly, blindingly, in that turquoise sky. Yet even when the rain and snow came, I had to admit it was beautiful. Like Mummy-Da's famous black pearls, shimmering with shades of mauve and silver and gold beneath the gray, the clouds all shifting shapes. Flowers, birds, rabbits, ribbons, caught on the mountains, torn by smoke from all chimanayos and horno ovens. At night there were sharp-edged stars like my new brooches and pendants, formed at my work-bench from what I saw all around me.

But I wanted no rain. Not today. "I forbid it!" I snapped.

"MR?" Violet said, puzzled. I glanced back at her, standing in the doorway with the breakfast tray of coffee and eggs and toast slathered in local honey. She and Ethel insisted on preparing all that food every day, even though I couldn't face eating in the morning. Or ever, really, not any longer. Food tasted like sawdust to me now.

"I'm sorry, Vi darling, I was just hoping it won't rain and spoil our day," I said. I reached for my mink-edged peach satin dressing gown, a bit of warmth until that ancient radiator could rattle to life. How I longed for the comfort of my own home, my Turtle Walk, at last! There would be new pipes and hot water there.

Violet laughed, and arranged the plates, the coffee pot, the linen napkins, on a table. She wore her green dress from Martha's, her violet brooch at the collar, her red hair tucked up in a coronet of braids with dark green ribbons, a new style. Unlike fading, old-growing me, she bloomed anew like her name. Serenity, content-ment, shone out of her like the New Mexico sun. I wondered, hoped, that gorgeous Mr. Rivers might have a teensy bit to do with that. He'd been very attentive in the days since he and Janet arrived.

"If anyone could order the rain back, it's you, MR," she said. "Now, have some of these eggs. Huevos rancheros, Ethel got the recipe from one of Mabel's cooks. You'll never get through the whole day without some sustenance, you know. And eggs make a person strong."

I poked a fork at the concoction, the eggs mixed with green chilis and potatoes. "You sound like your Iowa mother."

Violet laughed. She opened the wardrobe and glanced through the clothes arrayed there, my new calico and velvet and denim mingled with Dior satins and Charles James taffetas. All my life tangled up in fashion there. "You're lucky you've never actually met my mother. But yes, she does spend half her life commanding people to eat something."

I nibbled at some toast and gulped down some coffee, hoping

its strong darkness would fortify me. "Have you heard from your mother lately? Anything more about the grand wedding plans?"

Violet's hand went still on one of the velvet Navajo jackets. "It does sound like plans move apace. The bride's family insists on a reception at the Grand Hotel, which isn't quite as lavish as its name but *is* the nicest place in town. And the gown is coming all the way from New York."

"Weddings can be such an onslaught. I'm glad all mine were tiny after all. How is your brother faring in the middle of all the cakes and lace and flowers?"

Violet's brow puckered. "Mama doesn't really say. I hope he isn't—well, I hope he's still strong. Staying out of the way, I'd imagine."

I nodded, thinking of the stories of her brother's problems, the drinking, the vanishing into taverns, the falling into ditches. Like poor Benny, like her brother Harry. Like too many young men. "Will you go?"

"I don't know yet. My mother sure wants me to. I think her nefarious plan is to trap me there, marry me off to some neighbors' son in exchange for their cornfields."

"How medieval! Well, in that case, I won't let you go. I can't do without you." I nodded, thinking of my own "medieval" plan, to marry Violet off to that lovely lawyer. It sounded much better than cornfields.

"What will you wear today?" Violet glanced out the window, where a few pale rays peeked through. She held up one of my Charles James suits, chocolate-brown boucle wool with engraved gold buttons, a nipped waist and peplum that flashed peeks of orange silk. It had a matching swing coat, lined with more of that silk, with a mink collar.

Once it had been a favorite of mine. Now it just—didn't look right. I had always been a stickler for "the right fashion for the right event." It was the essence of style, really, engraved in me as a child by my ever-correct mother, and though I'd always had far more fun with my clothes than she did, that maxim couldn't change now.

I shook my head. "I've been thinking perhaps I should donate some of my clothes by dear Charles James to a museum. The Metropolitan, perhaps. They *are* great works of art, and deserve to be admired. I doubt I'll wear them again."

Violet frowned as she studied the suit. "But when you go back to New York ..."

I smiled at her gently. "You know I never will. Not to stay." Not Fifth Avenue, not Long Island, not Claremont, not Jamaica. This was it, my last great adventure. "We'll pack them all up when we move to the new house, and I'll write to the museum. What about one of my black sateen skirts and that red jacket? I can wear my ermine cape and that adorable Tyrolean hat I saved from Shulla, if you're worried about the cold. We must be properly dressed to visit someone's home, you know. Now, Violet darling, do sit down and have some coffee. I want to hear all the news of Iowa."

The station wagon was rather crowded for the ride out to the pueblo, but I didn't mind at all. Janet had gone back to California, but Mr. Rivers stayed behind. Business, he said, but what business would a California attorney have in Taos? No, my keen nose for romance said differently. He sat behind me me now with Violet, the two of them laughing as she pointed out sights through the window.

Brett sat next to me, the dogs crowded on her lap along with a large sketchpad, her pipe clenched between her teeth like always. She peered at the mountains, her charcoal sticks at the ready if a good view presented itself. Benny drove, sober fortunately. (I had some hopes the worst of all that was behind him; I'd seen no drink at all since that night at Los Gallos, and he seemed keen to learn more about making jewelry.) It was bad enough jolting over the rutted dirt lanes with no alcohol at all, every swerve and turn jolting my aching bones. Yet there was a lightness, too, as the town was left behind us and new vistas opened up with every turn. A sense of floating out of myself.

I glanced out the window, and saw fields rolling away at every turn, brown and dull-yellow as the cold part of the year closed in, but dotted with grazing horses, held in by split rail fences. The hills rose behind, purple against the gold, and I glimpsed a few low farmhouses, sheds, barns and rusting trucks, even a bathtub plunked down in the middle of milling-around chickens.

The car suddenly careened around a sharp curve, sending Violet tumbling against her beau. They both laughed, and I smiled to see it. My hopes, never terribly high for so many things, rose. Violet blushed and sat up straight, smoothing her pleated skirt, and Mr. Rivers beamed. Adorable.

Benny parked the car in a field just beyond a gate, among a haphazard collection of other vehicles and horses and wagons. I recognized Mabel's Bentley, and Martha's little coupe. "We'll have to walk from here," Benny said, and I glanced down at my new, high-laced moccasins. It was a good thing I left the Chanels at home, I thought with a laugh.

We all tumbled out of the car and made our way past a few low, small buildings, the rounded humps of horno ovens smoking as they baked breads and pies. The cold air smelled wonderfully of piñon smoke, fresh, yeasty bread, the metallic whiff of the morning's rain. Last night's showers had left the pathways muddy, rutted with dozens of footsteps, lined with scrawny dogs drinking from puddles, drying racks of meat and corn. We made our way past the nineteenth century church of San Geronimo, the whitewashed walls and gate, where bells tolled low, slow, sonorous.

And then there it was. Spread before me, exactly as I had dreamed it.

A river, tumbling, silvery, dotted with ice and crossed with plank bridges, divided it into two. To my right, the north build-ings, Hlauuma, four stories, as rosy brown as the earth it was built of with a fresh coat of adobe, the light glowing on the walls. The doors and window frames were painted bright blue, thrown open to the day. The flat roofs and stoops were crowded with blanket-wrapped figures, red, gray, green, blue.

Taos Mountain rose behind it, guarding it, creating it, as she had done for thousands of years, her snow-covered peaks alight. That building had been there, lived in, seeing laughter, music, sex, death, longer than Notre Dame or Westminster Abbey. Those generations past, stretching back and back, brought life to us now, in this moment. It was *our* turn to hear it, to love, then to leave. But maybe, like them, I could leave a trace behind for those after.

I thought of all this place had endured, and felt it, them, beside me. Wars, invasions. By all odds, it should have vanished long ago. Yet here it was, beautiful as ever. And I was here, too. I laid my hand gently on the wall of the church, and felt part of it.

I threw back my head and drew a deep breath into my poor, ragged lungs. Sweet and earthy, yet otherworldly, too. The rhythm of the sun, moon, stars, the earth and the wind. Peace. Peace at long last.

I opened my eyes and studied the plaza around the river. The climbing pole, the crowds, the dogs and people and smoke and life-life-life. As I watched it all, I felt something move inside of me, like something physical, as if my heart mended itself. Always, as long as I could remember, even as I always moved, always *did*, I wanted calm. Truth. And here it was, right before me, all around me. These people, unlike my own family, my husbands, just *were*. They were whole and serene in themselves.

Here I could be unknown. Free. A human among other humans. *I* could just be. It was dizzying, frightening. Wonderful.

I felt a touch on my arm, and turned to see Violet watching me. "Do you feel well, MR?"

I smiled at her. Couldn't she see? Didn't she feel it, too? This was *it*. This was our heaven. We had both come so far, in our different ways, to find it. "Never, ever better, Violet darling. Just look at it all. It's like the paintings, and here we are in it."

"The dancing won't start until sunset! You should come see this shop, you'll love it, the potter is wonderful," Brett called, waving at us frantically. Brett never did anything slowly, carefully; it was all here, time to see this, love these things, *now*. It was why I loved her, loved her vivid art. She had broken away from all that was before; she was her true self. Now I could be, too.

"I'm coming, darling," I called back, tingling with the excitement of what could be in that shop. Of the treasure hunt I always loved.

"Shall I come with you?" Violet asked.

I glanced past her at Mr. Rivers, who looked oddly shy for such a large, gorgeous man. Who watched Violet with such shining hope. "Oh, no, darling, why don't you explore a bit? Show Mr. Rivers around. He'll want to tell his California friends all about it, won't you, Mr. Rivers?"

He laughed. "I'm not sure they'd believe it, Mrs. Rogers. But there's no better tour guide than Violet."

"How right you are," I said brightly, and gave Violet another smile as she seemed worried. "I will be very well with Brett."

I drew my fur cape closer around me as she went off with her handsome swain, and I saw Benny slink away to look for his family (I hoped—no whiskey). The wind off the river was cold, but I was too thrilled by everything around me to care at all. The vendors with their tables of prune pies and bread, the shirtless, gorgeous men getting ready for the footrace, the women in their beautiful velvet skirts. I waved at the people I had met, and bought a small loaf of bread for suddenly I was very hungry indeed. Hungry in a way I hadn't been in so long.

I followed Brett over one of the plank bridges, near the low adobe wall that divided the village from the fields beyond. I glimpsed tall ladder poles sticking up against the sky, leading down to the underground kivas that concealed ancient secrets I could never see, no matter how the mountain claimed me.

We walked past a group of children playing on the riverbank, giggling together, reminding me of my own lonely, silent childhood.

Some of the girls, leggy as new foals, shining-haired, beautiful, were wrapped in lengths of black sateen, their lips stained red, waving twigs around as they paraded slowly by the water.

I laughed with delight. "Whatever are they doing?"

Brett laughed, too. "Don't you recognize it? They're playing Millicent!"

"Playing—me?"

"Of course. You're famous here already."

I waved at the girls, making them giggle and duck away. I wondered if there was a place to buy toys nearby, and I followed Brett towards the shop.

The south, Hlaukwima, side was lower than the north, only four stories, but the same earth-brown with blue windows, horno ovens, dogs, children. Several of the doors were open, hung with hand-painted signs. *Indian Things For Sale. Bread and Pies. Indian Jewelry.*

I felt like a child set free in Hambley's, delighted, overwhelmed, unsure where to turn first. Tables carefully laid with jewelry, weavings, pottery, every way I looked. It was dizzying.

"This way, MR," Brett called, brandishing Toby. "I want you to meet someone."

I reluctantly turned away from a spilling-over display of turquoise and followed Brett along a narrow alleyway. She knew this place, after all, knew its people and its back roads, its rooms and secrets in ways I longed to. She held something infinitely precious, the one thing I couldn't buy—trust. And *I* trusted her, too, trusted her as I did so few people besides my Violet. Brett wouldn't steer me wrong.

We stopped in front of an open doorway, blocked by a sleeping, yellow-spotted dog. *Indian Stuff* read the green-painted sign, which could mean—well, anything at all. I was intrigued. I glanced up at a curl of lavender smoke from a hidden chimney, and smelled the tang of juniper and—was that *manure*? I followed Brett, stepping carefully over the dog, who never stirred, and ducking through a low, narrow doorway.

At first, it was so dim after the dazzling day I couldn't see much, until I blinked away the gloom. As with all the pueblo apartments, this one seemed to be two rooms, one in front of the other. The one we stood in was the shop, with a calico curtain blocking off the living quarters. There was a rug, wondrously beautiful, woven of pearl gray, bright red, night-black, which could have graced the grand parquet floor of any grand drawing room. Here it covered a packed-down dirt floor, free for anyone to walk on. The bright-clean whitewashed walls were lined with shelves, and on them—it was Aladdin's cave. Bowls, vases, bean pots, two-necked wedding vessels, sparkling like diamonds embedded in its pale tan and black. They glowed in the faint light, a strange night sky.

I was utterly enthralled. I stepped closer to one object laid out on a table, a vase shaped rather like a wine decanter but with a shorter neck. I drew off my glove, compelled to touch, to feel, to *know*, but I fell back. It felt too presumptive, too rude to touch. And a Rogers was certainly never *rude*. Or not usually.

"Do you like it?" someone asked, a voice so low, so soft, almost like a shy child. I glanced back to see an older woman standing just in front of the calico drape. She must have slipped in when I was too enchanted to notice, but everyone here was so quiet, so calm. So filled with that peace I craved so much. I had to learn it, too.

"I've never seen anything so unique, so exquisite," I said, and it was true. No Cartier bracelet could be like this. The rim was as thin as my fingernail, slightly fluted, the neck like a swan, the base perfectly round. It sparkled with gold-like flecks.

"Micaceous clay, our Taos specialty," the woman said as she

walked, no, glided over the carpet. She was small and slim, as girlish as her voice, dressed in the traditional feast day garb. White, pleated blouse with one shoulder bare, a wide, bright, woven sash over a tulip-hem skirt, white deerskin boots I very much envied, her gray-streaked black hair up in a chignon and tied with red yarn. A red and blue shawl was draped over her shoulders, which she could draw up over her head outside. She didn't wear much jewelry, a loop of silver beads, a turquoise and coral pendant, a few bangle bracelets—Brett had said the Taos Indians thought the Navajo a bit vulgar to display quite so much wealth in their abundant jewelry! I could never quite understand that, being rather partial to jewelry myself. I touched my large squash blossom necklace, suddenly unsure it was quite right.

She smiled, a few wrinkles deepening around her brown eyes, and I saw she was even older than she appeared at first. Yet still surely too young for such skill.

"Micaceous?" I asked.

"The flecks are from the mica mineral from the Sangre de Cristos. The clay makes it very good for cooking, it heats evenly and stays warm longer. Most don't see it as a collectible object, just something for the kitchen."

"I can't believe that at all! It's so beautiful. You make them all yourself, then, Mrs ..." I gestured at the sparkling display.

"Mrs. Yazzie comes from a very long line of renowned potters," Brett said. "She's one of the first to be able to make the lines so thin and delicate, yet so strong. She won't give up her secrets!"

"My grandmother taught me," Mrs. Yazzie said. "But I'll never show anyone my first lopsided efforts from when I was a girl!"

"It looks so fragile," I said, daring to trace a fingertip over the opening.

"Lift it up," Mrs. Yazzie said.

I was terrified, but I very carefully raised it in my palms. It was like a cloud, like a feather, like nothing. Before I knew it, I held it high in the air, sure it would sail straight over my head and onto the floor, shattered in pieces. I had not felt so clumsy, so silly, since I first had Peter, my oldest son. He had felt like he would break in my hands, too, such a tiny baby. I hastily put the vase back down, making Brett and Mrs. Yazzie laugh.

"It's waterproof, too," she said. She picked up a nearby bean pot, black this time, but with the same glittering bits. "Pottery, Mrs. Rogers, is like your child. You try and give it something, and if you are lucky it gives back to you. But first you have to let go of something selfish inside of you, because if you keep it the pot is no good. If it's right, it comes alive, and you can feel it in your fingers, a kind of tingle, I think. It has a spirit of its own. And then you have something good in your home every day."

Something good in your home every day. Yes. That was what I wanted. I had enjoyed all my houses, put something of myself into all of them. But Turtle Walk was different. It was *all* mine, not to be someone else's idea of what a house should be. My home. Everything in it would be something good.

I smiled at Mrs. Yazzie. I always knew in an instant a true artist when I saw one, someone whose art was their one dedication. Like Brett. Like I wanted to be, but never could. I couldn't be a true artist. I could only show real art, real beauty, to the world. And this marvelous place was filled with it.

"How do you know my name?" I asked.

She laughed. "Everyone knows your name, Mrs. Rogers. And now I see why."

I wondered what she meant, good or bad, and thought of the girls beside the river. "Playing Millicent." I decided to use the lesson of silence. "I'll take this vase, thank you so much. Can I pick it up before I leave tonight?"

"Of course. I'll wrap it up." She picked it up in hands nicked and burned from firing pots, but graceful, elegant. She turned the vase thoughtfully in the dim light. "I'm glad you like it. Every piece finds its real owner. This one is clearly yours."

As we left the *Indian Stuff* shop, Brett grinned around the stem of her pipe. "I told you that you would like it there."

"Brett, darling," I answered. "From now on, you are in charge of all my *affaires d'art* ..."

VIOLET—ALSO AT THE PUEBLO

Violet sat perched on the low wall that separated the plaza from the open fields, from the mountain that watched over it all, munching on a prune pie and watching it all unfold. As the day grew later, the waning sun turning the adobe to rose-gold, the open area around the river grew more crowded, the drumming louder.

Charles leaned against the wall beside her, his golden hair ruffled in the wind. He studied the scene, too, but unlike her he seemed—not so enthralled. Curious, yes, but also somehow bored. He glanced at the Patek Phillipe watch on his wrist, fidgeting, and Violet handed him a chunk of her pie. He flashed a smile up at her, and she thought again how much her mother would like him. How perfect her family would think him. Handsome, polite, a successful lawyer! Even if he did live in California, that wouldn't matter so much next to all the perfection of him.

Violet let herself imagine it. A house in the hills, white with a red tiled roof, palm trees in the yard, a terrace looking down at the vast city lights. A coupe to take her shopping, a swimming pool, a washing machine and automatic oven, all the mod cons. Dresses and pearls and fur stoles. Dinner parties for rich clients—movie stars, even! Maids, a pool, some artwork. Not like Janet's house, of course, but very nice. Comfortable. What every woman longed for. And a handsome husband, too.

It was a tempting thought, a pretty image. Her job with MR couldn't last forever. Then where would she be? Back in Iowa? Charles was certainly nice. He seemed to like her. It wasn't anywhere near a proposal, but MR always said men were simple creatures who needed only the tiniest bit of encouragement. Easy for *her* to say, of course, she was a wealthy beauty. And she had that —that something. That spark Violet knew she lacked herself, that flame that drew everyone close.

And Charles smiled at her now; not just any smile. *That* smile. Warm, admiring. Maybe it was true that if she just pushed a tiny bit ...

She thought of Lorenzo again—quiet, still, unreadable, lovely Lorenzo. He seldom smiled at all, but when he did it was like the sunrise, sunset, moon, stars. It was like writing a perfect paragraph and *knowing* it was right. Not how it was right, not how it had been made, just that it was. The world stood still for just a second, and you saw the utter gorgeousness of what life *could* be. Then it all flew away again.

Her parents wouldn't like Lorenzo as they would Charles, for certain. He wasn't rich, he wasn't a lawyer, he had no house in the Hollywood Hills and couldn't care less about any of that. He was an Indian. He would never leave Taos.

Violet choked down another bite of the pie, the delicious crust suddenly catching in her throat. Lorenzo's family probably wouldn't like *her*, either. She remembered his lost sister and her white husband, together now at the Sierra Vista cemetery. Tony Luhan, and his exile from the kiva. She knew enough of Taos life now, of the pueblo, to know that family was everything. *We are in one nest*, they said, and yet they lost too many young people every year since the war, looking for modern work after they saw the world beyond. Lost like Benito, too, to darkness. They couldn't lose more of what made them—them.

She glanced behind her at the mountain. The sunset made the snowpack at its peak sparkle, as if it smiled down at her. How could she ever leave, either? She had only just found this place, found something of herself, found her words again.

Don't be silly, she told herself with a laugh. Charles hadn't proposed, nor had Lorenzo, and they weren't likely to. A woman could find her own way. MR showed her that. Violet might not have oil money in the bank, but she could live like Brett. Stray dogs and hot plates and art.

"This place is sure something," Charles said.

"Isn't it?" she answered, pleased he could see something of the magic there, too. The ancient walls that held, and hid, so much. Maybe there was hope for him, after all, despite his impatience.

"Like something out of the medieval world," he said. "Who knew anything like this was even left? I saw old castles in Europe, but I don't think anyone would dream of *living* in them. No heat, no running water, all that dust. Great places to see, though. They won't believe this back at the Samba Club."

"Yes," Violet murmured doubtfully. It *was* old, true. It didn't seem old, But she loved how it held everything, past and present, blood and love and laughter, even all the plants and animals and stars and mountains, within its arms. Nothing was separate. Nothing lost. Not just something to look at and tell your pals at the nightclub.

"How long do you think Mrs. Rogers will stay in Taos?" he asked.

She thought of Turtle Walk, slowly taking its shape atop the mesa. "I'm not sure she'll ever leave."

Charles laughed. "A lady like her? She'll get tired of it soon enough. Too quiet. She'll miss New York, Europe. Won't you?"

"You forget. I'm an Iowa girl. I don't miss Los Angeles."

He touched her hand, his leather glove warm and soft on her skin. "You don't miss anything at all there?"

She gently slid her hand away. "The beach, I think. But I never belonged there."

"You want to go back to Iowa, then?"

She shook her head. "Not there, either. I'm not sure what I want to do, really, not yet."

He smiled shyly. "Maybe you could think about California

again. It's not all like the city. People could make any kind of life there they wanted. Citrus farms, beach houses ..."

Violet nodded, but she knew what life she really liked—*this* life. She just had no idea how to make it happen for her yet.

The sun was sinking fast now, casting gold and purple and pink rays over the crowded plaza. The knots of people edged closer to the riverbanks and the stoops of the houses, and bonfires were being lit along paths that snaked around the buildings.

"Is that Senator Chavez?" Charles said, suddenly standing up straighter. His expression turned sharp and attentive.

"I'm not sure," Violet answered without much interest. "Which one? Who is he?"

Charles pointed to a tall man with slick, dark hair, incongruously wearing a suit, talking to the pueblo's War Chief. "He has several bills in the Senate I'm interested in, someone definitely worth knowing. I should go say hello, introduce myself. Shall we?"

Violet suddenly saw the other side of life as such a wife, the one of meeting "important people," charming them, drawing them in to help her husband's career. "You go ahead. I'm just going to finish eating my pie, and then I'll come find you."

He gave her a puzzled glance, a little frown, and she knew he also saw she was not being "businessman's wife" material. But she knew she never could, not really. He smiled again, and kissed her cheek. "Don't be too long," he said, and disappeared into the crowd.

Violet ate the last of her pie, and swung her legs against the old adobe wall, happy to be alone, happy to just watch the scene around her. A few others came to sit along her perch, and one of them was Eve, from the plaza shop.

"Violet!" she called merrily. "Great to see you. Is Mrs. Rogers here? Did she bring her gorgeous son?" She patted her hair, drawn up in a smooth chignon with silver combs.

Violet laughed. "Nope, sorry. That is, Mrs. Rogers is here, but Paul went back to school."

"Ah, too bad. He was a cutie."

"Hey, now!" the young man next to her cried, putting his arm around her. Violet thought he was rather a "cutie," too, with long black braids over the shoulders of his embroidered white shirt, and with laughing dark eyes. He wore a blanket over his shoulders of striped red and green, part of which he wrapped around Eve as the wind sharpened off the river. Violet felt a bit wistful, wishing Lorenzo was there to do the same with her. She wondered where he was.

"This is Pedro," Eve said. "He thinks I'm going to marry him."

Pedro laughed, totally unconcerned. "I'll persuade you, you'll see."

"Hmmm, we'll see," Eve said, and turned to Violet to chat about what was new at the shop, town gossip. As they talked, more torches were lit, laying out winding pathways. Even more people crowded onto the roofs and stoops, swathed in blankets and shawls, the windows squares of light in the gathering darkness.

"What happens now?" she asked Eve.

"Foot-races. Very competitive, a big rivalry between the north and south," Eve said. "Pedro came in third last year, even though it's not meant to be a competition, really. No one wins an actual place."

"I'd come in first now, if not for that dumb plow," he said, holding out one foot in a cast.

"Next year," Eve said as she patted his hand.

As they watched, the low hum of conversation and drumming suddenly quieted, and Violet heard the far-off ringing of small bells, silvery and mysterious, like something in fae-land in the old books she read as a kid. It grew closer, louder, and suddenly a great crowd of young men funneled out from an alleyway and spread around the church, running and running, so fast they were blurry.

They wore only brown breech-clouts and tall moccasins, their faces streaked with red and yellow and chalk-white. As they raced, a few broke away and streaked to the front, around the river.

Eve took a small pair of binoculars from her beaded pouch and passed them to Violet for a peek. She could make out Benito, further back in the pack but laughing for once as he pressed ahead.

And then she saw why she hadn't seen Lorenzo before. He was also racing, nearly in the lead, leaping gracefully, lightly over a fallen log and sprinting ahead. She suddenly couldn't quite breathe, her throat tight as she watched him.

She thought of MR, her handsome husbands, Clark Gable, the others. Was *this* how she felt with them? Like the whole planet suddenly tilted sideways, and something brand new burst forth. Violet loved it, felt like she could float up into the stars just winking on over their heads, lighter and lighter. It frightened her, too; she was becoming unmoored from what she had thought before. Becoming someone else. Or more herself.

"Looks like north will win," Pedro said. "Look, Lorenzo Serna is in the lead now."

Violet handed the binoculars back to Eve. "The north?"

"The north side of the pueblo," Pedro said with a little, happy fist pump in the air. "I knew he could do it! My cousin was always the fastest of any of us when we were kids, even up the sides of the mountain, like a goat."

"So Mr. Serna is your cousin?" Violet asked, even as she knew she shouldn't be surprised.

"Sure. We all are, in one way or another." Pedro leaped up on his good foot, cheering as Eve laughed. "But he hasn't raced at all since he got back from the war. Looks like he's back in action!"

Violet clambered up onto the wall for a better view of the finish line. The runners swarmed toward it, faster and faster, and Lorenzo did cross it first. She couldn't help herself, she clapped and clapped until her hands ached in the cold.

"Come on!" Eve cried, and grabbed Violet's hand. She had no choice but to follow, tumbling into the middle of the jubilant crowd. The warmth surrounded her, holding her up, carrying her forward, until she found herself face to face with Lorenzo, so close she could feel the heat radiating off him, smell the sweat like green, growing springtime things. He smiled at her, wide and happy, and she laughed.

"So—you're a runner, a silversmith, a blacksmith, a mechanic, a farmer," she said, trying to be light, to not be breathless, to not be *silly*, like some teenage girl clutching her autograph book at a movie premier. MR would never be silly. "What is there you *can't* do?"

His smile widened, and someone tossed him a striped blanket he wrapped around his bare shoulders. "Well, Miss Iowa, I think we both know I can't sing. Or dance."

"A bad failing, true." People jostled around them, congratulating him, clapping him on the shoulder, pushing Violet closer to him. He took her hand. "Come and eat at my aunt's place."

"Oh, I ..." Violet glanced around at the people, *his* people, and felt so shy. "I wouldn't want to intrude. And I should find Mrs. Rogers."

"She's probably already there. And my aunt will be insulted if you don't. She still thinks she didn't thank you enough for what you did for Benny that day in the alley."

"I didn't do anything anyone else couldn't have done."

He shook his head. "Believe me, not many at all would have stopped and done what you did. What you *do*."

"Well—I am pretty hungry, I admit."

He laughed again, and she loved the sound, like those bells. Like the best of life. "You won't be after. My aunties have been cooking for days."

Violet nodded, realizing she wanted nothing more than what was in front of her right now. Lorenzo, a home-cooked meal, a party full of laughter.

Mostly Lorenzo, if she was being really honest with herself.

She almost giggled aloud when she wondered what Jo-Jo would say if she saw Violet now. It all seemed so far away from when they sat in their LA boarding house, wondering about being secretary to a Lady Muckety.

She followed Lorenzo out of the crowd, all of them now dispersing to their family's places for the feasts. They made their way over one of the narrow wooden bridges and between rows of more adobe buildings, along paths so narrow they had to go single-file in places. The air smelled smoky-sweet, the sky like a swirl of light against black overhead, so close she was sure she could touch it. The noise of the plaza grew fainter and fainter, carried away on the wind.

Finally, they emerged at the back of the ancient structures into empty fields, where the mountains loomed like shadow-bursts against the stars, the silver-glow of the moon.

Lorenzo took her hand again, as casually as if he had been doing it for years, but it made her toes tingle. There was quiet between them, but it was as full as anything she had ever imagined.

He led her around another adobe wall, low, crumbling, chunks fallen off to land on the path. He kicked one out of the way before she could trip over it, and she glanced ahead of them. The vision she saw made her gasp.

Ruins, rising up majestically against the night sky, outlined by the moon. What seemed to be a bell tower, empty, gaping, of chipped earthen bricks, with heaps of tumbled-down walls around it, grown over with weeds.

White-painted wooden crosses, marked with names she couldn't read in the shadows, leaned crookedly against each other all around, surrounded by another tumbling wall. It was eerie, haunted, the most silent place she had ever seen, and yet one of the most beautiful. As if everyone who had ever been there watched her, considered her, tried to see if she belonged. If she should be there.

Violet wasn't sure where she *did* belong. She thought of Charles and that imagined LA hillside house, the car, the furs, and she knew that wasn't it, no matter what everyone else told her. But was it this?

She tipped back her head to look at the moon shining through the ruined belfry, a magical spotlight. "What is this place?" she whispered, not wanting to tear that perfect silence.

"The first mission church, built in the 1600s," he answered. "It was bombarded into ruins in 1847."

Violet was shocked. "But why?"

Lorenzo shrugged. "Mexico thought this place was theirs. The US Army disagreed. After Governor Bent was killed, they sent in hundreds of troops with rifles and cannons. Some of our warriors had sided with Mexico, in the simple version of the tale. They locked themselves into the church with the women and children, and the army shelled them for two days." He studied the scene with that unreadable look on his austerely sculpted face. "My grandmother said on the last day, one old woman saw the statue of the Virgin Mary through the smoke. She snatched it from the altar and ran outside. They shot at her, but she was never harmed. That's the statue in the new church now. She was lucky; a hundred and fifty others not so much."

"How hideous," Violet whispered. She could barely fathom it, the horror, the injustice. The way history circled around and around, never changing. She thought of the war, of Lorenzo's lost sister and her husband, of what happened in those ruined walls so long ago.

"And this is your cemetery?" she asked, thinking of that sister and her husband, far away across town.

He nodded. "Each grave is for a period of time, then moved to make room for others. Everyone wants to be near the spirits here, I guess." He gestured toward a row of crosses dislodged and propped again the base of the tower.

"But not your sister."

"Mary found something she loved with all her heart, something she was born for. She couldn't have turned away from it any more than we could change that wind from north to south. It made her very happy, no matter what happened in the end, and that's all we can hope for."

Violet thought of her brother, of the parts of himself he lost in the war. "Do you miss her?"

"Sure. She was like my second little mother when I was a kid, bossy and sweet and full of hugs. But you have to bury your grief sometimes, or the dead can't rest. That's what my grandmother used to say." He shifted the blanket around him. "I imagine I hear her once in a while, especially when I was gone in the war."

"What did she say?"

"She said—I'm all right. And you will be, too. You'll find your real meaning again. And I know she was happy with him." He gave an embarrassed laugh, and ran his long fingers through his hair, leaving the rough-cut strands to fall over his brow. The stars caught on the new silver bracelet on his forearm. "I've never told anyone that. Don't say anything, yeah? I'd get teased to pieces."

"Of course I won't," she said, amazed he would confide in her like that. Give her a tiny, hidden part of himself. "It's the loveliest thing I've ever heard. You should be the writer, not me."

"Me? A poet? Nah." He laughed. "But I didn't want to get all Byron on you here. I wanted to show you someplace before we go eat."

They circled around to the back of the old church, leaving its silent dead and echoes of old tragedy behind, and climbed a low, softly rounded hillock surmounted by the twisted, bare branches of a single tree. Violet could see that in the summer it would be shady and cool, with a view of the village all around.

"I used to come here a lot when I was a kid," Lorenzo said. "Benny and me and our gang, to eat apples we stole from that orchard just over there. We could see anyone coming before we got caught."

They sat down under the branches, leaning back against the strength of the trunk, and Lorenzo wrapped his blanket around both of them, just as Pedro and Eve had done. It felt safe and protected, so warm, just the two of them in the night. She leaned against him, watching the flickering lights from the windows below.

"Were you a very naughty child, then? I have a hard time picturing that," she teased. He was so very serious now, so self-contained. Yet she thought she sometimes saw flashes of old mischief, in the running race, in their dance.

"Oh, we were bad. We'd switch ladders, north to south, back and forth, at night, while everyone was asleep. Mixed the different lengths up. In the mornings, they couldn't get down if they'd slept on the roof. They'd holler at us, and we'd run and run. One time Benny climbed the San Geronimo pole, right in the daylight. Only the sacred clowns are supposed to do that on feast days, but he didn't care. Even when auntie was fined $10." He shook his head. "Eh. Kids."

Violet laughed so hard she fell against his bare shoulder, picturing him as child running away, giggling. "You terrible boy!"

"Didn't you ever get into trouble, Miss Iowa?"

She thought about when she was a child, school and grades being all-important, helping her mother with the chores. Wanting always to be praised for being good. How dull she must have been. "I stole a Cherry Mash from the five and dime once. But my mother caught me, and made me give it back and apologize. I felt *awful*. Could never look at a Cherry Mash again, and it was my favorite."

He laughed, too, light and happy as she had never heard him. She wished that night would never end, that it would go on and on, clutched between her fingers. "That was the worst thing you ever did?"

"I got a C in geography once." And she hadn't really wanted to marry Bill. Hadn't wanted what everyone said she should want, said she was so lucky to have. She felt tied there once, unable to escape. But no more. Millicent gave her that, showed her the bouquet of life all around her, the truth of her own heart.

Just like Lorenzo's sister. Sometimes people were born for something. But what about Lorenzo? What was he born for? She felt like she knew him better than she had anyone else ever, yet so much he kept inside.

"I think that's why I like working for Mrs. Rogers," she said. "I used to be scared of everything, of myself, the world, even though I craved it. I was scared of not being what I was told I should be. She's not afraid of anything. She's free."

A frown flickered across his face. "Money can do that. So many things people call courage, it just takes money."

Violet could see what he meant. It was easier to do what you wanted when you knew you'd never be thrown out on the streets for it, never lose a job, never free yourself from an unhappy marriage, all sorts of things. When rich people did strange things, it was "eccentric," "cute," clucked over in gossip columns. But she knew it wasn't only that, not with MR. "Money helps everything, no doubt about that. But it's not *just* money. It's ... it's like ..." She struggled to put into words what made Millicent—well, Millicent. Beautiful, yes, cultured, curious, daring. They were all true, but none were quite right. She just *was*. And Violet wanted to just be, as well. "I have no money. But I do have myself. My pen, my thoughts, my ideas. I have that mountain over there, just like MR, just like Mabel and Tony, or like you. I can find what I want, and I can grab onto it."

"The mountain won't spit you out."

"No. I hope she never will." She thought of her old home, the cornfields around so far you could see them forever, no anchor of mountains like here. No bright sky to catch onto. "I never want to be without her."

"You won't. When she decides you're hers, that's it. You're stuck, Miss Iowa."

Violet grinned up at him. "Miss New Mexico, if you please. I expect my sash and tiara any day now."

He smiled back, the most wonderful white slash in the night. "Miss New Mexico, then. Just remember that—you *do* have yourself. You don't have to rely on Mrs. Rogers, or anyone, for anything. No one can own you. No one can tell you what you should be."

She rested her head on his shoulder, listening to the steady thrum of his heart, like those drumbeats, counting out the perfect moments of life. "Why did you stop your mischief, in the end? Stealing apples and moving ladders."

"We got older, and then we only thought about impressing girls." He took her hand and raised it to his lips for a quick kiss, making her smile. Making her shiver. "Come on, it's getting cold. I kept you out too long. Let's go find some food."

Violet nodded, knowing she had kept him away from his family, his victory in the race, but she still wished she could just sit there with him. With the stars and the old stones, and that endless, endless night sky, just sit there forever. "You must be chilled after all that running."

"I forgot how it really felt, running, the earth under your feet, part of you." He wrapped his arms around her and held her close, so close they were like one. "I haven't felt so alive in years."

"Neither have I." In fact—she was sure this was the first time she had ever felt really, truly alive, ever.

CHAPTER 25

Violet

AT FRENCHY'S RESTAURANT

"Darlings, isn't it all so *boring*?" Millicent suddenly burst out. Surprised, Violet glanced up from the accounts she was checking for the new hand-painted floor tiles at Turtle Walk. It was a slow day, true, gray and misty outside the windows, the dogs snoozing on their cushions. Yet MR was almost never *bored*. There was always jewelry to make, stores to visit, books to read, house plans to change.

She'd been lying on the chaise for hours, wrapped in a cashmere blanket as Brett sketched her portrait. The small room smelled of Brett's pipe smoke, the piñon burning in the fireplace, Shocking perfume, cozy and snug.

"Well, what are you going to do about it, then?" Brett muttered around her pipe stem. Her charcoal scratched across the paper.

Millicent sighed, and kicked her feet up, bare but for a black silk stocking. "Weren't you supposed to drive out to the gorge with that gorgeous Charles, Vi?"

"Perhaps you hadn't noticed, MR, but it's raining," Violet laughed. "He stayed at the hotel to look at some legal briefs or some such thing."

"Darling, how dreadful! He's not going to be here long. You shouldn't leave him alone. Men are such distractable creatures, like children, really, always needing to be amused. Ronnie wouldn't sit still for a moment, always golfing, skiing, whatever."

Violet bit her lip as she listened to MR seemingly try to match-make again. Whatever had worked for the men in *her* life (and it had worked very well), Violet didn't think that sort of man would like her. And she wouldn't like them. Not that Charles wasn't nice, he was. He was just ...

Just Charles. And MR was right, he had so many good points, a million women would leap on him. But Violet didn't like MR's need to control everything falling on herself so much. She didn't like feeling as if her life was spinning into someone else's control.

"I think he might be okay alone for an hour," she said.

"But will I? Will *you*?" Millicent said, sitting up and tossing aside the blanket to reveal a blue velvet Navajo blouse shimmering with embossed silver buttons. She looked beautiful, of course, her pale hair perfectly curled, her diamond earrings glittering. But her eyes glittered, too, and her cheeks were very red. And she was getting so thin. The doctor had left more medicines, yet they didn't seem to be helping. Violet was very concerned, but MR always brushed her off. "I know, let's go to dinner at Frenchy's. I long for nice duck a l'orange, don't you? We'll fetch your Charles away from his dull legal papers. You come, too, Brett."

Brett stared at her, wide-eyed under her tangle of gray hair. "Me, MR? At Frenchy's? Don't you remember what happened last time? He tossed me out, the old bastard!"

"Of course I remember, and I think he needs taken down a peg or two. It will be fun." And when MR declared something "fun," it would be done, come what may. She pushed herself to her feet, and reached for a red woven shawl to wrap around her shoulders. She took off the bracelets she wore, stacks of turquoise, coral, and rose quartz to her elbows, and tossed them across the room. Violet barely dove to catch them in time, thinking of the time the maid at La Fonda found a diamond necklace on the ceiling light.

"Put those in the safe, Violet darling, and fetch my pearls instead. The triple strand with the ruby clasp. We might as well make it a real party!"

She swept out of the room, the dogs at her heels, thunder rumbling in the distance. Brett shrugged and went back to her sketch. "I guess we are going to a party," she said.

Violet sighed. She had been looking forward to a quiet evening at home, maybe getting a bit of writing done, but she was certainly used to quick plan changes by then. Yet since Charles had arrived, it seemed there were endless dinners at Los Gallos, picnics, hikes, cocktail parties. She'd had so little time to think about what happened at the pueblo festival, and how it felt like that one night changed so much. Nor had she seen Lorenzo. "I suppose we are."

She made her way to the little atrium at the back of the house, where trunks and suitcases and crated works of art were stored, along with the large J. Baum and Company safe. She whirled in the code and pulled open the heavy door.

Velvet boxes were stacked in its dark depths, stamped with Cartier, Tiffany, Verdura. New pieces, silver and turquoise, rested in linen bags, carefully labeled. There was also cash, and checkbooks from all the banks MR used. Violet tucked away the bracelets, and found the red leather case that held the pearls, which had once been MR's debutante gift from her father. There were also earrings, a bracelet, a brooch, clips, but Violet had never seen Millicent wear those pieces except the earrings.

She locked up again, and went up the stairs to take the pearls to Millicent and help her dress. She glanced out the window at the landing, to the now-dry fountain and the faded flowers, and noticed Benito out there. She started to open the sash and call to him, as MR would surely want the car, but he stumbled and nearly tumbled into the empty fountain. He had a hard time hauling himself up again, and his shirt was buttoned crookedly, his hair tangled.

Violet bit her lip, deeply concerned. Was his old problem coming on him again? She'd seen it so often with her brother. All would go well for a time, everyone would hope, only to see those hopes wrecked. But MR wouldn't have anyone question her about Benny, about any of her friends.

"Violet!" Millicent shouted, and Violet hurried toward her bedroom. They could always walk to Frenchy's, it wasn't that far. She found MR at her dressing table, her cream satin dressing gown over her shoulders, carefully outlining her eyes with Max Factor pencil. She still looked gaunt and pale, distracted.

"What will you wear, then? Since it's a party," Violet said, determinedly cheerful.

"The black Charles James cocktail frock, I think, with the three-quarter sleeves. It will do quite nicely, since he moved the buttons a quarter of an inch as I suggested." She reached for her lipstick. "Did you lock up the safe, then?"

Violet found the dress in the wardrobe, and smoothed the full taffeta skirt over its crinoline. "Yes, of course."

Millicent nodded. "We can't be too careful with security these days, you know. I'm not made of money, no matter what my sons think." She suddenly dropped the lipstick with a clatter to the floor, her slender hand shaking. "Damn it all!"

Violet put down the dress and hurried to find the new pill bottle. MR waved her away. "We don't have to go out, MR."

"Of course we do! Do things while you still can, darling, have I taught you nothing? Now hand me those shoes, the black satin stilettos ..."

Violet had only rarely been to Frenchy's with Millicent. It was no favorite of MR's, being "too much like a million other places I've been, darling. I want new, different. I want *me* at last!" she would say with a wave of her ivory cigarette holder. And *me* was now Taos, the mountains and the endless deserts and the pueblo and the people. And if they did go out, not to dinner in someone's home, they went to El Patio or the Sagebrush, or just sat drinking Mable's good red wine in Mabel's leather chairs. (When Mabel wasn't furious with MR, that was. Violet had seen her quarrel and make-up with MR, Frieda Lawrence, and Brett at least ten times in the last month.)

Sometimes, though, visitors to town wanted Frenchy's, and with Millicent they got it. It was an elegant place for Taos, with white damask tablecloths, proper crystal, classical music to go with classical (or classical enough) food. There were delicate sauces and fine wines, very popular with a certain sort of non-Mabel-ish clientele. Frenchy himself was actually Austrian, a man named Theodore Helton, large, mustachioed, high-handed, arrogant, bossy, like a country house chef in a Victorian novel. It wasn't what Violet would have called "fun," but she had to admit she *did* like the duck a l'orange and the floating island.

The sun set early now, making the nights long and silent. MR ate early at home, picking at her plates sparrow-like, but nights out were different. Violet had changed into one of Millicent's hand-me-downs, a gorgeous tea-length dress of lavender-blue silk and tulle with a matching swing coat, its deep shawl collar held with her violet brooch. And when she'd made her way outside, the car was waiting, but luckily no Benito in sight. Only Charles and Brett, no MR.

Violet shrugged. That wasn't so strange. MR had mostly mended her tardy ways in Taos; Frieda and Brett and Martha were amateur cooks who hated their creations to spoil, so Millicent showed up to their houses on the dot. But a restaurant was different. They tended to bring out the *Rogers* in her.

Violet pulled on her gloves, and glanced up into the dark sky. It was cold, wound-around with a sharp mountain wind, the whole sky seeming to lower right over the valley. But the rain had stopped, and a few stars peeked through.

She thought of that dance at the pueblo, lying under the diamond-net of those stars, held safely by the earth under her, the man at her side. Tonight, she floated free, alone, as she had been all her life. Different from what she should be, what everyone wanted.

She smiled at Charles as he kissed her cheek. He actually wore a tuxedo tonight, his shirt front blinding-white in the night, his golden hair glossy with pomade. The perfect city lawyer to the movie stars. "You look beautiful, Violet."

"You're not so bad yourself." She smoothed his satin lapel with her gloved fingertips. He really *was* lovely. MR wasn't wrong about that. Her mother would absolutely adore him. But how did she, Violet, feel? It wasn't at all clear, like it was in the books.

Brett leaned against the hood of the car, wreathed in pipe smoke, wearing her usual loose smock and battered sombrero, watching them closely as if they were a painting. "The hoity-toity ladies at Frenchy's will go absolutely crazy for you, Charles my dear. They never see men as handsome as you there, believe me. You should tell them you're Erroll Flynn."

Charles and Violet laughed, and chatted with Brett about movies and paintings and gossip from Los Gallos (of which there was never a lack), until Millicent finally appeared. She was beyond glamorous in her black taffeta and velvet gown, those gleaming pearls, every wave of blonde hair like the froth of the sea in the moonlight, lips red as if the tube had never tumbled to the floor. As if her hands had never shaken like that. Her mink coat concealed her thinness.

She took Brett's arm tightly, though, as if she needed the support in those beaded satin stilettos, and made her way toward the car. That was when Violet saw Benito did indeed sit behind the wheel, and she feared it was he that needed the help tonight. He could hardly sit up straight. Lorenzo's family insisted that this job was so good for him, was just what he needed, but now Violet wasn't sure. Paulie said his mother "couldn't get along" with the men she cared about. Maybe she was wrong about this, now. Maybe one of them, or both, would end up so hurt in the end.

Charles frowned. "Are you quite sure ..." Violet took his hand and squeezed it.

"Absolutely, my darlings, it's been ages since we went to Frenchy's. Maybe his bechamel sauce has improved," Millicent said, in that ultra-soft voice that brooked no opposition. "You are leaving us much too soon, Charles, so we must celebrate, and persuade you to return very soon. We'll miss you so much. Won't we, Violet darling?"

"Yes, indeed we will," Violet said. Benito swayed again against the car.

"Then how about I ride in the front seat?" Charles said. "I can even take a turn at the steering wheel, I've always wanted to try one of these models. Mr. Suarez and I can talk manly things and not bore you ladies."

Violet shot him a grateful glance. "You mean you don't want to hear about the new length of Dior skirts this season?"

"I want to hear about anything at all, if *you're* the one talking," he said gallantly. "But I'm a pretty good driver, even on roads like these. I'd love to give it a spin."

Violet nodded, and climbed into the backseat between Millicent and Brett before MR could protest. Even though ot wasn't far, she Millicent couldn't walk too much that night. They jolted over the rutted roads, Violet guiding Charles with directions until they got into town and made their way to the lights of the restaurant.

Frenchy himself waited inside the door, as if to guard his white-draped tables and candelabras and silver, domed trays from the unworthy. He was not a tall man, but stocky, clad in a dirty chef's jacket, his toque hiding the bald dome of his head, a flamboyant mustache flipping around his reddened face, cigarette perched in the corner of his lips.

He glanced down his long, purplish nose at Millicent's motley little party, even though he had certainly welcomed her floridly before. He flicked his stained fingers at Brett.

"We have a dress code, Madame Rogers," he snapped in his Teutonic accent. "Ladies *must* wear gowns. Being in the middle of nowhere does not mean standards can slip."

Millicent glared in return, her dark eyes narrowed, black as the night and twice as frosty. Without looking away from him, she took off her mink coat and draped it around Brett's smock-clad shoulder. Brett shrieked and swirled, brandishing Toby in delight.

"I'm sure a $20,000 mink is "standard" enough for your hole in the wall," MR said. "And don't give me your shit again, *Monsieur* Frenchy. Or shall I say Herr Hutter? You were probably my first husband's boot-black in Austria. Now, come along, darlings, I am utterly famished."

The young maitre'd scurried around Frenchy, who had been rendered silent and quite frozen for probably the first time in his life, and led them to a large, round table in the center of the room, sparkling with gold-edged china, etched silver, vases filled with fragrant hot-house lilies and roses. Everyone already seated stared at them, wide-eyed, whispering behind their napkins, but MR didn't even glance at them.

"Quite an entrance," Charles whispered in Violet's ear as he held out her chair, making her giggle.

"One things about this job—you can never say it's predictable or boring," she answered. She wondered if a California lawyer's wife could say the same thing.

She certainly admired this particular lawyer's *sang-froid*, though; every bit as *froid* as MR. He chatted casually with Brett about the British Museum, tasted and nodded as the wine bottle was elaborately presented, then discreetly moved Benny's glass a bit further away. He smoothed the evening over without even seeming to try, talking and laughing pleasantly. Even Millicent was smiling again when the duck was presented on its silver platter.

Millicent glanced around the room, twirling her pearls around one finger, and went still when she noticed a young man sitting alone in the corner. He seemed young, as handsome as a summer sky, gold-streaked brown hair, vivid green eyes behind spectacles, an open notebook in front of him as if to note down what those beautiful eyes saw. "Vi, darling, do we know him?"

Brett paused in taking heaping spoonfuls of caviar to study him. "Earl Stroh. Not Earl as in Strathmore or Spencer, just his first name, in your odd American habit. Quite a fine young artist. I heard he wants to travel to Bolivia, but he can't quite afford it. He's a great perfectionist about art, just like you, MR."

"How interesting." MR waved one finger to a passing waiter, who immediately came to a halt to listen to her whisper. The waiter went straight to Mr. Stroh, who turned to stare at their table in astonishment. He gathered up his notebooks, his glass, his patched jacket, and came to join MR, as men always did.

"It's a great honor, Mrs. Rogers, a great honor," he stammered. "I saw you once at the Melmont Gallery in New York, but was too shy to approach you."

"Aren't you a darling?" Millicent cooed, leaning closer to him, watching him as if he was the only person in the room. "Will you show me some of your work?"

As Millicent enthused over Mr. Stroh's use of color and line, Violet smiled ruefully at Charles. "Everything else does take a backseat to art here," she murmured.

He smiled back at her, and popped a lump of pate into his mouth as the waiter brought out platters of appetizers, poured out more wine. "Delicious. And I have to say I do like hearing about art. I'm getting quite the education on this trip."

"Same with me. I never imagined a place like this before." Or a life like the one she had found with MR.

"Law school has nothing on the School of Rogers."

Violet laughed. "Nothing else does. But surely your parents

must be so proud of what you do with that old education! Lawyer to the stars."

He shook his head. "I think they'd rather I just came home, to be honest. Take up my dad's practice, get married, buy a house down the street from them. Give them some grandkids."

She sighed in understanding. "I know what you mean. Not about the law practice, but about families and what they want as opposed to what *we* want. What we need." She took a bite of caviar on toast, thinking of her mother's letters, the hints that were becoming less and less hint-like.

"And what do you want, then, Violet Redfield?"

She opened her mouth to answer, even though she really had no answers yet. Not even to herself. But before she could say anything, a sudden ragged shout broke the hum of the restaurant. Benito yelled out incoherently, jumping up to shove Mr. Stroh off his chair, dishes clattering and shattering from the table. Brett shook her head and lit another pipe, while Millicent struggled to pull the strong young man away.

"You pay attention to that bastard, a stranger, and ignore me, like always!" Benito shouted. His eyes were bright, too bright, like he was caught in a ravaging fever. Which Violet knew he was. The fever of drink. "Like I'm just some stupid Injun who can't interest some high and mighty empress like you. Bitch."

"Benny ..." Millicent whispered.

He grabbed her arm and shook her like a rag doll, while Violet cried out desperately for him to stop. "You can take all your money and shove it up your lily-white ass ..."

"Hey! That's no way to talk to a lady," Earl Stroh interrupted, jumping to his feet and taking a swing at Benito.

Benito, despite his inebriated state, drew back his fist in one move and slammed it into Earl's jaw, catching him by surprise and sending him flying onto the table. Food flew around him. Charles shoved Violet behind him, protecting her as he and a waiter caught Benito. They twisted his arms behind him and wrestled him away as Millicent knelt beside Earl. Benito broke away and fled into the night.

Frenchy himself appeared, his face bright red, mustache bristling. "Madame Rogers! I may only be a boot-black, but there are rules of behavior in *my* restaurant. Leave now!"

Millicent had gone utterly white, her eyes burning feverishly, coals in the snow. Her fingers trembled as she took Violet's hand, and stumbled a bit on the edge of a carpet fringe. Violet took her weight against her own shoulder and steered her toward the door, Brett, Charles, and Mr. Stroh hurrying after them, surrounding MR like an honor guard.

"And *this* is why we must have standards," Frenchy snapped. Millicent opened her satin evening bag and took out a wad of cash, thrusting it into his stained fingers. Violet was pretty sure they would not be dining there again. She didn't mind too much, she just wished they could have had that floating island first.

Benny was nowhere to be seen outside, and she wondered what would happen to him now. Would even MR's patience be snapped, and he would be fired? What would they say, were already saying, out at the pueblo?

The car was still there by the curb, but of course the keys had somehow vanished with Benny, who had taken them from Charles when they arrived.

"Are there any taxis around here?" Charles muttered. Millicent was silent, vanished off into that Millicent World where she sometimes flew away, unable to be touched.

"I can drive you," Mr. Stroh said. "I'm right over there. Just a little, old coupe, but it still gets me around."

"You're so kind," Millicent whispered, and brushed his battered cheek with her red-tipped fingers. Her gloves had been lost somewhere in the scuffle, and Brett still wore the fur, but Millicent didn't even seem to notice the chill. She never did seem to notice, not when she was there in Millicent World. "I am so terribly sorry about all this. My mother would be appalled at such a scene."

It was indeed a tiny car, but they piled on top of each other, and it *did* get them back to the guesthouse in relative speed and safety. Ethel clucked and clattered, wanting to call the doctor over her employer's protests, while Brett paced the hallway. Violet spent an hour helping Millicent change into her nightgown, climb under the covers, close her eyes, and she waited until MR seemed to be asleep.

Violet found Charles in the tiny foyer, just the two of them in the faint light of one lamp. He had loosened his tie and unbuttoned the top fastenings of his dress shirt, his golden hair adorably rumpled.

"Wow, you weren't lying about this job not being boring," he said with a laugh.

She laughed, too, ruefully. "See? You never know what's going to happen next."

"But are you sure it's really safe? That guy—he's not the usual sort of chauffeur you see with someone like Mrs. Rogers."

"No, I guess he's not. But I'm not the usual sort of secretary, either. Mrs. Rogers does her own thing." She leaned against the wall, suddenly so tired, weary of the whole strange evening. She knew MR wanted to help Benito, as she wanted to help everyone, and Violet loved that about her. But Charles was right, too. Was it safe? "He only hurts himself, really. I'll watch closely over Mrs. Rogers tonight."

"But who will watch over *you*?"

She started to say that *she* would watch over her, that she always had. Suddenly, though, everything seemed to press down on her. The ceiling, the sky itself, this land where she felt so free, seemed to hold her captive, and she couldn't quite breathe. She was afraid she would start to cry, and closed her eyes tightly.

She felt his arms close around her, and he smelled so delicious, felt so warm. Felt so *normal*, part of a world she had never really known, a world of safe prosperity, of belonging. A place to hide in plain sight. It could never be hers forever, not deep-down real, but oh how lovely it felt just then. She leaned into him, letting him hold her up.

"Vi." His voice was rough. He tipped her chin up with the tip of his finger and kissed her. It was a very nice kiss indeed, exactly what a kiss in a movie would be. Sweet, soft, just a bit rough. Yet she felt so distant from it all, watching it from that ceiling. It didn't make the world crack wide open as Lorenzo did.

His head came up, his eyes full of questions. She had no answers for him, not yet. "Thank you," she sighed, and rested her forehead on the fine wool of his tuxedo jacket. It felt like the dumbest possible thing to say, yet there those words were, hanging between them. The whole strange night had driven all the words out of her head.

"I—damn it all, Violet. I like you. A lot," he said, that roughness still in his voice, a hint of impatience. "I know you're committed to this job, and that's very important. But someday ..."

"Someday?" she whispered.

"It's just—can I write to you for a while? Maybe meet up again soon? I've never met a girl quite like you, and I want to know more. I want to know—well, just everything, I guess."

Violet laughed. She wanted to know more about herself, too. It seemed impossible. "Of course we can write. I'd like that a lot."

He nodded hesitantly. "And—you'll be careful here, yeah? Let me know if you need anything. Janet and Adrian are worried."

She studied him carefully in the lamplight, and his eyes did indeed seem clouded. "Worried about what? They were the ones who sent her here."

"About their friend, of course. It's no secret that her health is, well, not great, and the altitude can't help heart problems."

Violet's throat tightened. "It's true there's no secret she's had some problems. But she loves it here, we both do. It might not have looked that way tonight, but everyone in Taos really looks after each other. I'll be fine here with her, as long as she needs me. She'll be okay, too."

He nodded, yet still there was that shade of doubt. "I'm glad to hear it. Just know you can turn to me whenever you need to. You're never alone."

"No." As if in a sudden flash of sunlight, she saw that was true. All the loneliness she felt when growing up, the loneliness of knowing she did not fit in, was not understood, no longer lingered inside of her. She had so much now. She even had herself.

He flashed her a sudden grin, and said, "And I'd be lying if I didn't tell you you're a beautiful woman, Violet Redfield." He kissed her again, this time a bit harder, a bit hotter, and she smiled against his lips.

"And you are a beautiful man, Charles Rivers." She could feel him watching her as she made her way up the stairs into the waiting darkness, but she didn't look back. MR's door was ajar, and Violet peeked in on her. The medicine bottle sat uncapped on the nightstand, and Millicent seemed asleep under her quilts, her bright hair rumpled, the dogs pooled around her. She glanced up at Violet with bleary eyes, then rolled around and went fast asleep, snoring softly.

"Well, Fan, I guess it's just us," Violet said to the dog. She shrugged off her evening coat and kicked away her high heels onto the woolen carpet. She was so tired, her head aching, but she knew she wouldn't sleep that night. She peered out the window to the glowing moon, the arroyo beyond. A coyote howled somewhere in the distance.

What if it was all LA, skyscrapers and glass and smoke wherever the eye could see?

She shook her head, and tucked the blankets closer around MR, listening to her shallow breath. She capped the pill bottle and turned out the light. "Someday," Charles had said, and Violet knew too well what that "someday" held. Her friend would be gone. It was a thought she couldn't bear.

"Be well, MR, darling," she whispered, and shut the door.

As she tiptoed toward her own room, she saw the night was not so still and quiet after all. The door to the small office was half-open. When she looked inside, she saw the safe stood open, too. She ran to peer inside, her stomach aching. The Cartier box containing Millicent's ears of wheat clips were gone, some emerald earrings, along with a stack of cash Violet knew was there when she fetched the pearls. Luckily the pearls themselves were still on Millicent's dressing table

Frightened, Violet ran out into the corridor, calling for Ethel. "We have to call the police," she gasped. "MR has been robbed!"

Ethel, wrapped in her dressing gown, still sleepy-eyed, just shook her head wryly. "I don't think we need to do that," she said. "I saw that Benito running by not an hour ago, a bag in his hand. I didn't think anything of it then, but now ..."

Now. Violet sat down heavily, sadness and anger bearing down on her. Now something, even if it wasn't the police, would have to be done. But how to tell Millicent what was happening under her own roof, without being incinerated in the temper-flames?

CHAPTER 26

Violet

"You're sure it was him?"

Violet stared up at Lorenzo. She couldn't read anything of his thoughts, he stood perfectly still, perfectly expressionless as he gazed steadily into the distance. She slowly nodded, and rubbed her hands over her arms in their gingham sleeves. It was a cool, brisk day, and they were sheltered in Mabel's garage, but she still shivered. She had hardly slept an hour, going over every situation there could possibly have occured in Millicent's house, only to know she had to tell Lorenzo the truth.

At least Charles had left early that morning, driving back to Santa Fe to catch a train home and take up his important business. She couldn't deal with him as well as all this.

"I didn't see him take it, but Ethel did, and she's not one to fib," Violet whispered. "He was awfully drunk after dinner, I'm afraid. That business at Frenchy's ..."

Lorenzo's jaw tightened. "I heard he was playing poker at the Taoseno last week, too. He must have lost a great deal. Damn fool."

"Mrs. Rogers won't call the police, and Ethel won't say

anything. Those pieces are not ones she wears often. But we did think Tony should know."

Lorenzo shook his head. "You're good people, Violet, all of you. Even your Mrs. Rogers, I admit. But it might do him good to sit in a cell, sober, for a while, and clear his fool head."

"So you think we *should* have called the police?"

"No." He hugged her close, some of the granite cracking. "You were right to come here. Where is Ben now?"

"I have no idea. We haven't really seen him since Frenchy's, and he hasn't shown up again. What should we do? We're actually supposed to go camping, if you can believe that."

His brow arched doubtfully. "Mrs. Rogers? Camping?"

Violet had to laugh. "I know. She says she really wants to see some of the Navajo lands, and she's found a guide to take us. Should I put her off the idea?" She hadn't been sure it was a good plan, anyway, with MR's health lately, but Millicent wouldn't be put off once she wanted to do something.

"Nah, it's probably good to get her out of the way, let Tony do his family work. I'll come camping with you, keep an eye on you all."

"Oh, could you?" she cried, afraid she sounded much too eager. To be with Lorenzo under the stars again sounded too wonderful to be true! "But your work ..."

"It can all keep for a couple of days. Besides, I heard you were keeping company with some movie star fella. Can't let him have the whole stage to himself."

Violet laughed giddily. "Jealous, then, Mr. Serna? How delightful." She felt like she should write it all down. Later. Once she kissed him.

MILLICENT—PLANNING ON GOING CAMPING

I leaned back on the seat of the Chrysler, insisting, despite the chilly day, that the top be left down, and the sky, clear—endless—empty blue, stretched over me. Catching me if I flew off the seat and into the ether, as I was sure I might. The shot the doctor gave me that morning before we set off toward Gallup, four hours away, made me feel distinctly weightless. Light as a puff of cotton. I would have to be certain to ask for that again.

The doctor hadn't been too happy to hear of my plans to attend the downs at the Gallup Stadium and then sleep under the stars. Dear Dr. Pond was always lecturing me about my diet and exercise and rest and ordering me new prescriptions. Like all the doctors, he treated me like I was about eight years old—"mustn't," "shouldn't," "can't." But it's true few were as good-looking as Pond. I never minded nodding along to his words even if I ignored them.

But I didn't tell him all my plans for this weekend. After we stayed at the El Rancho Hotel to watch the post-race dances, we would camp out under the stairs, the desert and the mountains all mine until sunrise.

"I will be terribly careful, doctor, of course I will. Violet will be with me, she is certainly prudent. And I did hear there was an extraordinary necklace for sale there, by a Zuni jeweler. I must have it. It calls to me, I'm sure." That was true enough. A Zuni necklace of two strands of turquoise tabs and a large pendant, three pounds or more. Wonderful.

The doctor nodded as he tucked away his instruments into his valise. "Tell me those plans again, Mrs. Rogers?"

I shrugged and drew my velvet bed-jacket around my shoulders. My horribly bony old shoulders. "We'll be quite a caravan, two cars and the station wagon. We'll stop in Santa Fe to fetch dear

Mirandi, you know her, she owns the Thunderbird Shop. She's helping Hal Bynner with his new volume of poetry, he says he'll come and he's sure to keep us entertained. Then to Albuquerque to fetch my son Arturo and his fiancée. Dusty is her name, though I'm sure it can't be her real one." I hadn't met Dusty before. She sounded quite the character, and Arturo would be lucky if he could hold onto her. Brett would come, of course, and that lovely Stroh fellow. "I'm sure they'll be speeding away while Violet fusses over me."

Dr. Pond hesitated. "Not your driver?"

I frowned and fussed with the lace trim of my jacket. No one had seen, or at least told me they'd seen, Benny since that spectacle at Frenchy's. He'd quite vanished into the blue sky, somewhere even I couldn't find him, help him, the beautiful boy. "Violet hired us a professional driver, and a guide. We'll be quite fine."

"Well, sounds like there are plenty of people to keep an eye on you, then, and at least I know a good doctor in Gallup," Dr. Pond said as he reached for his overcoat. "Don't hesitate to come right home, or even head to Santa Fe, if you feel the slightest bit faint again. I don't like your pulse today."

"I'm strong as an ox," I fibbed. I was getting so good at that. "Don't worry, doctor, potions will see me through, and your bills will be paid promptly."

As soon as he was gone, I reached for one of the pill bottles and swallowed three tablets, two more than I should. Once I felt steady, I dragged myself out of bed, out of my bed-jacket and nightgown, and into one of Martha's dresses, a red and blue print of tiny flowers, with a Charles James swing coat of black velvet over it, fastened with ruby-rose buttons. Thank heaven my pearls hadn't gone missing on that misbegotten night! But where were my emeralds, my clips, my money, my *Benny*?

I couldn't face any more of it. Tony's silence, Violet's accusing eyes, Mabel's gloating.

I sat down at my dressing table and slowly, so very slowly, started to paint on my face, curl my hair. Everything moved slowly now. Even walking across the room felt like a terrible effort. Climbing the Alps or something. Just as I had found my Taos, my Shangri-La, my spirit ebbed away from me! It rolled faster and faster every moment.

I longed for the wild, reckless, unknowing joy of my childhood again, just for a while. A second! Like falling all-in, no matter what, tumbling into new delights, new vistas.

I remembered how it all felt, but my heart didn't. It would cease all too soon. I felt the ice of death reaching for me too often now. Yet I could make a little more time. Time to finish my Turtle Walk, see my dances, have my own Thanksgiving party—make sure Violet was set right in life. The darling, foolish girl needed security, safety, then she would find lust. She'd see that.

And then there was time for just a little more Taos in my soul. A little more of the truth I'd found there.

I reached for my eyebrow pencil and carefully feathered in tiny lines, turning my head from one side to the other in the triple mirror, watching the sun catch on the spun-sunshine curls of my hair. At least *that* was still there. Beauty. My mother had always said if I had that, I had everything. I was her prize in satin hairbows.

Beauty, in people, mountains, art, jewels, it was all, everything. It was everything I would leave behind me.

And all I truly possessed, in the end of the day. All that waited for me, in one form or another.

The stadium at the center of the Gallup fairgrounds positively seemed to tremble as Lorenzo searched for a place to park in the haphazard acre of gravel yard, amid akimbo, dusty trucks and open-topped cars. Knots of girls with their glossy dark hair and velvet and calico finery, their gleaming turquoise jewelry, sipped orange sodas and giggled at handsome, gangly boys in jeans and printed cotton shirts, their long braids tied back with bandanas. Men more handsome than any she had ever seen, really, and she couldn't blame the girls for their giggles and dimples. Tall, slim, pretending aloofness, their skin and hair glowing like strong, youthful gods. Silvery bells whistled and sang in the wind, and drums called to her in the distance, along with the pounding of dancing feet, the neighing of horses, the swell of singing voices, rising and lowering. The rich smell of baking bread and sweets, beer, dust, people-people-people. Life life life.

She studied it all through her dark glasses, let it wrap around her like a sable stole, warm and eternal, as if it could bind her to earth always. That hovering sense of mortality that had hung around her all day and night tightened its ropes, yet always there was this beauty. The beauty here was surely the highest circle of life, a glimpse of the workings of the universe, such as Renaissance scientists sought, and it was enough for her. For now.

"MR?" Violet asked, and Millicent nodded at her. Violet and Arturo helped her from the car, one holding onto each arm, dear, pretty, blonde Dusty hovering behind, until she could find her footing on the gravel. To plant her moccasins in place. Violet turned away, but not Arturo. I hadn't seen him in quite a while, my tall, quiet, handsome son, and he had looked shocked and worried ever since he arrived. It was what I liked about Peter, too, he was quiet, hard to read, left me alone. Even they wouldn't be able to do that much longer.

I glanced back at Dusty, Arturo's newly-presented fiancée. I wasn't sure it would really last, she seemed too smart, tough, outdoorsy, so pretty in her Debbie Reynolds way, all sunny-gold in blue calico and velvet. "Dusty, my dear, perhaps you could hold my arm and help me into the stadium? I can show you where to go, and I know Violet is dying to fetch us some fry bread and cider, it was a long drive. Arty, darling, can you help Violet?"

The girl looked surprised, but nodded eagerly. "Of course, Mrs. Rogers."

I took her arm and made my way toward the music, the noise, the lights, toward what seemed like all of life itself in one moment.

CHAPTER 27

Millicent

I t was very late by the time we made our way to the El Rancho Hotel, with most of the rooms along the narrow, snaking corridors filled with dancers and horse racers. Millicent smiled and studied, and twirled one blonde curl around her gloved finger, examining each empty room that could be found until one was discovered at the back of the hotel. It was large enough for her, Mirandi, Violet, Dusty, Fanny, and a rollaway in the corner for Brett as she snored so horribly. As Lorenzo and Stroh carried in the luggage, Millicent examined each corner and crevice carefully.

Cotton draperies and bedspreads in approximations of Native patterns covered every surface, and the carpet seemed clean enough. There were no smudges on the glasses, and the bath was clean. The light bulbs in the leather lampshades even turned on and off. The worried-looking manager waited in the doorway with specially delivered bottles of hooch, too.

"Not the Ritz, is it, MR?" Mirandi teased. She sat down on one of the trunks, her yellow ruffled skirt like a jonquil.

"It's quite charming," Millicent answered, and the manager sighed in relief. She watched him pour out the booze with a grateful smile, lit a cigarette in her onyx holder, nodded when

Violet offered to draw a bath, but really she was so very, very tired. Aching deep in her bones. She just wanted to crawl under the blankets with her whiskey and her new, treasured necklace. It really was extraordinary, unique, like the Hope Diamond of the Southwest. She felt triumphant—but still that weariness. Damn it all.

"A warm bath will help," Violet said softly, as if she could read that pain on Millicent's face. Damn her, too.

As the others unpacked their nightgowns and cold creams and books, chattering about the day, Millicent let Ethel help her out of her heavy velvet skirt and jacket, and she slipped gratefully into the hot, rose-scented water. It always helped soak some of that pain away, and it was silent with the door shut, thin cardboard that it was. She slid deeper and deeper, listening to Violet and Mirandi gossip, Dusty talk about the gorgeous horses they'd watched race, Brett bang Toby on the table and Fanny bark-bark-bark. She gulped down her drink and reached for another, the steam wreathing her towel-wrapped head. How weirdly perfect life was in just that moment. How she wanted it to go on-on-on.

But it never did. When she emerged from the bathroom, fluffing her damp curls, wrapped in her peach satin dressing gown, the laughter in the packed bedroom had faded and Brett was clearly angry about something. Violet, Mirandi, and Dusty, such gentle, polite, Midwestern girls, sat in their crisp cotton pajamas and stared at Brett as she shouted in the corner.

"Whatever is the matter?" Millicent exclaimed. "Must I play nanny? You were all fine an hour ago."

"I wasn't told to pack properly," Brett snapped. She whirled around to reveal an old, graying nightgown patched and mended. Of course she had been told to pack nightclothes! Millicent realized with deep chagrin that Brett probably did not *have* proper nightclothes, and she should have sent her some. She never embarrassed her friends.

Thankfully, she had packed rather in a hurry herself. "Oh, that's nothing," she said airily. She took off her dressing gown and spun to reveal the long rip along the back of the matching satin gown, left by some long-ago lover and forgotten.

Mirandi clapped delightedly, sitting on her knees in the middle of one of the beds, while Violet and Dusty and then even Brett giggled. "Oh, my!" Mirandi said. "That must have been quite an exciting evening."

"I'm sure I don't know what you mean," Millicent answered haughtily. She went to the table where the box containing her precious necklace, as well as several bottles of wine, sat, and she poured glasses for everyone.

"I'm sure you do remember. You just don't want to say which one it was," Mirandi said, and lounged back on the pillows with her drink. "Look at us. An all-girls-together night. I haven't had one in ages."

Violet glanced at Millicent. "I'm not sure MR has *ever* had an all-girls-together night."

"Of course I have! I've had girlfriends," she protested. "Debs when I was young, ladies I meet at fashion shows. When I was young, when you were in your cradles, we went to speakeasies together, and hid behind boxes at the opera with our flasks, and went to shops ..." She stopped suddenly, thinking of the girls she had always read about in books, the Marches and the Brontës and such, and realized she had never had a night out with friends like *that*. "But we didn't whisper together at two in the morning."

"So no slumber parties at all?" Mirandi asked.

Millicent poured out more wine. "Not one. I'm not sure my mother or nannies ever said the words 'slumber parties.' What do we do?"

Brett lit her pipe and chewed on the misshapen end. "Well, don't ask me. I never did, either. Not proper in the best English homes, I'm sure."

"You read movie mags, and gossip about how dishy Cary Grant is," Mirandi said. "But you surely know him in person, MR, and everyone else dishy in the world, so that's no fun. We do each other's hair, trade lipsticks, tell fortunes and read palms ..."

"Wear someone else's lipstick?" Millicent gasped.

"Or play Never Have I Ever," Violet said. "Or Truth or Dare?"

Curious, Millicent asked, "And what are those? Something like bridge or mah-jongg?"

The others stared at each other. "Nothing like bridge, thankfully," said Dusty.

"Well," Mirandi said, opening another bottle. "Never Have I Ever—someone says something they haven't done, and if you've done it, you take a drink. Never have I ever kissed in an elevator."

"Never?" Brett drawled around her pipe-stem.

"I have never stopped at a fortuitous floor for such a thing."

"Neither have I," Dusty sighed. "Not many elevators where I come from! There's one at the Makeham's Department Store, but the elevator operator is a spotty fifteen-year-old. No Cary Grant."

"Brett?" Millicent asked. Brett just shook her head. "I bet Violet never has, either. What a dull lot you are."

Violet took a deep gulp of the wine. "Not quite true, MR."

They all stared at her with wide eyes. "Whhh-at? You, my Violet?" Millicent gasped.

"I'm hardly Melanie Hamilton! I've done a few naughty things in my life," Violet said. "The night before Bill went to war. We went to dinner at the nicest restaurant in town, which happens to be atop one of the only buildings with an elevator. A very slow, small elevator. I thought—well, I thought then that I should. In case."

"How was it?" Mirandi whispered.

Violet glanced away and poured more wine. "It wasn't exactly *Forever Amber* or anything. Didn't last long, since the elevator wasn't *that* slow. But it was—nice. He seemed happy about it. I was glad afterwards."

They all nodded sympathetically, and Millicent took a box of French chocolates from her suitcase to pass around. It seemed like the thing to do while trading confidences at a slumber party. "Oh, my darling Vi," she said, and gave Violet the best of the caramel centers. "That was all? He was gone forever after that?"

"There wasn't time to drop my silky drawers, MR," Violet said, her throat sounding tight. But she ate her chocolate.

"One day, my dearest, you will not be in an elevator of any kind, slow or not, and you will see how *delicious* it all is."

Mirandi kicked her hot pink-painted bare toes in the air. "I bet that LA lawyer could be deee-lightful!"

Millicent laughed. "No doubt about it. Those hands ..."

Violet laughed, but she wouldn't look at any of them, just gazed into her empty wine glass until Dusty refilled it. Millicent worried she had more matchmaker work ahead of her when it came to Violet. Or maybe Violet just needed more wine and a convenient elevator.

"I'm sure Millicent has done *lots* of things in elevators," Mirandi said.

"Of course I have, my dears. The Empire State Building, for instance. And as none of you seem to have recorders about you, I'll tell you all about it ..."

VIOLET

The whispers and laughter slowly faded as the light turned pale behind the patterned curtains. Brett did indeed snore from her cot in the corner, a symphony of crescendos that Violet had never even heard in a farmyard. Sheep, cows, violins, maybe a llama. At least, it all made MR giggle on the double bed with Violet, but then the deep shadows of night closed in, and Violet watched her sink under the weight of that insomnia that laid on her so heavily lately. It kept Violet awake, too.

She propped some pillows under her head and studied the

shadowed room. Mirandi and Dusty slept peacefully under their striped blankets, just as Fanny did on her cushions. Millicent lay quietly, yet Violet saw the shine of her eyes staring into the night, seeing who knew what.

Violet reached for the bottle of lavender oil Lorenzo's aunt gave her, distilled from her own garden, and softly, silently rubbed Millicent's temples until her shoulders relaxed and those dark eyes drifted shut. Hopefully she would sleep before they had to take out Dr. Pond's pill bottles. Millicent's breath was ragged, and when Violet discreetly checked, her pulse raced in her thin wrist. Violet feared the idea of camping in the desert was indeed a terrible one.

"Violet, have you really only ever kissed one man? Never more? Just kissed one man your whole life?"

Shocked by the question, her fears of camping forgotten for the moment, Violet glanced around to make double-sure everyone else slept. Not that they would care at all. They were women of the world who did what they wanted. "When you're not married, sexy-times can be hard to come by where I'm from. Someone is always watching you."

Millicent laughed softly. "And yet the movies love to show Midwestern square-jawed men and flaxen-haired women romping in haystacks!"

Violet laughed, too. "Only if you like an itchy backside, I guess, and I sneeze at haying season. And once you do have sex with someone, that's it—you're theirs for life."

"So you've never had sex?"

Violet hesitated for an instance. She'd never told anyone this, not ever. But this was Millicent. Millicent never judged. "There was someone once. At a canteen I volunteered at in the next town just after the war. He was from Rhode Island, on his way home. He didn't expect anyone to belong to him forever."

"Violet!" Millicent breathed, surprised but not surprised, not condemning, just as Violet knew she would be. "Was he handsome?"

"Very. And he was shipping out the next day. We'd had a bit to drink, I liked him, I—felt sorry for him, I guess. He'd had a hard time in the war. I'm not sorry I did it. It was nice. It's just—well, neither he nor Bill were like your own husbands. Counts and movie stars and skiers and South Americans. I've never wanted to try it again, really." Not until she laid wrapped in Lorenzo's blanket under the stars. But that was something she kept locked up deep in her own heart for now. Something she held back even from MR.

Millicent grabbed her hand, the platinum bands of the rings on her thin fingers cold and hard and steady. "Oh, Vi, you must! You are too young and beautiful to not try again. You don't *have* to be in love, of course, for it to be good, but if you are—oh, darling. It's a heaven I've never found for myself, not for long. If it's just a matter of contraception ..."

Violet felt her cheeks flame. "No! No, no—I understand how it works. And when I do find someone ..."

"Which you will very soon."

Violet shook her head. She *had* found someone. But she couldn't be part of his world, not really. "I will know what to do, MR. Don't worry about me."

"Oh, but I do worry." They leaned back against the pillows, Millicent's arm wrapped around Violet, holding them in a cloud of Shocking perfume.

"When I was a little girl," MR whispered, "I would make up stories about my future family. The gorgeous husband I would one day have, the son—because men need a son. The twin daughters. Those daughters, of course, never appeared, but I could see them so clearly in my mind. One dark, like I was back then, one with red-gold curls. Both of them so sweet, so smart, mine alone. My daughters. I would have done anything for them. Do you see, Violet?"

Violet stared at Millicent's cameo profile in the moonlight. "I'm not sure I do."

"I am loyal to those who are loyal to me, true blue through and through. I have plenty of faults, can be a great trial, but loyalty is not something I lack. You never have to worry, Vi. Not one moment. I will be with you."

After a few minutes, she went slack next to Violet, her arm falling away, as if she slept at last. As if some burden was gone. Violet drew in a deep, unsteady breath, afraid she might cry at the confidences only nighttime could bring. She turned onto her other shoulder and closed her eyes.

She herself had almost tumbled down into dreams when she heard Millicent whisper, "I feel it, too, you know. The beauty of that long black hair. It catches me somewhere deep in my tummy, that quiet, strong manliness. I've never known anything quite like it."

Violet squeezed her eyes more tightly shut, hardly knowing what she could ever say to that. Did Millicent talk about— Lorenzo? How did she know? How *could* she know the way he "caught Violet deep in her tummy," his smile, his understanding, his rare laughter, the way he kissed. The way he just seemed to know her, and she him.

Millicent went on. "But you must take care of yourself first, Violet. Be sensible. Charles is a rich man, he adores you, I can tell. He can see you through your own career, give you everything. Be careful, my dear one. I know how the world really works."

Violet couldn't breathe. MR did indeed "know how the world worked," more than anyone else. Violet was only just beginning to learn the world, her own world, her own heart. Her writing, her home in Taos, Lorenzo. He was an odd man, quiet, laid-back, hard to read—but he saw her. She knew he did.

Charles Rivers? What did he see in her? What life did he want to lead?

Above all, how could she ever leave, ever let down, MR?

She just nodded silently, and Millicent finally slept. But Violet couldn't close her eyes until dawn.

MILLICENT—CAMPING

"Go on, darlings, I'll catch up!" I called, waving everyone ahead as they left the car and made their way deeper into the desert. I felt deeply tired after the excitement of the fair, the half-sleepless night, the need to smile and laugh in the car as we drove and drove. But I had my precious packet of peyote tucked safely into my handbag.

My heart was pounding in that old, tiresome way, making even my feet heavy in their moccasins, my eyes ache behind dark glasses. It had been a hot day for the season, a long drive down dirt trails to that place called Canyon del Muerto, yet still I pressed ahead, eager to find something new yet again. Once I heard that name, I knew it was the place I needed. The place where I could find what I sought. The canyon of death.

The others climbed ahead of me up the steep walls of a canyon, Brett surprisingly spry as an old mountain goat in her flopping sombrero. The men joking as they carried the crates and tents, Arturo and Dusty giggling and holding hands. How adorable they were! Sweet and romantic in a way I had never been, could never be. Not really.

Violet turned and watched me for a moment, her face creased beneath her straw boater with its new coral and turquoise hatband that matched her striped jacket, her slim jeans. She was becoming such a part of this place, sun-touched, serene, my sweet Vi who didn't yet know her own strength. She could be, could do, all I could not. She had a young, strong heart; she had to live for us both for years to come. I just hoped she had listened to my advice last night. Thought about it carefully.

She held out her hand to me, as if she would come back to me, never leave me, but I waved her ahead, too. I wanted to catch my elusive breath first, without seeing any of that pity I so hated.

I sat down on a boulder near a fragment of shade, and pressed my hand to my aching side. I examined my surroundings though my dark glasses, as if it was all a painting. It was different from the soft meadows around Turtle Walk, the mother-like rolling hilltops of Taos Mountain. This was like Wagner's "Ring," all steep crags, rocky promontories, places cruel gods had made. Perfect. I scuffed the toe of my moccasin along the hard, dusty earth and listened to the harsh song of the crows, the echoed laughter of my friends.

I longed for Benny, for him to be there to kiss me and draw me down into his darkness. I'd longed for light all my life, craved for it, tried to find it, buy it, yet really darkness was all I understood. I could push Violet out of it, but Benito would stand there inside of it with me, because it was him, too.

I leaned back and stared up into the sky. That endless blue-blue-blue, lowering down onto me every day. What would it be like, if I could have a few more years and find a heaven on earth here in Taos, as Mabel and Tony had? Oh, sure, they (or Mabel) shouted and argued and threatened to leave, but everyone, including themselves, knew they were *it* for each other. They were a world together, in their perfect house, their true home. I thought of how they sat, together-together, alone in crowds, quiet, holding hands. Mabel would rage, and Tony would just murmur "I will take care of her." And he would. Always.

That was never meant for me, with my wild, damaged heart, my raging ways, my restlessness. There was no man like that for me, unless it could have been Tony himself years ago. Now I was going, slip-sliding down into that darkness we all saw, all met, but I had at least found that one vital thing—beauty. And maybe even a little truth.

I would put it into Violet's hands, and send her to that handsome, empty-headed man who could look after her, and maybe she would find The Way. My gift to her, for helping me as she had. My daughter-who-wasn't.

"MR!" Arturo called, and I noticed the sun was setting in Valhalla. The golden-blue softened to mauve at the edges, the light changing. It shone like the rose-gold flecks of those beautiful micaceous pots.

I waved at him, and stood up, careful not to faint. I brushed off my pleated calico skirt, and climbed the narrow, twisting path to our new camp.

It was nearly set up by the time my ridiculously weak legs reached it, the tents in a circle around a fire-pit where Lorenzo showed Art how to stack the piñon and tuck in the kindling twigs. I paused to catch my breath, watching them, listening to my son laugh as this man worked with him so patiently, with such good humor. I hated to think Violet's romantic instincts might be right, when she was just an inexperienced girl and the world was so rough, but—he *was* gorgeous. Even I could admit that. Reluctantly. It was no reason to throw your security away. Nights of display-dancing with Salmie in Paris cafes had taught me that.

Dusty and Violet sliced apples and carrots into a cast-iron stewpot, while Brett added bread and cheese and whiskey to the feast spread on a blanket. Stroh hacked at a haunch of deer for the stew while he talked about Gaugin in Tahiti, color and line and truth. Mirandi sketched some of the jewelry we had all bought, exclaiming over some of the best pieces, begging them for her store.

"I think I can see a Pacific influence in this, Earl," she said, holding up a shell bracelet strung on green beads. "You have to draw it!"

And *that*, I knew like a flash of lightning in that one tiny moment, was all that I sought in New Mexico. Desert sunsets, good food, fine art, lovely friends who understood, deep deep down, what this all meant. That this place was our paradise, for those who understood it, and it was now ours, together, for just this moment.

Mirandi spread the blanket wider for the platters of food, the bottles of wine, and everyone gathered around in the smoky night. Violet suddenly noticed me hovering there, and waved me over with concern in her eyes. I sat down beside her and let her wrap a shawl over my shoulders, watching as the sliver of golden moon crept up into the sky.

I carefully slid out the green baggie from my purse, unwrapped it from its cheesecloth. "Brett, dear, could you hand me some water? I understand this is most efficacious when made into a tea."

Brett's face, damp from the fire, went scarlet. My dear, comical Brett! "MR—whereever did you get that?"

"I bought it" I said blithely. "From a beautiful, and most obliging, young man that feast day at the pueblo."

"What is it?" Arturo asked innocently.

"Peyote," Lorenzo answered shortly. When Art still looked puzzled, he went on. "A small, spineless cactus with psychoactive alkaloids. Some people in my tribe use it for pain or toothache, colds, stuff like that, but also in some religious ceremonies. The hallucinogenic properties can invoke visions. Some people just think they're fun, though."

Arturo's face went as red as Brett's. "A hallucinogen? Ma! You can't mean to ..." He sounded as appalled as his fusty grandmother. I shouldn't have let them spend so much time with Mummy-Da when they were children.

"Oh, Arty, don't be like your own father," I sighed. "For all his Latin beauty, he could be quite the Puritan sometimes, no wonder he got along so well with my mother. You heard Mr. Serna. This has *religious* uses, too. And I am in need of a revelation."

"Just don't take too much, it's not so bad," Brett said. "Like a good worming or something, I suppose."

"You've taken it before, then, Lady Dorothy?" Dusty asked.

Brett waved her pipe. "Sure. I'll try anything once. What about you, Serna?"

Lorenzo shook his head, and turned away to fiddle with the

fire. "Not part of my own ritual. But it often helps a lot when someone seeks a truth."

"I brought plenty, if anyone wants some," I offered.

"I will!" Mirandi said merrily. "After dinner. Just don't let my tourist customers find out what a peasant I am!"

Everyone laughed, and gathered around to eat the stew and cheese, the dried cherry pies Dusty had bought. Brett and Stroh sketched as darkness closed around their little fire, and I was sure we were the last people in all the world. I wished we were.

Finally, I boiled my precious tea over the fire and let it steep before I took a sip. Mirandi, Violet, Brett, Stroh, and Art joined me, but Dusty shook her head, and went to sit next to Lorenzo, where the two of them watched us carefully as if they observed at a zoo.

I laid back on the silvery Two Gray Hills rug, Violet sitting at my feet, and stared up into the sky. So far away from any town, we seemed to be in the very middle of the stars, a swirl of silver and gold and blue any couturier would make a fortune to capture. I felt the wind catch around my face, catch at my skirt, smelled the dust and green and smoke. I wanted, wanted, for something vital to reveal itself to me, show me what I longed for. Reassure me—or maybe scare me out of my wits. I was ready for whatever came, as I always had been.

And—nothing.

Mirandi laughed abruptly, loudly, and Brett shouted "Bloody hell!"

"Do you feel anything, Vi?" I whispered.

"Erm—sleepy," she said hazily, as if she was a few glasses of champagne in. She laid down on her side.

Suddenly, I did feel something horribly familiar, a wave of nausea, drowning me like green, choking, slimy seaweed. I rolled over and vomited into an empty cooking pot.

"MR ..." Violet struggled to sit up.

"I'm quite all right. Clearly I went about this all wrong." I took a tiny sip, then one more, letting the bitter brew settle in my stomach before I laid down again. I watched that sky, as I would a mesmerist at a séance party, and soon a small clearing opened before me. The stars, always so clear and sparkling just like Mummy-Da's diamonds, joined together in a swirling, swinging, arcing dance, a ballet of pure light. As I stared, fascinated, they split into individual dancers, pairs and groups and one perfect prima ballerina, jolting and springing and twirling until the night itself cracked above them, revealing pale, perfect, pure light. Eternity?

"Violet!" I gasped. "Do you see this?"

"I see a cornfield," she whispered. "And a blue barn."

How dull, I thought. One's ultimate reality could hardly be a cornfield! It had to be a mountain of light.

I suddenly felt sad, so deeply, achingly sad for everyone who had never seen such a thing. My father, my lost soul of a brother, my ill-chosen husbands. The prosaic, isolating, ugly world that cut us off from everything that really mattered. Connection, beauty, *that* was what mattered. Serenity, stillness, laughter, silliness, joy. Art and truth. I had found all that here. What waited *there*? Could anything be out there? Nothing more beautiful than this, I feared.

I stared harder into that rose-gold dazzle, longing to know that there was *something*. To not be afraid any longer. But then it all closed up, swallowed whole, and the sky was just the sky again, awash with those stones of Valhalla.

Violet gave a hoarse cry.

"What do you see, darling?" I asked, desperate that those fields, that barn, not be her destiny. She was worth so much more.

"The corn—it all blew away. A tornado. The barn tumbled in. And there was this mountain. The mountain," she whispered. She laughed, almost hysterically. "Isn't that the most boring vision ever, MR?"

"No, it's just *your* vision, darling, your future, maybe." I slid closer, holding her against me in the chilly night, brushing her soft, damp red curls from her cheek, her neck, smelling the lavender perfume she wore now. I thought of how she was that day she came to me, in her hideous jacket and old shoes, unsure as a new fawn, and now she was just—her. Violet. She was learning her heart as I was learning mine. "You belong to the mountain, just as I do. It won't let you go. No more Iowa, ever."

"And you, MR? What did you see? One of your husbands?" Violet laughed on a hiccup.

Certainly not; none of them were worth the trouble. "I think —I think I saw the afterlife. Maybe. I know I'll be sure soon enough."

"No!" Violet cried. Her arms tightened around my shoulders, as if she thought her strength could hold me to the earth. She was strong indeed now, but I knew no force could ever do that. I was floating away, like those star-dancers.

I patted her head. "My sweet, sweet Violet. I wish it wasn't true. Yet we both know this is borrowed time, and every day it gets less and less. At least we found each other first, yes? And here we are, in Taos! I will take care of you, just as you take care of me." I glanced at Lorenzo Serna over her trembling head. He watched her in silence. "If you'll just listen to me, darling ..."

Violet laughed again and shuddered, turning away to wipe her face on a towel. I glimpsed Art and Dusty kissing just beyond the firelight, Brett snoring under her sombrero, Stroh sketching. I hoped he wasn't sketching *me*, I was sure I was an utter mess. And for once, I did not care at all.

"Mr. Rivers is a good man, Vi," I told her, feeling my strength ebbing with every second. "A rich, respectable man. He cares about you, appreciates you. You should go to him when—when ..."

Violet's eyes widened. "MR! Why ..."

I shook my head. "I know these games, Vi, and you do not. My family, strange as they were, had money I could fall back on. You do not. You need to write; you have a gift that must be seen, published, read. He'll give you that space." She looked at Mr.

Serna, those beautiful dark eyes of his meeting hers. "And he would surely build you a little vacation house here in Taos, where you will go whenever you want. Do whatever you want there. Make your own choices. So much of what we call courage in this life is just money. Money can get you what you want, no matter what the songs say."

Violet half-rose, shock on her pretty face. "MR, I can't be like that."

At least I knew she could see what I was saying. "You *can*. You must. You have to survive, thrive in this world. For us both."

She looked as if she longed to protest again, to argue, as I so often had with Mummy-Da. I reached for her hand and drew her down against my shoulder, wrapped the rug around us. We could hear the faint, ghostly beat of drums from beyond the next canyon, and they lulled Violet into restless sleep.

But I couldn't sleep. I wanted to grasp every, every second. I carefully eased her down onto a pillow, and went to take a sheet of paper and pencil from my handbag.

My dear Paulie, I scribbled, letting my words fly free into the sky like those dancing stars. *Did I ever tell you about the feeling I had a little while ago? Suddenly passing Sandia Mountain I felt I was part of the Earth, so that I felt the sun on my surface and the rain. I felt the stars and the growth of the moon, under me, rivers ran. And against me were the tides. The waters of the rain sank into me. And I thought if I stretched out my hand they would be earth and green would grow from me. And I knew that there was no reason to be lonely that one was everything, and Death was so easy as the rising sun and as calm and natural—that to be infolded in Earth was not the end but part of oneself, part of every day and life that we lived, so that Being part of the Earth one was never alone. And all fear went out of me—with a great good stillness and strength.*

If anything should happen to me, now, ever, just remember all this. I want to be buried in Taos with the wide sky. Life is absolutely beautiful if one will ... talk and live it according to one's inner light. Don't fool yourself more than you can help. Do what you want— knowingly. I've had a most lovely life to myself. I've enjoyed it as thoroughly as it could be enjoyed. And when my time comes no one is to feel that I've lost anything of it—or be too sorry. Take all the good things that your life and put them in your eyes and they will be yours ...

Under the wide sky. No matter what that other world held, this was the only place I really wanted to be. Forever.

CHAPTER 28

Millicent

THANKSGIVING, 1907

"Oh, Mary Millicent, do cease fussing like that! Your bows will be quite awry."

Millicent twined her fingers together in the lap of her fur-edged white velvet coat, and tried very, very hard to sit still. She hated it when Mummy-Da talked to her like that, all bitten-off and distracted and impatient, but it was so hard to keep her five-year-old mind from jumping about. Especially when they moved right now to the slow clippity-cloppity of the horses' hooves.

She tried to ignore the enormous moiré bows that held back her dark ringlets, and stared out the carriage windows. All the brownstones looked like gingerbread iced with snow, their lace-draped windows glowing with gold light to welcome Thanksgiving guests. Smoke curled and arched out of the chimneys and drifted over the gated parks where she wished *she* could run and skate. Anything but go to her grandfather's house. Days at Number 3 East 85th were slower than that dratted horse, slower than any other day by far.

Millicent sighed, and kicked her kid, buttoned boots. Sometimes they did have a holiday at home, where she could ride her new pony around the garden, faster and faster, or her brother

Harry would blast away on his new trumpet. But visits to the grandparents were positively royal audiences, and they brought out the finest carriage, the sleepy old horses who just wanted to snooze in their boxes and eat carrots. Stiff lace dresses, Buster Brown suits, seen-not-heard—it all seemed to zoom back in time to the Georgian days at the grandparents'. And Grandmother Emelie (who wasn't their *real* grandmother, as Mummy-Da reminded them, but just a step-grandmother; their real one, Granny Abigail, died ages ago) wasn't even very old. But she seemed so in that house.

But at least she could glimpse the whole city for once, not hurried along by an impatient nanny, or pulled through stores by her mother. No glimpses from the nursery window. It was all so exciting, towering buildings filled with people she didn't even know, people with their own stories and dreams. It all seemed so exciting, she wasn't sure why they always seemed in such a hurry. How did you see life at all that way? And life seemed to pass too fast as it was, even when one was a child and life stretched endlessly ahead.

Her mother looked beautiful, as usual, a steel-gray gown beaded with lavender peeking out from beneath a silver fox coat, diamonds and her famous black pearls gleaming, a feathered aigret wisping in her thick, dark hair. Millicent couldn't wait to wear such jewels herself, Her father, too, looked grand in his formal suit, a white rose in his buttonhole matching his hair, but there had been raised voices in the corridors that morning, and now they didn't look at each other. Mummy-Da barely spoke, expecting to keep little Harry from bouncing on the tufted leather seat. The silence—well, that was better than the shouting.

"Remember, Mary Millicent, you are practically a young lady," her mother said, tugging at those hair-bows again as the carriage rolled to halt in front of the grandparents' house. "Your first time in the grown-up dining room, so exciting! Remember *all* your manners."

Millicent didn't think it was *very* exciting. She and her cousins had loved peeking in at all the sparkle and splendor before a grand dining party, but it was surely more fun in the nursery. Roasted beef and Yorkshire pudding, chocolate, semolina pud, lots of games and laughter. No one laughed at grown-up parties.

Yet there was no going back, only moving forward, as her grandfather always gruffly declared. Blazing a glorious future, as he had. Being a lady was her destiny, whether she liked it or not.

Her mother twitched at the bows yet again, and her father threw down his newspaper with a loud *huff.* "For heaven's sake, Mary, the girl looks fine! We're going to be late. You know how my father abhors tardiness."

Her mother's lips tightened, but she nodded as the stern, black-coated butler opened the carriage door and a footman helped Millicent down the folding steps to the sidewalk. The snow had already been cleared and a beautiful blue carpet laid down the front steps of her grandfather's house. Outside, it looked like all its neighbors, four stories of chocolate-coated stone, white-draped windows, aristocratic, dignified, just spending its genteel days gazing out at the booming vulgarity of the city beyond. Nothing like her parents' new-fangled chateau of pale stone and mansard roofs on East 57th Street. Abigail Gifford Rogers, that old Knicker-bocker, had abhorred display, but her children did not share her taste. Once she was gone, anything went as far as "display."

Inside this house, though, it was very different, showing the taste of the new Mrs. Rogers, Emelie Hart. Millicent was always a bit startled, a bit dazzled, to step into that secret world. A planet of hothouse flowers, overflowing plant pots, garlands and swags made of white plaster and touched with gilt, pillars covered with stone fruit and leaves, portraits and landscapes and sculptures and antique furniture of all sorts, all time periods and styles and colors. The air was warm and smelled of lilies and carnations, and clean lemon polish.

A maidservant took her coat, and her mother held tightly to her hand as they went up the carved oak stairs, bought from a

Jacobean house in England, and moved through a series of reception rooms, sitting rooms, music chambers, libraries. Chatter and giggles grew louder as they reached the grandest drawing room, Emelie's pride.

Under Abigail's reign, it had been filled with dark Victorian pieces, heavily carved, covered in forest green velvet, an upright piano in the corner, potted palms, albums displayed on marble tables, fringed curtains holding out any light. Under Emelie, all was red damask, the silk-papered walls hung with three tiers of paintings she had brought from France, shepherds and nymphs, airy and funny, the rose and gold carpet dotted with deep, shiny, soft sofas and settees and armchairs, between two massive marble fireplaces carved with partygoers in Elizabethan ruffs. Tables were heaped with fashion magazines and novels and photographs, mostly of Emelie.

Her grandparents were seated on their throne-like red velvet chairs before the furthest fireplace, surrounded by Millicent's aunts, uncle, and cousins in their finest silks and velvets and rubies and pearls.

"Just in time for dinner, my dears," Emelie said, as Mary kissed her rouged cheek with a dutiful smile. Emelie did look nice, Millicent thought, in a gown of rose striped satin and gossamer she knew came from Paquin, and the Rogers diamonds. But the aunts ignored her to fuss around Henry Sr., wrapping him in blankets, flattering him until he chuckled.

"How pretty you are growing, my Mary Millicent!" he boomed. "You will be the loveliest of us all." The aunts scowled. "Come, give us a kiss."

She went and gently pressed her lips to his papery cheek. He smelled of camphor and pipe smoke.

"The toast of the town one day, just you watch," he said. He took her hand and led her through to the dining room himself, seating her next to him at the head of the vast table, even though she was far from the senior lady there. Her mother gave her a dire warning glance, but Millicent didn't care. She *felt* like the toast of the town as she perched on a pile of cushions, staring in awe at the dining room in all its holiday glory. The panels of carved black oak with gold edges, where the ladies' gowns of silks and satins could glow in the darkness. The medieval tapestries and crystal chandeliers, the long table spread with white damask and laid with gold chargers and gilt-edged crystal, pyramids of glistening fruit and nuts and peppermints in silver bowls, gold vases filled with red roses and holly. Silver-edged menus—*Blue point oysters. Clear Green Turtle Soup, Sorrell, Chicken Broth. Creamed mushrooms on toast. Boiled Kennebeck salmon with Cardinal Sauce. Saddle of lamb with kidney beans. Glazed ham with spinach. Tenderloin of lamb with stuffed artichokes. Sweetbreads in cases with truffles. Potted quail with brussels sprouts. Rum punch. Rhode Island turkey stuffed with chestnuts, cranberry sauce. Prime Rib. Suckling pig with sage stuffing. Green peas. Asparagus points. Mashed or boiled potatoes. Red-head duck with currant jelly. Tomato surprise. Green salad. English plum pudding, brandy sauce. Mince pie. Pumpkin tarts. Assorted petits fours. Strawberry ice cream. Camembert cheese. Champagne. Various wines. Port or sherry. Coffee.*

Usually, the menus would be in French, but Emelie had the taste not to do so on Thanksgiving.

Millicent studied the table, the beauty of it, the hospitality, and vowed that one day she would have something just so grand. No, even better! Her house would be fun and welcoming, and it would all center on the proper setting. She was determined to have nothing but the very best in her life.

VIOLET—THANKSGIVING, 1936

"Violet Anastasia! What are you doing up there? Come down at once and peel those potatoes, they won't fix themselves."

Violet sighed, and tried to sink down lower behind the old trunks, clutching at her library copy of *Wuthering Heights*. The attic was lovely and warm on such a dismal, gray day, perfect for huddling under a blanket and escaping into a book, into the misty moors. But she couldn't hide forever. Not now that she was old enough to *help*.

She hid the book under an old three-legged table, and brushed the dust off her skirt. It was her Sunday dress, pink pique with a white pinafore, her red curls ruthlessly brushed smooth and tied with pink bows. A bit out of season now that it was autumn, but they didn't have enough money yet for a new dark green plaid dress. She didn't mind dressing up for holidays. It made the house cozy with the scents of baking breads and pies and simmering stews, time for everyone to be all together with no chores at all later. But she did *not* like peeling potatoes, not when there were moors to wander with Cathy and Heathcliff.

She hurried down the stairs, the narrow, dusty, old wooden ones from the attic to the wider steps past the closed bedroom doors. On the landing next to her mother's prized fern, she peeked out the window to see the fields dusted with snow, the sky lead-gray, the dogs chasing each other around the yard.

"Violet!" her mother cried, and she knew time was up. She ran down to the kitchen, so hot and steamy even on that cold day that the back door was propped open to let snow flurries in on her mother's clean linoleum floor. The chickens clucked outside, the dogs woofing, and she heard her father chuckling with them all, staying out of sight. Who knew where her brother was. He was better at hiding than she was.

The air smelled of apples in cinnamon, roasting goose, and the dark, smoky tea that always bubbled in her grandmother's old Russian samovar.

"*Schastlivy den milaya devushka,*" her grandmother said, chopping at the pile of carrots in her usual corner, a black shawl over her thin shoulders, her best onyx combs in her thin, white hair.

Violet's mother slid a pan out of the oven, spreading the drippings over the goose. She looked much like a younger version of her mother, tall and thin and spare, with a poetic face, dark hair scraped back in enameled combs, looking worried as always. Violet always thought that was what waited for her, too. Worry worry worry. And cooking. "Your Billy's family will be here soon! Put on that apron and help your grandmother."

Her grandmother said something in Russian, making Violet's mother laugh. Her grandmother winked, and Violet felt her cheeks burn as if she stood right by the roaring oven. Her Russian vocabulary was rather limited, but she knew bawdy teasing when she saw it. "*Obushka*! I don't know if I want to marry Billy someday. I'm too young!" And, while he was nice and cute, he wasn't Heathcliff or Darcy. She'd never even met many other boys, had she? How could she know what she really wanted?

"You could do a lot worse, sweetie." her mother said. "His family's farm is nearby, and twice as big as this one! And don't you want to live close to your family? Have your own kitchen like this one soon, your own kiddies?"

"Sure," Violet said, but she wasn't at all sure in her secret heart. There *had* to be something she wanted to see out there, her books told her that. What if there was something she was meant to be, somewhere she was meant to be?

She glanced out at the kitchen yard as she reached for the apron and the paring knife, half-listening to her mother and grandmother gossip in Russian, trying to picture her own Thanksgiving dinners just like this one. Billy in the yard, her daughter peeling potatoes.

She silently shook her head. The future seemed so far away, more vast than all those cornfields. Who knew what might happen then?

VIOLET—THANKSGIVING IN TAOS

Violet studied the courtyard at Turtle Walk with a careful eye, trying to see it as Millicent had taught her a house should be for a party, not exactly as her mother would say it was. Her mother's house had always been scrubbed clean, sparkling and smelling of lemon, nuts in every small cut-glass bowl, not a cushion out of place, not to be touched. That was a "party atmosphere" in Iowa.

Violet laughed as she walked around the long table laid out in an H around the large garden at the center of the house. The flower beds wouldn't blossom for months now that the November mountain chill was in the air, but MR used large cottonwood branches to pretend there were trees, pots of sweet-smelling herbs, a bonfire laid to light after dark, musicians from the pueblo setting up their drums under the portal to make it seem celebratory. Violet's mother would have shuddered at it all.

But she would have loved the rest of it. Millicent's crates had arrived from her house in Washington, the Georgian manor of Claremont, and the tables were draped with rich damask cloths and dark red napkins, Meissen china in a flowers-and-vines patterns, edged in gilt, monogrammed silver, champagne chilling in buckets, hothouse roses in heavy crystal vases. Young girls hired as maids from the shops, dressed in hastily-fitted black dresses and crisp white aprons, hurried around laying out platters of food from La Fonda, turkey and sage stuffing, garlic mashed potatoes, green salads, vinegar-dressed cooked vegetables. In the kitchen, Ethel put the final touches on her pies and mousses, cursing anyone who dared get in her way.

"Where do you think this should go, Miss Redfield?" one of the girls asked, a very pretty, plump, pink-cheeked young lady Violet recognized from her time living at La Fonda. The maid held up a platter of pate and oozing cheeses. It was a bit surprising she had wanted to work at Turtle Walk for the holiday, since she seemed to spend most of her La Fonda time flirting with the bell-boys, but Millicent paid well for her temporary staff, so all hands were on deck.

"Just over there, thank you," Violet said, and gestured toward a carved Jacobean sideboard that held rows of jewel-like bottles of liqueurs and plates of appetizers. She twitched a tablecloth straight, moved one of the Navajo rugs laid over the flagstones into place, and hurried into the house. Her watch told her it was almost time.

Turtle Walk was quiet enough now, but Violet knew it was the quiet before a storm. Only, unlike at home, there would be no attic shelter to run to for quiet. She made her way through the warren of rooms, all at different sizes and elevations yet made spacious with high ceilings, large, sunny windows, and curved corners. All painted yellow, dark red, dull blue, with weathered vigas and kiva fireplaces, old carved Spanish chairs that matched the doors and window frames. Violet smoothed the striped rugs underfoot, checked that paintings—Renoirs, Fragonards, new scenes of Taos—hung straight, picked up books and dog toys and deposited them into Navajo baskets. Millicent's new corgi puppy tore past, barking madly as the dachshunds hid from her. Violet could hear clattering from the kitchen, shouts and curses.

Brett was already there, sitting calmly in the corner of the drawing room amid striped sofas and retablos and embroidered cushions. She smoked her pipe and sipped at some of Millicent's best port, humming as she idly paged through a new book of sketches Mr. Stroh had sent.

"Ah, there you are, Vi, darling. You are ever efficient," she said in her Jane Austen accent. "The feast almost ready? Do sit down, you look rather knackered."

Violet laughed, and gratefully sank down on a beaded cushion. She kicked off her new black patent court shoes, perfectly matched to her new black Hattie Carnegie suit, and wondered why she had worn such a thing to check on turkey and potatoes.

But she knew very well why. The new suit made her feel slim and elegant—and Lorenzo was on the guest list.

She rubbed idly at her heel while she thought of the last few weeks. MR had been so preoccupied with finishing (and re-finishing and finishing again) with the house, that there hadn't been a great deal for Violet to do once she was done with the day's bills and social diary organizing. She had come far along on her book, resisted her mother's letters entreating her to come back to Iowa, and explored Taos more. She walked down pathways and streets, just to see what she could find—an ancient tree, a beautiful old adobe house, a gallery, someone new to talk to. She browsed at Martha's shop, watched Brett work on a new painting. And spent time with Lorenzo.

She smiled secretly as she thought of those afternoons, having a picnic beside a mountain river, letting him show her the hidden spots of the pueblo, listening to the radio (Bing!) as Lorenzo worked in his garage. Kissing as the sun went down, and she would wish she could just stay there forever. When she leaned against his shoulder, listened to him laugh, let his calm smile into her soul, she never wanted to be anywhere else. Never wanted this late summer to end. As it surely would.

But not quite yet. No.

"I'll be glad when Thanksgiving is all over," she said. "Trying to organize what MR calls a 'proper holiday' hasn't been easy. Her idea of what 'proper' is changes every five minutes. And just try getting cranberry sauce in Taos!"

Brett shrugged and offered a slug of her port. "It's not usually a big event up here. Not like a saint's day or fiesta. Mabel has a dinner sometimes, but it's usually not one of her bigger 'dos'. And, no matter how long this old English lady lives in America, she will never understand what turkey has to do with the *Mayflower*. But no matter. A party is a party, and MR's are the best. Free food is always free food, so cheerio!"

Violet laughed. "I think Millicent just wants to give something back to Taos. Everyone here has been so kind. And she wants to show off the house."

"So she should. It's a triumph. From a crumbling wall and no roof to—this." Brett waved her pipe at the room, the beautiful mellow golden-tan walls, the books and paintings, the red silk curtains letting in the bright Taos sun. "And of course she makes jobs to be had. I'm surprised to see Gertie here, though. Should she be on her feet so much?"

"Gertie? Oh, yes." Violet thought of the girl she had just seen, plump and pink-cheeked in her black dress. Had she been rather out of breath? "Is she ill? Should we have her sit down?"

Brett chuckled. "Well, I am an old spinster so know little about it all, but I wouldn't quite say *ill*. Nothing a few more months won't take care of. And maybe a ring, if you care about such notions."

Violet felt her face turn embarrassingly hot. She remembered MR's recent lectures about birth control methods ("Cannot let things get untidy, Vi!"), and wished someone had said as much to Gertie. "I—I didn't realize. MR doesn't care about—rings and such. If she feels well enough to work today ..."

"Just as well, yes. I doubt he'd ever marry her anyway, or that she *should* marry him. She's better off on her own; some men just make more trouble than they're ever worth."

Violet tilted her head to study Brett curiously. This was one bit of local gossip that had passed her by. "Her boyfriend is no good, then?"

Brett leaned closer. "Vi, my darling naive Iowa girl. He isn't her boyfriend at all. He is Benny Suarez. Or so I hear."

Violet fell back in her chair, coldly shocked. She had known Benito was certainly not reliable, but a womanizer, too? She thought about how MR looked at him, protective, tender, puzzled, and Violet hoped against hope she had no idea about Gertie. "Does Millicent know?"

Brett shrugged, and reached for her tobacco pouch to refill her pipe. "Who knows with her? She's one of the best friends I've ever had, yet I know her not at all. I would suggest saying nothing to her. If she doesn't know, well and good, and if she's in denial about it all—she won't thank you to shatter that illusion."

Violet slowly nodded. She knew Brett was right. Millicent had a knack for seeing what she only wished to see; or at least only acknowledging what she wanted to see. Her temper could be fearsome if anyone let cold, hard reality intrude when she didn't want it. But what of Lorenzo? Did *he* know?

"Now then, who else is coming?" Brett said briskly. "I know they hired a bus from the pueblo, so many people are dying to see the house."

"Um—yes," Violet stammered, trying to make her mind move from "shock" back to "practical party planning." "The Romeros. Dick and Kay Dicus, of course, and some guests of theirs from the East. Ernest. Mabel and Tony. I don't think Mabel wanted to come, but she couldn't get over her curiosity! Oh, and Mirandi is coming from Santa Fe. We haven't seen her since that camping trip." She hid her snicker at remembering the drugs, the whirling sky, the giggles and the sickness. Violet doubted she would go camping again. "She's bringing a friend of hers who works for the BBC, Ludovic something, and his girlfriend. A famous actress!"

"Famous actress?" Brett said doubtfully. "Here? I thought we had our fill of that with Miss Gaynor."

Millicent swept into the room, the dachshunds swirling around her. She wore a red skirt from Martha's shop, with a crisp white blouse, red and blue Navajo shawl, and piles of silver and turquoise and coral jewelry. Her golden hair, turning more silvery now, was carefully curled and swept up, hiding how thin her cheeks were becoming. "Some English lady, I think, Brett darling," she said, kissing Brett's cheek and straightening a pile of cushions into a perfect pyramid. "I have completely gone off films since I left California, so I don't know anything about it."

Violet glanced at a guest list left on a Spanish mahogany side table, names crossed out and added in Millicent looping handwriting. Lists were useless in Taos; people showed up when they showed up, if they felt like it. But MR liked to keep them. "Moira Shearer is her name. She was in a ballet movie."

"My, but we are becoming posh! I might as well go back to the Home Counties," Brett smirked. "I hope she likes the pueblo dances later. Or she can join Mabel in her pouting, I suppose." She gestured with her pipe toward Mabel, who sat in the shadowed corner, swathed in her white caftan, arms folded and eyes narrowed as she watched a party that was not her own.

Violet laughed as she left Mabel to her Mabel-ing business, and hurried to the front door to see who else might be arriving. The light was growing mellower, more pale golden touched with gray at the edges, and the voices outside and winding through the halls and rooms were growing louder, more filled with laughter.

The door was open, but no newcomers seemed to be in the gravel driveway, just a haphazard cross-hatch of trucks and cars and bicycles. The laughter, chatter, shouts of the house were muffled, caught on the chilly breeze and carried away with a swirl. Violet knew more people would arrive later, all afternoon and into the evening, and she tidied up the front flagstone walkway, lined with banners in autumnal colors of burnt yellow and maroon, before she turned back to the house.

One person lingered in the foyer, straightening his tie in the Spanish silver-framed mirror, smoothing his hair, smiling complacently at his reflection. Benito.

Violet froze for a moment, completely unsure what to say. She hadn't seen him since the jewelry incident; she had heard he was working at a gas station on the other side of town, or maybe at an orchard or living rough in the mountains. She wasn't sure if MR saw him, if she did she kept it away from Turtle Walk, and Lorenzo didn't say anything.

He didn't look as if he'd been living in a mountain cave. In fact, he looked more handsome than ever, and he had always been the most handsome man Violet ever saw, including Clark Gable. His hair was as glossy and dark as the night sky and perfectly trimmed, tumbling in waves around his sun-touched face that emphasized his mountain-cliff cheekbones and dimpled chin. He wore a shimmery gray suit clearly tailor-made, a snowy white linen shirt, and modish blue and yellow tie that matched a silk pocket square. He straightened that tie, and grinned at himself.

Violet remembered the last stack of bills she had paid for Millicent—one for two suits at a Santa Fe shop.

"You're looking very fashionable, Mr. Suarez," Violet said, folding her arms.

He swung that smile onto her, and for a moment she glimpsed Lorenzo in his face, his eyes. But she knew that looks did deceive. Benny was not in the least bit like her steady, smiling, calm Lorenzo. At least Benny didn't look drunk right now. "Thanks, Miss Nurse Redfield. Folks like us—we do what we have to do, yeah?"

Violet's back stiffened. "Folks like us?"

"Folks who aren't born clutching the brass ring. We don't get many chances, do we? We see a door open, we have to push through it." He straightened his sleeves, onyx and gold cufflinks gleaming.

Violet frowned as she thought of that open safe, the lost jewelry. "Even if that door is a double-iron one with a combination lock?"

Benito laughed. "A challenge isn't so bad. Too many things are just too easy."

"I haven't found much to be so."

He leaned close, his eyebrow quirked in a confiding expression. "That's because you're just too nice, Nurse Redfield. The sort who finds lost causes in dirty alleyways and tries to fix them. You and Lorenzo, you're two of a kind. Looking for good in a rotten world when there just isn't anything good to be found. There's nothing but what you can grab for yourself. You could have so much more right now, if you weren't so fucking nice."

Violet's hands curled into fists at her sides, the fine wool of her suit skirt abrading. "What do you mean?"

He stepped closer. He smelled of expensive cologne and, underneath, whiskey. Not so sober after all. "People like Millicent —they open doors, yeah? And they like to be told what to do, no matter what they say, how they pretend to bristle. They like to have that steely control that hides behind money challenged sometimes." He idly picked up a silver-framed photo of Millicent from the side table, an image of a golden goddess on a yacht, one bejeweled hand raised to steady a wide-brimmed hat. "Still pretty, ain't she? For now. Not for much longer, I think." He glanced toward the doorway, where Millicent could be glimpsed chatting with some guests, her red skirt swaying. "She already looks like a scarecrow. You should get on her good side now ..."

Fury roared over Violet like mountain wildfire. She snatched the photo from him and slammed it back on the table. She caught a glimpse of herself in the mirror, her cheeks bright red, her eyes glinting.

"How dare you?" she whispered. "After all she's done for you ..."

Benny laughed again, heartier, louder. Yes, she could definitely hear the whiskey in it. "Come on, we're not so different, you and me. You're a lot nicer, I'll grant you that, but we'll end up the same. Thrown into the arroyo once we're not useful any more. Take my advice, get what you can now."

He patted her on the shoulder, and Violet twisted away, the expensive cloth of his sleeve brushing her arm. Good clothes now —what else did he hope for here? What had he "gotten" already? Violet thought of the other men Millicent would talk about, laughing but wistful—her husbands, her lovers, all who let her down in the end. Violet didn't want to see that happen once more.

The maid hurried into the foyer as Violet was leaving—Gertie, was it? Her pretty, plump cheeks glowed pink with eagerness, with a tentative smile. "Bennie," she sighed, and looped her arms around his neck. Then she glimpsed Violet standing there, and her pink cheeks turned brick-bright. She gasped and stepped back, but Benny's hands tightened at her waist and held her with him. His palm slid lower over her lush backside, and she giggled.

"No need to run off, then, Gert," he said smoothly, smiling down at her. "Miss Redfield here was just leaving."

The girl giggled again, and went up on the toes of her scuffed shoes. Violet glimpsed her distended belly beneath the stretch of her black dress, unmistakable now. Was it really Benito's? Did MR know? In such a small town, surely the gossip was flowing already.

Violet spun around to run away, to go somewhere, anywhere, away from this squalid little scene. Her loyalty was definitely to MR, and not, as Benito so grossly put it, for the Rogers' open coffers. She couldn't be a part of this, couldn't watch it. Captain Butler had been quite enough.

Yet it was too late. The front door opened and Millicent appeared, a case of champagne in her arms, the cold of the piñon-scented day clinging to her along with her "Shocking" perfume. She wore a silver fox coat now, fluffy around her throat, almost the same color as her hair. Her face went chalk-white as she saw Benito and the maid entwined in her own foyer, his hand on her backside.

The girl gave a squeal, and backed away to flee to the party. Benito grinned at Millicent, as if something very amusing had just happened. "Millie …" he cooed, and bent as if to kiss her.

Expressionless, she shoved the crate into his arms. "Take that to the kitchen, Bennie, like a good boy. And don't drink any along the way. It's Piper-Heidseick, much too good for you. It's for my select guests."

Benito's expression darkened, his eyes narrowed, but without a word he stomped away. The air in the foyer suddenly seemed warm and claustrophobic, despite the chilly day; the merry party noises slid into something sinister.

Millicent peered into the mirror, turning her face this way and that as if to search for a flaw. "Is Mirandi here with her movie people yet?"

Violet swallowed hard. "Y—yes, just a little while ago." She thought of Mirandi's English guests, the distinguished, if balding, Ludovic and his graceful, red-haired girlfriend. So polite, so soft-spoken.

"What is she like? Has to be the center of attention?"

"Not at all. Quite the opposite, I'd say." Miss Shearer was sitting in a corner with Brett most of the time, watching everything with wide eyes, her feet daintily crossed. "She is very quiet. Brett likes her."

Millicent sighed. "That's the English for you, manners, manners, manners. Pretty, though, I am sure. They say she's a ballerina."

'Pretty' didn't go far enough for Miss Shearer, really. Even against Janet and her Hollywood friends, there was something painting-like, elegant, otherworldly about Moira Shearer's pale skin and vivid hair, her elegant gestures. Violet wasn't sure she wanted Millicent to hear that. "Yes, she is pretty."

Millicent seemed to notice a fine line beside her rose-painted lips, and smoothed it with her fingertip. Benito was horribly right about one thing—MR was getting thinner, paler, more brittle. Violet blinked hard to hold back the sudden prickle of tears.

"Well, I am quite sure Benito won't be able to get so much as a glance from a woman like that! He'll have to stick to parlor maids," MR said, taking a tube of Elizabeth Arden out of her handbag on the side table.

"MR ..." Violet started, but she had no idea what to say.

Millicent laughed wryly. "You think I don't notice? I'm not so foolish as all that, though I admit I have made my share of terrible decisions when it comes to handsome men. I just can't seem to help it, it's my weakness."

She noticed a half-full bottle of vodka on the table, behind a kachina figure, and Violet was shocked to see the fastidious Millicent pick it up and take a long swig, and then another, straight from the bottle. It was a bit like watching Queen Elizabeth stuff down onion rings at Hamburger Heaven.

"My grandmother always told me being with no one was far better than being with the wrong person," Violet said. She couldn't think of any other words. "Of course, that doesn't stop my family from trying to betroth me to any nearby farmer."

Millicent laughed hoarsely, and offered Violet the bottle. "Easier said than done, darling, as you do well know. But shit. Do they all have to be quite so *wrong*."

Violet thought of Lorenzo, so, so right, yet so wrong. How could they ever fit into each other's worlds, ever really understand each other? But when he kissed her, and the stars aligned—she knew how Millicent felt.

"I did think he might be different," MR whispered. "A wounded soul I could help. I get so tired of being the one who always needs help! Poor sickly Mary Millicent. Here, *I* am the one of use. Sometimes."

"You *are* of use! Everyone here loves you," Violet protested. And they did love MR. How could they not? She believed in the beauty of this place, the importance of its art, and she showed the wider world that importance. She helped people every day. "Don't let one waster like Benito bring that down, make you feel that all that is unimportant. This whole town, this whole country, says you are important."

Millicent smiled, but it was tired, pale, despite the lipstick, the diamond clips in the perfect waves of her hair, the furs and red skirt and all the new jewelry.

Her lips tightened. "I will not be ignored! Not forgotten. Benito will be brought to see that."

She suddenly slid out of her heavy fur coat and tossed it to Violet. "Take that to my room, and make sure it's hung away properly. The last time I needed it, it was just crumpled in my closet. I don't pay you to be careless. You can be so sloppy."

Violet bit her lip at the sudden freeze-out, and forbore to point out that it was Millicent herself who had thrown it into the closet —along with all the satin shoes on the floor, the spilled face powder, the tangle of discarded jewelry. Neatness was not one of MR's qualities.

And being a wardrobe maid wasn't part of Violet's job, though Millicent did seem to make it one more and more. Demanding things be put away, ironed, laundered, shouting when it wasn't. Her temper had grown shorter lately, more fiery, less quick to subside. Violet sensed a new distance sometimes, but she put it down to MR's illness, and tried to keep her own patience. It wasn't always easy. So many things felt like a tug-of-war lately, control slipping beyond Violet. MR's world spinning beyond her entirely.

She turned toward the corridor that led back to the bedrooms. Outside the windows, she glimpsed the party, people dancing around bonfires as the sunset turned the sky a brilliant rose and gold. The drums made the walls vibrate.

She peeped in at the dining room, where Edith and a few of the hired maids (though not Gertie) were rearranging bowls and platters. The smells of roasted turkey, fresh-baked bread, and herb-laced vegetables mingled with the smoke and champagne and perfume. Mabel sat in one corner, a scowl on her face, tapping her cane on the floor, surely angry that she was not the queen of this particular hive.

Benito was nowhere to be seen.

Violet turned her back to the party and made her way to her room. It was larger than her space at the guest ranch had been, with a large canopied bed spread with a red Navajo blanket, a desk where her book pages waited, a large armoire for her new clothes. She opened the matching red woven curtains and threw open the window to let in the evening breeze, the music and voices. She laid the coat neatly at the foot of the bed and smoothed out its velvety pelts, still clinging with the scent of Schiaparelli. One of the dogs padded in, looking for peace and quiet, and plopped down on the coat.

Violet laughed, knowing she should make the dog move but she didn't. She went to her dressing table to smooth her hair, reapply her lipstick. She realized that, like MR, she was looking different. Her skin was pale gold from the sun, her freckles appearing across her nose, her hair thicker and more auburn, her eyes shining. She was blooming in Taos, expanding rather than shrinking, straining for—for more. For things she could barely even yet name. But Millicent ...

Millicent was fading.

Violet froze for an instant, staring into her startled eyes. Yes, MR was fading, and no matter how hard Violet tried to pull her back from the brink, to hold onto her, it couldn't be forever. Benito had been right about one terrible fact—this couldn't go on much longer. How would she know when it was really time to go? Where would she go? How could she leave MR?

"Not now," she whispered. This was no time to try and answer those questions. Surely she still had time, plenty of time. She dropped her lipstick and turned away, automatically reaching out to straighten the pens on her desk.

Her manuscript was out of order.

A breath seemed to catch in her throat, strangling her, as she stared at that stack of papers. It would surely look absolutely fine to anyone else, but she knew how she stacked the pages when she was finished writing for the day, each chapter turned a different way so she could find things easily for reference. Now they were skewed.

She hastily glanced through the close-written pages, and found one chapter, the next to last, was out of page order. She studied the rest of the desk, but could see nothing else strange. Her small jewelry box was still locked. Why would someone come into her room and mess with her papers? She'd told no one about her writing, and it wasn't interesting or valuable to anyone but her, anyway.

Still feeling that touch of disquiet, she put the pages back in order and tucked them in a drawer. She couldn't decipher it tonight. There was still a party going on. She smoothed her hair, straightened her jacket, and marched out to the courtyard. She left the dog on the coat.

The party had grown in the short time she was gone, noise and music, shouts and laughter, chaos spreading out into the night sky. She glimpsed Lorenzo across the crowded courtyard, and happily hurried toward him, hoping to forget her misgivings about her manuscript.

"Well, Miss Iowa," he said, with his usual calm, unreadable smile. It made all her doubts vanish in that moment, and she smiled, too. "You look busy."

"I am busy." She blew a loose red curl off her forehead, and took Lorenzo's cigarette from between his fingers for a long, stolen puff. "Did you know we have a movie star here tonight?"

Lorenzo laughed, as dark and deep as the sky above them. He was the one still spot in all this spiral-wild madness of a world, and she reveled in him. For a second she could forget MR and her changeableness, Benito, her manuscript, and all her doubts, and could just *be*.

"Of course there would be a movie star in Mrs. Rogers's house," he said, rolling another cigarette. The flickering firelight caught on a new silver bracelet on his muscled forearm, studded with tiny turquoise in an astrological pattern. He had been working at his art lately, too. "I wouldn't be surprised to hear that woodland goblins were dancing in the sitting room."

"They would be welcome if they had a good source for champagne." She laid a fingertip to the new bracelet, feeling the cool silver, his warm skin, under her touch. "A different design?"

"Just an experiment. I thought I'd get out some of my old sketches, see if they might give me an idea."

"I love it." She traced a line of stars etched in the silver.

A sudden crash echoed across the courtyard, louder even than the music. Violet jumped, and glanced back over her shoulder through the open doorway into the drawing room.

"Don't worry about it," Lorenzo said gently. "Just a Taos party."

Violet laughed nervously. "A party *I'll* have to clean up later. But MR did have to have a Thanksgiving."

"What about you, Miss Iowa?"

"Me? I had enough Thanksgiving to hold me forever back home. All that potato peeling. All those family quarrels coming up. In repressed, Iowa fashion, of course. My cousins would chase me around the yard with turkey intestines."

Lorenzo laughed, and caught Violet around the waist to whirl her around and around until she giggled, too, hopelessly, giddy, forgetting everything but the way he felt and smelled and sounded. The way she felt like she belonged *right there*.

"Should I go find some turkey innards, then?" he said.

She smacked him on the shoulder. "Don't you dare! This is perfect, just as it is."

He lowered her to her feet, and his face dipped to hers. His lips met hers in a just-right kiss, natural and bright and smelling of sunshine.

She heard a burst of wild laughter, a crack as a bat hit a ball, and Lorenzo's shoulders stiffened. She stepped back a bit, and rested her forehead on his chest, breathing in the clean cotton of his shirt, the heat of his skin.

"I—I am a little worried about something, actually," she said. It felt safe to talk there, holding onto his shoulders.

His arms came around her, and she felt him rest his cheek on the top of her hair. "Is the potato salad all wrong?"

Violet laughed despite herself. "As if Edith would make something so prosaic—and delicious!—as potato salad. No, Benito was here earlier."

His jaw twitched against her hair. "He's supposed to be making himself scarce, staying away from Tony, after all that jewelry business."

"I had suspected MR was still seeing him, though quietly. She never talks to me about it, of course. But there he was right now, in the foyer, bold as could be! And with a woman. A pregnant woman."

She glanced up at Lorenzo and found him frowning. "What did Mrs. Rogers say?"

Violet shivered to think of the strange scene. "She just threw me her fur coat and told me basically to mind my own business. I worry about her. Silly, I know, me worrying about her. I'm just her secretary, she's a millionaire, I shouldn't worry about her. But when it comes to men ..."

She bit her lip, and shook her head. MR's past—and present—with men, wise or not, couldn't concern Violet. Not if she wanted to keep her job. Yet she had been through too much with Millicent now, seen too much, to stand back and shrug her shoulders now. She saw MR as a friend, no matter how MR chose to see *her*. After that display tonight, she doubted it was as an equal and friend, which pained her. But she still cared. Too, too much.

She had the sudden, cold, sad feeling that this bright new life she had made wouldn't go much longer. And she had no idea what would come next.

Violet swallowed hard. "She is a big girl, I know, but I don't want to see her hurt. Too many people are walking wounded in this world, after the war. I couldn't help my brother at all. I can't just turn away from someone I care about now."

Lorenzo held her close again. "We really can't save anyone else from themselves, even the ones we love. No matter how hard we try." He closed his eyes for an instant, and she saw that alleyway where they met, poor, ill Benito, Lorenzo by his side. Her strong

Lorenzo. "Sometimes we can only save ourselves, not go down the gutter with them."

"Did you—go down the gutter?"

"Almost, after the war. After my sister." He held up his hands, his long, elegant fingers, narrow palms crossed with pink lines of scars, stained with oil. "But I managed to pull myself up in the end. It's too hard for some people, like Benny."

"And like my brother," Violet whispered. And, she was beginning to fear, too hard for Millicent. Millicent, with all her glamour and strength and beauty and sheer, burning life. It became too much for everyone eventually. Too much fighting was wearying.

A group of drummers had gathered in the corner of the courtyard, and started to play, low and hard and steady as a heartbeat. A tune, tiny and sweet at first, caught on a spiral of sound, up and up as if to reach the stars just blinking on in the dusty purplish night sky. Violet wished so much she could grab onto that sound and ride it away, go up and up just the same. She took Lorenzo's hand and let him lead her to a seat at the end of a table, let him pour her a glass of wine, and she studied the courtyard around them.

The table was scattered with the remains of the feast, empty platters, bottles tipped on their sides, laughter louder than ever, twining around the music. Tony sat by the wall, nodding at them placidly, a child asleep on each of his knees. Violet laughed, and watched more children play on the patches of grass beyond the courtyard, jacks and hoops and strange, made-up games kids always managed to devise.

She glanced at Tony. "Where's Mabel?" she wondered, remembering seeing her pouting in the kitchen earlier.

"Who knows?" Lorenzo said, catching one of the children's balls and tossing it back lightly. "Mabel goes where Mabel goes."

Even Tony—of course Tony—didn't seem to be concerned, but Violet wondered, especially with Millicent in a mood. "I think I'll just go check. I should bring out the last of the desserts, anyway."

Lorenzo kissed her cheek, and jumped up to join the dancers who had begun to circle to the drumbeats. The music was louder now, voices equally merry and quarrelsome, and Violet had to sigh to think it was really Thanksgiving everywhere.

She made her way around the garden toward the front portal. The door stood open, the driveway still a maze of vehicles, with a few added goats and a donkey poking around. The torches lining the covered portal were lit, but the night beyond was impenetrable.

Millicent was nowhere to be seen, and neither was Benito. But Mabel sat alone on a blue-cushioned bench, her white and coral striped caftan spread around her. A heaping plate was on the small table at her elbow, with a large bottle of wine, and she was happily munching on a turkey leg.

"Mrs. Luhan," Violet called as she climbed the portal steps, dodging two of the dachshunds. "Are you all right?"

Mable squinted at Violet through her thick glasses, and nodded. "Ah, Miss Redfield. Yes, I am quite well. Just wanted a quiet little spot to enjoy Edith's excellent cooking. These disorganized parties do overrun, I fear. My mother, oh, my mother, I'm afraid that dear lady was wrong about so many things, but she was wise about entertaining, and she said guests and fish always stink when left out too long. Mrs. Rogers will learn. This isn't Fifth Avenue." A large, crystalline crash came from around the corner, along with shrieks, as if to prove her point.

"Is it a fight?" Violet asked.

Mable calmly wiped her fingers on a damask napkin. "Mrs. Rogers will learn," she said again. "Unlimited alcohol is seldom an unalloyed good thing. But come, sit down, Miss Redfield. You do look tired, if you will pardon my saying it."

Violet half-sighed, half-laughed. She sat down next to Mabel on the bench, and kicked off her court shoes. Mabel handed her a piece of turkey, and Violet munched on it, enjoying the sudden quiet.

"I admit I'm not much of a big party person," she said, tucking her stockinged feet under her. "I like a few people I can really talk to."

"Ah, now you see the perfect essence of entertaining. Taos is not Palm Beach. Personality is all, not crowds."

"This isn't like anything I've seen before, or even imagined."

Mabel nodded. "You belong here, Miss Redfield, I could see it right away. Not everyone does. Not everyone can *see*." She took a nibble of frybread. "I tried to make a home out of New York and Italy. Italy *was* lovely, but it was made already. This I could mold into my home, make my house just as I wanted. Here I could do some good."

"It could make you fall in love?" Violet said, feeling bold.

Mabel gave her a sharp glance from behind her glasses. "Love, yes. Love I never thought was real outside of some silly play. Love where you are two halves of a whole. You quarrel, you disagree, but in the end you make a life together. You have more together than you could ever have apart. My mother, that grand Buffalo socialite, would have apoplexy if she saw me now!"

Violet laughed. "So would my Iowa housewife mother."

Mable guffawed. "So never tell her. Keep it for yourself. That makes it nicer, anyway. A secret."

"However long happiness lasts?"

Mabel took a sip of wine. "It can last as long as you like, Miss Redfield, Mrs. Rogers or not. What is it you *really* want? Not being a secretary forever, I wager. A wife to that handsome, rich, dull California lawyer who was here in the autumn?

Violet wasn't surprised Mabel knew about Charles. Everyone here knew everything about everyone else. Did everyone think she should marry him, just as MR did? "I really have no idea what's next."

Mabel slapped her knee through her caftan, her long strings of beads clattering. "No one knows—until they *know*! The mountain tells us. I see you aren't the sort to balance accounts and type letters and order clothes forever. What do you do when Mrs. Rogers isn't looking?"

Mabel glanced across the drive to Lorenzo, who was showing something under a truck hood to a group of men, all of them laughing.

Violet loved him, it was true. There, she admitted it to herself. Despite everything, the hard lessons he had learned when his sister loved a white man, Tony leaving the kiva to marry Mabel, the gulf between their pasts—she loved him. It was wonderful; it was terrible; she had no idea how it would end. How he felt.

Yet she had one more thing, a sure thing, her own thing.

"I write," she whispered.

Mabel's dark eyes widened. "Of course you do. Oh, Miss Redfield, you dark horse. No one comes here without a call to create something. Poetry? Plays?"

"A novel. Not finished yet." She remembered the disarranged pages, and frowned. "It's just a silly thing, about what happens to men and women when they come home from war and find home isn't home anymore."

"A family saga, I see," Mabel said happily. "Just the thing for the market now, especially if it has a little scandal in it."

Violet smiled, rather heartened by tidbits of encouragement, more than she had ever had for writing. "There is, a very little."

"Perfect. How far along is it?"

"Three-quarters done, or about that. I just write when I have a little extra time, mostly at night. It's slow."

"Oh, my dear Miss Redfield. It is true that plenty of fine authors have to write alongside other jobs—we all must eat. But it is not the best way to turn out one's finest work. If I can help at any time, in any way ..."

"You are very kind, Mrs. Luhan."

Mabel's head tilted like a bird's. "It's my life's work to bring art into the world. It is divine in itself to enable the beauty of others."

She adjusted her caftan around her. "Have you spoken of this to Mrs. Rogers?"

"Oh, no!" Violet recoiled. MR wouldn't understand; she would think it took Violet away from her work. Made her careless, like with the crumpled coat. "She certainly does value creativity so much, but I'm not sure she would understand how much it means to me—not yet. Well, not ..."

"Understand that her trusted right hand, her acolyte, has some greater calling?" Mabel chortled. "I daresay."

Violet was startled. She loved MR; she owed MR so very much. But—acolyte? Afraid of MR's reaction to an independent endeavor? She had never considered such a thing in her vague doubts. Millicent had shown her such kindness, had given her a chance. But would she let Violet go? Let her be her own person?

"I was planning to tell her when I finished the book," she said.

"Very wise. Just remember, Miss Redfield, there are plenty of people here who would love to help you, including myself. Don't hide your light under a bushel and all that metaphorical rot." The drumming in the distance had slowed, and Lorenzo glanced up from the truck hood to smile at Violet, his slow, sweet smile. "And, when it comes to love ..."

"Love?"

Mabel gestured with her glass toward Lorenzo. "I was married three times before I found my Tony. They were all milque-toasts." She grinned, and for a moment she looked as she must have thirty years before, when a young Tony Luhan came into her sight. "I knew he was the one for me, the *only* one, no matter what. That's a rare thing in life, the rarest, a man who loves you back for just who you are. Who gives you grounding *and* freedom, and never expects anything else. Only a ninny lets that go because society *says* we should, a ninny with no backbone at all. Are you a ninny, Miss Redfield?"

Violet remembered how nervous she was walking up to MR's Los Angeles door, how it felt even stepping onto that bus in Iowa.

She had come a very long way, and learned a lot. More than she had realized before that very moment. Millicent and Mabel were right —life was for grabbing, with both hands, while you could. She took up the bottle of wine and drank a deep gulp. "No, Mrs. Luhan. I am not a ninny."

Mabel sat back with a satisfied chuckle. "Just don't let that other part of you get in your own way. You only have one life, but it belongs only to you."

Before Violet could answer, a vision appeared on the portal. At first, after all the wine, Violet wondered if it was an angel. Tall, pale, with a cloud of red-gold hair, dressed in the height of fashion in pale blue Chanel and a white fur stole. She glided across the portal on her alligator shoes, and lowered herself onto an empty valance.

"Oh, thank heavens!" she gasped in a Mayfair accent. "I thought I would never escape that courtyard, it is filled with such a mob. May I have some of that lovely-looking wine? I'm Moira, by the way, remember? Ludovic and Mirandi brought me, I had no idea what a real American Thanksgiving was like! Such a riot. Most astonishing ..."

CHAPTER 29

Violet

AT BRETT'S HOUSE, A FEW DAYS BEFORE CHRISTMAS

"Well, now, Vi! What do you think of it all?"

Violet stepped back to examine Brett's courtyard, her boots crunching on the snow. She pushed back her scarf to tilt her head for a good look. Brett had been inspired by MR's Thanksgiving party (despite the disaster of it all, ending with drunken fights and many tears) to have a Christmas fete of her own. "Just like the ones I remember from Merry Olde England!" she declared.

Violet had never spent Christmas in England, but she wondered if this just didn't miss the mark a bit.

Brett *had* cleared out the courtyard, mucking out cracked flagstones, unidentified metal bits, and broken canvases, piling them to the side like some sort of avant-garde sculptures. A firepit in the center was cleaned and laid for a bonfire, surrounded by a mismatch of chairs and stools. A few dusty rugs were tossed here and there, sniffed cautiously by the stray dogs and cats, and tables were laid out along the crumbling adobe walls waiting for the food and booze to appear. The cold, dry air smelled of woodsmoke and Brett's pipe. She wore her least battered sombrero for the day, along with a nearly-new military cape of navy blue wool.

The studio, too, was decked in its best. Chains of looped red and green paper festooned every window, and a wreath of pine made by the kids at the pueblo hung on the door. A bright tissue donkey pinata, pink and yellow and orange, only a bit faded and dusty, was suspended from a viga, ready to release his riches of candy. The mountain, wreathed in cottony gray clouds in a pearl-gray sky, seemed to approve of the activity in her dominion.

Violet peered up at the figures on the roof, a papier mâché nativity scene someone had found in a basement. The shepherds looked unsure of it all.

"Oh, Brett!" she said, clapping her hands in their mittens. "It will be the best Christmas party ever, I'm sure."

Brett chuckled around the stem of her pipe. "It's the only Christmas party, here anyway! I can't believe I let you talk me into it."

"I do believe it was entirely your idea." Violet jingled a bell on the wreath and laughed.

"You're a doll to say so, Vi darling, but then you are always made of manners and sweetness and kindness."

Violet felt her face turn hot under those damnable freckles, and turned away to fuss with a bow. She thought of that night—just last week? It felt a millions years ago, but also just a moment. A minute too far away, a minute she wanted to happen over and over again, she and Lorenzo tangled in his old quilt, the smell of the sun and the dust, his tousled hair wrapped around her throat, his mouth ...

Well. That part didn't matter just now, did it? But Violet wouldn't ever forget that wonderful madness. Never forget shooting up into the deep turquoise sky, held to earth only by his callused hands, his kiss. That miracle mouth of his.

It would never have been like that with Bill, or with *anyone* at home. No sirree. She saw now why Lorenzo's sister, why Mabel and Tony, thought that nothing in the world was worth anything beside a feeling like *that*. Beside something meant to be like that.

"Vi?" Brett snapped. "Are you listening?"

Violet whirled around and smiled at her, still so giddy, giggling. She was afraid that Brett, that anyone in this town who spent their lives studying faces, reading minds, peering into souls to put them in brushstrokes and poetic words, would know. She took a deep breath, and smiled sweetly. "Of course."

"But you did forget to set the water boiling for coffee," Brett said.

Violet gasped. "I did?" Brett had set her that tiny task hours ago. She had just gotten too busy doing—something else. Daydreaming, probably. Most unlike her. "Oh, Brett, I am sorry! I'll get right on that. Now." She ran into the cottage, Brett and all her dogs following, laughing.

"No worries. As long as there's booze, everyone is happy." Brett gestured toward the long, bare table lined with benches, beer and champagne, bourbon and gin and unlabeled brown bottles from local stills waiting. Tubs of ice were shoved beneath, and a myriad of pottery bowls lined another table, tamales, potato salad, hunks of meat in red chili sauce, loaves of pueblo bread, pies and empanadas. Very different from MR's Thanksgiving feast of turkey and cranberry, her fancy bakery cakes. But Brett *had* swept the dirt floors, hung up a few more of her newest paintings for color, brushed her dogs, cleaned her curtains (which proved to be red!), and laid out rows of borrowed chairs.

Violet set about filling the coffee pots from the pump, dodging the herds of dogs as they tried their hardest to leave carpets of hair on her pleated crimson skirt. It was new, from Martha's, along with the silver-buttoned jacket and woven shawl, the engraved silver earrings that had appeared in a wrapped package one day, wrapping that smelled of Lorenzo's sunshine and juniper. An early Christmas gift. She'd so wanted to impress him today, to show him she belonged in Taos. If only that could be true ...

She paused to take a cookie from a tray, a star-shaped, amber-brown, so light and fluffy it melted on her tongue. It tasted perfectly of Christmas.

"What are these angelic things?" she asked around the cookie. "I've never tasted anything like them!"

"*Bisochitos*," Brett said. "Everyone makes them for the holidays. You'll get sick of them, they show up everywhere."

"I could never get sick of them," Violet vowed. She scanned the room, straightening cushions, emptying ashtrays. "How could anyone get sick of ambrosia!"

Brett watched her impassively from her chair in the corner, where a portrait of Millicent was half-finished on the easel beside her. MR stared out coolly from the painted scene, her emerald-green silk dress and diamonds impeccable, her face thinner, her hair more silver, her eyes wary. Even in paint, Violet worried about her.

"Vi, darling," Brett said, lighting her pipe again. "I may be an old spinster, but I have eyes. Are you in love by any chance?"

Violet froze. She slowly glanced back at Brett. Brett's brows raised. "Me? In love?"

"Perfectly natural. We all do it, from time to time. Except that crazy old Bynner. I think he really loves no one but himself. But you—you and your soft heart. God save you, my dear. You just give all your love away to all of us, even if we don't deserve it. You're devoted to MR, just as I am, selfish old witch that she can be." Violet started to protest, to declare that MR was so very generous, but Brett held up one paint-stained hand. "She is also an angel of generosity and beauty. She can afford to be witchy sometimes. But you, Vi, you are loyal to the very end, which does make one wonder. Are you in love with our Lothario, the dark and dangerous Benito, just as MR is?"

Violet couldn't stop her jaw from sagging. "Me? In love with Benito?" She thought of that dreadful Thanksgiving, the pregnant girl, MR's sadness. "No, certainly not."

Brett smiled. "You've got a level head on your shoulders. Martha and I were just worried ..."

Violet stiffened. "You and Martha were talking about me? How did you know anything about my personal life at all?"

Brett laughed so hard the pipe fell from her stained teeth, and she rocked in her chair. "Oh, bless you, my dear. Have you not seen where you live? Everyone here knows everyone's business, and just because they like to gossip the most about Mrs. Rogers doesn't mean they don't notice you. Martha and I are your friends, your true friends. We just worry."

Violet sighed. Brett did have a point. She wasn't blind; well, she wasn't *too* much of a fool most of the time. And Brett and Martha were really two of the best friends she'd ever had, along with MR. Unlike MR, they lived in the prosaic world of sense.

"Come on, sit down, have a beer or something, tell Auntie Brett all about it," Brett said, kicking out a chair and passing her a bottle. "So—if you're not in love with Benito, thank goodness, who is it? Your California lawyer? He was a handsome one."

Violet sat down and took a long gulp. One of the smaller dogs jumped up on her lap, and she didn't push him off. She cuddled him close. "I've been meaning to write to Charles to ask him if we can just be friends, but it's been hard to find the right words. He's so perfectly nice, so perfectly—perfect. But ..."

Brett shook her head wisely. "He can't stay here. And you can't leave."

Violet nodded sadly. "That's just it. I can't picture ever being anywhere but here now. And he can't. His work is in California. Just —don't tell MR I've decided anything yet. She seems so determined."

Brett shook her head. "You are well and truly caught by Taos, just as your MR is. Just like I was. No getting away now whether you want to or not."

Violet laughed. "That's just the thing. I *don't* want to go. I doubt even heaven itself could be as perfect as this. My family will never understand."

Brett poured more wine and shooed the dogs away. "Mine

never did either. Going from a deb's life in England's green and pleasant land to—this? Unfathomable! They would have sent me to an asylum if they dared."

"Luckily I don't think there are any asylums in Iowa. And my brother's ever-so-suitable wedding is distracting them."

"And now you're here, hundreds of miles from them! And you're in love! Not with Benito."

"No." Violet smiled, gazing down into her glass as she remembered certain kisses, certain whispers. The memory of his skin against hers.

"Then who? You can tell your Auntie Brett."

And Violet sensed she did have to tell *someone*. She was bursting with it all! The wonder and the fear. It was just what the poets said ...

But. But.

She drained her drink, and poured another one. "It's Lorenzo. Lorenzo Serna. Benito's cousin. But he's not at all like him!"

Brett's eyes widened so much it almost made Violet giggle. Brett took off her hat and slapped her knee with its battered straw. "Lorenzo Serna! Well, I never. Oh, my dear."

Violet shivered. "You hate it."

"Oh, no, no. I see it now. If ever two people were meant for each other, it's you and Serna. Two peas in a tiny pod. What beautiful babies you'd make."

Violet gave a choked laugh. 'Beautiful babies' had been far from her mind, thanks to MR's birth control advice, but everything else—everything that could keep them apart—she had willfully kept in the far background. Kicked the can. They were just getting to know each other, finding time together. But she knew she would have to face it all, and soon. Make decisions that would affect them all, just as Lorenzo's sister had, and shape the rest of their lives.

She closed her eyes and saw that forlorn grave, Lorenzo's sister who gave up all for her white husband, for their love. Family was everything to Lorenzo. She couldn't take that away from him.

"What does MR say?" Brett asked.

Violet opened her eyes, and took another drink. The heat of the alcohol was doing its job, blurring her thoughts, giving her a warm, wholly undeserved feeling of well-being. Of "everything will be gone by tomorrow and thus all right-ness." It was Christmas! How could things not be well?

"I haven't talked to her about it yet," she admitted.

Brett nodded sagely. "She thinks you will work for her forever, her devoted secretary, her servant ..."

"It's not like that!" Violet protested. "She pays me so well, I've never dreamed I could earn so much, and she's shown me so many things ..."

Brett laid a gentle, plump hand on Violet's arm. "MR *is* generous, to a fault. She will give you the Charles James shirt off her back in an instant. But she is always and ever about *her*, even with her children. You should be about *you*."

Violet knew that Brett was right, even if those words were the last thing she wanted to hear. MR was generous and lovely and stingy and selfish, sometimes all within five minutes. She relied on Violet, as she relied on Edith, but Violet couldn't stay bound forever. Not when she had glimpsed the free horizon. She slowly nodded. "The problem, my darling Brett, is I have no idea what I want to do. Not in a real way."

Brett studied her with lowered, doubtful eyes. "A girl like you must have a thousand talents you could use. Use for *yourself*. You had a dream of writing when you were a girl, yes?"

Violet, embarrassed, shuffled her booted feet in the snow. She didn't say anything about that pile of papers on her desk. "Yes, I did."

"Try that. A girl like you must have a hundred talents you can try or use or discard as you like. Use this time for *yourself*. It never comes again."

"Writing never comes again?"

"That's up to you, and only you. There are plenty of writers you could talk to here in New Mexico, heaven knows, and they do like to pontificate. You can listen, or not. Take what works for you and throw away the rest. Do what *you* must do to find the one art that belongs to you alone. Throw out bad stories, egregious poems, until you find what works well. Above all, see life, if you can. Design brooches with Millicent, travel around with Mabel if you can stand it, work in Martha's shop, talk to everyone or no one, above all just drive around the desert looking for art. Go to Paris! Rome! Cairo! Wherever! Whatever!"

Violet was laughing helplessly. Try this, try that. Whatever works keep it. Whatever you love, love with all your heart. It was the only way her writing was going to hold truth, as Brett's paintings did. "I'm not sure I have the money to get to Paris yet."

Brett waved this away with her pipe, as if money was a mere trifle. "We can help you find another job, no problem at all. You are too good to do MR's accounts forever, that's all." She fed a *biso-chito* to the over-excited dogs. "And how is MR? No one has seen nor heard from her in a while, not since that ever-so-fascinating Thanksgiving. They say Benito is off at Los Alamos with that maid, or maybe he's in Roswell. Maybe he isn't even in New Mexico now. Or was it Las Cruces? I hope the poor girl is near a hospital, anyway."

Violet carefully shrugged. She'd heard nothing of Benito since that party; Millicent never uttered a word, and she dared not pry with Lorenzo. "MR is working a bit. Working on her jewelry, a new falling star design. Keeping to her room." It was one reason Violet could sneak away to be with Lorenzo quite so often, but she still worried. Millicent always had days where her illness confined her to bed, but this seemed—different. Quieter, more tense, as if the whole house, the whole world, just held its breath. Waited. "She says she wants to have a Valentine's Day party in February."

Brett snorted. "That's an image, isn't it? A big pink and red party, when she hasn't seen anyone for weeks."

"She's just been tired." And that *was* the truth—but only part of it. MR had gone very quiet, not just over the dinner trays but deep in herself. She seemed to have gone somewhere no-one else could follow, or even fathom. Her dark eyes saw things far away indeed. "I would like your help, Brett. And Martha's."

Brett's craggy face softened. "And you have it, my dear. Always. I am not sure any of us can help MR very much now, but we would love to try. She, and you, mean so much to us. You're part of us, of Taos, now." She paused, relighting her pipe. "As for you and Serna—I beg you, darling, don't give up on him, no matter what pressure you come under. You will need all your strength, and then some, if you really love him and he you. Yet nothing worth having in life was ever had without a fight."

Violet slowly nodded. She did love Lorenzo; could she fight hard enough? Would he fight for her? They would face so very much, just as his sister had, just as the Luhans had. Would it be enough? She didn't know yet. She only knew how it felt when he held her in his arms, when they danced to his off-tune singing, and she knew happiness she never imagined could be true before. She knew perfection and purpose. Taos, Lorenzo, her book. It was everything she had ever wanted, if she could just be strong enough to hold it.

"And sometimes," Brett said gently, so very horribly gentle, "no matter how much we can love it, it can never be enough. Love can turn to resentment." A car horn sounded, and the dogs went crazy barking. Brett smiled brightly. "Ah—the holiday begins! Are we quite fortified, my dear Violet?"

Violet was quite sure she could *never* be fortified enough for what the cloudy future threatened to hold. But she had learned something very important from MR—the future could never, ever be held back. It was what we did with it when it came that mattered. The only thing that mattered.

"Good tidings of great joy," she muttered, and drank down the last of the wine before she hurried ahead to face the Happiest Season Of All.

CHAPTER 30

Violet

AT BRETT'S CHRISTMAS PARTY

"For that is the time to eat, drink, and be merry,
Til the beer is all spilled and the whiskey has flowed.
And the whole family tree you neglected to bury,
Are feeding their faces until they explode.
There'll be laughter and tears over Tia Marias,
Mixed up with that drink made from Gibleys.
Cause it's all we've got left as they draw their last
*   breath,*
Ah, it's nice for the kids, as you finally get rid of
*   them,*
In the St. Stephen's Day Murders."

Violet laughed as she watched everything around her, the whole scene that seemed like a fever dream, a painting, a surrealist poem. Everything had seemed a bit like that ever since she came to the mountains, ever since she rang MR's palm tree-shaded doorbell. Like life suddenly turned colors, turned lurid red and blue and green and sparkling silver. But this ...

"It's amazing!" she cried over the blast of the music, the Irish drums and voices that had come from who-knew-where. Brett's ancient gramophone had collapsed under the assault on its needles, given way to a live group of amateur, spur-of-the-moment musicians. Christmas songs went on and on, obscure and too popular alike (she'd heard "Frosty the Snowman" so much she was sure she would scream). Someone else had brought out a guitar, strumming out old Spanish songs in the courtyard, the sad chords clashing against all the snow and eggnog and snuggling against the frost, yet none of it mattered. They didn't even seem to be different things at all.

The lights strung around the courtyard sparkled and winked against the night, making the snowflakes that had begun to fall like sparkling diamonds. The space was surrounded by people, crammed, people dancing and swigging and singing and laughing. Brett's many dogs ran back and forth, into the house, outside again.

Frieda Lawrence, like a large, flowsy-haired Christmas tree herself in a green satin caftan and ropes of amber beads, exuberantly kissed Violet's cheeks and grabbed her hands. She waved across the courtyard to her Italian husband, who hurried over to hand Violet a glass of—she knew not what. Something red and glowing from the enormous punch bowls everyone had been pouring into and dipping out of all night. Violet had already had one—or two?—but drank it down anyway, laughing. Frieda was like that—an enormous ball of fun that carried everyone along with her.

"Vi, long time no see, *liebchen*! How hard the Frau Millicent must work you, yes? But we all must have fun at Christmas, it is universal law!" Frieda said. "How this town does agree with you. You look like—like Maureen O'Hara!"

Violet laughed, too. She looked not a thing like Maureen O'Hara, beyond their red hair, and she knew it. With Millicent, she had seen real stars, Janet, Moira. She had to admit, though, she *felt* rather lovely that night in a red taffeta gown handed down from MR, with her hair twisted up in a glossy chignon and a sable stole over her shoulders.

Or maybe it was just the punch. She was always sparing with alcohol, after seeing what it did to her brother, to Benito. Yet that giddiness, that giggliness! That floaty-freedom feeling. It wasn't so bad. It took her mind off MR's troubles, about what she herself would have to decide to do all too soon. She glanced back over her shoulder to see Millicent sat on one of Brett's chaises, smoking from her long holder, talking to Eva, no doubt about new jewelry coming into the store. She did still look too thin, too pale, too brittle, but more like herself in a gown of sea-green velvet and silver fox coat,rubies blinking at her ears. She saw Violet, and nodded and smiled.

Violet smiled back. Yes, on a night like this, everything—the music, the sky, the lights—it all drifted on a bright cloud of possibility.

"What do you think she is saying?" Frieda whispered in Violet's ear, her breath rich with drink, and for an instant Violet was confused. Then she followed Frieda's gesture back to MR. Eva had gone, and now Benito, the reappeared Benito, sat in her place, leaning close to Millicent, his face one large plea as she shook her head. He took her hand, raised her bejeweled fingers to his lips, and she seemed to light up like the bonfire. She was *too* bright suddenly, too tense, as if she might snap. Too close to the edge of control.

Millicent had always been changeable, of course, ever since the days by the LA pool. The days of Captain Butler. Peace had descended when they came to Taos, but lately Violet had sensed that tightness, that tension, growing again, a string drawn taut, taut, until it could snap. When he vanished after Thanksgiving, Violet had hoped that would be over.

She should have known better.

Violet took a sip of her drink and glanced around the crowded party. Millicent and Benito had always attracted attention; very soon they would surely be the star act. She took another drink, and said with a laugh, "Who knows with Mrs. Rogers? It's a party! Anything can happen."

"Anything, *ja*," Frieda said calmly. She was a woman who knew scandal very well indeed.

Violet felt a touch at her waist, and spun around to find Lorenzo standing behind her, his face all sharp planes and angles in the lights, his eyes narrowed. She had never been so glad to see anyone in all her life, and she almost melted against him.

"Care to dance?" he said.

"Would I ever!" Violet laughed, and let him lead her into the swirl and knot of people around Brett's broken fountain. Just as it always was with him, everything seemed transformed when he was near. The world was steadier, slower, more beautiful. More right. The song slowed into "I'll Be Home For Christmas," and he twirled her into the curve of his body.

She leaned against him, her forehead on his chest, inhaling the sun-clean scent of his cotton shirt, his softly woven wool vest, the smoke of the bonfires, the crispness of the snow. She felt small against him, but fierce, too, as if she could face anything at all. Be anything. There with him.

The press of the people moved close, holding her against him, and she could feel the hum of the song deep inside his chest, felt their bodies move together perfectly.

He spun her around again, her feet nearly leaving the ground, and she laughed and laughed. "Oh, this *is* fun!" she said. "Who knew Christmas could be like this?"

He caught her close, his hand warm and strong on her back, his smile crooked. He kissed her forehead, and she closed her eyes tightly, letting the music and that delightful tipsiness carry her higher into the clouds.

"Were your Christmases not so much fun before?" he said.

"No, not fun so much," she sighed, almost laughing to remember Iowa Christmases, and how they could not have been more different than this night was. The same foods on the same lace tablecloth, the same songs played on the pianoforte, the same sedate games, the same gift of a book and a doll and an orange, Bible readings, early to bed. "We would have a Boxing Day tea at my grandmother's house, where she would take out her samovar and her Russian tea glasses for the only time of the year, and we would nibble aniseed balls and bonbons and she would give us a half-dollar. To be invested, of course. My parents would have a sherry, also the only one of the year. Then we would sit quietly while my grandmother played the piano. That was it." She giggled, and held tight to Lorenzo's shoulders. "How shocked they would be to see me now! Drinking random wine, dancing. But I do miss my mother's apple tarts. I should make them for you sometime."

"You can cook, then, Miss Iowa?" he teased.

Violet smacked his arm before letting him twirl her again and pull her close. How perfect this was, she thought dreamily. The cold, the music—him. How it felt just like home. "Of course I can! It's not part of my job now, but I can make a decent roast chicken. Mash a potato. Bake a pie. Nothing like the luscious food at your aunt's house, though, I fear." She thought of the vast spread laid out on his aunt's table on the night of the races—red and green chili, tamales, stews, breads, cakes and cookies, pork posole, lamb in herbs.

"Come to the pueblo tomorrow," he said. "Dances in the morning, that food all day long until you can't move from stuffing yourself. I warn you, though—if auntie learns you can cook a Christmas spread, she'll make you teach her."

Violet frowned. Lorenzo's aunt was lovely indeed, but every time they met she felt a distinct chill from her, a suspicion. "I— don't know. It's just a family hobby ..."

"Christmas is an *everyone* hobby." he said. "Besides, who knows what you'll be in her home one day."

Startled, Violet took a step back, bumping into another dancer, and stared up at him. The bonfire cast flickering shadows over his lean features, making him unreadable. Could he—*could* he mean what he said? It was often so hard to know with Lorenzo. He was so mysterious sometimes. Did he mean he wanted her to be part of his family? Did *she* want that?

She moved into his embrace again, closing her eyes. She didn't think of that now, not with the night whirling around her. If she did, she feared she might grab onto his hand and drag him off to the justice of the peace, damn everything else that might happen. She suddenly felt so reckless, giddy even. And that wasn't like her at all.

Or was it? It wasn't like the old Violet. Maybe it was exactly the new Violet. The girl she was just starting to know.

"Sing to me," she said.

"Are you sure you can stand it?" he laughed.

She nodded, and he launched into "White Christmas." Bing again. Soon, everyone around them had joined in, a drunken chorus including the howls of Brett's dogs, and for a long time Violet forgot all about MR and her problems and everything else.

The song ended, and Violet sat down, suddenly exhausted, on a cushioned stool near the bonfire. Lorenzo went to fetch her a drink, and Violet stretched out her feet, aching in those new black stilettos. She scanned the crowd. She finally spotted Millicent along the wall, smoking, alone, a faraway look on her sculpted face. She looked gilded by the stars, as if she was far away from them all already. Violet started to stand, to go to her, but Millicent stubbed out her cigarette under her Vivier pump and left the courtyard. Violet stood up, as if to follow, and Brett suddenly sat down beside her, dragging her back down. Her face was red, her sombrero lost and her hair a wild swirl, but she looked exhausted and happy.

"I knew we were all wrong about her," Brett said, her voice more Jane Austen than ever with drink and pipe smoke, a deeply sad look suddenly clouding her craggy face. "But she is a grown woman. A woman who has never been told no. We can't be the ones to start that now."

"Surely ..." Violet started, then shook her head. Brett, in her own abrupt strange way, was right. Violet was MR's friend, as far as it went; she *wanted* to be her friend. Yet with a woman like MR, a woman Violet really had come to know so well, things could only go so far and no more. Just as at that night at Mabel's, when MR fell asleep in the car, she had to seek for herself, just as Violet had to seek for herself. Millicent would come back when she was ready, that was all.

Violet remembered what Millicent said to her once. *I have a mother who fusses over me. I don't need you to be one, too, Vi.*

Violet knew that feeling all too well. Too many mothers.

Yet—what if Violet did go after them? She could have stopped nothing, not really. MR was on a course no one else could fathom. What if. What if. What if.

It had grown late—or early? The sky was edging into pinkish-gray-coral from sheer black, the bonfire dying to smoke and embers, the snow lying in drifts on the ground, people lazing about as wild-drink laughter turned to sleepy murmurs—when Violet realized she hadn't seen MR in hours. Not since she saw her put out the cigarette and drift away, not since Brett told her Millicent was a grown woman.

Violet pulled herself up out of the old wooden deck chair where she was watching the stars blink off, one by one, and looked around at the courtyard. No Millicent, not in the studio where Brett shouted at Frieda through Toby, not where the cars were haphazardly parked. She thought of that night at Mabel's, MR asleep in the car as the sun rose.

Brett seemed to see something in Violet's eyes, something of panic, and despite her previous warnings to mind one's own business, she pushed herself to her feet and reached for Violet's arms. "What is it?"

"I can't find Millicent," Violet said simply.

Brett nodded, and in silence they hurried out to the rutted lane where the cars were left. More snow was falling, leaving stinging, cold, wetness. MR's station wagon was empty, but the keys were in the ignition and Brett used them to drive off slowly toward Turtle Walk. A few cars fell in behind them, and Violet recognized Benito's aunt, and—gulp—Tony in the backseat of one of the cars. A bitter wind beat at the car windows, and Violet slumped down in her fur stole and tried not think, not to worry, not to regret.

That was then they saw it. Violet sat straight up, her throat tight, her stomach so sour she feared she would throw up in fear. A small coupe, curled into a pole on the side of the lane, its wood and wires and steel collapsed onto the hood in a great tangle. The doors were crumpled.

"No!" Violet gasped., hardly realizing what she said. She leaped out of the car, Brett close behind her, and saw MR sitting by the side of the road. Blood matted her hair on one side of her head, and she had a bruise on her check. She cradled one wrist against her waist, but otherwise seemed unharmed.

"MR!" Violet cried. She knelt beside Millicent in the snow, and all the old first aid classes she took in the war came flooding back to her somehow. A strange, icy calm took over her mind. She checked Millicent's pupils, examined the scrape on her scalp, made sure the wrist wasn't broken before she bound it up in a scarf.

"Benny ..." Millicent whispered, biting her lip. "He ... he ..."

Brett was at the car, the crumpled driver's door open in front of her. She looked very solemn, especially for Brett. "Alive," she said. "Unconscious."

The car with Benito's aunt and cousins pulled up behind them, and as they carefully set about extracting him from the car, Millicent stood up and moved slowly toward them, like a ghost or a dream. She sat on the snowy ground and drew his bleeding head onto her lap, cradling him, looking at him in that dreamy silence.

"We'll take him back to town," one of his cousins said, his

whole demeanor resigned, as if he had seen this, dealt with it, many times.

"The hospital," Millicent said finally. "Brett, help me put him in the car. There is no sense waiting for an ambulance in this weather. I'll stay with him."

"Millicent," Brett said firmly. "You could have been killed here! People who are damaged like this—they destroy not only themselves but everyone around them. He needs proper help ..."

MR shot her a freezing glance, no less chilling for the streaks of blood on her forehead, her silver fox fur. "Hospital, now."

Benito's relatives carefully lifted him into her car, and MR moved to follow. Violet instinctively went behind her, wanting to help her, but so unsure what "help" could mean now.

"No, Violet, not you," Millicent said quietly, finally.

"MR?" she gasped, confused.

"I helped you once," Millicent said, not looking at Violet. Only watching the unconscious Benito, whose family ignored her. "Help me now."

And it was true. MR *had* helped her. Had changed her life completely. What could Violet tell her now? Ever? To be careful? It wasn't in MR to be careful, and it was all so late anyway.

"Yes," Violet said, and Millicent nodded. She threw a kiss at the end, a tiny gesture of apology, before she turned away. Even years later, Violet puzzled over that little moment. That moment when it all utterly changed.

VIOLET—TURTLE WALK

Violet stared down at the pan. It wasn't like her mother's, of course, Violet knew that. No matter what happened next, she would never run a house like her mother's. The perfect floors, the lace curtains, the china in the cabinet, the stylish furniture, all smelling of lemon polish. A woman's life work. Maybe she could learn to cook a few more things yet. It didn't look so bad, she thought as she examined the chicken pie in the pan. Pale gold on top, not burned, not white-raw. Not so bad.

Turtle Walk didn't seem right without MR there. Too quiet, too solemn, no waves of Shocking perfume in the air. Violet didn't quite know what to do with herself. So she was baking. She turned to the kitchen table, where Lorenzo sat with the dogs clustered at his feet. They hadn't gone to the feast at his aunt's house, but Christmas finally felt like Christmas just with the two of them together.

She smiled, and set the pan down next to him on the table, between the cold chicken and ham pie Edith left, the bottle of champagne Violet had dared to take from Millicent's own ice-box. "What do you think?"

Lorenzo laughed. How lovely it sounded after the strange few winter days, rich and warm and silly. "I think you'll make someone a terrific wife, Violet Anastasia. Someday."

Violet bit her lip. He had hinted at such things before, marriage in a jokey way, and she didn't know how she felt about it. How she *wanted* to feel about it. "I will make someone a terrible wife indeed. My head always seems to be up in the clouds these days, and I can't concentrate. But the pie doesn't look too terrible, I think."

"Your head's in your book?"

Violet sliced into the pie, making careful triangles. "Sometimes, yes. I admit that the book world seems more real than the human world sometimes. Or maybe I just want it to be. Ma writes me that I have to stop running away from life."

"Well, if Ma says it, it must be true. Or not." Lorenzo opened the champagne with a deft twist, a soft pop, and poured the golden liquid into their glasses. "But if there's one thing your friends here know, it's art. Real art. You can trust that."

"Real art." Was that what that stack of papers in her room was

—art? She dared to hope so. There were instants she even felt it. Yet that was all so far away. "Maybe so. I don't know. How is Benito?"

"Stable. We're grateful Mrs. Rogers wasn't hurt. She's insisting on paying his hospital bills."

"Of course she is. She's so generous that way." Violet poured out cream to go with her pie and arranged the plates carefully. "So many people think she's just selfish, like all beautiful, rich people. Maybe sometimes she is. No, sometimes she definitely is! But she does want to take care of the wounded birds. Even when that bird tried to kill her. Stole from her. Hurt her." Her hand stilled on the pitcher. "I guess love does that sometimes."

Lorenzo reached out and touched her hand, steady, warm. "You aren't a wounded bird, Vi."

She laid her hand over his. "I was once. Lost, unsure, lonely. I owe her so much."

He leaned back in his chair, his face thoughtful, unreadable. "Tony says—and everyone else agrees—Benny will have to go away when he recovers. Make a new start someplace. Tony knows a clinic in Colorado for a start."

"What does MR say?"

Lorenzo shrugged. "I'm not sure she knows yet, it's just been decided by the family. It doesn't matter. I know you have loyalty for her. Love for her. And your kind heart is amazing. She wants to help him, I suppose, but she can't any more. Her help only hurts."

Violet closed her eyes and thought of her brother when he came back from the war, how he seemed bent on drinking himself to death and no one could stop him. Not until he decided to stop himself. "Brett says the same thing."

"And you? What do you think, Violet?"

Violet bit her lip. "I think—Millicent is not well. She needs rest. She needs peace. She needs ..." She shook her head. "They are right. Of course."

Lorenzo just nodded. He was not a man of many words, but

she knew him now, just as he knew her. They both had people they loved who they had to hurt to help. Violet was glad she was no longer alone to face that knife-pierce.

"Here, try my apple pie," she said. "And pass that champagne."

MILLICENT—COMES BACK TO TURTLE WALK

Violet sat with Brett on the needlepoint cushion-strewn leather sofa in Millicent's library, the two of them silent in the twilight. The grandfather clock from Austria ticked by, one click at a time, bing-click-bong, the only sound beyond the ice in Brett's whiskey, Fanny's doggy snores, the wind over the roof. Surely Turtle Walk had never been so quiet before. So empty.

At last they heard it, the hum of a car pulling up the drive, the slam of the door, the tap of Millicent's heels.

Millicent appeared there, in one of her caramel-brown Charles James suits and a sable coat, her hair brushed under an amber taffeta turban fastened with a diamond brooch. Her face was thin, pale, her eyes lined with purplish shadows. She stared at them silently, drawing off her gloves.

"MR ..." Brett began.

Millicent gave her one of her patented frosty glances, one quick wave of her emerald-crusted fingers. "Haven't I been a good friend to you, *Lady* Brett? Haven't I done everything I could to support your art? To give you what you needed?"

Brett's face reddened in fury. "MR ..." she began, standing up.

"Go. Now." Millicent slapped her gloves on her palm, softening just a bit. Maybe she was just too tired to maintain her old magnificent levels of fury. "Please. I must speak alone to Violet."

Brett glanced at Violet. "I'll be right outside," she whispered, and Violet nodded.

"My manuscript, MR," she managed to say, even though she was shaking. "Did you take it? Read it?"

"Of course I did," Millicent said, looking absolutely incredulous she would be questioned about such a thing. "I wanted to help you. To make sure you had a good life. But you wouldn't listen to me, you silly girl!"

Violet felt her cheeks turn to flames, her anger at being controlled, at losing any ounce of privacy she had ever possessed, threatened to overwhelm her. "*You* tried to help *me*? While you and Benito ..."

"Who are *you* to tell me what to do?" Millicent said fiercely. She threw her gloves on the floor, hitting Violet's feet, and swept a vase off a table. It shattered into slivers. Millicent ignored it, and stalked off to the bar cart to pour out a full tumbler of brandy, which she tossed back. "You are just an employee."

Violet felt the sting of an arrow at her heart. After so long, so many things seen together, so many sacrifices, she was an *employee*. That was all. "I am your friend, I care about you. Millicent. I've seen the way Benito is, he is—is very ill. You must take care of your own health ..."

"I can manage myself, thank you, better than any farm girl could. You do not know him as I do. You do not know *me*."

Violet bit back a sob, remembering her brother, the terrible words he would spit at her when he was drunk, when he was in the darkness. "That girl—that pregnant girl at Thanksgiving ..."

"It is a lie! People are just jealous of him, of his beauty. Men are never faithful. They don't know how to be. For a clever woman, it never matters." Her expression twisted, and for an instant Violet didn't recognize her. "What would a dried-up spinster from Iowa like you know about it all? After all that I've tried to teach you, tried to help you. Charles Rivers would have helped you so much, given you a comfortable life while you wrote your book, did what you wanted ..."

"Wait," Violet whispered, the image of her manuscript, the

pages out of order, flashing through her mind. "You really did read it?"

Millicent's lips tightened, and she tilted her head. She knew best, that was what that expression meant, and she wouldn't be told otherwise. Violet saw it too often. "It's a good book, Violet, you have a gift. It could be better with help, with study. And Charles hasmoney, he would have supported you, introduced you to influential people. But you throw your affections away now. I've done that myself, and come to regret it, but at least I could afford it. You can't. I was *helping* you!"

A red mist seemed to rise before Violet's eyes, and anger such as she had never known threatened to turn her to cinders. Her book, her writing! And MR had interfered with it. Judged it. Thrown her toward a rich man so he could "help" her, no matter what Violet's own feelings. "How dare you?"

Millicent's lips thinned even more. "How dare *I*? I took you in when you had nothing, just a hideous jacket and terrible typing, and gave you a chance. A life. How ungrateful! How miserable!"

Violet's hands curled into fists. "Better a dried-up spinster than an old ..."

Millicent suddenly pulled back her hand, so thin now, so delicate, but heavy with those jeweled rings and cracked her open palm against Violet's cheek. The sound reverberated, echoed through Turtle Walk's elegant rooms like a firecracker.

Violet clutched at her stinging cheek and stumbled back, tripping on the edge of a rug. She was frozen with shock, fear.

Millicent stared at her expressionlessly. "Get out," she whispered, ice cold. "Now. I have had enough of your ingratitude, your foolishness. I've heard all about you and Lorenzo from Benito!"

Violet did not stay to hear one more word. She ran through the house, the lovely house she had helped design, had watched rise wall by wall into a paradise of beauty, all ashes now. She threw her suitcase on her bed and tossed in clothes, not the couture Millicent had pressed on her but her own Martha skirts and blouses and dresses, the bracelets Lorenzo gave her, the money she had saved. Her precious manuscript.

Her legs shook so much she wasn't sure she could move as she made her way blindly out of Turtle Walk, magical Turtle Walk, for the last time. She glimpsed her reflection in one of the silver-framed Spanish mirrors, her hair tangled against the collar of her new green wool coat, her cheek stained red with that handprint, her eyes damp. She dashed her palm across them and tilted back her head, refusing to show any more shock, any more misery.

Millicent was nowhere to be seen.

Brett waited in her ancient car in the driveway, chewing on the stem of her pipe. Her eyes widened in shock as she saw Violet, that red cheek, those glassy eyes. Yes, even Brett could be shocked, Violet realized. Amazing.

"Let's go to La Fonda," Violet muttered, slamming the passenger side door behind her. "I need a room. And then let's go to El Patio and order margaritas. I want to get very, very drunk."

Brett just nodded and started the car with a sputter. "Capital idea, duckie. Capital idea."

CHAPTER 31

Violet

MONTHS LATER, WORKING AT MARTHA'S

V iolet straightened a display of hand-painted silk scarves in the window, trying first to swirl them one way then the other. The brilliant blues and reds and golds and purples were a beacon against the dull, flat gray day outside, beckoning with hope of sunshine to return, but the shop was quiet. The whole town was quiet, visitors had gone to trek up the snowy passes and ski down, artists gone back to Albuquerque or Pittsburgh or New York or Paris. Only a few kids went sledding past, shrieking, one or two knots of sleepy groups braving the chilly winds, but that was all.

Not that Violet found Taos any less beautiful, less wondrous in the winter. In fact, she loved it more, loved the snow-muffled quiet, the feeling that the streets and courtyards only belonged to a few of them.

She finished with the scarves and went to polish the glass cases for the fifth time that day, rearranging the jewelry on the black velvet trays. Two of those pieces were Lorenzo's, an intricate turquoise brooch and an elegant silver bracelet. The other pieces had come in last week, and even though Martha had exacting standards in what she would carry they were slow to sell now in the quiet season. Violet wore one of the new creations herself, a turquoise and rose quartz brooch on the lapel of her black suit.

She took the clothes left in the fitting room and replaced them in the armoires, smoothing the calico and velvet and sateen, before she pushed the coffee-drinkers' sofas back into place in the corner. Every day, rain or shine, they came, the plump mistresses of town, arbiters of "society" as they saw it, despite there being no Society in Taos to speak of. They were a silly lot, those ranchers' and oilmens' wives, like squawking parrots, and they seldom bought anything, but it was only through eavesdropping on their gossip that she knew much about MR in those days.

Violet frowned down at a beaded belt. She hadn't spoken to MR since the day she left Turtle Walk, her face swollen, and she only glimpsed her as her new car (*not* driven by Benito now) roared past on Paseo. Violet's things had been delivered to La Fonda, and she had lived there ever since. "You must stay as long as you like," Mr. Karavas would say, patting her hand. "Let old Saki help."

Millicent, Violet had learned the hard way, was interested in everyone, would help anyone. But in the end she belonged only to herself.

Violet thought it wasn't so bad living at La Fonda. She had a cozy room made warm with a kiva fireplace, a large bed spread with a blue quilt, a desk where she could write, a view of the plaza from her window. The meals were delivered and generally edible, she was making friends, going to dances with Eva from the Reyna Shop and her crowd.

When her savings were low, she got the job at Martha's shop. Helping ladies choose the right dresses, unpacking new inventory, arranging the scarves, smiling, smiling. Still, she never saw MR. Millicent seldom shopped anywhere now, or was even seen at El Patio or the Sagebrush. Kay Dicus said doctors came in from Santa Fe and Albuquerque to Turtle Walk, and even MR's mother visited. Most alarming.

Violet couldn't help but worry, no matter what had happened

in that terrible last day. No matter how Millicent tried to organize her life, read her book without permission. MR's health was never good. Now it seemed that even her iron will couldn't hold it back. And Violet couldn't help.

"It is not your concern now," she told herself sternly. Millicent had made it abundantly clear she wanted none of Violet's assistance. Violet could still feel that sting on her cheek. That betrayal. That one gesture that severed what came before.

Violet's hands stilled on a vase she was dusting. What *was* Millicent suffering now, now that she needed help rather than giving it? How had she changed, that most changeable of all souls?

Sometimes Violet lay awake late at night, going over every day, every moment, every word she had with MR, worrying worrying worrying. At night, things were always worse.

Millicent had given her such a great gift. She had given her the confidence to live life in her own way. She would not squander those lessons now, no matter what happened after. She wasn't a scared Iowa farm girl any more. She was her own self. The self she had found at last, a Violet who could make up her own mind, live her own life, love who she wanted.

Find her own happy ever after, come what may.

She bit back a smile as she rearranged some silk roses in a silver vase. Ahhh, yes, romance. Now that was certainly *one* most important lesson she learned from Millicent. Courtship, love, *real* love, was a wild, unpredictable ride, like going up up up through the canyon and coming out to the deep, ancient, sunlit gorge. Or sliding faster and faster down an icy track. Who knew where it would end? A deadly crash, or a slow ease and contentment. A tumbling down into each other's arms, safe always. Known always.

"A quiet man is a boring man," Violet heard MR's voice say in her mind. *"But I'll say this, you'll get no trouble from a boring man."*

Violet laughed. If only MR knew.

She got into plenty of "trouble" with Lorenzo behind the

garage, in dark corners, in La Fonda's lobby behind the old suit of armor. (Herbert, Lorenzo had named him, their chaperone.) They hadn't gone all the way upstairs to her room yet, but that was because she knew him so well now. To him, a trip to the bedroom would mean a trip up the altar, and she wasn't quite ready for that yet. The sting of MR's attempted control of her love life was still there, lurking.

Though, when she did want to marry, she was sure it would be to Lorenzo. She'd never even imagined, pouring over novels in her attic space, that she could feel like this about one, real man. That his kiss could melt her, his laugh make the world bright, his brains and humor and calm nature make everything seem like it would be all right.

She knew what her family would say. He wasn't right for her, nor she him. They came from different worlds. But their souls were the same. And that could surely see them through. Couldn't it?

She dusted a display of hats and embroidered jackets in the window facing Paseo, and her heart suddenly pounded as she saw MR walking past. She was bundled in a heavy sable coat, her hair covered with a scarf, the dachshunds' leashes in her gloved hands, moving slowly, her lips turned down at the corners as if she was deep in thought. Violet had heard all that gossip all those months, and now here she was. Violet's stomach was tight, she couldn't suck in a breath. For one giddy moment, she thought MR might come in the shop. Yet she kept walking, not looking right or left, just slowly ahead.

Flustered, feeling silly, Violet hurried to the shadows at the back of the shop to dust another case.

She suddenly remembered something else Millicent once told her. *"My family love me in their way, they gave me roots, they gave me every luxury a child could know. But they did not understand me. I couldn't even understand myself then. Families are always strange. They always ruin us in some ways, as well as make us."*

And that was what MR gave to her. Violet's parents, too, loved her, their changeling child. It was as if a Pekingese had appeared among their house of Labradors or something. But MR knew. She saw. MR herself, though, was an eternal mystery. Like a part of Violet now, of her skin and bones and heart, but she knew she could never be like MR. She just had to be Violet now.

Whoever Violet might be. Yet she was beginning to see more and more of herself every day. Step by step. Every word written on her book, every dress displayed, every dance and laugh and kiss. She was growing.

At first, it was true, she had hoped Millicent might call. In a town so small, everyone knew where Violet was, that she lived at the hotel and walked across the plaza to the shop all week. But nothing had happened, and slowly, so slowly, that power over Violet that MR held vanished. The past, as wonderful and vivid and dramatic as it was, became hazy, like the cloud caught atop the mountain. Only *now* was real. She was making her life.

She couldn't be ripped in two again.

Violet ran her hand over a soft velvet jacket. Surely MR *had* cared about her, in her own way. Violet had thought she knew her, but in reality MR was a myth, even now while she was still alive. She could not be truly known. And Violet didn't want to be a myth. She just wanted to be a person. She could start to do that now.

She glanced out the window to find the snow falling a little thicker, fat, white, lacy flakes. The rooftops were covered, the walls obscured. "Do you need any help back there, Martha?" she called.

Martha emerged from the storeroom/office, looking shockingly knackered for a woman who always seemed like she had just emerged from a couturiers' showroom. She'd been going though inventory and balancing sales books for hours, and looked desperately bored. "Absolutely not. In fact, I have given up for the day. Once numbers start leaping off the page, throwing their little pen punches at my face, I know I must stop. You take the rest of the day off, Vi, you've been working so hard. See you at the pueblo on Friday?"

"Of course, the last dance of the year. Thank you so much, Martha."

"Nonsense. You're the best employee I've ever had! You are quite wasted behind that counter. Now go, go!"

Violet laughed. She didn't have to be asked twice. She changed her black suede court shoes for galoshes, wrapped herself in her new green wool coat, and hurried outside, stopping to snatch a hot chocolate from the Taos Inn bar next door. The street was even quieter now, practically deserted except for a few other people rushing home through the white deluge, and she dropped off her letters at the post office, unsure where to go next. Her book's pages waited on her hotel desk, a chapter to finish, yet somehow she felt too restless to work on them. Seeing MR had affected her more than she would have imagined.

A car slid past on the frosty road, the only vehicle in sight, and it slowed as it passed her. Violet glimpsed Tom McCarthy's tow head at the wheel, and Millicent in the back, apparently done with her walk. She was huddled down so deeply in her fur coat she could barely be seen, just a pale cheek, a red-lipsticked mouth.

To Violet's shock, the car stopped and MR's window rolled slowly down. A black-gloved hand eased the fluffy fur collar down. MR's makeup was as impeccable as ever, but it couldn't quite disguise how ghostly-white she was, how thin.

"Vi, darling," she said lightly, as if days and not months had passed since that cracking slap that broke everything. "How are you?"

"Very well, thank you, Mrs. Rogers." But MR was certainly *not* well. Violet could see it in her eyes, her tight mouth drawn against the pain.

"Working at Martha's shop, I hear," Millicent said tonelessly. "A counter girl. How it must remind you of your Los Angeles days."

Violet choked out a laugh. "Martha is a lot more easy-going than any glove counter dragon. No bottom-pinchers, either, and the hours are shorter."

"Helpful for writing, I would imagine."

Violet thought of those long hours in her La Fonda room, the scratch of her pen and clack of the typewriter, the scent of cold coffee, the world she created on those pages, just for her. The world as it should be. "Very helpful. The manuscript is nearly finished."

Millicent glanced at the post office behind Violet. "Dare I hope you are corresponding with the gorgeous Mr. Rivers?"

So that was it. MR could never stop controlling. It was not in her nature. "I was just sending a "no" response to my brother's wedding RSVP. And I sent a good-bye to Mr. Rivers a long time ago. He *is* gorgeous, and nice. Too nice to string along."

Millicent pursed her red lips. "Oh, my dear Violet. How sweet you are. How naive. He could have been of such use to you, if you only listened to me. I do know how these little things work. I wanted to help."

"I know," Violet said. And she *did* know that, now. Millicent really only ever wanted to help, whether her brand of assistance was what anyone needed or not. Violet thought of MR's husbands and lovers and movie star friends. Of all the artists whose work she supported. Of the town she loved and built on. It was a glorious parade that made a sparkling life. But Violet feared she herself was just plain old Miss Iowa after all.

But maybe being Miss Iowa, Miss New Mexico, was her very own dream, one she could grasp. Millicent showed her that.

"Ah, well, *c'est la vie*," Millicent said with a sigh, sounding so weary. "I am off to Santa Fe for a few days. Will I see you at the pueblo for the dance?"

"Oh, yes, probably." Lorenzo would be there, so of course so would Violet. Not that MR needed to know that.

"*A bientot*, then." With one last wave of her gloved hand, Millicent was gone through the snow, the end of the very first conversation they'd had since that horrible day at Turtle Walk.

Maybe this was the last conversation of all?

Violet shook her head. Confused, wary, hopeful, she turned and went on toward the end of town despite the weather, the end of the paved road, where the lane became gravel and snow and mud. She went past the gas station to the gates of Sierra Vista Cemetery and climbed up on one of the split rails of the fence. She stared up at the mountain, wrapped in clouds like a tulle gown, hoping beyond hope for an answer. A plan.

The mountain was silent. But maybe the peace was its own answer.

"Are you frozen to that fence, Miss Iowa?" a voice came out of the gray gloom, like some kind of other answer. Another dilemma. A most delicious dilemma.

Violet glanced back to see Lorenzo, his face shadowed by his wide-brimmed hat, wrapped in a sheepskin coat, loping along the pathway toward the gate. He held the wrapper of a flower bouquet, no doubt one he left for his sister.

"I'm afraid I just might be, so I'm glad my shining knight is here to release me," she said. She nodded at the wrapper. "Did you come to see your sister?"

"And to look for you. Martha said you left early and walked this way."

"The shop was quiet today, I was just a nuisance. I stopped to mail some letters, and then just—kept walking." She didn't tell him about seeing Millicent, not yet.

"I got a surprise for you," he said.

"For me? If you keep working so hard, my jewelry box lid will never close." Like her and her book, creativity seemed to have struck Lorenzo lately, he was working at his bench every spare moment.

"This one is a little more ephemeral than a bracelet or pendant." From the pocket of his sheepskin coat, he took a bunch

SECRETARY TO THE SOCIALITE

of mistletoe. As Violet laughed, he held it over their heads, and his lips touched hers. He tasted of tobacco and honey and Lorenzo, her favorite taste of all ever, and she curled her hands into his coat to hold him with her.

"That, Mr. Serna, was quite a lovely gift," she whispered.

"It comes with a bit of news, too."

"Hmmm," Violet said doubtfully. "Good or bad?"

"Just news for the moment. Could be either." He climbed up onto the fence beside her, his arms around her to shield her from the wind. "My cousin wants to lease out most of his farmland, move to Arizona. It's right alongside my own fields. I could expand my crops, maybe even build a bigger house, while I take over Pedro's garage on the weekends. I could build another workshop, too, Reyna's wants more of my stuff. It means more work, sure, but more money." He looked down at her with his lovely dark eyes, those eyes she wished she could read. "More possibilities."

Possibilities like—a wife? A family? "But that's wonderful for you, Lorenzo."

His lips quirked at the corners in that smile she loved. "I was hoping it could be—well, might possibly—shit, but I'm bad at this. Aren't we Indians supposed to be poets?"

Violet laughed nervously. "And we Russians are all Tolstoy."

"What I want to say is—I hope this news can be good. Can make a secure future. For us both."

"Us?" she whispered. She sucked in a breath through suddenly-numb lips.

Lorenzo slid down from the fence and knelt down in the snow. "I didn't plan on this now, Vi, I don't even have a ring, but, Violet Anastasia Redfield, you are the most amazing woman I have ever seen. Your kindness and calm that first night in the alleyway, your humor and patience and fun. I can't—I don't want my life to be without you in it. I'll do anything, work all the hours God gives me, never sing Bing again, if you will marry me. I know that the world won't make it easy for us. But I love you, that's all. I love you. And I'll follow you wherever you might want to go for the rest of our lives."

Violet laughed, and all those doubts, all those fears, everything vanished. There was only him. MR had been wrong. A quiet man was anything but boring once he started talking. "Well, lucky for you, then, Bing, because here is where I want to be. With you. Always. Now get up from there before you catch pneumonia."

He jumped up and caught her around the waist, twirling her around and around as they laughed and kissed and talked over each other.

"Oh, thank the stars," he muttered against her hair, her hat lost in the snow. "I would be embarrassed as hell if you said no."

"I can't say no," she said, and she realized that was the truest thing she had ever said, ever known. She wanted this man, this place, forever. Unlike with Charles, unlike with any of MR's husbands, this was real. This was true. This was hers. "I love you, Lornezo. This is it for me. For us. I know there will be challenges. Your sister, Tony and Mabel—they show us that. But I know we can do it."

"Because we have each other."

"Yes. Because of that."

The snow was thicker now, blanketing the world in clean white, and Lorenzo took her hand to lead her back to town. They didn't speak; they didn't have to. It was all right there for them.

As Violet looked up into the lowering sky, she felt something swift, sweeping, a chord of music maybe, inside of her, and she held tighter to his hand. She was brave then, beautiful, free. Alive. She understood so well then all that MR taught her; life was to live. It was to be true to yourself. It was to be savored every second you could.

She went up on tiptoe and pressed her lips to Lorenzo's, right in front of the whole plaza. "Lorenzo, I ..." she whispered.

He groaned in answer, his hands tight on her waist, holding her so, so close.

"Could you possibly," she said with a smile, "be a gentleman and walk a girl upstairs to her room?"

The light that peeked between the blue curtains was only the faintest pinky-orange. Still early-late. Still a moment to hold onto the most perfect instant Violet had ever known, or was sure she would ever know.

She shook back the tangle of her red hair, and rolled over in the rumpled sheets to stare at her sleeping Lorenzo. *Her* Lorenzo. Her lover.

How MR-ish.

Saki and everyone lingering in the lobby had seen them saunter up the stairs, hand in hand, laughing, careless. The old Violet, the old Miss Iowa, would have been appalled, but this Taos Violet could not have cared at all. She felt all covered with some new tingling, stardust sort of delight, just like that night in the desert when time had no meaning at all. Nothing mattered but life and lust and truth and beauty and eternity. There was this one life, just as MR always said, and it was Violet's alone. She would grab it.

And she would catch onto it with the man by her side, the man she could never have imagined existed. Her family loved her, but they didn't understand, they only wanted her to marry, bake bread, go to church, have babies. MR understood her, appreciated her (sometimes), saw they shared that love of beauty. But MR also believed Violet could do nothing without the help of money. Without a man's money. The *right* man.

Lorenzo, though, he saw *her*. Only her, and he loved that about her. He would help her, if she asked, she knew that, just as she would help him, always. But he trusted her to do it, be it, know it. It was strange. It was glorious.

She thought of Tony and Mabel, sitting next to each other,

holding hands, their gray heads bent together, not needing to speak because they were together. Always.

She glanced at Lorenzo next to her, sprawled in sleep, his dark hair tousled, a small smile on his lips as if he dreamed something lovely. His arm was flung out against the pillows, a rough, faded blue tattoo on his shoulder, silver bracelet gleaming. What did they mean? How much she had to discover. How she couldn't wait to do it. It was more than she could know in a lifetime.

She curled up close to him, breathing deep of his scent, the scent he shared with Taos itself—pine and rain and lemon and something dark and deep. She had, by some strange and marvelous chance, landed exactly where she had always belonged.

She closed her eyes and remembered Millicent's wave, that wave that seemed to say—she had passed on all she could. It was Violet's now.

Lorenzo stirred, his arm coming around her, tugging her into the curve of his lean body.

"Just think," Violet whispered. "This could be our mornings for years and years. Until the goats need milking, I suppose."

"Or the babies' diapers changing. Or your New York editor showing up on the doorstep demanding your manuscript."

Violet giggled. "Don't remind me of diapers! Still—we will be more than babies and goats and editors. We'll be us. And maybe *one* baby."

Lorenzo propped his head on his palm, smiling down at her in the brightening light, the new day. "So, are you saying you'll marry me for sure?"

Violet stared up at him, at those eyes, that smile. Everything. "I will marry you, Lorenzo Serna. For better or worse. And for never going back to Iowa again."

"I think I can definitely promise you that," he said, and kissed her. And the world was complete one more minute.

CHAPTER 32

Violet

AT THE PUEBLO, FULL CIRCLE WITH MILLICENT

"Just fold the dough like that, dear, and use the lard you melted to do this ..."

Violet dutifully folded the dough, used the brush dipped in the lard—and spilled the pork and green chili mixture right onto the linoleum floor. One of the meandering dogs snatched it up. Aghast, Violet looked up at Lorenzo's aunt, who laughed.

"Well, the third time will be the charm," she said.

"But that was the fifth time!" Violet almost wailed.

Wailing, though, was not the pueblo way. Getting on with things was. The dogs finished up the remains, and one of Lorenzo's little nieces fetched the broom, giggling. It made Violet laugh, too.

The last feast day of the year, the last dance. The first time Violet had been left alone to learn to cook properly, stews and breads and empanadas, while Lorenzo was off helping to prepare the plaza. She wanted so desperately for it all to be right. To be good. Dropping food all over the place didn't seem like quite the way to do that.

"So, what are your own traditions in—Ohio?" his aunt asked as she mixed up more of the dough.

"Oh—the usual, I suppose," Violet said, shooing off the dogs. She laughed to think Iowa and Ohio could be the same. "Mince pies and cranberry sauce and such. Turkey, roast beef. My grandmother's borscht. The best china, which I wasn't allowed to touch. For good reason, as you see now!"

Another of his many, many aunts gently squeezed her hand. "You will learn. You make Lorenzo happy, yes? That's what matters. This modern world ..."

Violet smiled, though her throat was tight as if she would cry. How kind everyone had been, through all her clumsiness and uncertainty and eagerness! Even Mabel had become, well, not *kind*, exactly, but helpful, chatty, wanting to hear all about her book. She had even offered to introduce Violet to literary agents. Maybe she understood what it was like to marry a man from this unique place. To find her own place in this world. Violet's first aid skills, her willingness to babysit, and the lessons of Lorenzo's sister and, as Tony said, "you can't fight real love" had certainly helped.

"Why don't you go watch them light the bonfires?" another aunt said, and Violet nodded. The cooking would surely go much faster, and everyone be a lot less hungry, if she got out of the way.

Then she caught a glimpse, pale and shimmering in the firelight, of silvery hair tumbling over the collar of an ermine coat. The swirl of sharp dachshund barks carried on the cold wind.

Millicent. She was there. Violet hadn't seen her since that snowy day on the road.

Violet glanced back over her shoulder, unsure what to do next. The Serna door was still open, amber light spilling out, the smell of the green chilistew escaping to mingle with the woodsmoke, offering retreat. She could run back there to her future, to her life now; or she could keep going, back into the past, at least for a while. She could set it to rest, if she could be brave enough.

And she knew she *had* to set it to rest, for the sake of her choices, of the life she wanted to have. Millicent had brought her this far. She had to take herself the rest of the way.

Yet still the cracking sound of that slap haunted her. Even more terrible was the knowledge that MR was disappointed in her. That she had not become what Millicent wanted her to be. And she had seen so many times how fast MR discarded what disappointed her. She couldn't face that again.

Yet she heard so clearly in her mind what Lorenzo would say, that to move forward she had to claim the past. Millicent took her into this new life, Violet owed her a good-bye. She owed it to herself.

Squaring her shoulders in her green coat, the collar pinned with her silver violet brooch, she marched forward through the gathering crowds until she reached the open-top car. She didn't know what to expect when she saw Millicent, spoke to her again after all this time, but MR just smiled and gestured for Violet to climb in and sit beside her. The dogs went crazy barking and whining, jumping onto Violet's lap.

"I think of all the dances, this is my favorite," Millicent said, softly, far-away, her eyes gazing out at something no one else could see. "The last is the best, surely."

"MR, it's not your last," Violet cried in alarm, in cold fear. "This place can't do without you."

Millicent gave her a strange, crooked smile. "Oh, Vi darling. You are as sweet as ever. You'll never completely get the Iowa out of you. Look at me. I can barely stand upright. I have nowhere to go now. No more adventures. But I'm glad I'm stopping here. I'll have the mountain to watch over me forever."

Violet didn't know what to say, what to do. She held MR's arm as they listened to the drums, the heartbeat of the world.

"But you, Vi," Millicent said, suddenly brisk, hoarse. "It won't be the end for you for a long time. You will stay here, yes?"

"Yes. Lorenzo and I are getting married," Violet said slowly, wondering what MR would think of that.

But she just nodded. "Of course you are. Oh, my Violet. I

thought I knew how to take care of you. That my way was the only way. My path the only one. What a foolish thing to think!"

Violet was deeply shocked. Millicent, saying she had been wrong? "MR ..."

"You have a freedom I never had," Millicent went on. "A real freedom. It won't be easy."

"No." Violet knew it would not. Lorenzo's family was kind, polite, but they had doubts. Reservations. She did, too. But Tony was right; love would not be denied. "We do love each other. We will be fine in the end."

Millicent smiled, bright and perfect, like summer sunshine one more time. "You will. I see that now. No matter what comes."

She suddenly swayed, her pale face even whiter, and she let Violet take her thin arm. "I think I should go home, Vi darling. Help me? One more time?"

Violet swallowed her cold panic, all her old anger and fears, and nodded. "Yes, MR. Of course I will."

CHAPTER 33

Violet

BY HERSELF, WEEKS LATER

The hospital, all white and clean and smelling of bleach, filled with mysterious machine-beeps, hushed footsteps, ringing bells in the distance, didn't seem like the place for MR, Violet thought as she made her way toward the closed door at the end of the corridor. It was too antiseptic, hushed, closed-in, claustrophobic. But here they were all the same. Here it all ended up. She took a deep breath, and pushed the door open.

A nurse checked the chart at the end of the bed, smoothed the crisp sheet, brought a chair—so quick, so efficient, so impersonal. So unlike anything else about Millicent's life.

How thin MR was, like a wisp, a nothing, a sprig of winter chamisa, a disappearing cloud in her white gown. Blue veins showed through her skin, and her waving hair was white, bound with a bandage. Deep purple ringed her closed eyes, and her chest barely rose under the blankets, tucked amid a thicket of tubes.

On a bedside table was a forest of amber pill bottles, vases of beautiful roses and lilies and orchids bearing cards from Mabel, Millicent's mother, Paulie. A silver crucifix and rose quartz rosary were among them—so the rumors were true, MR had converted to

Catholicism, finding a comfortable faith in the end, a spot in Sierra Vista.

"I'm afraid the cold she was suffering late last year turned to strep," the nurse whispered. "It moved quickly to her heart, it had become so enlarged and weak. She was dyeing cloth in the bathtub, they said, and had a heart attack. She hit her head as she fell. A blood clot on the brain had to be removed. She is doing better, though—her sons have been to see her, and her mother calls every day. She will certainly be glad to see you."

Violet wanted to laugh and sob all at the same time. Dyeing fabric! So like MR. Beauty always. But if only Violet had been there! She would have stopped it happening. She would have been there to take care of MR.

"Do sit down. She won't sleep long," the nurse said. She gathered up a bundle of blankets and hurried away, leaving Violet alone amid the beeping machines, the smell of bleach and flowers.

She longed to run away, to scream, to do *something*, to mess up this perfectly scrubbed nothingness and have the old days back. To have Millicent back. This should not be how a woman like MR ended up! Never, never. Not the woman made of beauty.

But Violet could not leave. Could not run back to her new, happy life and leave behind the woman who gave her all of that. She put down her own flowers beside Mabel's and perched at the edge of the chair, staring at the mountains outside the window. The Sandias. Not like Taos Mountain. They were sharp and massive and dominating.

She turned away and saw a few prints hanging on the wall where Millicent could see them when she woke, Japanese woodblocks of streams and temples and ladies in flowing kimonos.

Suddenly, Millicent's eyes opened, as dark and fathomless as ever. "Violet."

Violet smiled, though it felt tight, forced. "Yes, it's me, MR."

Millicent blinked. "So strange. I was dreaming of my father, of

Ludi even. I was sure I was among them again at last. But I'm still here. Unless *you* are dead, too."

"No, not yet."

"I'm glad for it. You can give my love to Taos one more time." Millicent reached for Violet's hand, tracing the new ring on her left finger, a thin silver band inlaid with turquoise. "Mrs. Serna now, yes?"

"Yes. Just a little courthouse wedding." Violet thought of that afternoon, her dress from Millicent, Lorenzo in his suit, the nerves and laughter and joy and smiles, the champagne after at La Fonda. No lace or orange blossoms or confetti, but perfect.

"That's better than all that nuptial fuss. And he is gorgeous, I admit. You have better judgment in men than I did. Did you wear the dress, at least? The one I sent?"

"I did. Everyone swooned over it!"

A small smile whispered over Millicent's chapped lips. "So they should. It's a Dior."

"I remember wearing it that night at Janet's dinner. I was so nervous I would ruin it."

"Oh, Janet. Such a darling, but so silly sometimes. She keeps sending me Religious Science tracts. As if ..."

"I see you found comfort somewhere else." Violet nodded at the rosary.

Millicent waved her hand. "I had to, to be buried just where I want, to have my funeral at Our Lady of Guadalupe. And who knows what comes after, really? Better safe than sorry. You will be there, won't you? At the funeral. Make sure the flowers are just right?"

Violet smiled, but she wanted to howl. She could barely imagine MR's funeral, barely imagine that soon it would be real, she would be truly there, and her friend would be no more. That spot of beauty and perfection empty. "I will do anything you like, MR, but surely that won't be for a long time."

Millicent sighed impatiently. "Everyone plays those games with me. I am tired of fighting. I had only one more thing to do."

"And what is that?"

"To tell you that I am sorry." Millicent scowled, and stared out the window, at those solid, unmoved mountains. "I never apologize. But I was wrong, so wrong, to drive you away. And over a man, of all things! You were my friend—sometimes I think you were my only friend. I have—have missed you."

"Oh, MR." Violet choked back the tears, sure if she started wailing she would never stop. "I have missed you."

"Then take this, and I will know you have forgiven me." Millicent took a box from under her pillow and pressed it into Violet's palm. "And always live your life *only* for you. Only as *you* desire it. And I will be with you, cheering you on. Your book, it will be a great success, I know it, and so will your marriage. Because you are you, with your good heart and kind soul."

"Millicent, I ..." Violet had no words for what she wanted to say, what must be said. Yet there were no words that could make anything different. "I love you."

Millicent gave a radiant smile, and closed her eyes. Her hand fell away, as if every ounce of her fierce strength, her fiery fight, had gone out. Violet sat there for a moment, an eternity—until the nurse returned, visiting hours were over, and she had to leave.

She didn't look back, but when she reached a bench at the edge of the parking lot she fell down onto it, and broke utterly apart. She sobbed and sobbed, until she had nothing left, until there was only the blue New Mexico sky above to wrap around her and hold her safe. She fell back, empty, depleted, and saw the box still in her hand.

She opened it, and inside was a piece of Millicent's own handiwork, a shooting star of silver and garnets, flashing always through the world and making it ever more beautiful.

MILLICENT—BY HERSELF

She closed her eyes, and let herself soar up through the ceiling of the horrid little white room, soar up into the sky as she had that night in the desert when everything seemed possible. She was on the edge of something now, something she didn't understand, something she couldn't control as she had struggled every day to control her world. Control her heart. Yet it all came to this, like the sea in Jamaica—blue and green and gray and black, forceful and perfect and cold and utterly indifferent. She took comfort in that, at least.

The wave that seemed to drag her out and toss her back was warm, salty-clean. So much easier, so much harder, than she had imagined.

She floated on that wave, giving herself up to the pain that now never left her. She broke through to the surface, to the sun, and opened her eyes. She half-hoped to see Violet still there, but she was gone and Millicent was alone. As she always had been, really.

She sighed, and closed her eyes again. What a lovely life it had been, all she could have wanted. All she had wanted but length of days, of years. Of more time. Now she only wanted to crack off this horrible shell of illness until the true Millicent flew free again. Until she was that girl on the veranda at The Port, everything ahead.

She turned her head slowly and gazed out the window into the sunset. There were no sunsets anywhere she had seen like the ones in New Mexico, soft and fiery all at the same time, pink and lavender and gold, fading into dusty blue. She had found her home, her purpose, and now she held tightly to those truths. She'd found them late, but, oh, they had been hers for a time. It had all been hers.

She floated on that sea, that light, carried out and out, so far she knew she would never find shore again. She heard Indian drums, voices—her sons, Benny, Brett, maybe Violet, who had come back to her at last. Music, music, always music. Every tale she had ever read, ever told, every dream she ever cherished, every beautiful thing, pulled her up into that light. She floated again, floated, floated, until she was nothing. Until she was free.

Author's Note

I've had so many questions from early readers about "who is real" in my story, so I thought I'd make a quick note (and use some of my notebooks full of research!). This was such a fun story for me to write, because Taos has been a special place in my own life. When I was very young, about 4, my parents decided to spend part of the summers in Taos, and so that was my vacation spot every year. One year, we visited a beautiful museum in an old house just outside of town, the Millicent Rogers Museum, and on the gift shop wall was a *Vogue* photo of a gorgeous blonde woman in a Charles James blouse and piles of turquoise and silver bracelets. I had to know more about her!

The Museum was started by one of Millicent's three sons, Paul Peralta Ramos, in 1956 to showcase his mother's collection of nearly 2000 pieces of local art—jewelry, pottery, weavings, carvings, and her own work as well, as she was a jewelry designer. It's now grown to over 7000 pieces, and moved to its current location in 1968, where it's continued to grow and expand.

Violet Redfield is fictional, but Millicent Rogers was very real! In her short life (1902-1953) she was a socialite and heiress (her grandfather was a co-founder of Standard Oil), fashion icon, art collector, and later an activist for Native American rights. She contracted rheumatic fever at age 10, which shortened her life and plagued her will illness, but she managed to marry three times, fall in love with men like Clark Gable, Roald Dahl, and Ian Fleming, and live in New York, Virginia, Jamaica, and Austria before making her final home in Taos in 1948. She was buried in her new hometown at the Sierra Vista cemetery on January 1, 1953.

Mabel Dodge Luhan (1879-1962) was, like Millicent, a socialite, daughter of a wealthy Buffalo, New York family, who married several times (four!) and was a patron of the arts. She lived in Florence, at a famous Medici villa, and ran a counterculture salon in New York before landing in Taos in 1917 to establish her own arts colony, attracting people such as DH Lawrence, Georgia O'Keefe, and Ansel Adams. She married Tony Luhan from the Taos Pueblo in 1923, and is buried in the Kit Carson Cemetery in Taos. Her house is now a National Historic Landmark and run as a conference center.

One of the great Taos characters is Dorothy Brett (The Hononorable! 1883-1977). Daughter of a viscount, she was raised amid Queen Victoria's court, but became an artistic bohemian who attended the Slade School and became friends with the Bloomsbury Circle before befriending DH Lawrence and moving with him to Taos in 1924. She stayed there for the rest of her long life, creating her own unique art (some of which can now be seen in the Smithsonian, as well as the Millicent Rogers Museum and Harwood Museum).

Martha Reed (1922-2010) actually opened her famous shop in 1953, so I fudged it a bit for my story! Daughter of artist Doel Reed, she got her own Arts degree in 1944 and worked at the Philbrook Museum and Dallas Museum of Art before moving to Taos. She first worked at the Pink Horse Shop on the Plaza, where she became well-known for designing her "broomstick" skirts and blouses in calico and velvet, before opening her own shop. She was a very sociable person, famous for her "soirees with hooch" all over town. I am lucky enough to own a painting by her, as well as Martha of Taos original bought by my aunt in the 1960s!

Lorenzo is fictional, but his cousin Benito was real, a man who (like so many others) was tormented by what he had seen in World War II and was helped by Millicent. The Karavas brothers first bought La Fonda in the 1920s, and it came to be run by one of their sons, Saki, until his death in 1996. He was an art collector and (as his tombstone says) "a great Taos character." Tom McCarthy is also real, and if you visit Taos you can stay at his family's beautiful B&B, Casa Benavides! They have the best breakfasts, and he is full of stories of his long life in Taos.

These are just a few of the sources I used! I have to thank the Historic Santa Fe Archives for all their help, too.

The Mabel Dodge Luhan Papers Collection at the Beinecke Library of Yale (much of which is online)

Mabel Dodge Luhan, *Winter in Taos* (1935) and *Edge of Taos Desert* (1937)

Lois Palken Rudnick, *Utopian Vistas: The Mabel Dodge Luhan House and the American Counterculture* (1996)

Cherie Burns, *Searching for Beauty: The Life of Millicent Rogers, the American Heiress Who Taught the World About Style* (2011) and *Diving for Starfish: The Jeweler, the Actress, the Heiress, and One of the World's Most Alluring Pieces of Jewelry* (2018)

Judith Nasse, *A Life in Full* (2022)

Annette Tapert and Dana Edkins, *The Power of Style* (1994)

Sam Hignett, *Brett: From Bloomsbury to New Mexico* (1985)

Lois P. Rudnick, ed. *Mabel Dodge Luhan and Company: American Moderns and the West* (2016)

And you can visit my own website for more behind-the-book tidbits, as well! http://ammandamccabe.com

Also by Amanda McCabe

Standalone

Secretary to the Socialite

Kate Haywood Elizabethan Mysteries

Murder at the Princess' Palace

Murder at Westminster Abbey

Murder in the Queen's Garden

Murder at the Queen's Masquerade

Murder at Whitehall

Murder at the Royal Chateau

Flora Flowerdew Victorian Mysteries

Flora Flowerdew and the Mystery of the Duke's Diamonds

Flora Flowerdew and the Mystery of the Purloined Papers

Flora Flowerdew and the Secret of the Sarcophagus

Daughters of Erin

Countess of Scandal

Duchess of Sin

Lady of Seduction

Scandalous St. Claires

When She Was Wicked

Two Sinful Secrets

Regency Rebels

About the Author

Amanda McCabe wrote her first romance at the age of sixteen—a vast historical epic starring all her friends as the characters, written secretly during algebra class (and her parents wondered why math was not her strongest subject...)

She's never since used algebra, but her books (set in a variety of time periods—Regency, Victorian, Tudor, Renaissance, and 1920s) have been nominated for many awards, including the RITA Award, the Romantic Times BOOKReviews Reviewers' Choice Award, the Booksellers Best, the National Readers Choice Award, and the Holt Medallion. She lives in New Mexico with her lovely husband, along with far too many books and a spoiled rescue dog.

When not writing or reading, she loves yoga, collecting cheesy travel souvenirs, and watching the Food Network—even though she doesn't cook. She also writes as Laurel McKee. historical Elizabethan mysteries as Amanda Carmack., and Eliza Casey...

Please visit her at http://ammandamccabe.com